Night Terrors

Night Terrors

By

Randall Lane

"Oh my goodness!!! I just finished Devil's Den. What a roller coaster of a ride!!! I LOVED this book!! I can't wait to read your other stories, thanks again!!" — **Sherrie W Review for Devil's Den**

"This is not a book that I would have normally read, but I went to a reading by the author and was mesmerized by his incredible skill at drawing you in with sensational detail. I was right there in the story and was spellbound by this affecting and powerful book! The writing is excellent, the story is compelling, and the book has a message that touches your soul, one you will not forget! Looking forward to more from Randall Lane! I give the Devil's Den five big stars!" — **Janet B Review for Devil's Den**

"I loved Devil's Den. It was scary and quite intense as I read through it. I could not figure out, "who dun it." I really enjoy a book that has me guessing until the very end. I can't wait until your next novel is published! Thanks for such an enjoyable read." — **Sandra N Review for Devil's Den**

"I recommend this book highly. Devils Den. Can't put it down!"—**Marybeth L Review for Devil's Den**

"Awesome read! Once you start it's hard to put down! The way he tells the story keeps you captivated throughout the entire book." —**Tammy P Review for Devil's Den**

"I really enjoyed this book. The plot grew with an intense "who dun it" while surprising me with a twist I didn't anticipate.
It's a great read in good vs. evil. You will find yourself questioning the validity of each character." — **Happy Amazon Customer's Review for Devil's Den**

"Mr. Lane writes with the eloquence of a storyteller. Deep, profound and superbly imaginative." — **Mark M Review for Devil's Den**

"This author's imagination will leave you spellbound! These stories will excite your senses, give you pause to think and excite your very soul! Can't wait for more!!!!" — **Happy Amazon Customer's Review for When Darkness Hides**

Table of Contents

"The Light shines in the darkness, and the darkness has not overcome it."

—John 1:5

Bloody Bones

57 miles West of Wilmington, NC

Winter of 1893

Arthur and Josephine Rice live in a quaint, three-bedroom home with cedar shake exterior and an outhouse in the back yard. The married couple has raised four children so far, with a fifth on the way. Arthur's elderly and alcoholic mother has lived with them for the last two years after his father's death. Arthur and Josephine are seated at the kitchen table. An oil lantern with a weak flame light their faces. It's just passed the midnight hour, and all four children and Arthur's mother had long since turned in for the night. Arthur sat in his white long johns and rested his elbows upon the table. He looked into Josephine's eyes as he spoke.

"Look, we have enough food to last for four weeks. That'll give me time to go into town and work a job long enough to get us through the winter. I read in the paper there's a new textile mill hiring."

"I don't know Arthur. That's a long time for you to be away. Isn't there something you can do that's closer to home?"

She watched as Arthur lowered his gaze and tightened his lips, "I wish they were. This textile mill thing is about all I know of." He raised his head and pointed toward the field behind their house, "If we hadn't of had such a terrible drought this year, we wouldn't be having to think like this. I's was talking to Old Man Rigsby last week and he say it was the worst one he seen yet. You and me both know he done seen his share of years."

Josephine hugged herself and shivered. The thought of Arthur leaving them sent her stomach rolling.

Arthur rose from the table and crossed to the pile of firewood next to the wood stove in the living area. The iron door creaked open, and he tossed in a log. Embers danced as the flame licked at the fresh wood.

"You would have enough food and supplies for four weeks. I double checked." He shut the door and rose to his feet.

Josephine sighed.

"What is it?" He asked her as he drew near.

She shook her head and looked away.

"No. Now c'mon, don't be like this Josey. What's on your mind?"

She looked back at him as if questioning whether he really wanted to hear her thoughts.

"Why go on. Let it out."

"I don't want to be here that long with your mother. It's bad enough when you're working out in the field all day. You know me and her ain't the best of friends."

"Aww please. Josey, you'll be fine. She's not that bad."

"That's easy for you to say, you're not the daughter-in-law that's never good enough for her."

"Now Josey, you know there ain't no truth to that. I know she might have an odd way of showing it, but she really does think a lot of you."

Josephine wrinkled her nose and gave a bewildered glare.

"Okay, well maybe she doesn't think a lot of you, but she does think of you."

Josephine slapped his chest and the two shared a laugh as he took her in his arms. He kissed her neck and said, "You'll be fine. Trust me."

Josephine agreed to Arthur's plan. Three weeks later she came to regret the decision. She hated herself with passion each time she heard the voice of one of her children crying out with hunger pains. Arthur had undoubtedly miscalculated their oat and grain supply by a wide margin. Josephine had rationed it out as best she knew how, but they were now down to one meal a day and would soon be lucky to have that. Josephine had created a makeshift hog trap yesterday morning. She and Arthur's mother, Margaret, had argued over its effectiveness most of the day. It'd never be strong enough to kill a hog, Margaret had protested. Josephine had watched her father kill many a hog using the very trap. She knew good and well that it'd kill a hog. The question was not whether it'd work, but whether a hog could be found in what was beginning to feel a lot like a barren wasteland.

The children cried and begged for supper. Even the baby kicked and squirmed within her. No doubt feeling the lack of sustenance.

Margaret had been short tempered all day and often lashed out at the children. Josephine had all she could take at one point and told Margaret if she didn't control herself, she'd kick her out to fend for herself. Margaret snickered and said something about it being a cold day in hell before she'd let her daughter-in-law do such a thing. Despite her dismissiveness of Josephine's words, Margaret never raised her voice at the children again.

Josephine rounded up the last of the grain and oats and did her best to make a meal. She returned to her room afterward with a growling stomach as she only allowed herself enough to keep the baby healthy and nothing more. Had it not been for the baby in her womb, she would have fasted before eating what could have gone to her children. She was skimpy with Margaret's portion too and the two argued over it for most of the meal. Her disdain for that woman was only growing by the hour.

As she knelt by the bed to pray, her mother-in-law called for her from her bedroom. Josephine ignored her for a moment and continued praying to the Almighty. At last, Margaret's voice irritated her more than nails across a chalk board. She finished her prayers with a huff and asked for forgiveness. She rose to her feet and crossed for Margaret's room. The door was slightly cracked, and Josephine nudged it open.

"What is it?" she asked with an edge to her tone.

"Step in here for a moment."

Josephine eyed her suspiciously, wondering where this was leading. She stepped in and shut the door.

Margaret drew a deep breath and stood with her arms crossed at the foot of the bed. She rested her hip against the medal frame.

"You disrespected me back there, little lady."

Josephine batted her eyes and tilted her head. "I beg your pardon?"

"You heard me. I didn't stutter."

"Margaret, I don't have time for this. There are more important things to tend to." She turned and aimed for the door.

Margaret rushed her and grabbed her arm.

"Don't you walk away from me when I'm speaking to you," Margaret growled through clinched teeth.

Josephine yanked from her grip and Margaret lost her footing. Josephine watched it all as if it were in slow motion. Margaret stumbled head long, full force into the door. Her temple thudded against the heavy, metal handle. Josephine gasped and placed her hands to her mouth. She watched as a deep laceration formed across Margaret's head. Blood gushed and spurted out. Her eyes were glossy and dazed like a stuffed animal.

Josephine stared in shock at the sight before her. Margaret didn't move or bat an eye. She was as good as dead.

Oh my God.

Josephine stepped closer and squatted down to check for a pulse. She never found one. Margaret was gone.

IT HAD TAKEN Arthur a week longer to return home than he'd expected. In his four and a half weeks of working at the new textile mill, Arthur earned enough wages to buy food to last through winter and on into spring. He had made the trip to and from Wilmington on horseback along with three other men. He'd departed from those men an hour earlier and is now only minutes from home as he trudges along the narrow path. Trees line the edges and hang over the trail like arms stretching forth to snatch someone up.

Arthur smiled as a giddiness filled his spirit. He couldn't wait to tell Josephine the news and show her the money he'd earned. They may even have enough left over to buy her and the children new clothes. He clicked his teeth and nudged the horse forward.

Their home came into view. Smoke billowed from the chimney, and he thought he caught a faint whiff of stewed meat.

He'd worried for the last two weeks how his family was doing with the food he'd left behind. The past week had weighed heavily on his mind as he feared what the extra week may have done. He trusted Josephine would ration things as best she could until he returned. His thoughts were swept away at the sight of his four children playing in the front yard by the swing beneath the tall oak.

His two younger daughters, ages five and seven, glanced up and began running towards him. Their tattered dresses were dingy at the bottom from dragging the dirt and in desperate need of a good wash. John and Gabriel, the older of the four, were close behind their sisters.

Arthur hurried forward to meet them. He hopped from the horse and squatted to a knee as all four of his kids rushed to wrap their arms around him. He squeezed them tight and kissed each one on the top of the head.

"Oh my goodness. I'm so glad to see you."

He was ecstatic to see the energy they exhumed. He'd long feared everyone would be weak with starvation and shriveled in bed. Praise God Almighty, that isn't the case. They each beamed with joy and life.

They pulled back from him, and he asked, "Where's your mother?"

John pointed to the house and said, "She's inside. She's cooking supper."

"What is she cooking? Does she have meat?"

"Hmm mmm. It's so good too."

"Where did she get it?"

"Mama said she caught a hog in her trap last week. We've been feeding off it ever since. We ran out of food about three weeks after you left. We were all starving until she got that hog."

"Is that right?"

Mary, the youngest daughter, mumbled, "It's so so good."

"Mmm, it sure smells good. How is your grandma?"

"She's been staying in her room a lot. Mama said she's been sick and running a fever. She doesn't want us near her. Said we might catch something." Said John.

Arthur rose to his feet and walked towards the house with the reins of his horse in one hand and Mary's hand in the other.

He reached the porch and tied his horse to the railing. He removed his hat and stepped inside.

The house was dark as it was lit only by a dim lantern.

He scanned the darkness to find Josephine standing in the kitchen with her back to him. Her arm stirred a pot of stew.

He crossed toward her, "Hey honey. I'm so sorry it took me so long to get back."

She didn't acknowledge him but continued to stir the pot.

He walked up behind her and squeezed her waist, kissing her neck and cheek. She didn't respond. He pulled away and stepped to the side to look at her. Her eyes were distant and glossed over. Her hand worked vigorously to stir the stew. He swallowed hard and batted his eyes.

"Honey? Are you okay?"

She gave a gentle nod.

"Hey. What's the matter with you?"

"They were starving. We all were. The old hog has kept us alive." She had yet to blink.

Arthur squinted at her and said, "So I heard."

"Its meat is really tender and moist. You'll love it."

He took hold of her arm and gave it a shake.

"Hey. Honey? Josey? Are you alright? What's going o—"

She blinked hard and snapped her head side to side. She cleared her throat and finally looked at him. The distant stare had left, and his Josey had returned. She hugged him tight and began to cry. They embraced for a moment.

Arthur pulled her head to his shoulder. She wept as she sunk her nails into his back.

"I didn't think you were coming back. I thought something happened to you." she said with hitches and gasps for air.

"Sshh. Sshh. I'm sorry honey. I'm sorry. It's okay. You're alright now. I'm here."

She sniffled and pulled back.

He wiped the tears from her eyes.

"I have some good news to share. Where's Ma? Is she in her room?"

Arthur stepped from Josey and headed for his mother's room.

Josey grasped at his hand and called out, "No. Wait. WAIT."

Arthur had already reached his mother's room and had his hand on the doorknob. It was locked.

He turned to Josey who had marched up next to him, and said, "What the hell is this? Why is her door locked?"

Josey only gave a blank expression. He watched a shadow cross her face as the blood drained from her flesh.

He turned to the door and began to knock and call for his mother. No answer.

He rammed his shoulder into the door.

Josey clung to his arm and pleaded with him to stop. He shrugged her off and continued banging against the door. The children had now huddled around their mother.

Finally, the door gave way and Arthur stumbled into the room. He was instantly smacked in the face with an acrid odor that stung his nostrils and made his eyes water.

He buried his face into the crevice of an elbow. He turned and glared at Josey who stood in the door frame, trembling.

He turned back and scanned the room. The bed was empty. The covers were pulled back and ruffled into a ball near the foot of the bed.

"Ma?"

Nothing.

"MA?"

Josephine had tears dripping down her cheeks, "I'm sorry, Arthur. I'm so so sorry."

"What have you done?"

In frantic desperation, he began searching the room.

He crouched and checked under the bed. There was nothing there. He straightened and crossed for the closet door.

"Wait. Arthur. No, I can explain."

He turned and looked at her. Tears puddled to the floor at her feet, and she covered her mouth with her hands. The children were also crying and clinging to their mother.

Arthur gulped and turned to the closet door. He took hold of the handle. He heard something shift behind the door when he began to open it. He worked past his fears and yanked the door. It swung open and out spilled the decaying body of his mother.

The children screamed.

Arthur yelped and leaped backwards.

Her forehead had a large gash and was shaded with a ghastly bruise. Her mouth was drooped open in a drawl. Her eyes were sunken deep within their sockets.

His heart banged like a drum as his pulse quickened. His eyes fixed to his mother's arms and legs. Large chunks of meat were missing. A thought flashed across his mind as the words of his oldest son, John, screamed in his head:

Mama said she caught a hog in her trap last week. We've been feeding off it ever since. We ran out of food about three weeks after you left. We were all starving until she got that hog.

"Dear Jesus, what have you done, Josey?"

He turned to look at her. Her shoulders sagged. Her voice cracked as she said, "It was an accident, I swear.

We would have starved, Arthur. I didn't know what else to do."

57 miles West of Wilmington, NC
Present Day

MARIA FAULKNER had been saving for a down payment on a home for the last three years. She and her nine-year old son, Sammy, have lived in an apartment ever since they lost their home to foreclosure when her husband died. Maria spent countless hours combing every Zillow, Realtor, and Craigslist ad she could find. Yesterday she stumbled upon a nice, new doublewide sitting on two acres of land well within her budget. She wasted no time calling the buyer's agent she and her husband had used in the past.

She signed the necessary agency agreements and scheduled a showing later that day.

"So, this one is a two bed two bath. It comes in just shy of fifteen hundred square feet. There are luxury vinyl flooring throughout, and as you can see, you have brand-new stainless-steel appliances," her agent said as she gave Maria and Sammy a tour.

Sammy clung to her side while working on a blue sucker. Maria noticed he seemed particularly fixated on the closet of what would be his bedroom. He'd locked eyes on it the second they stepped into the room. Almost as if he'd heard or saw something. She felt him grip her arm tighter when her agent opened the closet door.

Maria rubbed her hand through his hair and patted his back.

"It's okay sweetie. There's nothing to be afraid of. See. It's just a closet. Look how big this room is. You'll have twice the space here as we do at the apartment." Maria says to him.

Her agent smiles and waves her hands throughout the closet. "I remember I used to be scared of closets too when I was a kid. I bet even your mom was at one time."

"I sure was."

"I remember my mom said she had Bloody Bones when she was growing up. My grandma used to tell her that Bloody Bones was going to get her and her brothers if they didn't behave." The agent whispers past the side of her hand to Sammy, "It was just scare tactic kid. There's no such thing as monsters in closets. There all just as empty as this one. Here's your proof."

Sammy still stares at the closet.

"I'll bet you're a big Lego guy aren't ya? Huh? I just bet you are."

She looks at Maria and grins.

"He hasn't spoken since Sean died on deployment. That was three years ago."

The agent places her hand to her heart and says, "Oh my God. I'm so sorry to hear that."

"Thank you. Yeah, he was just starting to talk before Sean was sent to Iraq for a second tour. His doctors say couple his autism along with such a traumatic event at a young age, may lead to him never speaking again."

The agent squeezes Maria's arm and says, "I'm so sorry. Maria, you are strong woman to endure what you have. You're doing amazing. Sean would be so proud of you."

Maria sniffled and said, "Thank you. I try my best. That's all I can do."

Maria would go on to get an offer accepted on the property and a month later she and Sammy were moving in.

On the day of the move, with boxes scattered through the home and furniture quickly arranged in the living room, Maria and her best friend, Brittany, spend the evening chatting and sipping red wine as Sammy plays with Legos in the floor.

"You guys are going to love it here. This is so much better than the apartment. Like look at how much more space you have. And you have two acres too. Girl, you hit the jackpot with this place."

"Thank you. Yeah, I knew I couldn't pass this one up once the numbers made sense. I just have to get Sammy to overcome his fear of the closet. He's never been that way before, but for whatever reason, that closet in his room gives him the creeps or something. He sort of creeped me out the day of the showing."

"Really? What do you mean?" Brittany asks with a chuckle before sipping more wine. She crosses her legs like an Indian and turns toward Maria as they sit on opposite ends of the couch.

"I don't know. He's just going through a phase, I guess. I mean all this is new to him, you know. A few years ago, when Sean was still here, he went through a stage where he was afraid there was a monster under the bed. He'd go around saying, 'Monk monk. Monk monk,' and pointing under every bed."

Brittany laughed and said, "I remember that. He did that at my house a few times too."

"Yeah, he did, didn't he?"

The two continued chatting for another half hour before calling it a night. They hugged and said their goodbyes. Maria and Sammy stood on the front porch and watched Brittany back out of the driveway. After waving her off, Maria turned to Sammy and said, "You ready to tryout your new bed?"

Maria read to Sammy from the Adventures of Tom Sawyer, and within twenty minutes he was fast asleep. She laid in bed with him for another ten minutes or so to be sure he was out, before planting her feet to the floor.

She flicked off his lamp and crossed for the door. She watched him for a moment as she peered through the darkness. Maria smiled and let out a sigh before easing the door shut.

IN HIS DREAM, he was sailing down the river on a homemade raft. The wind brushed his hair back and water splashed his face. Something rattled loudly but he could never place where the sound was coming from. It reminded him of the antlers his dad used when he took him deer hunting. He had watched him clank and rattle them together from the tree stand or blind. That is what the sound reminded him of. His dream began to fade as reality blended in to confuse the two states of consciousness.

The dream turned to darkness with a faint red hue as he stared at the back of his eyelids. The sound of rattling bones continued. He flashed opened his eyes and jolted up in bed. The bed sheets were thrown to the foot of the bed during his movement. His breath came in short gasps. He blinked as he tried to peer through the darkness. The rattling came once more. It ceased when his eyes fell on the closet. The folding doors were left open as he had begged his mom not to close them.

All he could see was the faint outcropping of a few shirts hanging in place. Then his heart knocked. He swore he could make out a face staring back at him. He fumbled for the flashlight on his nightstand. He found it and brought it to his chest. The bone rattling started again. He struggled to find the on switch for a second. He panted for breath and felt himself wet the bed. He started to whimper before finally switching on the light. He jerked it to the open closet. Nothing. Just clothes.

The light winked, flickered, then burned out.

He smacked the side of it, but it never came back to life. He remembered the night vision option on his iPad's camera. It lay on the nightstand next to him. He reached over and snatched it. He flipped over the cover. The screen burned his eyes for a moment. He swiped to the camera and clicked a few buttons before the screen turned black and white. He angled the iPad to his closet and held it there. The hanging clothes came into picture. It was blurry at first, but then the lens focused. Something round drew his attention. He felt his pulse rachet up again as he slowly began making out the features of a face. The nose. The lips. The eyebrows. THE EYES! The lids flashed opened to reveal bright white eyes. The lips pulled back to show big white teeth. The figure hissed and rushed from the closet with its bony hands outstretched for him. He gasped and tossed the iPad. He yanked the covers over his head and clinched them tight within his little hands. The bone rattling sound filled the room again.

His whole body quivered. His bladder released a deluge. He felt the bed sink beneath something's weight near his feet. The thing's breath was raspy and smelled like sewage.

He could feel it crawling closer towards him. The bed squeaked with the added weight. He drew a deep breath and yelled with all he had in him.

He didn't stop yelling until something yanked the cover from him and turned on the lamp light. It was his mama. She hugged him tight and tried to console him.

He wept and pointed at the closet.

"Sshh. Sshh. It's okay. I'm here, honey. I'm here."

She rocked him in her arms as he clung tightly to her. After a few moments, Sammy finally began to settle. She stood and walked with him back to her room. She changed him out of his soiled clothes and sang to him until he fell asleep in her bed.

THE NEXT DAY she called Brittany to tell of their first night. Brittany mentioned she had an aunt who claimed to be a medium. She said she could come out and walk around the property to see if anything was going on. At least to ease Maria's mind a bit. She was hesitant at first, but since it was her friend's aunt, she gave in and agreed for Brittany to schedule an appointment.

The next day around noon, Brittany and her aunt, Valerie, pulled into the driveway.

Maria watched from the window as Brittany helped her aunt out of the car. She was a heavy-set lady with long gray hair and by the looks of it suffered greatly with bad knees and hips. She walked with a wooden cane to help with the hitch in her step. She wore numerous necklaces and bracelets. Brittany helped her towards the door. Maria watched her stop in her tracks after only taking a few steps.

Maria stepped out onto the front porch with Sammy clinging to her side.

"Hey Britt."

Brittany looked at her and placed a shushing finger to her lips. Maria looked on as her aunt Valerie scanned the land with squinted eyes.

A breeze rustled the leaves and birds sang while hopping from one branch to another. A dog barked in the distance followed by the crow of a confused rooster.

Finally, the lady broke her gaze and spoke, "There's a dark energy here. Something tragic has taken place upon this land. It weighs heavy on my spirit. I can feel it." The last two sentences she said while looking at Maria.

Maria's mouth went dry. She licked her lips and swallowed. She cleared her throat and added, "I'm not sure how to respond to that, but my name is Maria Faulkner. This is my son Sammy. I appreciate you agreeing to come out here on such short notice."

Valerie nodded and said with a tight smile, "It's a pleasure to meet you both. When Brittany told me this morning about your son's condition and behavior, I felt it was important for me to visit to see for myself. My instinct has always served me well, and from the moment we pulled into the driveway I could sense something was off about this place."

"I don't understand," Maria said with a wry smile and tilt of her head before continuing, "This is a new house. No one has ever lived here before."

"Your thinking's all wrong ma'am. Houses are not the only things that can be haunted. This here dirt is older than all of us combined. Something has happened here. It's not the house, but the land it sits upon."

"But why us? Why would anything want something to do with us?"

"Children like your son are exceptionally sensitive and vulnerable to the spirit realm. As are the young and elderly. Animals too. A dark spirit may attempt to attach itself to your son to draw from his light. Every dark being craves the light within such pure individuals. It will often intimidate or harass the pure and vulnerable to push them into a weakened state so it can draw from that light."

Maria sighed and rubbed her tear ducts.

"Do you mind if I have a walk around the property?"

Maria waved her around and said, "Be my guest."

The four of them angled for the back yard. The old lady's jewelry jingled when she walked. Once they rounded the corner of the house, Valerie stopped and scanned the land again. Maria watched her closely. After a few minutes the old lady grimaced before closing her eyes and swaying in place. She dropped her cane as her hands balled into fists. Brittany took hold of an arm and motioned for Maria to grab the other. The old lady rocked side to side while mumbling incoherently under her breath. This went on for five minutes or more. It ended when the lady slumped and dropped her head towards the ground. Her body hung limp for a moment before jolting straight. The old lady began an ear-piercing wail. She shook violently in Maria and Brittany's arms.

Brittany consoled her and patted her on the cheek. Maria watched Valerie's eyes flash wide as she panted for breath. She took hold of Maria and Brittany's hands, squeezing tight.

"Sshh. You're okay Aunt Valerie. We got you. We're here. Easy now. Catch your breath."

Sensing she was beginning to settle down, Maria stepped away to be with Sammy who stood to the side with wide eyes. Maria embraced her son as Brittany helped Valerie come to her senses.

From a dry throat came a cracking voice, "It's a female spirit. Her name is Margaret. She's haughty and narcissistic. I don't know what happened to her, but she feels she was wronged and defiled at her death. She is a vengeful and bitter spirit. I believe she had grandchildren in her lifetime, but she despised them and considered them a nuisance. I believe that may be why she has been giving your son trouble. She is strongly connected to closets. I don't know why that is the case, but there is something about closets that she is connected to."

Maria's mind instantly went back to the real estate agent's mention of the folklore her grandmother believed in. Maybe there was something to it.

Valerie stepped close to Maria and took her by the hand. She looked deeply in her eyes and said, "You will need to stand up to her and rule over her. You have to assert your dominance with her, or she will with you. She must know she has picked the wrong child to terrorize."

"Are you sure about all of this?"

"As sure as I've ever been in my life. I would advise making a salt perimeter around the entire house and make a line at the front and back doors. You may want to cover up your mirrors for the next few days as well, just to be sure you close off any portal in case she tries to bring along other spirits."

"My God, should I call a preacher or something to bless the place?"

"It certainly wouldn't hurt."

That night Maria had Sammy sleep in her bed. She left all the lights on throughout the house and kept the closet doors open. She'd also done as Valerie had said about the salt. A preacher from the local Freewill Baptist Church was scheduled for a visit tomorrow.

Sammy had stayed awake with her for most of the night while keeping a watchful eye on the closet. Maria reassured him numerous times that everything would be okay. Mama was here now.

It must've been around midnight when Sammy finally drifted to sleep. Maria wasn't far behind. She dreamed of a family beach trip much like the one they had taken shortly before her husband's death.

As she entered that distant land between dream and reality, she began to hear noises. It started as a faint creak like the working of a rusty door hinge waving in the wind. Then it turned into a horsed whisper with a raspy undertone. Her dream of the beach quickly faded to black as the gravelly whispers grew louder. They begin to be accompanied by the sound of rattling bones. She felt herself stir as she swam to the surface of consciousness. She opened her eyes. The room was pitch black. Her nose felt like an icicle. Her cheeks stung as if she were walking in a blizzard. She watched as her breath steamed into the darkness. The bones continued to rattle, and something began to growl.

She tossed the covers back and felt for Sammy. Her hand hit the mattress. The space next to her was empty. Her heart leaped into her throat. She found him sitting up in bed with his gaze fixed towards the closet. Her eyes went there too. A silhouette formed in the darkness. She stared until the features came into picture. She could see the shape of a woman's face with long hair and bony hands stretching for her son. The woman growled as her bones creaked and rattled.

Maria jolted to her feet and shouted at the spirit. Margaret snapped her head around and hissed. Maria snatched Sammy from the bed and held him close to her side. The old hag roared. Her bones clattered together.

"Go away. You hear me? You're not welcome here. This is my house. This is my land. THIS IS MY SON!"

The spirit let out a long, piercing wail before something popped as air rushed in to replace where she once stood. The lights flickered and hummed before coming to life. The temperature of the room returned to normal. Maria squeezed her son and kissed his head.

"It's okay sweetie. Mommy's here."

The next morning Maria called and told Brittany of their experience.

The first thing Maria said when Brittany answered was, "Well, I think I got rid of Bloody Bones."

That she did. Margaret never returned after that night. That isn't to say Maria hasn't caught herself checking the closets from time to time or bolting awake every time something goes bump in the night. So far, those bumps have been nothing more than the house settling or a branch tapping a window. It would be nice if things stayed that way.

The Dog of Deadwood

November 17, 1958

7 miles south of Deadwood.

4:58 p.m.

The day slipped away as the sun peeped over the clouds for the last time. It disappeared and gave way to a dreary overcast which covered the land. Slithering patches of fog meandered their way in and out of the trees before resting atop Cedar Lake to create an array of apparitions. Sparrows rummaged about in the bush, shifting and crackling dead leaves with their tiny feet. A chubby squirrel with a mouthful of acorns skittered down the same tree, raking off the bark before leaping to the ground and bolting away into a briar thicket. A hungry carp rolled at the surface of the lake, sending a ripple trailing to the banks. A gang of Ravens rested in the top of a tall cedar. They glared down and cawed a dozen warnings of the coming darkness.

Sitting on his haunches with his back pressed firm to a large oak, the hunter looked on at the stirring animals less than a hundred yards away. His deer rifle rested across his lap with a round chambered and the safety engaged.

The hunter scratched his beard, sighed, and glanced at his watch. He had another half hour before the sun would officially set. Better get moving while he still had enough light to see his way out. He had about a half mile to reach the trail, another mile to reach his truck, then at least five miles to make it to Deadwood.

Conceding victory, the hunter rose to his feet in a huff then glared down the long path leading to the edge of Cedar Lake. As he was about to turn and head for the trail, the crackling of leaves and twigs stole his attention. He froze in place before leaning his shoulder against the oak. The hunter steadied his grip on the rifle as he waited and listened.

The bush stirred once more. It came from a few dozen yards away in the thicket. If a deer stepped out of the woods where the sound emitted, he'd have a perfect shot.

There was more thrashing and crunching of dead leaves and twigs.

He could feel his heart pick up pace as the palms of his hands became moist. He swallowed hard, then raised his rifle and propped himself up against the tree. He steadied his aim and waited for the moment of truth.

After minutes had passed of the deer's rummaging, it stopped. Dead silent. Did it smell him? Couldn't have, he's down wind. Why did it stop?

That's when he noticed how eerily quiet everything had become. The birds were still, and not moving or saying a word. Nature was listening.

He pulled back from the rifle's aim, scrunched his brows and began to scan the area in slow sweeps.

Pop!

His heart got a start at the crack of a large branch directly behind him. Before he could even turn, every hair on his body was forced to stiffen at the sound of a long, deep howl blasting through the air.

Owwwwww-wooooollllll!

His blood turned to a slush as a thousand bumps scattered across his flesh in rapid fashion. The carotid artery along his neck thumped like a plucked fourth string on a bass guitar. His heart knocked against his chest as the animal continued its long and guttural howl. Its booming voice echoed through the forest.

The hunter leapt into action. He dashed through the thicket, tearing past limbs and briars, and leaping over logs as he raced for his truck. Heavy feet pounded just behind his heels, thrashing through the woods after him. The air had filled with an inky blackness. It smothered him and stole precious oxygen from his lungs. He began to gasp for breath as his air steamed off into the ebbing day. His eyes darted to and fro to scan the plethora of passing trees. He sought desperately for the trail leading back to his truck. His knuckles turned white as he clinched the rifle. He leapt over another log and landed hard on the other side. It sent a flash of pain snaking from the arch of his foot up the side of his calf. His face twisted with pain.

Can't stop! Must keep moving!

The thudding foot falls crashed even louder behind him. The thing was gaining ground!

A string of deep grunts and growls from what sounded like a rabid dog tore through the air, thumping against his ear drums.

What the heck is this thing?

His lungs screaming in agony, burning with an unbearable pain from the lack of oxygen. His muscles were aching and tiring, but he continued bounding through the forest. He snaked in and out of the trees, dodging their punches and swipes.

Another howl drummed from behind, and sent a splash of ice water down his spine.

Owwwwww-wooooolllll!

Oh, dear God!

Onward he fled, racing with labored breath, pressing for the trail. He ducked beneath a branch and side stepped the trunk of a small tree. His heart found relief at the sight of the trail just ahead. That hope was quickly snuffed by the loud growl emitting just behind him. The thumping feet were close, and scraped at his heels.

A flash of hot searing pain ripped across his back, pushing him face first to the earth. He landed with a thud, knocking the air out of him. His chest and lungs throbbed as they begged for breath. His back screamed and pleaded for attention. He could feel warm liquid sliding down his back and sides.

Blood?

The rifle landed a few feet in front of him.

His body wrecked with pain, he forced himself into a crawl towards his weapon. His fingers dug into the cold soil as he pulled himself closer. His face twisted with terror and agony. He struggled to catch his breath.

Owwwwww-wooooolllll!

Oh, God no!

He stretched forth his hand. Took hold of the rifle. Brought it to his gut. Pushed off the safety. Rolled onto his back side, leaned up, and took aim.

Nothing.

He darted the rifle's aim side to side in frantic sweeps.

Nothing.

The snarled growl from a demon loosed from hell rumbled just behind his ear. The blood drained from the hunter's face as his heart came to a screeching halt.

Before he could even flinch, his death already began.

A mile to his truck and five and a half miles from the town of Deadwood, his blood curdling screams could continue until tomorrow's dawn and no one would ever hear.

As the creature enjoyed its kill, smacking and slurping up the goodness, the moon peeked out from behind the patch of clouds, shining its light upon the carnage below.

The creature stood to its feet with blood streaked across its face, raised its vision to the full moon and let out another sequence of its booming howl.

Owwwwww-wooooolllll!

7 months later

June 27, 1959

I REMEMBER WELL my first encounter with the Dog of Deadwood. It happened late one Saturday night. I was sitting on the couch watching a rerun of Superman on our new boxed television set when my mama, who was seated next to me in her rocker and working on something with her yarn and needle, asked if I'd fed Wilber.

"No Mama, not yet. Can I do it as soon as this is over?"

She tilted her head and sighed, "Yeah, but soon as it's over I want you out there. Don't want the poor dog starving all night," she said, then went back to her knitting.

After a climatic action scene filled with bams, pops, smashes, booms, and Superman saving the day, I rose from my seat and headed for the kitchen.

I opened the pantry and searched for the bag of dog food.

"Mama . . . I think we're out of dogfood."

"Oh, well take him that plate of spaghetti in the fridge. It's probably bout spoiled anyhow. He'll like it."

I rummaged through the fridge and pulled out the foil wrapped plate then crossed for the back porch.

"I'll be right back."

"Okay, hang on, I'll watch you from the porch."

I shut the screen door and bounded off the steps. I made my way down the hill towards Wilber's doghouse.

As I neared, I heard his tail wagging and smacking against the walls of his home. The chain rattled, and I saw him emit from the box.

The screen door slammed shut, and I heard Mama trying to sweet-talk Sylvester as he must've been rubbing against her legs, striking up his purring motor. He was the only cat we had left. The coyotes must've gotten all the others.

I sat the plate of food down and stepped within Wilber's reach. I gave him some strokes across his head and under his chin. He always loved the attention. I picked up Wilber's food bowl and crossed to empty the remains against a tree at the edge of the wood line.

A crowd of crickets were in mid-chorus as a soft breeze tickled the leaves above me. The hoot of an Owl off in the distance echoed among the trees, joined by a thousand screechy cries of tree frogs singing into the dark night.

I banged the metal bowl against the tree and looked in awe at the full moon above. It shined bright among a million stuttering stars before wispy clouds crossed in front of it and blocked its light. I was covered in darkness. The words of the town's gossip about the hunter they'd found shredded down near Cedar Lake filled my mind and caused me to pick up my pace.

I swallowed hard and hurried back to the plate of spaghetti resting on the ground a few feet from me. I unwrapped the foil and picked up a stick to rake it into his bowl. I hunched at the back as I began to fill his bowl.

Pop!

My heart knocked at the sound of a cracking branch. I darted my eyes to the edge of the woods. My feet were frozen to the ground.

Snap! Thud!

I couldn't move. My entire soul was engulfed with fear as my body began to tremble.

Wilber let out a quick bark then entered a soft whimper before retreating to his doghouse. I could still hear my mama talking to Sylvester on the porch, she had no idea what was going on down the hill.

I heard one last crunch of leaves . . . and that's when it stepped out of the woods. All I saw was a big black silhouette with pointy ears. It had bulky shoulders with long arms that dangled to its knees. It was covered in thick wavy hair that danced with the breeze. The moon poked out from the clouds and sent its light swimming to the beast. Starting at its feet then slowly rising to its face. It was covered in thick black hair from head to toe except for its face. Its face was twisted and snarled like that of a dog but with big red glowing eyes and a mouth full of oversized teeth, and a small spot near its navel that was bald.

In that instant, my chubby body broke from its glitch to send my heavy feet pounding across the earth. I grasped for ground and bolted to the house. Tears blurred my vision and choked my breath. I had to reach the back porch. I had to reach Mama.

Hearing the ruckus coming towards her, she began to call out, "What is it? What is it? What-what?"

I pounded up the steps and crashed into her arms, prodding her inside.

"What? What is it?" she kept asking.

We entered the backdoor and I slammed it shut behind us. I slid the dead bolt home and pulled back the curtain to take a quick peek out the window.

"Jackson Everett. Tell me what's going on right this minute."

I pulled away from the window on the door and pressed my back to it, still gasping for breath.

"I saw some-I saw some-some-something."

"Ssshhh. Now calm down, catch your breath. You're going to end up hyperventilating," she said as she took my hand and sat me down at the kitchen table. She pulled out a chair and sat across from me.

I couldn't look at her, my eyes were trained to the door and window as if it were a magnet. I felt her fingers on my chin as she gently pulled my attention towards her.

"Jackson. Tell me what you saw out there."

My lips quivered as I stuttered out the words, "Big-big-monst-monst-monster-hai-hairy-hairy-monster."

My mother sighed and looked at me with a tilted head as she released my chin.

"Please. You have to believe me. I really saw something."

"Son, I'm not saying I don't believe you, it's just—"

"That you think it was my imagination?"

"Well, yeah. You got spooked and your mind played some tricks on you. That's all there is to it."

I dropped my head and looked back at the door, "I'm not ever feeding Wilber at night again."

"That's fine. You don't need to wait so late anyhow. Don't worry. There's nothing to be afraid of."

I looked back to my mother, dressed in her gown with a dozen hair rollers scattered atop her black crop of hair, "What about the hunter from Cedar Lake?"

"Jackson."

"I'm just saying. Something got him, didn't it? That wasn't someone's imagination."

"And it was probably just a bear. Not a monster."

I sighed and used my thumb to pick at a few fingernails in my lap.

"Well, I think it's time we turn it in for the night. What do you say?"

I nodded.

My mother stood from her chair and hugged me.

"It's okay, there's nothing to be afraid of. The night will pass, and you'll forget it ever happened."

She kissed my head.

But that night and the coming days have haunted me ever since.

1 week later

July 4, 1959

AFTER I TOLD a few buddies in the neighborhood of my encounter, word quickly spread that little Jack Petarson had lost his marbles and started seeing werewolves. Word even got to the locals and on two separate occasions while I was about town with my mother, people stared and gawked at us as if we had three heads or something. You'd feel someone watching then turn to catch them whispering near the milk fridge or produce section. You'd pass someone along the street, and they'd turn and give you the stink eye as if I'd conspired to kill Eisenhower.

People were already stressed out over the dismembered deer hunter found near Cedar Lake, and I guess my claims of seeing a werewolf didn't help. I heard

Sam Cartwright, our local gun and ammo salesman, had sold out of rifles and bullets shortly after they found the shredded deer hunter. He of course made another nice profit after the rumors of my werewolf sighting spread like the plague among Deadwood.

The paper in Wilmington even wrote an article about it. They contacted my mother, but she denied them any press coverage. Last thing she wanted was for my chubby cheeks to be in the Wilmington Star in regard to a werewolf sighting. I was already bullied enough at school. I didn't need any more unwelcome attention. Especially something like that. So, I missed out on a chance of becoming an overnight celebrity and received a detailed lecture from mother about gossip and choosing better friends instead.

And with it being the Fourth of July, a pool party at my Uncle Bill's seemed like the best thing for ending a hectic and embarrassing week.

"Will Gabe and Scarlet be there?" I asked looking to my mother from the passenger seat in our burgundy 1947 Ford Super Deluxe V-8 2 door that my mother had paid for in cash from her savings a summer ago.

"They should be. Uncle Bill said he and Melanie were working things out and expected her and the kids to be there. We'll see. You know how that goes."

"Yeah."

"We'll need to stop and grab a few things from AL's before we get there. Watermelon, some Pepsi . . . oh and some hotdog buns. Don't let me forget, okay?"

"I won't," I said while watching the trees streak by and looking up to the bright blue sky. Not a cloud in sight. I could hear Uncle Bill's pool calling my name and I could hardly wait to do a cannonball off the deep end.

As we rumbled our way down the secluded two-lane stretch of road that wound its way along a few S curves here and there, I found myself retreating back to that night. The big black outcropping of that ... *thing*... pounded at my mind's eye over and over again. What the heck was it? I'd never seen anything like it and prayed to God I never would again. But that was one prayer that went unanswered, because I did see it again.

AFTER ENTERING AL'S, my mother and I split. She went for the hotdog buns and Pepsi while I went in search of the world's largest watermelon. The gawking glares of the town's folk had mostly ebbed, but there were still a few exceptions. Like the old man in overalls and a straw hat leaning against the music box playing Hank Williams's *Kaw-Liga* from staticky speakers. His searing eyes were too sharp for me to look into, so I diverted my eyes directly in front of me and forced my feet to march for the produce.

Ole Al, busied himself stacking new crates of tomatoes. He had thick black hair and a chiseled frame despite his age. He was dressed in jeans and a white tee rolled at the cuff which held his smokes.

"Hey Mr. Al," I said while looking out the corner of my eye, not really sure if I spoke loud enough for him to hear.

He stopped his stacking, "Oh, hey there Jack. How's it going? Ain't seen ya in a while? Everything all right with ya? How's ya mama?"

I nodded as I picked up a nice melon with a golden spot on its belly, "Good."

"Well, that's good. Hey ... about the uh ... um ..."

Oh boy.

"... well why don't ya just say it Al. About what happened. The talk going around. Did you really see it?"

It was the tone in his voice and look in his eyes that said maybe I wasn't alone in all of this.

I nodded.

He stepped closer and placed an arm around my shoulder, before walking me towards the back. We passed the music box. The old man watched with his angle brows shaded under his hat. His face was stern and unmoving as if he were a wooden sculpture.

We reached the back of the store where bags of grain and beans were stored and stacked. Al stood on his tip toes to look over the aisles to be sure no one was eaves dropping. He leaned down and for a long time looked me in the eye, deciding whether he should say what was on his mind or not.

He swallowed hard then whispered, "I've seen it too. That hunter near Cedar Lake . . . wasn't no bear that got him. No sur. That was something else. That was the beast. The werewolf, dogman, or monster, whatever you want to call it. What you saw was real. I know. You're not crazy and don't let anyone ever tell you, you are. Just because you encountered something they can't explain doesn't mean it didn't happen."

I nodded.

"But I want you to be careful, you hear? There're some things out there we've yet to discover and I think this might be one of em. Don't go out at night and be sure your doors and windows are locked. He seems to have trouble with doors. And he don't much like fire either."

Jackson!

My mother's voice called from the other end of the store.

Al rose from his crouch and patted me on the shoulder, "I believe you kid. You're not the only one to ever see the Dog of Deadwood and you probably won't be the last.

C'mon let's get you back to ya mama," he said with a grin, "He's with me Miss Petarson, don't ya worry."

I heard her heels clicking across the tile as she rounded the edge of an aisle a few feet over from us.

"Oh, thank heavens. Jackson, I told you to stay at the produce or come to the bread section. You scared me."

Before I could even answer, Al had started talking, "Oh, my apologies Miss Petarson, I was showing him the new shipment of grain we just got. Told him I could use another hand this summer. Maybe on the weekends?"

"Yeah. We'll talk about it. I'm sure he wouldn't mind making a little money."

I bobbed my head and shuffled my feet across the tile.

Al gave me a good slap on the back. I looked up, he smiled and winked, "C'mon let's get you folks rung up."

My mother never asked about Al, and I didn't tell her what he said until after everything happened.

WE FINALLY MADE it to Uncle Bill's. He was standing by the grill when we arrived. Talking it up with a few pals while flipping burgers and sipping a cold Pepsi. He tossed his hand up when he saw us come through the wooden door of the fence surrounding his ginormous swimming pool. He often joked that he once caught a king mackerel out of it. God knows it was certainly big enough for such a creature.

I toted the watermelon behind my mother and sat it down in the kitchen where she got caught in conversation with a few lady friends.

I then headed back outside for the pool. Gabe and Scarlet, my two eleven-year-old twin cousins, were splashing around with a few of the neighborhood kids as the aroma of a summer cookout and sunscreen lotion filled the air.

I was always a big kid around the waist and the summer of 59 was no exception. I'd particularly packed on a few extra pounds during the last year after my dad was killed in Korea. Though I'd never tell my mother this, I think she may have gained a few pounds that year as well.

Always conscious of my weight, I was never one to rush into shedding my shirt. But after taking a few breaths, marinating what others would probably think of my flabby skin, and seeing one of the neighborhood kids, who was even bigger than me jump and splash without shame, I peeled my shirt off and ran for the diving board.

Cannonball!

I landed with a *boowoosh* sound that nearly put out the fire to my uncle's grill. Yeah, I was that hefty. My history teacher always said I should've been a lineman on the football team.

Anyhow, I spent the next hour or so being a kid with my cousins and making friends with the others. After winning the biggest splash competition, my cousin Gabe and I were treading water near the deep end when he asked the big question, "So, you saw a werewolf, uh?"

"What? How'd you find out?"

"I've got my sources," he said with a side grin.

"Yeah, we heard you may have lost your marbles. You haven't have you?" Scarlet said as she came paddling up behind me, before spewing a gush of water to the sky.

I kicked my feet and flapped my arms to keep afloat as the hot Carolina sun beat down upon my neck and shoulders, "No. I haven't."

"Good. That's good to know," said Gabe.

"So, what did you see?" asked Scarlet.

"I don't know. I just know I don't ever want to see it again."

"You think that's what got the feller at Cedar Lake?" asked Gabe.

"Maybe."

Scarlet with her eyes in a daze looking at the fence behind me, "You're going to need a silver bullet."

Me and Gabe chuckled.

"What? A silver bullet?" I scoffed.

"That's what they used in the books."

"What books?" I asked.

Scarlet flipped her wet hair with a toss of her hand then went back to treading water, "Oh, you know. *The Werewolf of Paris, Man-Wolf and Other Tales, Darker Than You Think*, there's a few others, but those are most memorable."

"I don't know if a silver bullet would stop this thing. I think you'd need something more than that."

"Like what?" asked Gabe.

"Maybe fire." I said.

Scarlet chuckled, "Yeah, that could work."

I scanned around the pool and found my mother and Uncle Bill seated at a table talking with a few of the neighbors.

"Let's see if your dad will get in with us," I said to Gabe and Scarlet.

Scarlet rolled her eyes and gave a twisted smile, "You can try, but I don't think he wants to get his hair wet. Trying to look like Elvis I think."

I chuckled then swam my way to the shallow end and conquered the steps. Gabe and Scarlet followed me.

Mom and Uncle Bill were laughing with the others as we approached them.

"C'mon Uncle Bill, come swim with us," I said tugging at his hand. He wore a white polo shirt with black swimming trunks, his gold necklace riding just below his curly black chest hair.

"Oh, I don't know. Might get sick. You know you're not supposed to swim on a full belly."

He said while smiling at the adults.

I wouldn't let him rest.

"C'mon." I said while pulling on his hand.

After seeing my persistence, he finally obliged.

"Okay. But not for long," he said standing and pointing to each of us.

I went running back towards the steps of the pool then turned around to see him taking off his shirt. My heart sank at what my eyes were showing me. Every bone in my body rattled as I was instantly doused in ice water.

Just next to his navel was a mark. A scar.

In the exact same place as the creature's bald spot.

My feet were cemented in place.

I was taken back to that night.

The flash of that black silhouette filled my mind. Then the moonlight shining on it to expose that bald patch in the same spot as Uncle Bill's scar.

It seemed that for the longest time, we just stared at each other, just like that night.

I could feel my hands begin to tremble as my knees knocked against one another at the sight of my uncle stepping towards me. I watched as the expression on his face changed at the realization that I'd spotted the scar. He came to me and plopped one of his big hands on my shoulder. Skin on skin. The smack stung.

"What's the matter? Looks like you've seen a ghost. You haven't, have you?"

I swallowed hard and wagged my head.

"Good. Well, what are we waiting for? Let's swim," he said pushing me onward to the steps.

I stopped and pulled away, "You know I'm not feeling so well."

Uncle Bill didn't say a word. His sharp eyes said enough. I half expected his ears to turn to a point and those thick chest hairs to spread across his body right there in front of everyone before he went on a wild feeding frenzy.

"What's the matter? You were fine a second ago," said Scarlet.

"I just don't feel good," I said turning away and heading back to my mother seated at the table.

I glanced over my shoulder to see Gabe and Scarlet racing past Uncle Bill, heading for the steps. His face was stern, eyes locked on mine. In a slow wag, he shook his head while keeping a firm jaw and angled brows.

I jerked my head back around in time as I reached my mother's side.

"I don't feel so good. Can we go now?"

"What? Are you okay?" she asked while feeling my head with the back of her hand like most mothers would.

She grabbed her bag and said goodbye to those at the table.

When I looked back to Uncle Bill at the poolside, he was gone. My eyes found him in the deep end, swimming with Gabe and Scarlet.

We locked eyes once more as my mother and I were leaving and again, he looked at me with a set jaw and scrunched brows, slowly wagging his head.

I TRIED TELLING my mother on the way home why I *really* wanted to leave Uncle Bill's pool party, but she laughed at my theory of him being a werewolf. Got to say,

I probably would have laughed too if my kid had told me my brother was a werewolf.

We made it home around six or so that evening, and I wasted no time feeding Wilber. The last thing I wanted was to have to be out there at night again.

It wasn't long before the fireworks began. My mother said we didn't have enough money to spend on fireworks that year and she didn't want me risking a finger or hand anyway. We made our way out to the front porch and rested in the rockers as we watched the night light up with sparkling booms and blasts from the neighborhood. She toted our small Victrola record player out and put on some Everly Brothers tunes. We ooh-ed and aw-ed with each explosion as the Everly Brothers sang *All I have to do is dream.*

Then I remember her leaning on the arm of her rocking chair and saying, "Jackson . . . I want you listen to me for a moment."

Oh boy. I remember thinking.

". . . I know we might not have the best of things or the most of things, but one thing I can assure you . . . we don't lack love or trust. And that is what will get you through the hardest of times. I want you to remember that you hear?"

I nodded.

She placed a hand on my forearm.

I looked her in the eye.

"I love you son. I always will. No matter what. I want you to believe in yourself. Just because we might be poor now, doesn't mean you have to be when you grow older. I want you to do better than this. Don't you ever settle for less than what you're capable of. You dream big and be all that you can be. Ain't nothing you can't do. You can do anything you set your mind to."

"I know mama."

"Good," she said with a sniffle as she patted my arm.

A moment passed.

"So that's not a scar on Uncle Bill?"

"No honey, it's his birthmark. Had it for as long as I can remember. Mama used to say it was where he got shot or stabbed during a past life."

"Past life?"

"Yeah, just some old folklore. Some people say your birth mark is the wound that killed ya in a past life before you entered this one. It's an old wives tale, I guess. Lots of people have them, some just stick around longer than others. Mine went away when I was just a kid."

"Really? Where was yours?"

"Between my shoulder blades," she said pointing with a thumb.

"Did I ever have one?"

"No, sure didn't."

"Did dad?"

She blinked a few times, then drew a deep breath and said, "No, he didn't either."

A firework crackled overhead, splashing the dark sky with pops of light.

We didn't say another word for a good while after that. Words weren't needed, our presence was good enough.

The vinyl record ended, and I remember mother flipping to the other side and lowering the needle. As *Bird Dog* blared through the air with the flashing colors of exploding gunpowder sparkling in our eyes, I entered a daze and said, "I'm not the only one to ever see this thing."

I continued to look straight ahead but could feel her turn and look at me.

I added, "Al has seen it before too."

I heard her sigh.

"Jackson."

"Mama, you gotta believe me."

"I do honey, I do. I believe you saw *something*. But I don't believe you saw a werewolf. They don't even exist."

"You weren't there. Mama, please. Please believe me. I know what I saw. And Uncle Bill has the same . . . scar, birth mark, whatever you want to call it, in the exact same place."

"Sweetie," she said with a sigh before adding, "I don't know what you want me to do. If this is some way to gain my attention then baby, you don't have to do stuff like this. I know we've had it rough since your father died, and I've been working a lot here recently, but baby you know I love you and you know I'd do anything to make things better for us. I'm trying with everything I know how..." her voice trailed off at the end as she brought a hand to her mouth and entered a soft sob.

I rose from my rocker and wrapped her in my arms. She wept against my shoulder as her hot tears soaked through my shirt.

"I know that Mama. And I'm not doing and saying all of this to seek attention. I don't have to. You're the best mother I could ever ask for. I'm saying all of this because it's true. I know it down to the core of my being. I know what I saw. And Uncle Bill knows I know. You have to trust me."

She sniffled and nodded against my chest.

I kissed her on the top of her head and pulled back.

"Please, Mama."

"What should we do?"

"Secure all the doors and windows and make sure the gun's loaded. Do we still have gas in the can?"

"I think so. Why?"

"We could use it to make a fire."

"A fire?"

"Yeah, with all that hair, I don't think he'd like fire too much. I know I wouldn't."

I FOUND A HALF empty metal gas container underneath the lean to against the house. I sat it just outside the back door, but within arm's reach. Then, with my mother by my side, we went down and got Wilber to bring him inside for the night. With her help we pushed some furniture against the front and back doors, then hammered a few nails into the windows to be sure. My mother found dad's rifle and a box of ammo. She sat them both on her dresser.

The fireworks were still booming outside but slowing to a halt as we crawled closer to the dawn's early light. Must've been just after midnight when we were satisfied with our work. Our bodies half drug us to our beds as our eyes were growing heavier by the second.

"Honey, I don't think an army could get through tonight, let alone some half man and half dog thing."

I chuckled.

"You can sleep in my room tonight if it makes you feel better."

It did and I didn't argue.

MUST'VE BEEN AN hour later when I was awoken to the sound of something banging up against the side of the house. It hit so hard it knocked off one of my mother's pictures she had hanging on her wall. We both raised up in unison. I looked at her, she looked to me. Our faces each asking, "What was that?"

Wilber stood at the foot of the bed, staring at the outside wall that'd just taken a punch. He entered a soft whimper like he did the night I saw the creature. He started backing up slowly as his toenails ticked across the floor.

My heart pounded and knocked against my chest. My lungs were taking in air faster than I could function.

I felt my mother's hand squeeze around my wrist. Her palm was greased with sweat. I heard her breathing from her mouth.

Bam!

The whole wall rattled and vibrated. As did my innards.

I felt the bed shift. I looked and found my mother standing to her feet before crossing for the gun on the dresser.

"You know how to use that thing?" I asked.

"Your father taught me a thing or two," she said while sliding the bolt back and chambering a round.

Bam!

My flesh must've leaped a foot.

Owwwwww-woooooollllll!

The hair on my neck stood straight.

My world came to a halt. Everything entered slow-motion.

I looked at my mother standing to my left at the dresser. She had the gun clutched within her grasp. Her mouth hung open, and her eyes were wide.

Bam!

The wall shook again.

Wilber let out a bark that I think was more out of fear reflex than aggression.

"C'mere," my mother said in a quick whisper.

I bolted from the bed and ran to her side. I threw my arm around her waist and stared at the wall.

Bam!

This time it hit the wall the bed was against and knocked off a picture above the headboard.

Owwwwww-woooooolllll!

My hands took on the tremors again as my spine grew cold.

The howl ended but was proceeded by long, dragged-out scratching noises along the side of the house.

Wilber barked again, but my mother was quick to shush him.

The scratching stopped. Everything got quiet. I swear I could hear blood pulsing through my veins.

Crash!

A window shattered. Sounded like the one over the kitchen sink.

Owwwwww-woooooolllll!

Mama spun and faced the open bedroom door. She aimed the gun from her hip.

I heard the window on the back door explode.

With our breath racing out faster with every gasp, Mama slammed and locked the bedroom door, then stepped back and trained her aim to it.

Crap! The gas can. I left it at the back door. We'd have to get it.

"Mama! The gas can."

"What about it?"

"I left it at the back door."

"Well, I don't think you want to go get it now, do you?"

Everything got quiet again.

Wilber crawled under the bed and vanished from the scene. I couldn't blame him.

A long moment passed of eerie silence.

"C'mon. We have to make it to the phone. I'll have to call the Sheriff and report a burglary."

"No! What if it's inside?"

"Didn't sound like anyone came inside. They'd had to have crawled through the windows. Those are small windows. C'mon, let me get to the phone."

I watched as she reached for the doorknob and twisted it open. The door creaked on its old hinges as it swung. The floor moaned when we stepped across it.

We eased down the hall, then peeped around the corner into the living room. It was dark. Only the light from the moon shining through a double window behind the couch shone as it created a halo of light on the living room rug.

We looked in the kitchen and saw the window busted above the sink, just like I'd imagined.

Taking baby steps and constantly looking over our shoulders, we reached the back door. The kitchen table and chairs were still pressed against it, but the little window was shattered, and deep claw marks were raked across the wood near the doorknob.

"We have to get that gas," I said.

I knew we needed it, but for the life of me I didn't want me or my mother having to step a foot outside to get it.

"And do what? Burn the house down. Gas ain't going to do us no good unless we're outside and away from the house."

I parted my mouth to speak, but my words were cut short by another voice. Not from my mother nor me.

"It's safer in here. Don't go out there."

I gasped and bolted around searching for the source of the voice, but my eyes found only darkness.

I felt my mother jump as she gasped as well.

"Please. Don't go out there. It's safer in here. Trust me."

My eyes darted to every shadow as my heart sank to my gut, weighing me down, pulling me to my soon to be grave. My veins were cold as blood raced through them in an effort to keep up with my pounding pulse.

"Bill?" my mother asked with a crack in her voice.

"See Mama, I told you."

"Stay back, I've got a gun."

"That won't do you much good. I'm your only hope tonight. You'll need more than a gun against what lurks beyond these walls. Trust me."

"Mom! He's lying!"

I pushed past her and hurried to pull away the table and chairs.

"Marilynn . . . please. Don't go out there."

"Don't listen to him, Mama. Please. C'mon help me."

I'd moved the two chairs but was struggling in removing the table. I watched my mother stand frozen in place as Uncle Bill filled her mind with his lies.

"Bill, I don't know what you're up to, but I have to trust my son with this one. Stay where you are. Don't try me. Not now."

I heard him sniffle.

"I'm not going to hurt you. I'm here to protect you," his voice sounded strained and weird. Distorted even, but he remained in the shadows of the living room.

Mama braced the rifle against her right hip, keeping it aimed to where Uncle Bill was hiding, and helped with her left hand to drag the table away from the door.

With the door cleared, I took a moment to marinate our situation.

I knew Uncle Bill was the werewolf because I saw the birth mark. But is there truth in his words? Is he here to protect us from something? After replaying his demeanor at the pool, I had my doubts. The only thing I could think of at that point was the gas container.

"C'mon. We got to go," I said to my mother as I tugged at her arm.

She took a moment, no doubt having the same thoughts as I only moments ago.

"Please, Marilynn. I can protect you better in here," Uncle Bill's voice seeped out of the darkness.

"I'm sorry Bill, I can't trust you right now. I have to go with my son."

With that, I flung open the door, reached down and grasped the container. Its cold metal handle filled my palm.

We raced off the porch and couldn't have bounded three or four steps when the sound of the most devilish growls stung my ears.

I heard my mother grunt behind me as if the wind had gotten knocked out of her. Before I could turn to see, I heard her smack the dirt with a thud. The rifle clambered across the ground.

All I could see was a black silhouette crouched over top of her, growling and tossing her side to side like a rag doll.

Tears sprang to my eyes as my heart felt as if it'd gotten stung by a hornet. The awefullest growl ripped through the air as my mother entered a loud shriek, filled with what sounded like mortal agony.

I forced myself into action, bolted and nearly tripped over my own feet in efforts for the rifle laying between myself and the atrocity taken place just feet away,

I stumbled for it and crashed to my knees. The gas container was still clutched in my grips as I reached for the rifle.

My mother's screams and the beast's murderous anger tore at my psyche. I dropped the gas can and was bringing up my aim to the beast, but at that instant all I saw was a flash of blackness streak by, knocking the beast from my mother. A black ball of growling animals rolled across the dirt, tearing at one another's flesh with claws and razor-sharp teeth.

With the rifle in my grips, I picked up the can of gas again and crawled to my mother's side. She moaned and whimpered with words I couldn't understand.

I sat on my haunches next to her and looked on as not one, but two of these hair covered creatures scrambled and fought, tearing at one another's throat right before my eyes.

"The gas," my mother wheezed out.

I looked at the gas container in hand, then looked up at the beasts rolling and growling like rabid dogs less than a stone's throw away.

I pulled back and tossed the gas container as far as I could throw it. It tinged off one of their bodies. I took aim and fired. Miss. The creatures didn't faze. They even bumped into the can, causing it to spin and move about a foot.

"How do I reload? How do I reload?"

My mother took the gun, slid back the bolt, chambered a round then steadied her aim and waited. The creatures moved closer to the can.

One of them stopped and looked dead at us, then bolted to the side the instant I heard the shot ring out. An instantaneous boom and a flash of exploding light licked up the darkness, sending red and orange flames dancing to the moon above. My face flushed with heat. One of the creatures belted out a long screech from a scratchy throat as it was covered in flames and throwing its arm about as it twisted in circles.

I heard my mother chamber another round.

The shot rang out.

I heard the creature grunt.

It stumbled away from us then crashed to the earth with a loud thud, fully engulfed in the flame.

I looked on in shock, unable to think or say a word. Other than her labored breathing, my mother was quiet as well.

I turned to her, "Are you okay?"

"Yeah-yeah, I think so. My arm's cut pretty bad."

I took off my shirt and wrapped it around where bloody claw marks were streaked. The orange glow of the flame gave me just enough light to see. I found myself glancing upward. I scanned the yard for the other beast.

"Are you sure you're okay?"

"Yes, I'm sure. Did he get you anywhere?" she asked.

"No-no, I'm fine."

"I told you I'd protect you," the voice crackled.

I jerked my head, searching the darkness once again for the source. My eyes found something to the left of us. A large figure came closer and stepped into the light.

Uncle Bill.

I gasped.

"Ssshh . . . it's okay. I'm your protector. This one's been following you for a while. I've watched him as you've fed Wilber. He's the one who killed the hunter at Cedar Lake."

"Who-who-who is he? What is he?"

Uncle Bill drew a long breath as he squatted down beside my mother, tending to her wound. He was dressed again in the clothes he wore at the pool earlier.

"Butch Ferguson."

My mother gasped.

The name didn't register to me.

"Butch Ferguson with the chicken farm?" my mother asked.

Uncle Bill nodded.

Then it dawned on me.

Butch Ferguson with the chicken farm is the old man I saw at Al's store. The one in the overalls and straw hat, leaning against the music box.

"He was the same as me, only evil. I'm from a different breed."

"How-how did this happen? How did I never know?" my mother asked.

I heard voices coming down the road. I looked and saw a trio of flashlights bounding our way. The neighbors.

"I'll explain all of that later. Right now, we have to deal with explaining why Mr. Ferguson is shot and burnt to a crisp in your back yard."

Forty Years Later

1999

LOOKING BACK ON it now after all these years, I still don't know if I believe what happened that summer. Just feels kind of like a dream. I can't tell whether it was real or not. All I know is, my mother went to her grave with scars on her arm from that night. Of course, only I, her, and Uncle Bill ever knew what really caused them. Everyone else was told she cut herself on the glass somehow during a scuffle with Butch Ferguson. He was always sweet on the ladies anyhow, so wasn't all that hard in fooling the authorities into believing he'd gotten drunk that fourth of July night and wandered out of his crevice for some loving. And after forcing himself into the home and causing trouble, things turned south.

It was considered self-defense and my mother was never charged, neither was Uncle Bill.

As for Uncle Bill's explaining, which he did give a few days later. He told us that late one night towards the end of his tour in Korea, that him and a few buddies stumbled upon this palm reader on the streets. They dared each other to sit down and have a chat with this little old Asian lady that was dressed with enough beads around her neck that must've outweighed her own body.

She went on to tell my Uncle Bill about his past life. Saying that he was once a guard dog to a high ranking official for the Austrian Army during World War One. And that it was his job to be the last line of defense against any enemy sneaking into the Officer's chambers. Uncle Bill was stabbed and killed while defending his owner from an intruder. She told him of the entry wound along his belly, near the navel. She'd said all of this without him ever telling her of his birth mark in the exact spot where she described him being stabbed in his past life. She then went on to tell him of certain evils lurking among us, just behind a *Veil of Grace*, she called it. And that he was bestowed with the honor of protecting the innocent from such evils.

That was his rationale for the whole werewolf thing. He said the reason I saw him that night while feeding Wilber, was because Butch was stalking me and about to pounce. He said, "if only you'd have seen what stood behind you that night."

So, as I cruise down Ocean Boulevard here at Ocean Isle in my convertible Ford Mustang, with aviator glasses adorning my eyes, and my ears graced with some good old tunes from Elvis, and the Everly Brothers, I often find myself wondering . . . why us? Why were we chosen for all of that? Then I also wonder if my uncle's genes were passed down to Gabe and Scarlet and what kind of secrets they may be hiding. Who knows?

And so, after all that craziness, I became a writer. God knows I have enough material to draw from. I'm glad I took mama's advice that night out on the porch. I dreamed big and because of that I finally broke the New York Times Best Seller list. What's my bestselling novel, you might ask? Of course, it's none other than . . . *The Dog of Deadwood.*

Wailing in the night

New York City
October
1942

I keep it locked in the basement. It eats like you and me.

It talks like you and me, but it doesn't sleep like you and me. When I forget to feed it, I'm reminded of my mistake by its long, throaty wail. It becomes angry when ignored. Before I changed the locks it would roam about and hide in the darkness while craving another meal. I know it has more than once reached for me from the shadows of my home with its curled hands that look like bird claws. I have felt it caress my soul with its ghostly touch, and I have heard its whispers during the midnight hours. It knows my name. Yes, it most definitely knows my name.

I tend to believe it followed me home nine years ago on the thirteenth night of October. I remember that night very well. The days prior were rather difficult as I'd prayed earnestly for a life-long companion to accompany me the rest of my living days. My plea was granted that night, although not in the way I'd wished. As the years have passed, I now know I shall never be alone if I'm on this side of heaven. It has been with me ever since and shall be forevermore. It is an ailment of which I'm convinced no amount of prayer or pleading will ever be able to cure. It is decided. It is final. And it is here.

Thank goodness the new locks have kept it caged because for the past week, sleep had become a distant memory. If tonight is successful, it'll mark the second night in a row of no roamings. We shall see. I have some errands to tend this evening, and how I do wish the locks will have held when I return.

†††††††††

THOUGH I HAVE recently withdrew myself from the congregation, I find it fills my soul with comfort to attend a confession of sorts as often as I can. Despite the tragedy which has befallen me, I have somehow managed to cling to what little faith I have left. The stained-glass windows and hollow sanctuary have become my sense of refuge as of late. The thing has almost driven me to my mind's limits. If I can continue to keep it locked in my basement, I believe there may be a slither of hope for me.

I can hear my footsteps echo among the walls of the cathedral where the patron saints are sculpted. Mother Mary eyes me as I pass between the pews while heading for the front door. Before reaching forth my hand to take hold of the handle, I turn to look into the eyes of Christ as he hangs limp upon the cross at the altar. I take a deep breath, return my top hat to its rightful place, secure my scarf and rosary beads, and open the door.

A brisk wind greets my cheeks, and I watch my breath steam into the night. I retrieve my pocket watch to see that it is a quarter past ten. The streets are dark and lifeless as the curfew has been met. The dimming of the city has come. No lights, or big city entertainment in fear of being bombed by our enemies across the pond. The dark quiet gives the streets an eerie vibe. Almost feels as if we've been rushed into an apocalyptic aftermath.

I angle down the steps of Mother Mary's and begin my trek home. Halfway down the dismal sidewalk, I begin hearing the voices. They grow louder the further I go. I squint my eyes and rub my tear ducts. I tell myself it's my recent depravity of sleep which is causing the voices to multiply. The voices become so loud with their sharp

53

edged chitter chatter that they cause my head to throb just behind my eyes as if tiny creatures are scratching upon the backs of my eyeballs. I grind my molars and continue to angle down the sidewalk. With one hand tucked tightly beneath an armpit, I rub my forehead with the other, trying desperately to soothe the inevitable.

Please, for heaven's sake, not again!

The chatter continues and so does the throbbing behind my eyes. I pass under a string of lifeless streetlamps and walk by a group of apartment complexes. A wrought ironed gate separates the apartments from the sidewalk.

I notice a couple up ahead walking arm in arm towards me. I squeeze my arms tight to secure my coat. My cheeks and nose are beginning to sting. Icy tears continuously pour from my eyes as they fight the harsh wind. I feel my body jolt when the loud scream of a woman gives my heart a start. I jerk my head up towards the source of the sound. In the fourth story apartment building to my right, a lady leans out of her window and yells at the young couple passing below her on the street. The couple stops, smiles, and waves back at the woman in the window. As I near this couple, a gust of wind rushes across our path, sending leaves skittering over the pavement.

A tingling sensation spreads throughout my body. No, please don't let it happen again! I angle my head down, wrap myself tighter in a hug, and quicken my steps to pass the couple. I try desperately to avoid making any eye contact. I edge closer and attempt to pass but the man takes a step back. Now directly in my path. I accidentally brush shoulders with him, and as I turn back to offer an apology . . . that's when what I had just prayed would not happen, happened.

The man and woman now stare directly at me. Their faces are drooped with death and decay. Their necks are swollen with dark and protruding veins. Their eyes are black and sunken deep within pale faces. Their lips are pulled tight to reveal nothing but teeth. A black swirl of smoke surrounds their skeletal-like bodies. But it's their words that frighten me most. In tight, raspy tones, the young couple says: *Better hurry home Father, for she's waiting.*

I feel a scream well up within me, but it's held captive by the bone chilling fear of what my eyes and ears have just witnessed. Cold fingers trail up and down my spine. A light rain begins to descend. Fog snakes its way from the heavens and settles into the street.

I spin around and try to enter a trot, but I'm almost knocked to the ground by the large belly of a man dressed in a ground dragging black trench coat. "Hey, watch it will ya!"

I gather myself and stumble past him. My throat is still clinching any would be words for an apology. As I turn, I catch glimpse of the young couple again. Their faces and bodies have returned to normal. Thank God. However, their words continue to haunt me as I stride closer to my home. *Better hurry home Father, for she's waiting.*

†††††††††

I REACH MY home and quickly make my way inside. I shut the door behind me, unwrap my scarf, and place it and my coat upon the rack. I leave the rosary beads about my neck as well as my white collar. I stand silently in the foyer and listen. The wind rips about outside, blowing in wailing gales as it thrusts and beats upon my home causing it to creak and groan. I stand still and try to listen past the noise. I'm desperately hoping there will be no sound of it running about my home with its feet slapping and thudding upon my floors.

The locks had to have held. I do not know how much more I can withstand to behold the sight and sounds of that ungodly creature. There must be a better way, for this is not what I had in mind. I take three timid steps forward to reach my staircase which leads to my bedroom. With one hand on the railing, I lean to look up the stairs. It's dark and quiet.

"Hello?" No answer. "Are you up there?" Only the sound of wind and rain answer my question.

Satisfied that the home is quiet and void of any darting shadows, I carefully make my way out of the foyer. I pass the dining room and find it neatly set with silverware as it should be. As I near the kitchen, I notice an amber glow as if from a small flame. I swallow hard and press onward.

I enter through my saloon style doors and stand in the kitchen. A small candle burns upon the tile next to the sink. It sits within a candle holder and rests atop what appears to be a neatly written note. I feel my heart pick up pace as I slowly and carefully angle closer. All while darting my eyes about every shadow, hoping not to see one come alive and reach out with her curled claw of a hand.

I take hold of the white piece of paper and slide it out from beneath the candle holder. I hold up the candle to light the words. Scribbled with neat penmanship is the following:

I missed you, and I'm glad you're home.

I rub my face and curse beneath my breath. I clinch my fist tight around the note, wadding it into a tight ball. I throw the crumpled paper to the floor and march off for the basement. I snatch up the candle to light my way.

The locks didn't hold. They couldn't have.

Using the candle flame as my guide, I reach the basement door and turn the handle. Unlocked. Judas Priest! The door swings open with a soft creak. Dusty air fills my nostrils and tickles my throat. I cough into the crevice of my elbow. The basement awaits me. Only the decline of stairs stands between us. I crane my head low and gaze at what the candle flame bids me to see.

I take slow, soft steps as I begin the descent to where she should be waiting. The floorboards creak beneath my weight. I make my way down one heel to toe step at a time. The home creaks above from a gust of wind. I swallow hard and rub my face with my free hand. Is she down here? Has she escaped? She wouldn't leave me like that though, would she? She's too attached, right? Yes, she's too attached indeed.

A distant growl of thunder rumbles the bones of my home. Tiny patches of dust fall from the floor joist above me. I take another heel to toe step. The steps creak again. I descend further. More creaking. I reach the last step and stand a moment to listen before stepping onto the basement floor. I scan the room with my swaying candle flame. Despite the light of the flame, the room feels darker and colder now. I feel the hairs on my arms and neck begin to straighten. Chill bumps spread up and down my body. That's a good sign though. She must still be down here.

I turn to my left and step toward the cage. The amber glow reveals the black bars and door with all the locks. Her bed is neatly made as it is sandwiched in between her two favorite nightstands. A replica of the setting in which she'd spent a third of her living days. I can see from this distance that the locks have held. I feel a slight bit of tension release in my throat and chest, allowing me to breathe again. I dare not step any closer. I squint hard to check the corner shadows of the cage.

"Are you in there, sweetie?" I say with trembling jaws.

No answer.

More thunder rumbles in the atmosphere. More dust settles to the floor.

I scratch the back of my neck and search the floor for words.

Soft and melodic at first, I hear her turntable record player begin to play her favorite album. The one by Dinah Shore. *Blues in the Night* starts to play, drifting slowly from the cage and lingering into the dusty air. I clinch my eyes and shake my head while saying through grinding teeth, "No. No. NO. NO! NOOOOO!"

Warm tears snake down my cheeks. I sniffle and wipe my face.

"Please honey. Don't do this."

Dinah Shore sings from the record, "A man is a two faced . . . a worrisome thing who'll leave you to sing the blu-uu-uues in the night."

I look up and stare into the darkened cage to say it again, "Please hon—"

"Sshh." Her raspy voice rises over Dinah Shore's to pierce my heart. The record player comes to a screeching halt. I feel my hands and knees begin to tremble.

"I died alone with no one there to hold my hand. No one there to send me off into the light. You weren't there, and for that I will forever be here."

"Please, sweeti—"

My words were cut short by the sound of her growling. She rushes out from the shadows towards the bars. All I saw was her misshapen figure emitting with a curled hand from the dark. I drop the candle to the dust and bolt for the stairs. Leaving her in the darkness while she screams and wails. I hear her beating upon the metal bars as Dinah Shore sings again about men leaving her to sing the blues in the night. Halfway up the stairs, my feet tangle and send me clashing into the wooden boards. I bang my knee and shin, and just narrowly avoid cracking my chin on the rise of a step. I gather myself and hurry up the remaining steps.

Her piercing wail rises behind me. I burst through the door and crash to my knees in the hallway. I push myself up as fast as I am able. I then turn and ram my shoulder against the door. I rush to send the dead bolt home. The instant the door secures, her wailing ceases, and so does Dinah Shore's soothing voice.

Gasping for breath and trying to decipher a million thoughts rushing through my head, I bend at the waist and place both palms to the tops of my knees. With adrenaline beginning to wane, the pain of my tumble on the stairs raises its ugly head. I wince while rubbing my injured knee and shin. A chill washes over me as I try my darndest to forget what just happened in the basement. I hobble off towards the kitchen sink. Grasping through the darkness along the way.

I can hear the rain and thunder have grown more intense. Lightning now lights up my darkened home in sporadic strikes. I'm lucky not to have been visited by an officer regarding the candlelight left in my kitchen. With the war being as intense as it is right now, they take the curfew rather serious. Last thing they want is for someone to light the way for the enemy to make an easy bombing raid.

My train of thought gets sidetracked as I enter the kitchen. The candle and note! She'd gotten out! Judas Priest! The locks didn't hold. They couldn't have. She tricked me.

My breath leaves me, and I rush to the sink to splash water on my face. After three dousings, I retrieve a glass. I gulp down two cups and take a third with me to bed. I don't want to have to face her again. Not tonight. I need my sleep. I need to crawl beneath the covers, close my eyes, and pray for daylight. At least in sleep there will be peace. I just hope and pray she doesn't crawl into bed with me as she did last week.

Dear God, not that again.

††††††††††

IT COULDN'T HAVE been a few hours later when I was roused awake by the sound of loud knocks in sharp succession. Accompanying the knocks was the tune of Dinah Shore followed by a shriek from somewhere beneath me. I jolted up and threw the covers from me so fast it caused my head to spin as my eyes struggled to decipher the shadows swirling about my bedroom.

Bam! Bam! Bam!

I swallow and blink away the slag in my eye as I go to stand. Who the heck would be knocking at this time of night? Had an officer saw the candlelight from earlier? Had she escaped and lit another one? Regardless, I reach for my robe on the back of my chair in the corner. I secure the ties around my waist and take two steps to pass through my door. Dinah Shore continues to sing the blues in the night from deep within the basement. Then there came another kind of noise. At first I thought it was more knocks, but these weren't knocks. No. This was the sound of someone running. Feet pound across the floors below me, reverberating throughout the house. She's loose! She thuds in quick strides as bare feet slap against the cold floor. She's going towards my front door.

"Coming," says a soft voice.

Dear God, she's going to open the door! I can't let her open that door. I can't let anyone see her like this.

My heart pounds as I bolt towards the stairs. Coming to the top of them, I hear the front door unlatch before swinging open. A rush of wind swooshes in to send a cold chill throughout the home. I'm halfway down the stairs when I hear a familiar voice say, "Tom? Why good heavens, what are you doing? Where'd you go?"

I continue down the stairs and can now see my friend Steve closing the door behind him. His big, bulky back is set to me. He secures the door and removes his top hat.

"Steve? What are you doing here?" I say while stealing side glances about my foyer and dining room. I wonder if she'll be brave enough to reveal herself to an outsider?

Steve gasps as he flinches at my words. He utters a curse and says, "I thought I heard you run towards the kitchen. How the heck did you get back so fast? I heard you unlock the door. It came open and then you ran off. What are you doing? Are you alright?"

I nod and come down the last riser. My wounded knee and shin remind me of the whole shebang from earlier. "What time is it?" I ask as I rub at my eyes.

"It's a half past twelve." Steve says while scanning my home. "Are you sure you're okay, Tom?"

"Yeah. Yeah. I'm fine."

"Well, what was all that noise and running around? And is that Dinah Shore coming from the basement?"

His questions were becoming like nagging mosquitoes and I attempted to fend them off, one swat at a time.

"The house moans and groans ya know when it's bad windy out. Been doing it a lot lately with the recent storms. And yeah, that's Dinah Shore. Listen though, it's not what you think. I need it Steve. It helps me sleep at night. Makes me think she's still with me."

"Listen, whatever gives you comfort Tom. You got to do what you got to do."

I nod, "So, why are you here again?"

"Oh, right. Have you been by the church tonight?"

"Yeah, I was there a few hours ago? Why?"

"The front door was open. I noticed it on the way home from my shift at the mill. Don't worry, I closed it up for you and used the spare key on the porch. I checked everything to be sure no one was messing around. The wind must've opened it. Maybe you forgot to dead bolt it and it didn't latch all the way or something."

"Huh, yeah I guess so. Well, I appreciate you taking care of it for me and stopping by to let me know."

"Yeah, I hated to drop in on you at this time of night, but figured I'd check to be sure it was you."

"Well, thank y—"

In midsentence, Dinah Shore's voice turns loud and screechy while transitioning up and down unnatural octaves. I feel my blood turn cold as it seems to have trouble swimming upstream. My feet glue me in place, and I begin to pray beneath my breath that she will not scream. I feel Steve looking at me for an explanation, and I hear his lips part to question me, but she screams before the question comes. Loud and shrill, she begins to wail.

Bam! It sounded like the door to the basement slammed shut.

"What the heck was that?" Steve asks.

My lips stammered as words became scarce. I can't answer him. I can't move.

"For heaven's sake, Tom, who is that? What have you done? Are you off your meds?"

"It's nothing. And I told you before I don't take the pills anymore."

"You never told me that." Steve said with his eyes growing wider by the second. "And like hell it was nothing. That sounded like a woman screaming. Oh, Tom what have you done?"

He marches down the foyer towards the source of the screams, but I step in front of him and place a hand to his chest. "Now hold on, I can explain this, Steve."

He swats my hand away and says, "Then you can explain while we go see what that was."

"Steve. No, listen. Please, you have to listen." I say while finding myself back stepping through the foyer. Past the dining room. This bull of a man continues to push onward toward the basement. I can't let him see her. No one can. "Steve, stop. You have to listen to me!" I curse out loud and shove him back. "Enough! I can't let yo—"

She wails again. This time longer and louder.

Steve draws a deep breath through his nose and angles his head down at me and says, "Tom, I'm going to see who that is whether you like it or not. So, please, before anyone gets hurt, step aside."

Biting at my lip and darting my eyes about the hallway, I feel my pulse pound against my ribs. My hands turn numb. I can now taste blood in my mouth from where I'd bitten too hard on my lip. I cross my arms and cradle my chin in one hand. A million thoughts tumble through my aching head. I shut my eyes and draw a deep breath. I rub my face and place my hands to my hips. I look up at Steve and nod before saying, "But promise me you'll listen to my story."

"I promise I'll listen, but I can't promise I'll understand. Now, take me to the basement."

With that, I turn and head for the door. Steve follows just behind my heels. The music stops below us. The home is quiet now besides our own footfalls. We reach the door. I place a hand to the knob and rest my left ear against the wood. Silence. Will she show herself?

"Tom, c'mon now. Open that door."

I dip my head and slowly twist the knob. The door swings open with its familiar creaking. The stairs disappear as they lead into darkness. I hear a metal chink and flick. The darkness flees at the flame from Steve's lighter. Together we make our way down. One step at a time.

Heel to toe. Creak. Heel to toe. Creak.

All the way down. Our little circle of light taking us deeper into the chamber. We step off the last riser and stand still upon the dust covered floor. I turn to Steve with a finger to my lips. I can see the tension and fear growing in his eyes. His Adam's Apple takes a bob as he looks past me while extending his hand holding the lighter. The room is quiet and dead. Tomb like.

I nod and step toward the cage tucked away in the corner shadow. Slowly . . . Steve's light begins to reveal it, and I hear him curse beneath his breath before finally cursing aloud when the cage comes into full view.

"Goodness, Tom. What have you done?" He says while rushing to the cage. I stand ten feet back and watch him bang on the cage as if to awaken her. At the moment, it appears she's chosen to remain on her side of heaven.

"What is this? What the hell is this, Tom? Are you keeping someone in there?"

"It's a holding cell. Something I started using a few years back when she began to turn."

Steve squints his eyes and shakes his head. "What? Do you hear yourself, Tom?" Holding the lighter in one hand, he plops the other atop his head and looks back into the cage.

"If you look hard enough at the bed, you'll see where she rests."

I watch as he moves closer to the cage and extends his hand between the bars. I hear him gasp and curse as his lighter pushes back the darkness. The bed comes into view.

"Tom, tell me that's not who I think it is. For heaven's sake, tell me this is not what I think it is."

"I wasn't there Steve. I wasn't there the night she died." I feel my throat constrict the words. "I couldn't live with myself, so the night after her funeral I dug her up while the grave was still fresh. That way no one would ever know. I brought her home and kept her here. When she began to decay, I took to learning how to lessen the process with the proper chemicals. Then once she dissolved to bones, I nailed and screwed things together to keep her intact. I begin placing her in bed with me at night. I'd tuck her in beside me to keep me company. It helped me cope through the loss."

"Christ Almighty, Tom."

"Don't say that, Steve." I look down and run my fingers through my hair. "I found that if I didn't take my meds, I'd hear her talk to me. It brought me great comfort to have her back. It was as if she'd never left. But as time went on, I noticed a change. She was becoming irritable. Our conversations often ended in arguments. She was always mad about something.

"Then she started moving on me. I'd come home to find her in another room. It wasn't long after she started moving around on me that I began hearing her roam the floors at night. I'd wake to the sounds of her running through the home. That eventually was accompanied by her screaming. I tried taking my meds again, but that only made things worse for some reason. So, two years ago I built the cage. It worked for a little while. Until she learned to pick the locks. Though I've never seen her skeleton move, I have seen something else. Like I said, I think she's turned."

Steve rubs his forehead. The lighter goes out. He hurries to flick it back on. "What are you talking about, Tom?"

"She's turned into something else. Something otherworldly. Not of here. A creature or ghost of sorts. I've never seen her fully, but I've seen enough. She likes to hide in the shadows. I'm waiting to see if she'll reveal herself to you like that. For your sake, Steve, I hope not."

"Listen Tom . . ." he says as he takes a look back to the bed where her skeleton lies tucked beneath the covers. "You need your meds. You need to see the doctor. We have to get you some help. Does your doctor know you've quit taking your medicine?"

I shake my head. "No. I make sure I get it filled on time and stay up to date, but I toss them down the toilet when I get home."

"C'mon Tom, let's get you out of here." He says as he places an arm around my shoulder.

"Are you going to tell?"

Steve takes a moment to answer, but says, "I don't know. I haven't decided yet. Let's get you some help, then we can figure the rest out from there. Okay?"

I nod.

Together we climbed the steps and left her by herself in the basement.

† † † † † † † † † †

One month later

November 15^{th,} 1942

THE ALLEGHENY STATE HOSPITAL, formerly known as the Allegheny Asylum for the Insane, is a 10,000 square foot red bricked building that was built in 1868 and is located some two hundred miles north of the Big Apple. Here in the north country, time is slower, the air is fresher, and the night is quieter as the animals watch various shapes of fog slither down from the saw-toothed mountains.

The Adirondacks stand for miles to the north and the Catskills lie jagged like shark's teeth to the south. Here the wildlife outnumbers humans, hunters outnumber men in business suits, trees outnumber streetlamps, and mentally disturbed patients in white gowns and sometimes shackles, outnumber orderlies and nurses.

The first patients to arrive at Allegheny were received via a steamboat from Geneva Lake on October 12, 1869. After removing the irons and chains from the incoming patients at the docks, they were transported by horse and buggy along the hoof trodden trails of the Catskill mountains. A stone's cast from these trails the transporters and patients would have passed numerous Indian Burial grounds.

Along those trails, a dozen or more patients escaped and fled into the vast wilderness never to be seen again. It's often rumored that on full moon nights you can hear them talking to one another as their voices ride the wind to meander among the valley residents below.

With this night missing its moon, it won't be the voices among the trees you'll hear, but rather the voices coming from within the institution.

The stars are scarce as they hide behind thick, low hanging clouds pregnant with winter's first big snow. A dusting has already taken place, but a blizzard will soon be coming.

Viewing from the wrought ironed gate, with razor wire curled inward along the tops of the surrounding fence, the Allegheny State Hospital is a daunting site to behold. A black silhouette with lit windows that look like a plethora of golden spider eyes glaring out of the shadows. Black figures pass back and forth by the windows. Some are orderlies making their rounds, or nurses giving the patients their shots and pills. The majority of the movements though are patients extinguishing the remainder of their energy as they prepare for "lights out."

If you were to dare enter through the big looming doors, your ears would likely be met with screams, laughter, repetitive chatter, and soothing elevator style music. Your eyes would behold white walls, white floors with pepper flakes, and red rugs with gold trimmings.

Walking along any of the curving corridors snaking to and from the three-story wards, each with the capacity for 125 residents, you'd pass numerous framed paintings of a big boned man dressed in a three piece suit, a top hat, and a pocket watch attached to his breast. This would be the founder, Dr. Willard Doth.

Doth passed away three years after Allegheny opened. A group of wealthy doctors from the Midwest soon took over. The doctors were known for their rather strange strategies in treating the mentally ill. They believed in harsher treatment than did Dr. Doth. For a period of four years following Doth's death, the patients at Allegheny were treated with brutal disrespect for their life and well-being. Often beaten, electrocuted, and stretched to their joint's boundaries, many of the patients did not survive the new treatments.

After a thorough investigation, one such patient was noted as being "deformed and demented," from having been chained in her cell for three years without a bed or change of clothing. Three other patients, all male, were found bound in three-foot by four-foot iron crates built for toting chickens. After these horrifying discoveries, the three doctors were relieved of their duties and sentenced to prison. All three died in their cells within the first two years of their sentences.

Rumors say the spirits of the tormented patients still roam the floors of Allegheny. Of course, it's always difficult to recognize them as they can blend in with the current patients. Some say you can tell the difference by the sounds the ghosts make. Chinks and rattling tings can sometimes be heard as if the ghosts were still bound in their iron shackles as they roam the halls of their previous home.

With the elevator style music beginning to fade the further you walk down this long corridor, the sounds of your heels clicking on the tiles now become evident. You are here in this place. You begin to pass by the nurses in their white uniforms and caps, and the orderlies in white or blue janitor suits. The place is loud with voices, screams, and giggles. You pass by many doors on your left and right. A golden line rests at the bottom and you see feet shadows pace to and fro within the rooms.

At the end of the hall, you see an open door and begin to hear more music. Only this music has a voice. A woman's voice. You know this voice well. You come closer to investigate. The music is soft and melodic, and it draws you into the room. Above the music you hear a man's voice with a questioning tone. You see a small bedroom arrangement. One man with wire rimmed glasses, who is dressed in a white gown, sits with a hunch in his back upon the mattress. His white hair is thick on the sides but fades away at the top like a monks would.

Another man, dressed in suit and tie with a long white coat and glasses, sits on a stool across from the bed. He has his legs crossed and is busy scribbling upon a clip board. You go and stand beside him, but he doesn't notice. They rarely do.

††††††††††

"DOCTOR MONTGOMERY, I'm telling you the truth. I'm taking my meds. I promise." I say before secretly asking for forgiveness for the lie I'd just told.

"I hope for your sake, Tom, you're being honest with me. As I've told you before, you know what can happen if you get out of routine with your medication. I can't stress it enough. I believe you, but we will continue to monitor that. Okay? And we'll know if you're being truthful. We always find out eventually."

I nod, "Yes, Doctor."

I look down at my feet which dangle off the bed. I take a deep breath and allow my mind to wander for a moment. I hear Doctor Montgomery speaking, but my mind goes back to the night I brought her home from the grave. I replay the plea and prayer I'd uttered about her forever being with me. I thought I was doing what I had to do. There's no telling what I would have done if I'd not found a way to cope with the pain.

With the doctor's words playing in the background of my mind, I feel a sudden breeze enter the room. The flesh on my arms is immediately ravaged with chill bumps. My throat constricts, and my heart bangs hard.

I raise my head, hoping and praying the doctor had opened my window to cause the draft, but deep down I knew this breeze didn't come from no window. I feel myself jolt before freezing with dread and terror at the sight before me. Doctor Montgomery is too busy speaking and looking at his clipboard to notice her crouching next to him. Her eyes are sunken deep within her skull, and her lips are pulled tight to leave her teeth exposed in a wide grin. Her hair is matted and stringy with visible sticks and leaves stuck in it. She's crouched with her bony, bird-like claws dangling to her knees. A sulfurous odor like boiled eggs and swamp water, surrounds her.

My heart hammers fast, my hands and legs tremble, and my teeth begin to quiver. My eyes are glued to those black holes where hers used to be. She smiles big and hard, then raises a hand and curls a finger towards herself. I feel a warm tear slip down my cheek, and the inside of my bottom lip begins to throb as the taste of blood fills my mouth. I swallow a gulp of blood-filled saliva, and I look to the stereo in the corner of my bedroom.

"Turn that off, please." I say as I bury my head into my hands.

"Pardon?"

"Please, turn the stereo off. That's Dinah Shore, my wife's favorite singer. Shut it off. Please. Just shut it off! Shut it off! SHUT IT OFF!"

"Okay. Okay. I will." Montgomery rushes over and turns the dial. The music dies slowly with popping static.

"I'm sorry, Tom. I didn't notice. Are you okay?"

I only nod.

He returns to his stool and fixes the flap of his coat. "Now, I only have a few more questions before our session is complete. Think you're up to a few more?"

I bob my head again.

"Okay. Good. You're doing good, Tom. Now, as for the hallucinations . . . have you had any lately?"

I hesitate to answer. I rub my face and spend extra time massaging my eyebrows. For the life of me, I don't want to look up, but something draws me like a moth to a flame. I open my eyes and slowly . . . raise my vision.

The doctor is alone.

I swallow another gulp of blood and saliva mix. With quickened breaths, I look straight into the eyes of the doctor. He has a face that looks like a turtle as his nose is upturned. I begin to form a sentence. Out of the corner of my eye, I see a shadow move by the stereo. I dare not look over there, but I know it's her. I can feel her. Doctor Montgomery squints his eyes and angles his head as he awaits my answer.

I lick my lips . . . and shake my head. "No."

Doctor Montgomery dips his head and returns to writing on his clipboard. At the boundary of my right eye, I see the shadow move. She rushes closer, floating over the tile. She crouches at an angle to my right, staring at me with those hollow, black eyes. I see her mouth droop open as if to scream. From somewhere deep within the chambers of the asylum a woman begins to wail. The woman stops when my deceased wife closes her mouth.

I watch as Doctor Montgomery sighs and removes his glasses. "I'm afraid I will need to tend to that. That will do for tonight. We'll pick back up two nights from now." He stands and crosses over to me. "You're doing well, Tom. Keep it up." He says with a pat to my shoulder before angling for the door.

Now alone with her, I dare not look her way. I just keep her in my peripheral. I watch as she moves back to the corner shadow next to the stereo. I hear her click and turn the dials. Static spits from the speaker, and Dinah Shore's voice returns to singing about the blues in the night.

With a trembling hand, I pinch my tear ducts before curling into a ball upon my bed. I tuck my feet beneath the bed sheets and pull the covers up to my chest. This is my curse for disturbing the dead. My plea was granted, and I'm afraid she'll forever be with me. Roaming these floors and wailing into the night. I shut my eyes and pray for sunlight.

Out Beyond the Pines

Devon Garrison's dream since childhood has been to venture deep into the secluded Blue Ridge Mountains on an extended camping and fishing trip. When a high-risk high-reward crypto bet paid off this past summer, Devon blocked out two weeks' time to check this coveted item off his bucket list.

The drive up from Florida had been long and exhausting but the reward waiting for him would make it all worth it. He arrived in Asheville late last night and stayed in a motel. He was up before the sunrise this morning and finds himself winding up a mountain towards his destination. The plan is to camp and live off grid for ten days. All the while hiking almost ten miles from various fishing spots he had scoped out and investigated through numerous online forms and YouTube videos.

His eighty-seven Ford Bronco crawls over the gravel as the pavement had ended long ago. Rocks ping against the undercarriage and wheel wells. The radio is tuned to a classic country station and ole Hank Williams moans out *Howling at the Moon.*

Fog slithers over the path as the headlights pierce into it. A swift breeze bends a few limbs and breaks off their leaves. Devon glances into the rearview mirror and sees orange and pink skies flooding the horizon as the sun shines through all the growth. He trains his eyes back on the road ahead and sees nothing but black sky as the night fights for another minute of power. A raccoon scurries across the path.

Devon smiles to himself and takes a deep breath to relish the moment. He would do anything if his brother Mike could have made the trip with him. The two had often talked about doing such a thing but were never able to get around to it. Mike died last May after a prolonged battle with ALS. Mike made Devon promise him he would take the fishing trip they had often talked about. Devon looked him in the eye and promised. If Mike hadn't of done that, truth be known, Devon may not have chosen to make the trip. He was torn. Part of him wanted to do it, but another part of him felt a little guilty for going without his brother.

He ran over a dip and the whole cab jiggled and squeaked. Devon lowered his foot onto the peddle and continued deeper into the mountains.

HE REACHED the checkpoint and eased the Bronco in front of the cedar hewed split rail fence near the visitor restrooms. He stepped out and gathered his gear, checking and rechecking everything as he went. He wore a Springfield XDM chambered in ten millimeter on his right hip and a hunting knife on his left. The Springfield had a capacity of sixteen rounds. The bullet entered like a quarter and exited like a cash register. He had enough fire power to bring down anything walking on two or four legs in the Northern Hemisphere two times over. He fitted into his heavy backpack, locked the Bronco, and headed for the trail.

Three wooden signs were nailed to a pine at the entrance. One said ½ mile to Devil's Pass, another said 3 miles to Crazy Woman Creek. The creek had received its name from a local folklore about an insane woman who had lived her whole life in the mountains before turning feral. She had lost her mind after her husband's passing. Legend says she's often heard wailing and moaning for her husband late into the night. There's countless tales of men being chased off the mountain from her piercing, hair raising screams. While interesting, Devon had never been one for any woo woo crap. The likely scenario was of course a mountain lion as they are known to sound strikingly similar to a woman in distress. Many Natives and early settlers thought the woods to be haunted and forbode anyone from meandering where the screams were heard. It wasn't some lonely ghost that Devon feared as much as it was a sneaky mountain lion creeping up behind him. Which was why he felt inclined to carry his Springfield.

His plan was to take his time hiking to Crazy Woman Creek, enjoy the scenery and fresh air, and make camp downriver at a place he heard was good for Rainbow Trout. It's there he plans to spend the day hunting for a big one. He'd head out in the morning for Johnathan's Creek which was another place known for good fishing.

Devon took out his cellphone and snapped a picture of the three signs. He sent it over to buddy and lady friend in Florida with a simple caption of:

Day 1 . . . Wish me luck!

He turned off his phone and slid it into a pocket in his backpack. A trio of crows began to caw overhead in a tall pine after he zipped it shut. The sun had risen enough to light the trail. Devon pulled his beanie further over his ears and blew into his hands. He clapped them together and huffed out a breath. He watched it steam into the cool morning air before beginning the trek to Crazy Woman Creek.

The leaves rustled to his right. He turned and watched a chubby squirrel dart up a pine tree with a mouthful of acorns. It climbed to a high branch and angled for its nest.

Another squirrel sat on an even higher branch and barked down at Devon as he passed.

The woods grew thicker the further he travelled. The pines eventually gave away to gumball trees, oaks, and spruce. Hillside blueberry, black huckleberry, and mountain laurel take advantage of the sunlight filtering through scarce gaps between the tall trees. A vast assortment of birds sing and call to one another as they light from one branch to another. Every so often, Devon hears the cawing of crows above the chatter of the other birds. The crows follow him as he goes.

The trail steepens and turns a bit rocky. He trips once and nearly twists an ankle. That's the last thing he needs is to twist an ankle in the first hour of the trip. Wouldn't that be something? It would be his luck too.

As he nears the top of the incline, he hears people talking. Two heads poke above the horizon of the trail. He sees an older lady and gentleman with hiking sticks heading his way. He nods and says hello. The couple do the same.

The man and woman are the only people Devon sees along his journey to Crazy Woman Creek.

A LITTLE OVER an hour and a half later, he reached Crazy Woman Creek. By nine o'clock he had found his spot and set up camp. With his tent set, he turned his attention to rigging up his rod. He tied on a small, white rooster tail with black and yellow spots and a gold blade. The rippling water filled his ears and made him feel like a kid again in anticipation of catching the big one. He made his way down to the creek bank and quickly made the first cast from his spinning reel. He'd thought about taking fly fishing lessons but decided it would be more aggravating than it was worth and chose to stick to his old and trusted spinning reel. He'd caught more fish than he could count with it and figured it'd be enough to do the trick here in the creeks of Southern Appalachia.

He'd go on to spend the next three hours walking up and down the creek bank making his casts. By lunchtime he had enough trout for two meals. He'd also missed a nice one that stole his rooster tail. He'd cursed loudly when the line snapped. It was shortly after that incident when he felt the eerie feeling of being watched. It had settled over him like the shadow of a dark storm cloud. He made a few quick glances over each shoulder and scanned across the creek for any movement. He chuckled at himself and hurried to tie on another rooster tail. This one was yellow with black feathers. He finished tying the lure and went about making his casts. Devon tucked the thought and feeling of being watched deep into the far corners of his mind.

After getting back to camp, he made quick work of cleaning the two big Rainbows. He roasted them over a fire and saved the leftovers in a baggy for later. As he sat on log next to the fire, letting his lunch settle, he took solitude in observing nature and listening to the sounds. He'd brought along a small bird book and busied himself with identifying each one he saw. Most of them he could name without the book's help, but a handful had him stumped.

The Purple Finch and American Kestrel were two in particular he had never seen before and wouldn't have been able to name had it not been for the book.

With his lunch settling, he turned to store the booklet into his bag but was frozen in place when a high-pitched shrill cut through the air. Every hair on his body jolted upright and he felt a chill slither down his spine. His eyes flashed wide as he did a quick scan of his surroundings.

"What in the hell was that?"

As he questioned the sound, it did it again. Long, guttural, and yet piercing. It sounded like a woman being murdered. The screams lasted only for twenty seconds or so, but it was enough to send gooseflesh spreading across his body. He'd never heard anything like it in his life. He had lived in the Florida everglades for the last thirty years and had heard all sorts of wildlife late in the night. Even heard a wild panther in the swamps one time. Sure, it'd spooked him, but it hadn't had half the effect of whatever animal this was. His primal instinct had kicked into high gear and everything in him wanted to high tail it back down the mountain to the safety of his Bronco. He felt himself brace at the knees as his pulse soared. His fists clinched at his sides, and he began to smell his own body odor. His fight or flight mode was in full effect.

He swallowed hard and darted his eyes about his surroundings, waiting for it to scream again. With his right hand resting on the butt of the pistol by his hip, he chuckled and wagged his head. It was probably just a big mountain lion letting him know he was encroaching on its territory.

"I hear ya big guy. I don't mean ya no harm. I promise. You don't bother me, and I won't bother you, deal?" He said to the forest.

He smiled as he thought about all the stories he'd read and heard about grown men retreating off the mountain from that sound.

"A bunch of grown men scared of a big cat. Humph. What a bunch of wimps?" he said to himself as he patted his pistol. He gave a good scan of the woods before picking up his fishing rod and heading back to the creek.

HE WENT ON TO fish for another four hours. He caught three more of decent size. The biggest he decided to keep. He snapped a picture of it and sent it to his friends in Florida. He returned to his camp as the sun began to sink behind the trees. He built another fire and filled his gut with roasted trout once more. With his belly stuffed and his morale filled to the brink, he retrieved his grandpa's harmonica he had tucked away in his bag. He lay on his back by the fire with his head propped against a log and played some tunes on the harmonica. He knew *Oh Susanna* and *I'll Fly Away*. He could also play bits of *I Saw The Light* as well as *You Are My Sunshine*. He tried a few blues licks his grandpa had taught him when he gave the instrument to him one Christmas. He was never able to get it down pat though.

Man, Mike would have loved this.

He thought to himself after pocketing the harmonica and staring at the stars. He spotted the big and little dipper and was then able to find Orion's belt. His mind went back to his childhood when he and Mike used to climb on the roof of their father's building during summer nights and count the stars. After a while they started naming them also. Devon laughed as he remembered the name his brother had given one. Carl. For whatever reason, he used to think a star named Carl was the funniest thing. He finds himself chuckling now at the thought. He shakes his head and smiles. He felt a deep pain for his brother. Somehow though, he liked to think maybe he was with him here after all. He had no way of rationalizing the feeling, but somehow, he just knew. He could feel him. He reasoned it must be due to the love and memories he has for him.

After a while, Devon felt sleep begin to settle over him, so he stood and crossed for his tent. Not before putting out the fire with a before bed piss though. Moments later he was crawling into the tent and tucking into his warm sleeping bag. The sounds of nature flooded his ears. Over the rippling water of the creek and way off in the distance, he could hear a whip-poor-will. He loathed the thought of hearing the crazy woman. It sent a shiver down his spine at the recollection of that shrill. He hid away all the stories of haunted forest, creek devils, and mountain demons to the far reaches of his mind. He focused his mind on his childhood with his brother and fell asleep to the sound of water and whirring crickets.

HE DREAMED he was a kid again as he and his brother played in the woods pushing over dead trees. They laughed and hollered as each one fell with a thump. He watched through a blur as they must've pushed over a half dozen or more of these dead trees. After the last one fell, an even louder crash sounded behind them. Their laughter halted as they both spun towards the sound. They leaned down and peered through the forest towards the noise. All was quiet. Devon took a few steps forward. The leaves and twigs crunched beneath him. His brother stayed put. With his attention fixed to the spot of the loud crash, a branch snapped under his foot. At that exact moment he heard his brother begin to scream and a flurry of commotion rattled behind him. Devon's heart pounded and his blood turned to ice. He spun on his heels. The sight before him stalled his racing heart. Every hair on his body stiffened. His brother was being dragged from his hair through the woods by a huge, black figure with hulking shoulders and long, slender fingers.

As his mind tried to comprehend what his eyes were showing him, the monstrous beast let out a guttural howl.

At that, Devon jolted from his sleeping bag. His heart pounded so hard it made his chest ache. He panted for breath. Sweat trickled down his forehead and leaked into an eye. He wiped away the burn. He rubbed his face with both hands and took deep breaths. His heart began to slow, and he swallowed hard. He clinched his eyes and massaged his tear ducts.

A branch snapped somewhere out beyond the pines. Devon opened his eyes and raised his head. He listened to how quiet the woods were. Even the crickets were silent.

Another branch popped. Devon grasped in the darkness for his backpack. He danced his hand around a bit and found it. He unzipped it as quietly as he could. He felt for his Springfield and found it. He drew it out and gripped it tight.

Snap!

He jerked to the right. Another broken twig. How did it move over there so fast? Are there two of them? Two of what?

Leaves rustled behind him. He was being surrounded. But by what?

His heart skipped a beat when he heard something grunt followed by heavy breathing.

He adjusted his grip on the pistol and aimed it towards the sounds. More movement to his left this time. It wasn't a deer or anything on four legs. He could tell by the crunching leaves and sticks it was on two legs.

It stopped. Everything went silent.

He listened. Nothing. Just an eerie stillness.

The wind whispered through the pines and a pinecone fell to the earth. He flinched when he heard it drop. He scoffed at himself and listened again for more movement. Nothing.

He rubbed his forehead and checked his watch. "Damn, it's two o'clock in the morning. There ain't nothing out there, Devon. You're just spooking yourself." He said aloud.

No sooner than he finished his words, a glass shattering shrill blasted into the night. He clinched his teeth and winced. His chest vibrated from the noise. Leaves and sticks stirred as something began to run circles around his tent. He could hear heavy feet slapping and pounding the earth. It huffed for breath and grunted with every stride. A tall, wide shadow flashed by the tent. Devon rose to a squatted position and trained his gun to the shadow on the tent wall. He followed it as best he could as it dashed around his tent, grunting and huffing. Its breath rattled with a rasp, coming from a mucus filled throat.

Devon centered his aim on the daunting silhouette and pulled the trigger. The inside of his tent flashed white, and his ears rang from the blast. The silhouette disappeared the instant his bullet left the barrel. Silence filled the air.

Devon panted for breath and held his shaking gun at eye level. He cursed and blinked hard. He flexed his jaw as sound slowly crawled back to his ear drums. A quarter sized hole in his tent allowed a slimmer of moon light to filter through the opening.

In the far distance, he could hear a voice. A scream. A call for help. It was faint but grew louder with each cry. He stepped closer to the bullet hole in his tent, turned his ear and listened. It was his brother's voice. He jerked back and stared at the hole. He shook his head.

"No. No. No. This isn't real. This isn't happening." He pinched his arm and slapped his cheek. He felt it all. This is real.

Help! Devonnnn! Help me!

His brother's voice called for help, drawing out the words.

Devon beat the heel of his hand against his forehead. His brother continued to yell as he drew closer with each scream.

Devon grinded his molars and steadied himself. His breathing quickened. He crossed to the opening of his tent and made quick work of the zipper. He stepped through and planted his feet on the hard soil. The creek rippled down the bank. His brother's voice continued wailing.

With his gun gripped tight and in a ready position, he angled around his tent, stood at the back of it, and listened.

His brother's screams ceased.

He stood there for a moment longer.

All he could hear was the breeze playing on the leaves and the rippling creek. The forest was tomb quiet. He had that strong feeling of being watched again. Devon scanned the darkened woods, looking for something peering out from the cover of a tree. He searched for leering eyes but never found any.

He lowered his gun and looked up at the full moon. He saw a wispy cloud pass in front of it.

Snap!

Before he could lower his eyes in time to investigate the noise, the beast was upon him. He caught a glimpse of black, wavy hair. He thought he saw an antler or a tree branch near its huge head. He heard it growling and felt its hot breath against his face just before it sank its teeth into his neck. He heard it make slurping sounds as he felt his rib cage being torn open. His world turned black as he fell into a deep sleep.

THREE DAYS later Devon Garrison's camp was discovered by a group of hikers. Everything had been ransacked and torn to shreds. There was no trace of the man nor any drops of blood. His pistol and a boot were found a few yards from his tent. A spent shell casing was discovered inside the tent. Ballistic investigators were able to match it with the size of the hole on the tent wall. His friends and closest relatives were informed of his disappearance a week later. Devon's off and on girlfriend in Florida, Caroline Brown, had contacted the North Carolina police after she hadn't heard from Devon in three days. He'd promised to call or text once a day. Her last conversation with him was when he had sent pictures of the trout he'd caught on the first day. Her call had put a name and face to the missing man.

DNR and forest rangers launched a search that lasted for a total of five days but had come no closer to finding him than they had the day his camp was discovered.

Caroline Brown along with Devon's best friend, John Beaty, had spent the better part of a month researching missing people cases near the Blue Ridge and Appalachian Mountains. There were hundreds if not thousands of cases of hikers, hunters, fishermen, kids, you name it who had vanished over the years in that region. Following the internet rabbit hole, Caroline and John stumbled across everything from Bigfoot, serial killers, aliens, ghosts, and pretty much everything in between. One scenario stood out among the others though. It was a tale they had come across on more than one occasion. It was the story on the origin for the name of Crazy Woman Creek.

Caroline had remembered Devon joking once that he hoped he didn't get killed by the ghost of the lonely woman who was said to roam the hills near Crazy Woman Creek. He had only mentioned it in passing late one night after they had both had a few too many drinks. They laughed and joked about it, never saying any more on the subject.

Caroline dug deeper and eventually found another origin story behind the name. She discovered a YouTube video of an elderly Native man sitting on the front porch of a log cabin in a rocking chair. He had two long braids of hair over each shoulder and wore a brown hat with feathers stuck on the side. He leaned forward in his rocking chair and placed his hands atop a wooden cane with an eagle carved into it.

He said many men had heard the crazy woman over the years. None had ever claimed to have seen her and survived. The old man said there were countless stories of men who had been spooked while out in the woods by something they couldn't identify. It would start with the feeling of being watched. Like something was hovering over your shoulder and breathing down your neck. Then you would hear phantom footsteps nearby in the woods. Many even claimed to hear the cries of passed loved ones as the entity mimicked the voices of those close to the victims. Some men claimed to have caught glimpse of something huge and bulky in the corner of their eye, tearing through the woods after them. Wailing and screeching like a dying woman during the pursuit. Someone behind the camera asked the man what this creature was.

Caroline and John watched the old Native in the video turn his gaze from the mountains ahead and look dead into the camera.

"You have to be careful when talking about these sorts of things. You must be sure your heart is right with the Creator so you can have his full protection over you. The creature at Crazy Woman Creek is what us Natives know as a Wendigo. It's an evil entity that roams the woods in search of human flesh and spirit. Many believe it all started with a wicked medicine man shortly after we discovered the land. He was claimed to have lived in a cave deep in the mountains. He was a very large man and was often made fun of by the tribesmen. Though he healed many of their sicknesses, people were ungrateful for his help. He was visited one night by the devil himself who promised to seek revenge upon the people in exchange for the medicine man's soul. The medicine man was no match for the devil's charm and quickly agreed to the offer. Ever since, the wicked man has roamed the woods in search of sustenance. He is of his father the devil and has a way of deceiving many. He often mimics the voices of passed loved ones, children, or women in distress. He's not something you want to mess with."

The old man coughed and wiped his mouth with a handkerchief before continuing.

"I hear many people talking about the missing in these hills. I hear them say all sorts of crazy things as they wonder what may have gotten them. I don't wonder what happens to them. I know."

Caroline felt a shudder pass over her body at the thought of Devon encountering such a creature as the old man described. Is that what happened to him? Did he see it? It's now been three months since his disappearance, and it seems he'll be another number to add to the growing pile of victims.

Caroline raises her head from the laptop and looks at the wall in her office. It's covered in a six-foot by eight-foot map of the United States. She'd stuck various colored tacks across it and weaved string from one to another. She has over four hundred printed pictures of missing people pinned to the board. But that's only scratching the surface. She printed just a fraction of the stories she'd read online through news articles and blog posts. Some stories she'd read where hikers had disappeared from a group in mid hike. Many times, they'd even left their clothes behind on the trail. She remembered reading numerous times where the clothes were found neatly folded and stacked where the person had vanished seconds ago just behind the back of another hiker. Those stories always sent a cold shiver down her spine.

What's happening out there? Who or what is snatching up all these people?

She rubs her temple before downing a shot of scotch. She huffs out a breath and rises from her chair. She flicks off the lamp light and enters the hall for her bedroom. She lives in a small two-bedroom home with two acres of swamp land that backs up to a nature preserve. With the whole state of Florida having a warmer than usual winter, for the last week Caroline has slept with a window cracked in her bedroom.

She slides out of her house shoes and looks at the alarm clock on her nightstand. Red digital numbers reflect back at her. It's a quarter to two in the morning. She sighs and crawls beneath a thin sheet. She punches her pillow and rolls onto her side. Crickets chirp outside the window and an army of tree frogs screech into the night.

Her mind swims with stories she'd read and listened to online. She imagined being there with Devon when things happened. She forced her mind elsewhere and fought for sleep.

When she finally drifted into that dark place of nothingness, she thought she heard the distant cries of her missing boyfriend. She had entered that space of no return, and her mind convinced her she needed her sleep. Besides, it must be part of some dream, right?

Lady of Chapel Grove

Near the NC/SC border
October
1962

I grew up in the small town of Chapel Grove. We were forty miles to Wilmington, North Carolina, thirty miles to Myrtle Beach, and about twenty minutes from the ocean. Chapel Grove was a quiet little town. The kind where you knew everyone you passed on the way to the supermarket, the cashier knew you on a first name basis when you got there, the town pastor visited when you were sick, and the mayor walked the same streets you did. The town was founded in the eighteen hundreds by a group of devout Baptists, so we had our own town charter and such. The original church still stands to this day. It's a quaint little church with white planks, black shingles, a red door, and a black steeple with a cross on top. It's nestled between a grove of pines hence the name of the town, Chapel Grove. The schools had strict dress codes, and staying out late at the movies or parties was vehemently forbidden. Our crime rates were some of the lowest in the region. The running joke was that the Andy Griffith Show was modeled after Chapel Grove. At least it seemed that way. But things changed the day Donnie Wells disappeared by the Martha Rivers ballfield. That was the day our town lost its innocence.

I remember it was a cold day, but the sun was out to give a welcome warmth as it cast its rays down to encompass you like a blanket. The periodic breezes were crisp as it picked up the leaves and swirled them about in tiny tornadoes.

The ball field where I, Donnie Wells, Cindy Wheeler, Robby Fisher, and Astrid Lyle played was within walking or biking distance from our neighborhood. Us boys usually took our bikes, the ones with Mantle and Aaron flapping in the spokes, while Cindy and Astrid followed behind us. Of course, we were always popping wheelies and bunny hopping over things to impress them. They'd snicker to one another about how dumb boys can be when they're competing for love. We weren't any older than eleven or twelve. The age when love seemed foreign and distant, yet you could tell the chasm was shrinking.

With little league being the town's pride and joy, me and my friends never missed a season. And we rarely missed a Saturday evening practice either. Boy, did we love baseball. The girls always tagged along to cheer us on from the ragged, sunbaked dugouts. Other times they'd bring a blanket to sit on a patch of grass behind the fence. We'd bring a cooler full of Coca-Colas and candy bars we'd bought from Sealey's Market downtown. In between innings we'd chug on our bottles of coke and munch on the bars like we were the Babe chowing on hotdogs or something. As if all that sugar would give us the strength to hit the ball as far as he could.

A thick patch of woods, which was overran with pines and Kudzu, served as the outfield wall. Since there were only three of us who played, we'd take turns rotating between pitcher, hitter, and fielder. We'd play until we tired out or became drowsy from the sudden spike and plummet of insulin. We'd come home all dirty and sweaty and couldn't wait to get back out there the following Saturday. Then when winter came, we'd stare out the window and wish for Spring.

But it was that one Saturday in October of sixty-two when all of our fun came to an end. I remember it so clearly. It's something I'll never forget.

We'd spent most of the afternoon and evening down by the ballfield. With our jeans cuffed at the ankles and our baseball shirts stained a grungy yellow, I remember looking up from the pitcher's mound and watching a cloud pass in front of the sun. A shadow crawled over us. We had about half an hour before our parents expected us for dinner. I remember Donnie had the lead over me and Robby. I was pitching to Robby, and Donnie was playing in the outfield. He was stationed in right center because with Robby being the big lefty that he was, he tended to be pull happy. I was to hit after Robby. He was down to his last out and needed three runs to take the lead.

"You can't hit worth a crap, ya big sissy." Donnie teased from the outfield. Astrid and Cindy snickered behind the fence.

Robby raged and his face flushed, "Oh shut up! I hit better than you and you know it."

I giggle and look over my shoulder to see Donnie belly laughing with a hand on his gut. He pulls in a breath and screams, "Then how come you're losing?"

"Shut up!" Robby waves Donnie off and says to me, "C'mon Larsen, serve one up for me."

I work to gain my composure. I shake off the imaginary catcher not once, not twice, but three times to agitate Robby even more. I go into my wind up, reach back, and give it all I have. A crow caws in the pines behind home plate as I release the ball. It tumbles from my fingertips and speeds away. Robby loads. His eyes are as big as saucers, and he clamps down on his tongue. I watch as the ball tails low and away like a Gaylord Perry sinker. Robby swings and misses, spinning himself into the dirt.

The girls laugh. Donnie collapses to the ground behind me, gasping at air for more chuckles.

Robby picks up the ball and fires it back at me. It stings my palm. "Quit throwing them dang sinkers. Give me something good to hit."

"I've been throwing them all day. Donnie didn't have a problem with them."

"Well, he's not a lefty now, is he? C'mon, you know I can't hit nothing low and away. I got one out left, give me something good. Toss me a cookie, will ya?"

I snicker and lower my head. Donnie's still heckling in the outfield as he now gathers to his feet. I fiddle with my grip and go for the four-seamer. *You want something good to hit? Let's see how good you can hit it up and in, huh?* I think to myself. I pat the ball in my glove with my hands held out in front of me like the old timers. I enter my wind up, rare back, and throw it as hard as I can. I blinked when I released it, but I knew by the crack of the bat he'd hit it good. I didn't throw it where I wanted.

I hear the girls gasp. Robby starts laughing. I spin around and see Donnie's back as he's in mid chase. The ball must've been twenty feet over his head. He had no chance of catching it but could only hope to run it down in time to throw Robby out at home.

I watch as the ball finally lands and takes several bounces before disappearing into a patch of Kudzu. Donnie chases after it. Robby's laughing as he powers toward second. The girls are cheering behind the fence. I'm screaming for Donnie to hurry as I watch Robby round second. His big feet pound for third.

Donnie reaches the wood line. He stares at the thick Kudzu and hesitates for a second.

"Hurry up. Hurry up. C'mon!" I scream again.

Donnie ducks into the Kudzu. It swallows him like a shark whoofing down a baitfish.

I'm screaming and waving my hands. The girls are jumping up and down. Robby rounds third and chugs for home, slowing down as his breath comes now in quick bursts. Donnie is still in the woods. I spin around to see Robby stomp on home plate before falling to the ground to catch his breath. I see Astrid and Cindy smiling as they give each other high fives.

"That was for you, girls." Robby says as he tries to collect his breath. He lies on his back with his meaty forearm covering his face.

I turn back around to face the outfield. Still no Donnie Wells.

"What's he doing out there, Jacob?"

I hear Cindy ask me. I scratch my head and say to her, "I don't know, but he's going to have one heck of a case of poison oak if he isn't careful. That Kudzu is eat up with it in there."

Cindy comes over to me while Astrid pulls Robby to his feet.

"Donnie. Hurry up man!" I call out from the pitcher's mound.

No answer.

Astrid and Robby join me and Cindy in the middle of the infield.

"Don't worry about him, Jake. I'm sure he's just trying to pull our leg," says Robby.

Astrid says, "I don't know, what if he fell or something? You know there's that cliff on the over side of that."

"It's like a forty foot drop down that bank," says Cindy as I feel her clinging closer to me.

Robby laughs and says, "It's not even half of that. You girls are always exaggerating things."

"No, it's more than that Rob. It might not be quite forty feet, but it's as high as my two-story window," I say to him.

"You think?"

I nod and with a nudge of my head I say, "C'mon, let's go see what he's up to."

Together we march out of the infield and make our way to this patch of Kudzu where Donnie disappeared. The sun descends a little further below the trees, leaving us with less than an hour before giving itself completely to the impending darkness.

We call out for him the whole way to the wood line, but never get an answer. Cindy and Astrid begin to express their worry that he may really be hurt. We reach the border of woods and stand before the Kudzu. "Donnie!" Again, no answer. We listen for any movement, but it's dead quiet.

"We've got to go in after him," I remember saying.

I watch as Robby swallows hard. I can see fear swimming about his mind as his eyes convey it. Cindy and Astrid say we should go get help.

"It'd take us all of fifteen minutes to go get help and then come back. What if he needs us now? Like right now?"

"He's right, girls. We need to go after him." Robby had suddenly taken on a hero's persona as if this may be his chance to win Astrid over for good. I angle my brows at him and almost laugh when he tries to puff his chest out.

I look into the Kudzu and try to find a path in, then look back to them and say, "Seriously. I think he needs us."

They each nod, and together we enter the woods.

We step over branches and logs as we crunch leaves and tamp pine needles. Sparrows and Cardinals disperse from the trees as we encroach upon their domain. In the distance, I can hear a crow cawing as if to warn the others of our presence.

I pick up a stick and wave it through the spiderwebs woven between the trees. The others follow close behind me.

"Donnie!"

Nothing.

The embankment that Astrid had mentioned lies about twenty feet ahead of us. I can tell because the trees thin out and give way to the others below them in the distance. Nehi, Coca-Cola, and liquor bottles are scattered here and there. Some are broken and their glass shines among the earth. There are the remains of a barbed wire fence post which leans to one side with the wire curled like a snake waiting to strike another victim. We step over it, and I hold Cindy and Astrid's hands when it's their turn.

"Donnie!" we cry out but get no answer.

We stop about ten feet from the ledge and listen. Other than the birds in the trees and some barking squirrels, everything is quiet.

The canvas of light behind the tree's fingers is quickly dimming to a dark shade of gray. The temperature is dropping. Any moment our parents will begin to worry.

We continue to the ledge. We reached it and look down to be sure Donnie hadn't fallen. Nothing. We look out over the trees below us. Nada.

"What are we going to do, Jacob?" Cindy asks.

I wipe my face with one hand while my other is stationed on my hip. I hear the crow caw again in the distance. I look up to the sky which is half blocked by the tree's bony hands as they loom over us.

"It's getting dark. I think we should head back and get h—"

My words were cut short by the popping of a branch below us. We each yank our attention to the source. I remember it was like getting punched in the gut. My heart sank hard and landed with a thud in my stomach.

Below us and about twenty yards into the thick of trees, a woman dressed in a black cape walks with her back to us, going deeper into the woods. She hums to herself calmly like trying to put a baby to sleep.

Neither of us say a word. We were frozen in terror. I felt my body begin to quiver, my knees and thighs taking to tremors. Cold chills flowed up and down my flesh. Gently, the lady in black continues to walk through the woods, humming with tight lips. Her hair is long and dark but with a hint of gray. It cascades down her back. She walks with her hands clutched to her gut as if she's carrying something.

I didn't even notice Cindy was clinging to my arm until I felt the blood being squeezed from it. I look over and see Astrid clasping tightly to Robby. His eyes are as big as baseballs and his jaw hangs slack. I look down at Cindy and try to soothe her as she'd began to whimper.

Another branch cracked, and the others gasped. The lady's humming stopped, and the forest grew silent.

I look up and see the lady in black looking back at us. I only got a glimpse because as soon as I saw her we began to run. But what I saw was a sickly-looking lady who looked like a drugged-out hippie. The kind that the folks of Chapel Grove always warned us about. Just before I turned and joined the others to race out of the woods, the lady in black hissed at me. I'll never forget it. She even had a wild, animal-like look in her eyes.

I've never run so fast in my life.

We stumble our way through the woods, rushing past branches and blocking their swipes. Wiping cobwebs from our eyes and tripping over logs.

We finally make it out, and we can hear the lady behind us as she now sings instead of hums. The words are inaudible, but her voice is there. Crying out like a lonely bride in the night. Her voice comes in long and sorrowful octaves.

We race for our bikes. Astrid took Donnie's and Cindy did her best to ride behind me on mine. I rode standing up, so she'd have the seat. My legs and lungs were aching by the time we reached my house. I thought Robby was going to have a heart attack as his asthma was raving like a mad demon. His breath now came in ebbs and flows of raspy wheezing.

We ride into my yard and throw the bikes down. They crash upon the leaves under the tall oak. We darted to my front door. I burst in with the others trailing behind me.

"Mom! Dad!" I cried out.

I can hear my mother's Victrola playing a Sam Cooke record in the kitchen. I also hear running water from the faucet, but it stops as I come closer. When we entered, I found my mother with an apron tied about her as she dries her hands with a dish towel. The savory aroma of meatloaf fills the air.

"What is this?" she asks with wide eyes and a toss of concern stamped across her face.

I can barely speak as I can't seem to catch my breath. Robby's wheezing gets louder.

I hear footsteps coming from another room. Dad.

Mom leans over and takes me by the shoulders. "What happened? Honey? Jacob, you have to tell me what happened."

Her brows angle at me.

I hear my dad enter the kitchen. Still dressed in his suit, tie, and slacks, he stands next to my mother and says, "What is this all about? You kids alright?"

I shake my head as my tongue is finally loosened from the strings which bound it.

"Donnie. Donnie. Donnie's missing."

"What?" both of my parents say in unison.

"What do you mean he's missing?" my mother asks.

"There's a lady in the woods."

"Huh?" my dad says as he cranes at the waist with his hands to his knees. He looks me in the eyes and places a hand to my forehead, using his thumb to peel back each eye lid.

Cindy speaks up with a shake to her voice, "Donnie went into the woods after a ball and never came out."

"Oh Jesus." My mother says as she straightens and places a hand to her forehead. "I need to call Deborah. Jim, don't you think I should call Deborah?"

My dad scratches his clean-shaven cheek and says, "Yeah. Yeah, call her up. See if her boy's made it home yet." Dad looks back to us, "You said there was a woman in the woods?"

I bob my head.

Within the hour our entire town was crawling with police cruisers, each flashing their strobing lights. Officers canvased the area, going door to door taking notes from the occupants. Martha River's ballfield was swamped with officers and K-9 dogs as they combed through the woods with their flashlights and guns. This went on for over a week. Not once did they find any evidence. No clothing, no blood, no sign of a struggle. Nothing. It was like Donnie Wells had been eaten whole by a monster. Taken right under noses.

You'd go into town and almost every light pole you passed had Donnie's photo stapled to it. We were told even the neighboring towns and counties had done the same. Donnie's mom was interviewed at multiple press conferences, each aired on live tv. His mother pleaded over and over again for someone to bring her baby home.

Preacher Waltrip of Chapel Grove Baptist held vigils three times through the week and twice on the weekends. His sermons changed into lectures about how to trust God in trying times and how to never give up hope, regardless of what our eyes may be showing us. I remember one time he'd said something along the lines of, "We all go through a season of shadows from time to time, but I promise you it won't last forever. Sooner or later, the sun will shine again."

But for those trying two weeks that Donnie Wells was missing, it seemed the sun had left us for good. The days were filled with bleak and rain, filling the town with fog and dread. The darkness seemed to last longer when it came. The nights felt sinister. Like an evil presence came out to lurk among our streets, plotting who to take next.

Even the dogs noticed as they were restless during those two weeks. Every night you'd hear them whine and howl as if sadness was overtaking them. Something was different about our little town. You could sense it in the air. We'd been visited by something dark, and I think the thing that scared us was that neither of us knew what it was. It was the unknown that frightened us most.

When Donnie began visiting me in my sleep, is when things changed.

I remember so clearly as if it were yesterday.

It was almost two weeks after his disappearance that I found myself woken in the middle of the night with the sudden urge to pee. I got up, walked through the darkness, and stumbled my way into the bathroom. I rubbed my eyes and squinted with pain when I turned the bathroom light on. I yawned and began to relieve myself.

I flushed the toilet, turned out the light, and walked back into my bedroom. My eyes were half open when I came near my bed. I was almost ready to dive in beneath the covers, but the dark object lying where I lay, stopped me. I pulled up and felt my heart plummet to the floor. I swallowed and blinked away the slag. I rubbed my face, expecting this dark object to be gone, but it wasn't. It was still there, lying where I lay, CURLED BENEATH MY COVERS!

It moves over to lie on its back. I gasped. It's me! I'm looking at a sleeping me. Then something stirs from the other side of my bed, and it was at this time I first noticed the lump beneath the covers. Something or someone else laid beside me. My heart races so fast it causes my head to spin. I stumble backwards, trip over my own feet, and crash to the floor. Only there was no thud. It was like landing on a pillow. Am I dead? Am I dreaming? What in the world is this?

I blink and rub my face again. I can still see myself lying in bed, stiff as a corpse. Yet, I hear something moving between the covers. It's coming closer. Creeping over the bed sheets. I hear them wrinkle and rub. My hands are pressed hard against the cold, hardwood floor. I can't move. My eyes are fixed to my bed where I laid. I watch my foot twitch as if tickled by a ghost. I see my knee shift upward, closer to my body.

Then I see black movement. It's like a big shadow, but in the shape of a person. It comes closer to the edge of my bed and leans toward me as I sit on the floor. I watch as it presses down upon the other me. I begin to make out the features. I can see the head, neck, shoulders, and so on. I hear a smacking sound as if someone is slowly moving their tongue around their mouth and opening and closing their lips. I remember thinking it sounded like grandpa when he was in that nursing home near the end.

The lip smacking stops, but my pulse continues to soar. My arms and neck crawl with gooseflesh.

I hear heavy breathing. The breathing is turned into whispers. I can't make out the words at first until I hear, *"Be-neeaaatthh."* The pronunciation was like rolling off a serpent's tongue. Then I remember hearing a loud clap sound which was followed by a burst of light.

The next thing I know I'm jolting awake in bed. The room was dark and held an eerie chill to it. Like a presence lurked within the shadows. Remembering what I'd just seen, I jerk to the left of me and yank back the covers. Nothing's there. I began patting myself all over, then pinching my cheeks to be sure I was awake. I felt the pain, and I felt the urge to pee. I swung my feet off the bed and hurried to my feet in fear of something grabbing me and pulling me under it. I hurry and turn on all the lights in my room. I take my time looking around it. The only eyes in the room beside mine where the ones belonging to my Babe Ruth and Sandy Koufax pictures.

Beneath? Beneath? Beneath what?

I push aside my bladders cry for relief and rush to my parent's room. I told them of my dream, which they say sounded like a nightmare, and they promised we'd talk more in the morning. After some pleading, they allowed me to sleep in their bed for the night. I found it hard to go back to sleep as all I could think about was my dream or whatever you want to call it, and those words which I believe Donnie was speaking to me.

Beneath.

The next morning, my parents took me down to Sheriff Dubois so I could tell him of my dream. I remember he sat behind his mess of a desk, with his feet propped upon it and his hands interlocked in his lap. His mustache and long sideburns were freshly trimmed, and a steaming cup of coffee sat within a hand reach away. His badge had a shine to it when the sun hit it just right as it filtered in through the half-open blinds. I don't think his desk was usually that messy. Sheriff Dubois didn't strike me as that sort of man. What made his desk so messy was all the scribbled notes, photos taken of the woods where Donnie vanished, and school or family photos of him.

There were also a bunch of names and numbers. Some I recognized, some I didn't.

When I finished telling him of my dream, he took a deep breath and rubbed his mustache on each end with his pointer and thumb. He chewed hard on a wad of peach tobacco, reached for his cup of coffee, took a sip, and then leaned over and spit into a small trash can next to him. He raised back up, wiped his chin with the heel of his hand and said, "Now boy, I know this must be hard on ya. I can only imagine what you and your friends are going through. I can see how this could weigh on your mind and get ya to start dreaming all sorts of things."

I heard my dad take in a deep sigh. The sheriff directs his eyes to him for a moment, then looks back at me, clears some things from his desk and leans his elbows across it. He takes a deep breath and scratches the left side of his head with one finger. He squints his brows and looks at me with a tilted head. "Beneath, you say?"

I nod.

"Beneath? Beneath what?"

"I don't know, Sheriff. But I promise you it was Donnie that I saw. It scared the living bejesus out of me, but I know it was Donnie because he makes that same smacking sound when he's sleepy. It drives us nuts every time we have a sleep over."

"I see," the sheriff pulls back and crosses his arms over his chest with one hand rubbing the mustache again. He looks off to the side at a file cabinet. His eyes are vacant and in deep thought.

"What about this lady they all saw, Sheriff? Haven't you found anything on her yet?" my mom asks.

Sheriff Dubois chews a little more on his tobacco, spits into the trash can, and says, "No ma'am. We can't find anything on a woman of that type. She must've been a transient or something. We've already spoken with all of our neighboring counties. They know to be on the lookout for a lady and boy who match our descriptions. You know in case they're travelling by greyhound or thumbing their way across the state."

"Lord have mercy. This isn't looking good, Sheriff," my dad says.

"I know." Sheriff Dubois goes for another sip of coffee which is followed by another spit into the can. "Listen Mr. and Mrs. Larsen, I'm going to have my boys search those woods like their lives depend on it. If Donnie Wells is out there . . . well as God is my witness, we'll find him."

"Let's hope you do before it's too late, Sheriff. This would be one heck of a stain on our town." My mom says as she rises from her chair.

Me and Dad follow suit. The sheriff remains seated with his hands folded in his lap, still chewing on the wad of tobacco. "I appreciate you folks coming in. We're going to continue looking, and I guess now we'll start looking beneath things a little more."

My dad says, "I think that'd be a good idea."

We each shook his hand before leaving the office. We make it to our ugly yellow 1950 Crosley station wagon, which I always called the *school bus.*

"I'd like to think the sheriff is taking this seriously, but I kind of got the feeling in there that maybe they're losing steam," says my mom.

"Honey, it's been two weeks without any trace of the boy. They can't go on looking over them woods forever. Sooner or later as cruel as it seems, they're going to have to move the folder to the cold case cabinet. If they don't find him soon then I'm afraid they may never find him." Dad says as he shifts into gear.

Meanwhile, my mind is in a daze as all I can think about is Donnie's visit and that word.

Beneath.

It lingered in my brain the rest of the way home, and I hardly heard anything my parents were saying. When they asked if I were okay, I'd just give a vague reply like, "Yeah," or "I'm fine." We made it home and though it was Saturday, two weeks since Donnie went missing, I had no plans of going down to the ballfield to practice.

Neither did Robby Fisher. Cindy and Astrid were torn up over everything too. The few times I'd spoken with them over the landline, they could hardly finish without crying. Robby was more scared than anything. He was worried about the wild-eyed lady in black coming back and picking us off one by one until there were no more witnesses. I think all those horror comic books had gone to his head. Not that I hadn't had the same thoughts myself, I just fought them off quicker than he did, I think.

I remember for the second Saturday in a row, I spent the evening in my room lying in bed. I either listened to Elvis or Muddy Waters on my little turntable or took turns reading my paperback of Huck Finn and the biography I had of Babe Ruth. My mom would step in and check on me throughout the day. She'd sit on the side of my bed and offer soothing words to ease my grieving. Then she'd pat my leg and tell me to get up because supper was ready.

I remember we had red beans and rice with thin slices of steak that had gravy drizzled over top. Then of course there was homemade cornbread and a fresh glass of milk to round it off. I went to bed that night with a full stomach but an empty heart.

I was awoken sometime in the middle of the night to the sound of tapping. At first, I was afraid it was another nightmare. I didn't want to open my eyes to find the source of the sound. But the tapping continued and the more my brain awakened, the more I began to realize that it was coming from my window. I listened with my eyes shut for a moment, afraid to see what it was. I was also afraid of what may be lying next to me in bed.

Tap. Tap. Tap. Tap.

Realizing that the tapping wasn't going to end, I pushed away the fear and opened my eyes. My room was dark except for the ray of moonlight swimming in from my blindless window. I throw the covers back and turn to face my window on the left side of the room. My heart jolts at the sight. Looking at me through the window and tapping with his pointer finger is Donnie Wells. I could only see from his shoulders up as he bobbed gently like a cork being played by a panfish. He smiles and continues to tap the glass.

My gut twists into knots and my hearts races in circles like an indwelling tornado. Blood rushes through my veins at the speed of light. The room is freezing, and the glass begins to fog with frost. I swallow hard and fight for another breath. It comes and then escapes into a small cloud of smoke, lingering about the room like a ghost.

Donnie continues to smile and tap. His face is dirty, and his curly blond hair is grungy and matted like. His red and white striped shirt has mud stains blotched here and there.

I watch as he slowly opens his mouth and begins to smack his lips like he does when he's sleepy. He stops tapping and is now drawing with the same finger. I watch as little by little each letter begins to appear on the fogged window: *L E A V E S.*

I rub my face and squeeze my eyes. When I open them, Donnie's gone but his word remains painted on my glass. I bolt out of bed and rush down the hall to my parents' room. I scare them half to death but manage to convince them to get up and come look at my window. I was hoping and praying the whole way that'd the word would still be there. Amazingly, it was. I wasn't crazy. I'd really seen Donnie Wells floating outside my two-story window and watched as he drew the word . . . Leaves.

"Oh, Jacob. Honey, you must be imagining all of this. You had to of slept walk or something. You used to have night terrors when you were younger. You remember that?"

"Mom, I promise you I didn't draw that," I say as I look at the window where Dad examines it.

I watch as he reaches out and touches where the L is. My mom is saying something, but I'm not listening. I'm struck by the way my dad is acting. He turns and faces us with a look on his face I'd never seen before.

"This wasn't written from the inside. This is on the outside."

His words send a chill racing through my veins. My mom breathes out a stunned, "What?"

Dad nods his head and tries touching the letters again. None of them smudge. "Someone wrote this from out there. Jacob didn't do it." He looks at me and says, "Son, I don't know what to tell you, but I think maybe Donnie's trying reach out to you."

"Oh, have mercy, this is crazy," says my mom.

"Beneath. Leaves." My dad says looking out the window with his hands to his hips. "Beneath. Leaves. For heaven's sake, Margaret, I think that boy is out there in them woods. I can't explain any of this, but I could never live with myself if I didn't do something about it."

"Jim, what are you talking about?"

He turns and faces us, "I think someone needs to go out there and have a look for themselves."

"Honey, the sheriff and his men have been out there looking for two weeks—"

"I know that, but what if they've overlooked something? What if Donnie is really communicating with Jacob somehow? You know me, I'm not much for the supernatural, but how else do you explain that?" He turns and points to my window. "If I call the sheriff and tell him my boy saw Donnie Wells floating outside his window, why he liable to send us all to a doctor. He and his boys are likely finished for the night anyhow. I say I go and have a look myself."

"Jim, no. You're not going out there. You can't."

"Why not?"

My mom sighs and crosses her arms.

"You'd want someone to do this for me if I were out there, wouldn't you?" I said.

"Now Jacob, that's low of you to say. You know I would, but you have to understand this is something the police have to deal with."

"Mom, you were questioning the sheriff yourself earlier when we left his office. What if Donnie is really reaching out to us and needs our help? We have to do something."

My mom covers her face with a palm and shakes her head as she looks to the floor.

"Marge, he's right. Let me go out there and have a look for myself. At least so we know we did our part in all of this."

"I'll go with you."

Mom snaps her head and says, "No you won't either, mister. You're staying put right here."

"But what if Donnie reaches out to me while we're out there? He might help lead us to him."

She takes a deep breath.

"He might be right, Marge."

She looks away from my dad and stares at Donnie's word scrawled across my fogged window. Finally, she bobs her head. "But make it quick. If you're not back within an hour, I'm sending the sheriff out there."

"Give us two. Two hours tops. We'll be fine. I'll take my guns."

With that, Dad crosses the room and gives Mom a kiss then looks down at me and says, "Get dressed and find your flashlight. We'll head out in twenty minutes."

It was almost three thirty in the morning when we pulled the Crosley into the driveway of the Martha River's ballfield. Gravel crunched beneath us as the stereo played Howlin' Wolf's *Smokestack Lightin'*. His deep, whiskey and cigarette beaten voice crying out into the night. The headlamps beamed out over the baseball field below us. The moon was full, and a thick fog hovered atop the grass in the outfield. Our breaths steam into the air and begin to fog up the windows. Patches of fog pass by the headlights like ghosts on their way to another land. Dad quiets the radio. Howlin' Wolf and all the guitars, drums, and harmonicas give way to a static hiss followed by a pop. Dad looks at me and says, "Alright now, we're going to go out here and look beneath the leaves for anything out of the ordinary, okay? We've got two hours before ya mother starts worrying and for the record, we're still in the bed asleep right now, right?"

I nod.

"Good. Last thing we need is to have people knowing we're out here snooping around. Let's try to make it quick but worth our while being here. You got your light?"

"Yeah," I say as I reach beneath the seat and retrieve the big thing. The cold metal stings my palm.

Dad reaches over and lets down the glove box. Two revolvers lie asleep next to each other. He takes them out and checks their cylinders, then stuffs them in his coat pockets, one on each side. "Okay, well c'mon." Dad says as he climbs out.

I met him at the front of the car. We stand for a second and look down the hill at the ball field. The wind blows softly through the trees, just enough to cause the leaves to rattle and a slight whistle to pierce the air. Clouds pass in front of the moon, casting shadows across the pitcher's mound. Crickets chirp in the rocks beside us, and an owl sounds off in the distance.

Dad pats my shoulder and says, "C'mon son. Let's get this over with."

As we make our way down the rocky trail leading to the outfield, I couldn't help but think of Donnie's visits. What was he trying to tell me? Is he dead and is now leading us to his body? Oh God, please no. Anything but that. Or is he alive and somehow God helped him communicate with me? Either way, I wish he'd done a better job instead of appearing like the ghost in that Charles Dickens story. Goodness Donnie, why couldn't you have just showed up during the daytime and been a good little boy?

" . . . about where you last saw him?"

I hear my dad in mid-sentence.

"Huh?"

"I was asking if that is about where you last saw him? Looks like the sheriff has it taped off."

"Yeah. That patch of Kudzu where the yellow tape's at is where he went in. We went around though to avoid all of the poison oak."

"I see. Well show me the way. And don't turn your light on until we get into the woods a little bit."

"Okay." I marched on and found the spot where me, Cindy, Robby, and Astrid had stepped in at. We duck into the wood line about twenty feet to the right of the Kudzu patch. Leaves crunch beneath us and twigs break under our weight. We turn on our lights and begin sweeping them about. The fog is thicker inside the canopy of woods and the air feels chiller. The fog swirls about our feet like lost souls reaching out to feel something alive again.

We canvas the woods, kicking our feet across the earth and dispersing the leaves. We didn't know what we were looking for but somehow, we knew we'd know when we found it . . . or him.

And it was the thought of finding him that scared me. I was afraid we'd find him buried in a shallow grave with leaves piled on top, his flesh rotting and turning colors as it began to stink. I was afraid we'd find him just like the words said: Beneath. Leaves. I was afraid he wouldn't be breathing when we did.

I pushed on though and continued raking leaves with my foot. My cheeks were beginning to numb, and I could no longer feel my fingers or toes. My breath became thicker each time I let it out. Behind the sound of leaves, I thought I heard the wind begin to howl. But the more I listened the more I could tell it wasn't the wind. It was something different. I stopped moving the leaves. My dad did too. We both stood there quietly with our lights. I watched him as he listened with squinted eyes. There it was again. What is that? It's distant but sounds like it's moving closer.

My heart leaps as if struck by a bolt of lightning. The sound wasn't the wind. It was the sound of that lady in black humming. I gasped and looked to Dad in time to see a knot bob in his throat. He looks at me with a hint of fear in his eye.

"It's her. It's the lady in black." I say to him.

As soon as I say it, the humming stops.

"Turn out your light," Dad says.

"Huh? No way. Uh-huh."

"Do it. She won't be able to see us."

"But we won't be able to see her."

"Trust me. Turn out the light."

We flick off our lights and allow the moon to guide us. It's quiet and eerie. After a dozen seconds pass, her voice returns but this time with singing. Low, soft, and in long, drawn out syllables. Her voice has a unique pitch to it that almost feels angelic in a way.

My dad takes one step and then another. I follow closely behind him. We continued to walk softly through the woods as she sings, but each time she stopped, we stopped. When she picked back up, we continued. We did this for about five minutes or so. Walking as she sung and pausing when she rested her lungs. I noticed her voice was becoming louder, and I realized how close we were getting.

My dad was quiet and almost trance-like. It was as if he was being drawn against his will in a way. I felt it too, just not as much. The further we walked, the louder she got, and the slacker my dad's jaw became. It was like life was slowly being pulled out of him. Just as I was about to tug his arm and shake him from this odd state of slumber, he stopped. His hands hung loose by his sides, his shoulders were slouched, and his face was drooped. The life in his eyes was evaporating.

I feel my heart begin to race. My throat constricts and squeezes off my air way, causing my breath to come in short gasps.

As I go to shake his arm, he raises his other one holding the light. He holds it straight out in front of him. I follow his aim and can begin to see a silhouette sitting about twenty yards ahead of us. I try to peer through the darkness but can't make anything out. The lady is quiet and so is my dad. Even nature is caught in a holy hush. No wind. No crickets. Just dead, utter silence.

Click.

My dad's light flicks on and lights up the shadow before us. It's a small cabin made from cedar logs. It seems out of place. Like it'd dropped from the heavens, descending like lightning the way the devil did. That angelic voice returns. It begins low and soft before rising and falling in pitch and octave.

My dad moves forward while still dazed and in a trance. I feel even myself drifting away as my head begins to spin. My vision blurs slightly and my feet move without much of my command. It's almost as if I'm gliding forward, hovering above the ground the way you often do in dreams.

We come to the door of this cabin. Hanging from the little shed overhang are numerous stick made ornaments. Each spin and dance with the wind. My dad turns out his light. The singing is loud and crisp, but there's still no intelligible words being sung. I watch as the door swings open on its own. Slow and steady until it rests against the wall. We stand there for a moment before venturing inside.

The floor is wooden with flattened and skinned logs. The walls still have cedar peelings. The cabin is empty, but each corner is dark and undiscernible. I look up towards the ceiling and for whatever reason, I see leaves. It was like looking at the bottom of a pile of leaves. A funny thought occurred to me then: This must be what worms see. Yet, that thought also scared me. It made me feel like I was losing my mind. Then two words appeared before my mind's eye, each scribbled upon my fog covered window: Beneath. Leaves.

Oh God, we're beneath the leaves!

Bam!

I spun around and saw the front door had slammed shut. I heard a match strike and ignite flame. I see an amber hue lighting the walls beside the door. I hear someone blow the match out and the smell of it fills the room.

Feeling my hands and knees begin to tremble, I turn around and face the center of the room. Standing before us is a beautiful lady with long brownish-blonde hair that drapes past her shoulders. She wears a white dress similar to what a bride would wear, but slightly different. Different I don't know how, just different. She holds a candle with both hands in front of her waist. Her hands are delicate and feminine. Her face is perfectly symmetrical. Her complexion has a golden sheen to it. Her eyes are blue and almond shaped, strikingly captivating, sparkling like cherished diamonds as the flame plays upon them. She smiles and her smile seems to brighten the room even more, giving the flame more glow.

I look at my dad, and he is still in a trance like state. Then I hear the smacking sound that Donnie makes, followed by soft whispers. I look back at the lady. She smiles at me and says, "Hello Jacob Larsen. It is lovely to finally meet you. I have been watching for quite some time." Her voice is smooth as honey, soft and elegant.

My throat tightens and traps my voice. I want to scream but can't. My head spins, and my pulse pounds like machine gun fire. My heart takes on deep and painful beats. My eyes are drawn to her enticing smile and beauty. I can see her mouth is shut, but for some reason I continue to hear whispers. It's like serpents hissing in my ear, their forked tongues sending warm breath brushing against my flesh.

I pull my eyes from her and look at Dad. I tug hard on his arm and say, "Dad, wake up. I need you."

He draws in a long breath through his nose. He blinks twice and sneezes hard. I see the mucus spray into the air. He wipes his face down with a palm.

I shake him, "Dad. Wake up!"

He blinks again, and I can see reality return to his eyes. He swallows, looks at the woman, looks to me, then back to her.

"What is this? Where am I?"

"Sshh." I watch as she says with a finger to her ruby lips.

"What have you done to Donnie?" Dad asks.

She smiles hard and chuckles, "No need to worry about Donnie. He's just fine, Mr. Larsen."

"How? How do you know my name?"

"I know a lot of things, Jim. Margaret is lucky to have a man like you. So strong. So masculine."

"Where's Donnie?" I say with a hint of malice.

"Your friend was too easily enticed, Jacob. It's a shame because so many of you are. So few can resist me. I'm not complaining. It certainly makes my job a little easier. Though I wouldn't mind a challenge from time to time."

"What do you want?" Dad asks.

The lady takes a step closer. Her bare feet glide gracefully across the wood floor, almost like she floated rather than stepped.

I feel my soul retreat from such darkness. Somehow, I knew, even at that age, that what was standing before me was nothing but pure evil. An unholy thing that feeds upon the innocent.

She looks each of us in the eye and says, "You. I want you. All of you. I crave you. I long for you. You are what gives me life. Your lust which I evoke gives me strength. It gives me life. Your lust becomes my lust."

"You sick, wicked, abominable thing." Dad says. Her face recoils as if he'd just tossed acid onto her. "You're a deceiver, that's what you are. You hear me? A deceiver!"

She hisses loud like a cat. I watch in horror as her face shifts from the beautiful young woman and slowly contorts into the lady in black we saw in the woods that day. Her skin stretches tight about her face, pulling her lips back to reveal ugly and rotten teeth. Wrinkles ravage every inch of her skin. Her hair turns from wavy blonde to stringy dark gray. Her figure conforms to a shriveled and bony lady who looked like she'd taken one too many trips with the mushrooms. Her hiss turns into a loud screechy wail. Behind her wail I begin to hear moaning and whimpering.

The candle goes out, leaving us in the dark. I hear dad scramble for his light, and I hear feet pound across the floor toward us. She screams louder and drowns out the whimpering. Dad flicks on his light. The screams stop. The footsteps are no more. He darts his light about in quick sweeps. The lady is gone.

I hear the whimpering get louder. "Over there." I point to the corner on our left-hand side. Donnie Wells comes into view. He sits on his butt with his knees tucked tight to his chest. His mouth has tape over it, and his hands and feet are bound with rope. Dad and I rush over to him. We race to free him. As I'm undoing his hands I notice his eyes shift from us and go to the ceiling. His eye lids disappear, and his head begins to quiver. Dad yanks the tape from his mouth. He's free now, but fear still binds him.

Dad and I slowly turn and follow his eyes to the ceiling. Dad shines his light. Pressed firm to the ceiling with her arms and legs spread out, is the lady in black! Her hair drapes down with gravity but the rest of her body defies it. She smiles big to reveal those ugly, yellow teeth. She begins to chuckle as her eyes turn blacker by the second.

"C'mon!" Dad says as he yanks us up by the arms. As the three of us race out the door, I hear a heavy thump land upon the floor. She must've dropped from the ceiling. As we begin to pound our way through the woods, Dad drops the light. I kick it with my feet, sending it spinning every which way.

"Leave it!" Dad screams as he pulls us onward.

I hear the lady cackling as she runs tight behind us.

Dad slows a bit as he jerks his arm away from me. I hear him fidget in his coat pocket. He stops and allows us to continue on.

"Get to the car!" No sooner than he said the words, I heard three cracks of gunfire ring out. The booms echo among the forest. Donnie and I raced onward for the car. Another blast of gun fire. Then I hear more footsteps pounding closer behind us.

Oh, dear God, please let that be Dad.

The steps are gaining ground faster than we can outpace them.

I feel myself tense as I prepare for the worst.

The steps come up right behind us. I hear heavy breathing, followed by my dad's voice, "Keep moving, we're almost there."

† † † † † † † † †

THE THINGS THAT happened during those two weeks will remain with me for the rest of my life. I think the same can be said for the others too.

After Dad, me, and Donnie reached the car, we raced to the police station and reported the shooting. Dad didn't tell them everything, just enough so they wouldn't think we were crazy. When the sheriff and his boys went out there, they found the lady lying in a pool of her own blood and barely clinging to life. Though they searched the entire patch of woods, there was never a report of any cabin.

The lady somehow survived taking two rounds from a .44 revolver and decided to fess up to avoid any more added prison years than what she was already facing. She claimed to have experimented with black magic since her high school days. She spent most of her years travelling around from town to town, working as a palm reader and spiritualist. But during the course of the six months leading up to Donnie's disappearance, she took things deeper and darker.

She claims she'd begun communicating with the devil and soon found herself equipped with supernatural abilities and gifts. Examples being levitation, shape shifting, and creating grand delusions. Which I think explains what happened to us the night we found Donnie Wells tied up in the corner of that cabin. After having learned what the lady had to say and with there being no evidence that the cabin ever existed, I believe we were deceived into seeing it. Also like the way we saw her transform from the beautiful woman back into her true self. Grand delusions indeed.

When asked what her plans were for Donnie, she said, "I don't know. The devil hadn't told me yet."

One can only imagine what may have happened if we hadn't found him when we did.

Now, I know you're probably thinking I'm crazy and just making all of this stuff up. I can totally understand where you're coming from. I'm not asking you to believe me. It makes no difference to me whether you do or not. I know what I saw and experienced. I will never be able to forget or unsee those things. To this day, almost fifty years later, I rarely venture near the woods alone. Donnie is the same way. I'll go hunting and stuff, but I never do it alone. Even when someone's with me, I still find myself on edge. It's like I'm just waiting to hear her begin to hum and sing again. That lonely, angelic voice lifting among the trees. Whew. It's giving me goosebumps just thinking about it.

Anyhow, that's our story. I don't question whether there's supernatural things out there, or if there's true good and evil. I don't have to question because I've seen it first-hand. I know evil exists in the world, and I believe it can give people supernatural abilities. But I also believe there is good in the world too because I see it every night in my wife's eyes when I kiss her good night. I hear it in the laughter of my kids and grandkids as they run around the makeshift bases in our front yard during our Saturday whiffle ball games. I feel the light of God's love when they run up and give me a hug.

As I look back on it now, it was like a shadow covered our town of Chapel Grove for those fourteen days, but like Preacher Waltrip said, "We all go through a season of shadows from time to time, but I promise you it won't last forever. Sooner or later, the sun will shine again."

I find those words to be true, especially with the older I get.

The Beach Bum

Gulls squawked overhead as they floated along in a swift ocean breeze. Waves beat against the slopping beach as they spread to caress the old man's toes. The sun peaked out from the horizon. Oscar Campbell caught a glimpse of a pelican in mid free fall as it searched for a morning pogie. The pelican diverted Oscar's mind from his dying wife, Abby.

She had fought and beat cervical cancer twice already and the stubborn thing had decided that wasn't enough. The evil beast came back last month with vengeance. Abby was given six months to live just yesterday. Oscar had cursed and called the doctor an unfriendly name. Abby had scolded him with one of her looks. She finished scolding him the rest of the way home from Wilmington. She had fought like a prize fight for the first two rounds, but this third bout had her seeming to accept defeat. Oscar loved her more than anything in the world, God as his witness, but the fact that woman was somehow okay with leaving this world in six short months had stirred an unusual anger in his heart. He kept reminding himself he should cherish every moment he had left with his wife and sweetheart since grade school, but he found himself with a case of resentment towards her he had to fight to ward from growing. He had argued with her and others more times in the last month than he had in the last decade. Abby had been his world for the last forty years of his life and they had travelled the country and globe together, raised three kids, and once ran an antique shop before the cancer took over their lives. The one place they never were able to make it to was Egypt. It had always been Abby's dream to see the pyramids and ride the back of a camel. They had booked an appointment with a travel advisor a week before the cancer returned. She was rushed to the hospital with stomach pain the day of the appointment. Oscar promised her she would see the pyramids.

"Come hell or high water, little lady you're going to see those pyramids."

He'd told her that as she sat in his lap on the recliner. He squeezed her tight and planted a big wet kiss on her forehead. She giggled that cute little giggle of hers and that was that.

They'd planned in the past to use a decent portion of their retirement account to spend on a month-long trip to the middle east. They'd planned to visit Egypt along with the Holy City of Jerusalem. Oscar didn't have the guts to tell her he'd lost the majority of their retirement funds making a risky bet on a small cap stock he'd read about from a Facebook ad. It was a semiconductor chip maker out of Massachusetts which was running for a couple bucks a share but was expecting to explode when China finally invaded Taiwan. Which so happens to be the king of semiconductor chips. With the king then dethroned, this little chip maker from good ole Massachusetts had its eyes on the prize, and so did their investors.

Oscar sold over eighty percent of their IRA and dumped it into this up and coming can't miss opportunity. That bet turned south quick when a month into it, the company's CEO was fired for sexual misconduct. The stock plummeted eighty-nine percent and has yet to make any attempt at a recovery.

A sharp stinging pain ripped through the bottom of his foot. The injury brought his mind back to the present. He winced and bent to tend to the wound. A broken seashell was to blame. The jagged edge had gouged right into the soft spot of his arch. He grimaced and rubbed at it. Fresh blood oozed into the sand. He removed a handkerchief from his pocket and tightened it around his foot. He dropped his flip flops onto the sand and slid into them. He grit his teeth and shook his head at his misfortune. He gave a quick side glance to the heavens and mumbled under his breath. If he listened hard enough, he imagined he could even hear the big man laughing at him. He sighed and turned around to head back to his truck parked two miles away at the end of the road.

Something on the other side of the dune caught his attention. A white trash bag rattled in the wind. He squinted and removed his sunglasses.

What the hell?

A boat tailed Grackle hopped upon the sand near the bag before squawking and taking to the air. Oscar stepped forward for a better look at the odd object. He felt his heart knock when the rest of the trash bag came into view. It was partially hidden next to a shrub, but the shape of it sent a ghostly hand caressing the back of Oscar's neck. He gulped as his brow furrowed. It can't be what he thinks it is, can it? He began to check his surroundings. He was all alone. He had only seen a few people this morning when he started his walk. They had all been down the beach in the opposite direction he had chosen to go. The bag rattled again as it was brought to life with the breeze.

He crept closer, keeping his eyes peeled along the way. The bag was long and slender with black electrical tape wrapped around it in three places.

"Good Lord, this can't be."

It has to be some sort of evil prank by mischievous teenagers. It has to be, right? There's no way he just stumbled upon a dead body. No way.

His mind raced with a million thoughts as it tried to convince him why this can't be happening. Somehow, he knew in his gut he was in the presence of the deceased. He could just sense it in his spirit.

He angled next to the bag and stood over it for a moment. He nudged it with his foot. It gave slightly and rolled back into place. If it is what he thinks it is, they hadn't been dead long enough for rigor mortis to set in. He peered over the dune and looked again for any beach goers. No one was around. He drew a deep breath and took out his Swiss army knife. He grunted when he bent down to slice open the plastic. The slit spread to reveal the pallid, gray face of a man who was left in the middle of a scream. His eyes were glazed like a fish, and he had salt and peppered stubble.

Oscar jerked back with a yelp. He nearly tripped over his own feet. He placed his hands on his head and panted for breath.

"Oh Jesus. Oh Jesus. No. No. This can't be happening."

He retrieved his cell phone and walked back to the body. With his phone in hand, he was about to dial the three magic numbers before he noticed something in the man's mouth. It was white. He leaned closer. It looks like a folded note. He grimaces and growls at himself. One side of his brain screamed to leave the body and scene alone for investigators to deal with while the other side just had to know what this note was all about. He straightened his spine and looked again over the dune to see if anyone was coming. The coast is clear. He leans back down and reaches out a timid hand toward the dead man's mouth.

The damp paper touches his fingers. He snatches back as if the man were about to bite him. He gently unfolds the note and begins to read. Four words are written in thick swirly letters: *LOOK AT MY TOE.*

Oscar squints his eyes and glares at the note then glares at the dead man. He looks towards the man's feet and makes a small cut in the plastic. Investigators will wonder why he made two cuts. He could easily explain the first as the curiosity had gotten the best of him, but the second cut would need a little more thought. He'll think of something to say later. He tears the plastic away to find two lifeless feet bound together with rope. On one toe hangs a folded tag. Oscar opens the note.

Text this number for instructions to the money. $1 mill if you bury the body in your back yard. Up for the challenge?

Oscar stared at the note. He read over the words at least a dozen times, trying to soak it all in. Finally, he began to laugh. His shoulders hitched. Tears filled his eyes. He placed a hand to his hip and the other to the bridge of his nose. He sucked in a gust of air and looked heavenward.

"Oh, that's a good one. You almost had me there for a minute."

He lowered his eyes back to the body and crossed over to it. He chuckled along the way and said, "Look man, I'm assuming my brother put you up to this shit. That was a good one. You can get up now. You got me."

He kicked the man's legs.

Nothing.

Oscar sighed and said, "C'mon, quit yanking my chain. You ain't no dead man. I know Ronnie put you up to it somehow. The joke's over."

As much as he tried to rationalize it all as a twisted prank put on by his childish brother Ronnie, the thought didn't really make sense when he let it sit in his mind for a moment. How would his brother had known he was going for a walk this morning? Of course, there's the fact that it's not unusual for him to do so, but how did Ronnie know he would be here at this exact moment? Better yet, how did he know this is where he would turn around at after stepping on that damned seashell back there? He wouldn't have. Which only means one thing . . . this ain't no joke.

Oscar's eyes widened at the thought. He swallowed hard and nudged the body again. This time with more force. The dead man remained dead.

"Oh Jesus, he ain't playing."

He drew closer and bent over the man to feel for a pulse. He couldn't get anything at the neck, so he tried his wrist. The flesh was cold to the touch and no thump ever came. The man was dead as a frozen fish.

Oscar scratched his chin and chewed on the inside of his lip. He took another look at the note.

Text this number for instructions to the money. $1 mill if you bury the body in your back yard. Up for the challenge?

He shook his head.

"This is silly."

He retrieved his phone and texted the number. He punched in three simple letters: *Hey.*

He lowered his phone and looked out at the rising sun as it glistened off the water's surface. His phone vibrated. He flinched. He looked at the screen. The number had texted back.

Wise choice old timer...

Those words pierced his heart like fangs from a rattle snake. He felt their venom seep into his blood stream, poisoning it with fear.

"How does he know I'm an old timer?"

Oscar jerked around, looking in every direction for prying eyes. The phone buzzed again.

It's a simple proposal. You take care of me. I take care of you. You bury this body. I pay you $1 mill. Up for the challenge?

Another text came in on the heels of that one. It read:

You should stop jerking around before you hurt yourself. I can see you, but you'll never see me. Don't believe me? You're wearing Blue Jeans with a red and black checkered button-down shirt. Short sleeve. You have black sunglasses and a tan straw hat. I had hoped someone younger would have come along to make things easier, but hey I always enjoy rooting for an underdog. Think you're up to it old man?

Oscar's breath had ceased. His heart had dropped to the pit of his gut. He felt it thump against his colon to almost cause an instant bowel movement. With trembling hands he struggled to keep from dropping his phone. His eyes scanned the beach across the inlet. It was empty. He blinked and looked at the houses in the distance. Even with a young man's sight it would have been difficult to see anyone, let alone with a seventy-six-year old's eyes. He turned around and looked behind himself. He scanned the trees and shrubs. Nothing. He looked up over the dune once more to the beach front. He even looked skyward for a spying drone. He was all alone.

He focused back on his phone. The stranger's words glared back at him.

A bead of sweat trickled into his eye. He blinked and wiped it away. His trembling thumb began to text.

ThIs Has to be a jok. How do i know your for reel?

A moment passed and the phone rattled in his hand.

Does this help?

Below the words was a picture of ammo cans full of banded ten-thousand-dollar stacks.

Oscar gulped and felt his heart flutter at the sight. He licked his lips as his pupils dilated. His pulse soared at the thought of what that million dollars could do for him and Abby. Hell, they could spend the rest of her life in Egypt if she chose to. They could even afford better doctors and treatment who may be able to extend her time on this earth. And all he has to do is find a way to bury this old feller in his back yard to earn all that? Why this is the easiest decision he's ever had to make. He could cut Ronnie in on it too to be sure it gets done. He would need some help anyhow and Ronnie was about the only person he could trust to help him. He could never drag the body back to his truck without being seen. His eyes lingered to the inlet. His brother does have a boat.

Another text came through.

What will it be old man? Are you up for it or should I wait for another?

Oscar rubbed his Adam's Apple and thought for a moment.

He texted back: *I'll do it but not without a 10% deposit. I'll need my brother's help to do this without getting caught. You leave $100k in the trash can at the boat landing. You put it in McDonalds bags. He gets the money and drives his boat over here to help with the body. No deposit. No deal.*

It took him a few minutes to type it all out and he read it over more than once. He chewed on his lip until he tasted blood. He scratched the back of his neck. He hit send before he could talk himself out of it. He removed his hat and ran his hand through his hair.

It seemed like an eternity had passed before his phone buzzed again.

Deal

"Oh my God, what am I getting into?"

He scrolled through his contacts and found Ronnie. His brother answered with a groggy tone on the fourth ring.

"Ronnie, I need to ask a favor of you."

AS OSCAR HAD expected, Ronnie thought it was all a joke. It wasn't until he heard the shake to Oscar's voice that he came to understand the predicament. He argued at first with Oscar that he should contact the police and not take the risk the stranger was offering. Oscar was able to change his mind by offering to go in fifty fifty with the money. Ronnie had always been the slightly more level-headed of the two, but like Oscar, he had a weak spot for money. Within ten minutes, Oscar had persuaded him to chip in. Being the avid fisherman that he is, Oscar's brother owned a twenty-foot center console they often went deep sea fishing with. On board the boat is a YETI 350 cooler perfect for storing the days catch. Or in this case, hiding a body.

Thirty minutes or more passed before Oscar heard his brother strolling up the inlet. The half hour felt more like seven days as he spent the entire time peeking over the dunes and checking the thin wood line behind him for any witnesses. When he finally saw his brother's boat angling around the bend, Oscar marched towards the beach and scanned for any early morning scrollers. The coast is clear. For now, at least.

His brother beached the boat and angled to the cooler in front of the steering wheel. He opened the lid then walked to the front and tossed out an anchor. Oscar watched it sink into the soft sand. He glanced up and down the beach once more and did a quick scan of the homes across the inlet. He rubbed the back of his neck and chewed on a lip.

"This is crazy, Osc."

Oscar nodded as he watched Ronnie hop down from the boat after killing the engine.

"Yeah, but you willingly agreed to it, didn't you?"

Ronnie arched his brows and tilted his head.

"If we get caught, this was all your idea."

"I figured you'd say something like that. Do you have the cash?"

Ronnie let a sly grin stretch his face, "All hundred k of it. I just hope it's all real."

Oscar swallowed as he rubbed his palms and looked around. He turned for the dune which hid the body.

"C'mon. Let's make this quick." Oscar said as he and Ronnie headed for the body.

They climbed the incline and stepped behind the dune.

"Oh my God," Ronnie said as the white trash bag came into view, "Shit, you weren't kidding."

"Did it sound like I was kidding?" Oscar said as he bent and grabbed the feet. "You're younger and stronger, you get the head and shoulders."

Ronnie cursed again as he strained lifting the body. Together, the two took three stumbling steps. Oscar lost his grip and the legs smacked into the sand. Ronnie grimaced as the jolt likely jarred his back.

Oscar regripped.

They started off again.

Oscar could feel sweat beading on his face as the biting flies began to swarm. He blew air towards his nose to ward them off. Not before he took two good bites near his eye. He blinked and scrunched his nose to try and relieve the itch.

About that time, Ronnie began cussing again.

"Those damned things biting you too?"

"Yeah."

"It's those no see ums. The wind dies down any at all and those things come out in droves."

Oscar felt one pierce the flesh on the back of his neck.

"Hold up a second. Let's stop right here. Let me check the beach one more time."

Oscar dropped his end of the body and scratched his face and neck. He caught a glimpse of Ronnie scratching too.

Oscar walked down to the beach and scanned it before looking across the inlet. Nothing.

He came back to Ronnie and the body. Oscar gripped the legs with a grunt.

"We good?"

"Good as we'll ever be."

A million thoughts flashed through his mind, but all he could picture was Abby riding a camel with a pyramid in the background. That image gave him strength and helped him rationalize his crazy plan.

The two struggled and stumbled, almost dropping the body more than once before hefting it up onto the bow of the boat. The dead man smacked into the floor once they shoved him over the side wall. Ronnie climbed aboard while Oscar panted for breath with his hands to his knees. His heart was beating harder than he had ever felt before. The carotid artery in his neck thumped like a plucked bass string. His lungs burned as they groaned for precious oxygen.

I swear if I have a gosh darn heart attack, I'm going to poke somebody in the eye when I get to heaven.

Ronnie's voice called out to him.

Oscar drew two deep breaths and rubbed his face before straightening his spine. Saltwater pooled around his ankles and soiled his socks.

"Huh?"

"I say hurry up and get your ass in the boat before someone comes around that bend. Get up here and help me put this ole sucker in the cooler."

"Well, you'll have to help me in the boat first."

Ronnie angled to him and stretched out his hand. They locked forearms, and Ronnie pulled him on board. They took each end of the body again and heaved it into the cooler. Oscar snapped the lid shut. Ronnie crossed to the front and began pulling in the anchor he'd tossed out to the sand. Once he had it in, he manned the stern and went to turn over the engine.

Oscar sat in the passenger seat still trying to catch his breath.

The engine growled but struggled to turn over.

Oscar watched Ronnie's Adam's Apple bob.

Ronnie hit it again. Same thing.

Oscar glared at his brother. Ronnie turned his head toward him slowly like an owl.

"It'll turnover this time. Sometimes it takes three tries."

Oscar clinched his teeth and angled his brows at his brother.

The last thing they need is to be stranded on the beach with a dead body in their fishing cooler. That'd sure be a hard one to explain.

Ronnie turned the ignition. The engine roared to life.

"We're in business," said Ronnie.

He threw it in reverse and moments later they entered the ICW and headed for the boat ramp.

This might just work after all.

Oscar thought to himself as he sat behind the captain's glass with the wind hitting the top of his head, sending his curly gray locks flapping behind him. He held his straw hat in his lap.

The sun beamed off the water as ocean spray lit his lips. He saw the picture in his mind's eye again of Abby at the pyramids.

I'm gonna get you there honey. You're gonna see those pyramids.

He mumbled to her.

About that time, a siren sounded off. His heart skipped a beat as it locked up in his chest.

No way. Please, don't let that be what I think it is.

He turned around to find flashing red and blue lights. The siren went off again. *It's a Game Warden.*

Oscar looked up to Ronnie and they met eyes. Neither said a word, their shared look said enough. Ronnie eased back on the throttle and began to pull out of the boat channel as he angled near the bank.

Oscar's heart began that unfamiliar thump again. His fingers trembled as he hid it by gripping tighter to his hat.

Ronnie eased to a halt. The DNR boat slid up next to them.

"How we doing there fellas?"

Oscar and Ronnie nod before returning the gesture.

"You were going a little fast back there weren't ya?" One game warden asked as he gripped the metal pole on the center console. Another warden stayed behind the wheel and watched the brothers closely behind his dark shades.

"Was I?"

The warden nodded, "Yeah, but that's not the reason we stopped you."

"It wasn't?"

"No. We were sitting back there—"

Oscar's pulse quickened at those words.

They've been caught. The wardens saw what they did. They had to.

"When you went roaring past us. I noticed it didn't look like you had a registration sticker." The warden pushed his glasses up and pointed at the side of Ronnie's boat. "I see I was right."

Oscar's shoulders slumped in relief. Those words were like music to his ears. Oscar watched Ronnie lean over the boat to have a look for himself.

"Why hell, that stupid thing just won't stay on. I tried glue and tape, you name it. I guess that sucker must've fell off this morning."

"Mm hm. You fellas do any fishing while you were out?" the warden asked with his eyes lingering to the cooler.

Oscar began to stutter as Ronnie looked to him for help.

"No. No sir. We—"

Ronnie cut him off and said, "We've been working on the fuel pump on this thing for the last week. It's been a real devil, I tell ya. We finally got it working though so we wanted to give her a test spin this morning."

Oscar chimed in with, "Yeah, we plan to go out this afternoon when the tide and winds turn. We prefer fishing an incoming tide."

The warden bobbed his head as he soaked in their words. Finally, after glaring at the cooler long enough, he said, "Yeah, me too. My granddaddy was the same way. The winds and tides can make or break a fisherman."

Ronnie nodded, "You got that right."

"Alright, well listen. You guys have been gentlemen, so I'm gonna let you go with just a verbal warning."

Oscar exhaled for what felt like the first time in this whole ordeal.

"But if I see you out here again without that sticker..." the warden lowered his head and angled his eyes. "I'm gonna get ya. Fair enough?"

Oscar and Ronnie couldn't nod any faster.

"Alright, you men enjoy the rest of your day and good luck later."

Oscar and Ronnie offered their thanks and parted ways with the wardens.

It was just after eight o'clock when they reached the boat landing. They had two hours before Abby would be up and wondering where her husband was. He hadn't told her about taking a walk on the beach this morning. That was something he decided to do after being woken at five worrying and thinking about their situation. If he was lucky, she might sleep till eleven, but worse case he had until at least ten. Which he figured would give him and Ronnie enough time to bury the man without her ever knowing. He planned to cover it up by planting the garden atop him. He knows how sick and twisted it is, and even Ronnie protested his choice, but it's the perfect disguise. Oscar and Abby had talked just last week about it being time to get the old tiller out and churn up some dirt. What better day to till a garden than the day you've been tasked with burying a dead man in your back yard?

Ronnie eased his truck and trailer into Oscar's driveway, and they made their way around back. Oscar got out and peeked into the bedroom window. He was relieved to find Abby sleeping with her back to him. He crossed to Ronnie and the two climbed into the boat to gather the body.

An hour later, and plenty blisters to show for, the two had dug a big enough hole to lower a casket into. Oscar climbed out and wiped the sweat from his brow. Ronnie placed his hands to his hips and leaned to crack his back. Oscar rubbed the blood blisters on his palms and grimaced.

Ronnie sighed and said, "Who the hell is this guy anyway?"

"I don't know, and I don't want to know. I think it's best that way."

"Yeah, but ain't it like shooting a man when he's not looking at ya or something? Won't he come back to haunt ya or something like that?"

"Shut up, Ronnie. Let's just get this over with. C'mon, help me roll him into the hole."

Ronnie shook his head and tightened his lips.

The two dropped the man into the hole. He landed with a hard thump. If he was alive, it'd likely knocked the breath from his lungs.

Oscar retrieved his phone and was in the process of snapping a photo when a voice called out from behind them. He nearly tossed his phone in the air.

"Honey? What're y'all doing out there?"

The sound of Abby's voice sent him leaping out of his flesh. He spun around to find Abby standing on the back porch, a silhouette behind the black screen. He cut his eyes to Ronnie then looked at the shovel. Ronnie got the message and started shoveling dirt onto the body. Oscar crossed the yard and started yapping up a lie.

"Hey sweetie. Yeah, Ronnie caught some fish this morning. We buried the scraps beneath where I'm going to plant the garden. It'll make the ground nice and fertile."

He watched Abbey wrinkle her nose before squinting her eyes at him to question the idea. He opened the screen door and gave her a kiss before taking her in his arms.

"Really? He went fishing without you?"

Oscar searched for words.

"Uh, yeah can you believe it? That sorry rascal. I guess he felt guilty, so he thought he'd offer to help with the garden. He only caught three fish. They weren't all that big. He offered me one, but I told him he could keep em."

"Well, at least he offered it." She waved at Ronnie, and he waved back. "That's an awful big hole, isn't it?"

Oscar gulped. "Well, you know, I mean we had to make sure the scraps were deep enough in the ground so an animal wouldn't try digging them up."

"Hmph. Well, I'm going to make some coffee. You want one cup or two?"

"I'll take just one." He kissed her again and watched her go back inside.

He whistled out a breath and thanked the heavens. He went out the screen door. It slammed behind him. He picked up a shovel and helped Ronnie cover the hole.

Twenty minutes later the job was done. Two blood blisters had popped on Oscar's palm. Another bled in the crevice of his thumb and forefinger. He sucked on the wound and watched Ronnie wipe his brow with the back of his arm. Oscar walked to his building and pulled out the tiller. Half an hour later, he'd done enough to cover the recent hole. He shut the engine off and took out his handkerchief to dab the sweat on his face.

"Now what?" His brother asked.

"I guess I text this feller back and show proof of what we did. He's supposed to send instructions or a map for the rest of the money."

Oscar pulled out his cell and began texting.

Ronnie scratched the back of his neck and wrinkled his face as he peered at Oscar, "Makes ya wonder what in the world this guy did to be worth a million dollar cover up, doesn't it?"

Oscar waved him off and said, "Oh don't go talking like that. All that matters is we did our part. Worse case at least we're both fifty grand richer than yesterday, right?"

"I guess."

Oscar looked up from his phone and squinted at his brother. "You guess? What the hell you mean 'you guess?'"

"I mean what if we're being set up somehow? You don't know who's on the other end of that phone." Ronnie pointed to the device in Oscar's hand. "Hell, that could be the Mafia, the Southern Gentlemen, a Clinton hired hand...what if shit goes sideways and they come after us for something?"

"Ronnie, it's too late for all that. We're in deep and they ain't no getting out now. The least we can do is make sure things follow through so we can get the rest of this money. Can you imagine what you could do with five hundred k of cold hard cash? C'mon, Ronnie. We've come this far, they ain't no turning back now."

"I'm not talking about turning back, I'm just saying we gonna have to be watching our backs from here on out less we end up like the feller we just buried in your backyard."

Oscar nodded and sent the text.

A moment later his phone buzzed.

Nicely done! I knew you had it in you.

Oscar responded with, *Okay, now what about the instructions for the $???*

Ronnie came close and hovered over his shoulder as they glared at the screen.

Patience my fellow man. Patience. I was just getting to that. See the attached map.

Another text came through right after that one. It was a hand drawn map of marshland and tidal creeks. A single black line snaked its way through the marsh to what looked like a large tree. A bright red X sat at the base of the tree.

Just like any old pirate story, X marks the spot. Here you will find seven sealed ammo cans with the reward. Thank you for your business. Maybe we can do it again sometime.

"I know where that's at. Look there's the old church that burned down and right there's Dink's service station." Ronnie said as he pointed at Oscar's phone.

"Yeah, I think you're right."

"Look, if we drive here in the boat we could enter the marshland there. That's a shorter walk than going at it from the parking lot at that public fishing dock. Plus, there would be less chance of us being seen with all those ammo cans."

Oscar thought about it.

"That's a good idea but remember you ain't got no registration sticker on ya boat. If that warden sees us again, he'll hall our asses to jail."

Ronnie cursed and stomped the ground.

"But hey, we could park over here. Ain't there that old dirt road that runs out beside Dink's? If I remember right, it seems like oyster hunters used that road for years before the DNR shut it down after that bad algae bloom one year."

"Hey, yeah that's right. I forgot about that. It's pretty secluded too. Yeah, that'll work. I'll drop the boat off and we can ride up in there."

"Alright then, let's hit the road."

"What about Abby? Won't she be wondering what you're doing?"

"Yeah, I'll just tell her you and me went up to the store to get some tomato plants."

"Alright then, well hurry your ass up."

Oscar turned and marched to the back porch. He opened the back door and yelled for Abby. He told her the plan and said goodbye.

Twenty minutes later, after the two unloaded Ronnie's boat back at his house, they were winding up the old dirt road, inching closer to the treasure.

Oscar stared at his phone. That big, red X glared back at him.

The truck bounced as Ronnie did his best to dodge the potholes and miss the branches hanging out into the path.

Oscar kept checking the mirrors to be sure they weren't being followed. He saw Ronnie doing the same.

The path began to open up a bit as the marshland came into view. The sun glistened off the tidal creeks beyond the tall Spartina grass. A narrow trail cut through the weeds and grass and led to the big live oak standing in the center. There were no houses or boats anywhere in sight. Just like Ronnie had said, it's pretty secluded out here.

Ronnie parked his truck and the two stared out the window for a moment. They checked all their surroundings for any ambush or lookeylews.

Satisfied that the coast was clear, they climbed out of the truck. Oscar checked his phone once more to verify they were at the right spot. There's no denying it. This is where the money is.

They began their trek towards the live oak and stole glances over their shoulders the whole way. The stench of decomposition filled the air the closer they got to the marsh. The live oak stood on the last of the hard soil and fifty yards from there was where the creeks began.

Gulls flew overhead and called to one another. The air was hot and thick with humidity. A dark storm cloud formed near the horizon as it grumbled its way toward the vast Atlantic.

The live oak came into full view and so did the army green ammo cans sitting at its base.

"Fried monkey on a stick, the stupid bastard left a million dollars just sitting in the shade of an oak? Who the hell does that sort of thing?" Ronnie said with bewilderment.

"The same sort of guy who pays a million dollars for an old man to bury a dead body in his backyard I reckon." Oscar replied.

They stood under the oak and glared at the ammo cans. Oscar scanned around one last time before bending down to open a can. After a slight struggle with his arthritic fingers, he was able to pry the can open. He pulled the lid back and felt his heart leap at the sight of banded, crisp Benjamin's looking back at him. He craned his head up to Ronnie and smiled as he took out a wad and flipped through it. The air lighting on his cheeks.

"Well, I'll be damned." Ronnie said.

Oscar and Ronnie checked the other cans and were delighted to find them much the same way.

After two quick trips, they'd loaded all seven ammo cans of cash into the truck and were hightailing it out of there.

On the way back, Ronnie dropped Oscar off at the beach so he could pick his car up from where he'd parked it earlier for his morning walk. Oscar followed Ronnie back to his house where the two took the cans inside and divided it out. All one million was accounted when you included the hundred k they already had. They eyed the bills carefully and even compared them to bills of their own but were unable to spot any differences. They googled ways to spot counterfeit money and tried every trick they could find, but each one they did only verified the authenticity.

Satisfied, Oscar took his share, gave Ronnie a brotherly hug with a slap on the back and headed home to Abby. He grinned like a schoolboy with his first crush most of the way home until he heard something in the back seat of his car. Climbing the hill towards home, he chuckled to himself before glancing into the rearview mirror. He screamed and jerked the wheel. The dead man sat in the back seat smiling from ear to ear. His flesh was ashy gray and decaying as worms slithered out from his teeth and nostrils.

Oscar's car fishtailed and the wheel yanked violently out from his grip. A guardrail with a bright yellow sign warning of the sharp curve ahead, rushed towards him. Oscar's heart pounded as his mind shouted at what lied on the other side of that guardrail. It was at least a fifty-foot drop straight onto a rocky shoreline with crashing waves.

The dead man began to let out a deep, knee slapping, belly aching laugh and Oscar watched his shoulders hitch in the mirror. He tried to correct the wheel, but the guardrail only came faster. His car smashed through it and took a nosedive for the rocks. The dead man's laugh grew louder in Oscar's ears until gravity finished its job and the car crumbled like a piece of tin foil into the rocks.

Cash floated with the breeze as Oscar's spirit joined the dead man in the afterlife.

Them

June 3rd, 1935

24 miles southwest of Charlotte, NC

7:48 p.m.

The amber hues of a Carolina sinking sun filled the sky amidst the wispy clouds. The fields of Old Man Starling had seen their share of rain which had resulted in abundant crops that were taller than his helper. Coming to the end of a hard day's labor, Old Man Starling climbed onto his tractor and watched as his helper, Joseph Conrad, finished up.

"You know Joe, with my kids being off and grown, doing their own thing, you'd be bout tha only one I reckon I'd want to leave this here to," Starling said with a wave of his hand about the field.

Joseph Conrad grunted as he dropped a bag of wheat onto another, sending a puff of dust fluttering into the air. He straightened his spine and wiped his brow. His white sleeveless shirt and blue jeans were stained with dirt and sweat.

"Why, that's awfully kind of ya, Mr. Starling. But you sure you ain't got no other youngins to pass it down to? Grandkids and what not?"

Old Man Starling wagged his head and rested his arms on the wheel of the tractor.

"You bout the only kin folk I reckon I could say I got left. You've always been like a son to me. This here be yours when I'm dead and gone."

Joseph Conrad continued stacking the last of the bags in between the conversation. By the time he was finished, the sun had fallen away to leave the sky black with specks of white light tossed here and there like pinches of salt.

Old Man Starling waited on the tractor as Joseph locked the barn doors. Angling from the back of the barn, Joseph stopped and turned his palms upward, glancing at each forearm with squinted eyes. He took to scratching, trying to soothe the sudden tingling and itching sensation spreading up his arms. His whole body buzzed with an inward vibration as if he were standing too close to an electric fence. The hairs on his arms stood straight and were fuzzy feeling.

"What the heck?"

He clawed his arms, then followed the irritation to the back of his neck.

"Must be dadburn fire ants or somfen," he said as he thudded around the corner of the barn.

Coming to the front where Old Man Starling waited on his tractor, Joseph Conrad was stopped dead in his tracks.

A loud hum pierced his ears as his whole body tingled with the vibration. There was a buzzing with an electric current that he was sure would drop him dead any moment. But it was what filled his sight that sent his heart knocking against his ribs.

There sat Old Man Starling on the tractor, engulfed in a radiant halo of light, staring heavenward at three ginormous glowing beams.

The piercing hum was joined with a loud rumble which was similar to that of the tractor, only louder.

Joseph covered his face with the crevice of his arm. He crouched and stumbled backward.

The light grew brighter to encompass every inch of Starling and his tractor.

Joseph opened his mouth and went to scream . . . nothing came out. His voice was silent even though he should have been screaming to the tops of his lungs. He felt his mouth to be sure it was open. He raked a finger along the jagged crowns of his bottom teeth. He drew a deep breath and went to scream again . . . nothing.

Old Man Starling was frozen in his seat, glaring at the light. Not moving. Not speaking. Just there.

The hum and rumble intensified and forced Joseph to cover his ears and turn away. A horrible stench of rotten eggs and death ripped through the air, stinging his nostrils, and turning his stomach.

He puked and heaved.

The ground entered a tremor. The barn began to rattle, clapping the tin roof, and shaking the wooden siding.

Boom!

An explosion blasted through the air sending a shockwave that shoved Joseph Conrad across the earth.

His chest ached as his lungs were in desperate search of oxygen, begging for another breath. His head spun in a wild haze and throbbed like he'd been struck by a hammer.

He lay still, not saying a word. He listened to the silence. No birds, no creepy crawlies, no frogs, no hum . . . just dead . . . utter silence.

He opened his eyes and peeked through his fingers. He rose and formed an L on the ground. His eyes found the barn, then scanned and landed on the tractor.

No lights, no hum, and no Old Man Starling.

October 27, 1982

AFTER A LONG NIGHT of catfishing down by
Crowder's Creek, two childhood friends, Hank Bigsby
and Bo Wright, were travelling along a windy secluded
road with the windows down in Hank's Chevy S-10
pickup truck. A Waylon Jennings song played through
the radio with a staticky whine as the signal came and
went.

"Can't believe we only caught those three. Figured we
might do better than that," Hank said with one hand on
the wheel before bringing the other holding a cigarette to
his lips and stealing a long drag.

Bo craned his head, "Yeah. Better than nothing though
I reckon."

Hank bobbed his head and flicked ashes out the
window.

Reaching the bottom of a long hill where a short
bridge crossed over a part of Crowders Creek, Hank
lowered his foot onto the gas pedal, sending them
chugging up the other end. Both sides of the road were
dressed in tall cornfields. The sky was dark but clear. The
moon shone bright along with a thousand stars.

Cresting the hill, Waylon's voice turned up a few
octaves and entered a long, loud, screechy whine. Hank
and Bo winced.

"What the heck?" Hank said as he hurried and dialed
the knob down to save them both from going deaf.

The headlights of Hank's truck dimmed, then winked
out. The engine puttered and spit, then dyed and sent the
men easing to a stop off the side of the road.

Bo cursed.

Hank slapped the wheel and threw his cigarette onto
the pavement, "Must be the dang alternator again."

He sighed, curved his spine, and reached for the lever
under the wheel to pop the hood.

As his hand reached the door handle, he felt another hand grab his forearm. Hank turned to Bo.

"What?'

"You feel that?"

"Feel wh—"

A sudden tingling chill crawled across every square inch of his body and turned his skin to gooseflesh. Hank pulled from Bo's grip and hurried to crank the window up.

"Alright. What the hell?" Hank said as he rubbed his fingers across his arm, feeling the hairs standing stiff as if he was only inches from a TV screen.

"Something's not right, man. Something's not right," said Bo.

A distant hum filled the air. It grew in volume and sounded like a plane flying over.

The headlamps flicked on. They were brighter than before. Waylon Jennings boomed over the stereo, vibrating the cab of the truck. A gushing wind tore at the windows, howling as it thrust itself against the glass. The truck began to rock and squeak on worn shocks.

Bo screamed and clutched the hand grip above the passenger window. He shifted in his seat and darted his eyes about.

Hank was frozen. His body was cold along the flesh yet burning with a flame within.

Boom!

Three bright balls of light erupted in the sky. They blazed to earth with trails of flame behind them. They started over the cornfield on the right side of the road, then quickly crossed in front of the truck before disappearing behind a grove of pines off the road. A dome of transparent light bubbled high into the sky then winked out.

Other than Waylon's deep voice, the purring of the truck's motor, and Hank and Bo's gasping breath . . . it was silent.

A moment passed.

Hank swallowed a long gulp, then looked to Bo, "What the hell just happened?"

Bo wagged his head, eyes wide, mouth drooped in a pant for breath.

Hank shifted the gear stick and eased his foot onto the gas.

"What are you doing?" Bo squeaked out with a cracked voice.

"I'm going to go see what that was."

"Not with me you're not," Bo said fumbling for the door handle.

"What? Are you going to walk home in the dark, all alone, after all that?"

Bo got quiet, looked at Hank for a long moment, then pulled his hand from the door.

"That's what I thought. C'mon, we got to see what that was."

Bo cursed under his breath.

Hank eased back on the road and putted along. He had his hands and head up on the wheel with his eyes peering into the midnight sky.

"I think it went over the dirt road up here, didn't it?"

"You mean, Mr. Conrad's driveway?" Bo asked.

"Yeah."

"Great. Just great."

"Chill man, don't be such a wimp."

Bo scoffed out a breath, "A wimp? What and like you weren't scared back there? I saw that look in your eyes."

Hank gave a side grin and kept chugging along, searching for the dirt road which led out to the field where the balls of light had landed.

"Ah ha, here we go," Hank said as he whipped the truck onto the beaten path. They were greeted by a tunnel of trees which leaned over and interlocked bony fingers of branches. Hank half expected the headless horseman to come charging for them any moment. The two could only see to the edge of the headlamps reach. Which, by his guess, couldn't have been any more than a few feet. The darkness along the trail was thicker than usual. It felt like they were entering a sea of inky blackness so thick, you could feel and taste it as it seeped through your skin like an invisible flesh-eating bacteria.

"Man, are you sure we should be doing this? You know the stories about this place. We'll be lucky to make it out. Either Conrad's going to shoot us, or those things are going to get us."

"Shut up! Don't go talking like that man. Not now."

"I'm just stating the facts," Bo said with raised brows and a shake of his head as he glared into the darkness ahead.

The truck bumped and jolted as they traversed over rocks and sticks littering the dirt drive. Hank reached and quieted the stereo. He ran his hand along his arm, "You feeling anything?"

Bo gave it some thought, "No, I don't think so. You?"

Hank wagged his head.

"How far is this place?" Bo asked.

"He's a good way off the road. We should be getting close though I think."

They continued along the dark and narrow road. Their hearts got a start once at the sight of a trio of deer jolting across the path.

A gust of wind caused the leaves to sing with agitation as they quivered in the tall trees.

Frogs, crickets, and other night critters screeched away in harmony as they tucked themselves away in the darkness. Rocks tinged off the under carriage as the truck crawled onward. In the distance, a tiny light came into view. It looked like a porch light.

The curved trees over the dirt path began to lose their reach as the men emitted from their grasp. They entered an open patch of flat land which was filled with crop fields.

The porch light grew as did the silhouette of a small shack of a home. A 1950's blue Ford pick-up truck was parked next to the cobbled stones leading to the front porch. Another trail to their right cut into a cornfield and disappeared into the dark.

"I guess I'll go knock on the door, see if he saw anything."

"Are you crazy? He'll blow your stinking head off. Don't do it man."

"Bo, you need to chill. I got to try and talk to him. I ran into him once when I was a kid. He's a reasonable man. He just doesn't put up with non-sense."

"And you don't think that two dudes in the middle of the night, claiming to have seen three balls of light crash into his cornfield, ain't gonna come across as non-sense?"

Hank craned his head and sighed, then popped open the door and climbed out.

He wasn't more than two paces away when he heard the door lock behind him. He spun around to see Bo pulling away from the driver's door, returning to his seat. Bo tossed his hands in the air, palms first, and shrugged his shoulders.

Hank wagged his head then marched on for the front porch.

A frenzy of windchimes jingled in the breeze. The man must've had a dozen or more draped from his porch.

A trio of cats scurried and bounded from the bannisters, streaking into the shadows. One hissed along the way.

The home was small, worn, and quiet. The gable was sagging, having seen its better days. The white paint along the sides was chipping and, in some places, missing large flakes to reveal the bare cedar shake beneath.

One of the panes on the front window was shattered. Inside, the home was dark and vacant.

Hank reached the front door and leaned his ear to it. Nothing. He sighed and gave three knuckle wraps, then stepped back and waited.

Nothing.

Hands in his pockets, he turned and gave a glance to Bo in the truck. They locked eyes. Hank shrugged his shoulders and knocked once more.

Again, nothing.

He angled off the porch and marched back to the truck.

"Either he's a sound sleeper, or he ain't in there," said Hank as he entered the cab.

"Or something happened to him."

Hank sighed and pulled the truck to the trail cutting between the cornfields.

He sat for a moment, headlamps beaming on the stalks of corn as they swayed in the breeze as if in some accordance with a ritual.

"I don't know about this man. I got a bad feeling."

Hank drew a long breath.

"We got to see what that was. We can't leave now."

"Uh, yeah we can. Road's that way," said Bo as he tossed a thumb over his shoulder.

"Now what if the old man's out here and needs our help. We can't just leave him like that."

Bo dropped his head and shifted in the seat.

"C'mon. We've come this far. We can't chicken out now."

"It's not about chickening out. It's about making sure I get to see the sunrise again."

"Look. I'll drive out here and if we don't see nothing then we'll head home and call ourselves crazy."

A moment passed.

"What if we do see something?"

"Then we'll wish we were crazy."

Hank eased on the gas and entered the trail. Stalks of corn towered over the truck on both sides.

They bounced and rocked as they went over the dirt path. Water from a mud puddle splashed the under belly of the truck as the shocks squeaked again with the tires dropping into the hole.

"Man, I didn't realize the fields were this big out here. He's got a lot of money sitting right here."

Hank craned his head, "You could say that again."

They traveled along the bumpy path, dodging holes when they saw them in time and plunging into them when they didn't.

A gust of wind ripped through the air, sending the corn stalks bowing in reverence.

"Hey, look at that!" Bo said as he shot up from his seat, stabbing a finger at the front windshield just in front of the steering wheel.

"What? What is it?"

"Looks like a trail through the corn up there."

"What?"

"Yeah. You might not be able to see it from your side, but I swear, it looks like the corn is laid over or something up there. It looks like a path."

They continued onward, searching the left side of the corn for this path.

"Stop! Right there. See it?"

"Yeah."

Hank parked next to a narrow cut into the field. It's not something a farmer would have done deliberately.

The corn laid flat on the ground to create a long road which was only about shoulder length wide.

Hank killed the engine and pocketed the keys then reached behind him and pulled off his rifle from the gun rack along the back window.

"What are you doing?"

"I'm going to see where this leads. You coming?"

Bo swallowed hard. His face twisted with indecision. He cursed, then opened the passenger door.

"Grab the lantern, will ya?" Hank asked as he chambered a round in his lever action rifle.

Bo took a deep breath then reached into the bed of the truck and rummaged through a large duffle bag. "I can't believe we're doing this. I can't believe we're doing this," he mumbled as he brought the lantern to life.

"Alright. Stay on my tail. We got to stick together."

Bo nodded.

"And don't blind with that thing either," Hank said as he winced and gently pushed the lantern from his face.

"Sorry."

They trudge along the narrow cut among the corn stalks. Crickets rubbed their wings and sent chirps into the air as they hid among the shadows of the field. The moon shone above as it gleamed before a small cloud passed in front of it.

They'd followed the path long enough for them both to become winded when Hank stopped on a dime. Bo crashed into his back, sending them both stumbling forwards.

"Dadgummit! Can't you see I stopped?"

"What'd you stop for?"

"That," Hank said as he pointed a finger.

Bo raised the lantern and peered ahead.

About a stone cast away was a large clearing.

They took a half dozen paces before stopping at the edge of the opening. It was a circular cut in the field about the size of a large parking lot. The stalks were laid flat to the earth, not cut.

"For heaven's sake, what the world could've done a thing like that?" Hank wondered.

"Alls I know, is we best get moving," Bo said as he turned with the light to head back the way they came.

Hank spun and took hold of his arm.

"Hold it!" a deep gravelly voice boomed into the night.

A chiseled faced old man dressed in overalls and a jacket, stepped out of the corn with his gun drawn and jaw set firm.

"Mind telling me whatcu boys are a doing out here in my cornfield? I give ya five seconds to explain, else I'ma fill ya both full of lead."

Hank and Bo both waisted two precious seconds before blurting, "Hang on—"

Hank released Bo's arm and held up his hands.

"I can explain."

"Ya got two seconds for I'ma locking and loading."

"We saw the light. We saw what made this," Hank said turning and waving a hand behind him.

"I swear Mister, we ain't mean no harm. I tried knocking on your door. We was afraid you might be in trouble or something."

The old man glared at them with angled brows and searing eyes. He clenched his jaw and didn't say a word.

"I swear it's the truth."

Bo nodded, "We ain't never seen nothing like that before."

"You saw a light, huh?"

Hank and Bo nodded.

"Just one?"

Hank wagged his head, "Three actually, sir. Looked like meteorites or something. They crashed, then a big dome of light filled the sky," Hank demonstrated with his hands, "But before all that, my truck conked out on me like the battery died or something. And our skin got all tingly feeling and staticky like."

The old man sighed and lowered his head and aim.

"You boys feel itchy?"

Hank and Bo looked at each other.

"No, not really. Just tingly I guess."

"You best get moving. You don't want *them* coming after you too."

"Who?" Hank asked in a low tone.

The old man looked slowly to the dark sky and pointed to the stars, "Them."

Hank swallowed hard, "I'm sorry mister Conrad. We didn't mean to cause you any harm. We just wanted to be sure you was all right."

Mr. Conrad nodded, then waved his gun, "Go on, git. Forget this ever happened. And go get you some cats and windchimes . . . they don't seem to like it much. At least for me it seems to work." He raised his head and looked them both in the eye, "Promise me, you won't tell anyone bout this?"

Hank and Bo nodded.

"They'll get me if word spreads too much. They don't like too much attention. You boys get out of here for it's too late."

Hank nodded before the two of them headed for the narrow trail leading back to the truck. Hank stopped by Mr. Conrad's side and gave him a pat on the shoulder, then crossed to Bo waiting at the edge of the trail.

Once on the trail, they bolted along, climbed into the truck, and threw dirt to leave Mr. Conrad and his crop circle behind. The two hardly spoke a word the rest of the way to Bo's house. When Hank pulled in the driveway to let him out, he turned and said with his right hand extended, "Not a word to anyone. Right?"

Bo nodded and shook his hand, then climbed out and headed inside. Glancing at the dark sky more than once along the way to his front door.

Hank drove home and replayed the night's events over and over in his mind.

Who was the "them" that Mr. Conrad spoke of?

Were all those rumors really true about him and that old fella named Starling? After what he'd seen that night, Hank couldn't help but wonder.

A WEEK HAD PASSED without anything weird taking place. No strange lights, humming sounds, or tingling skin. It was like it'd all been a dream. Had it?

That question was answered the night Hank was roused from his sleep late one night to the sound of that loud hum, meowing cats, and dancing windchimes.

When he woke, he found himself lying on the floor next to his bed, dazed and confused. The hum pierced his ears. The tingling sensation once again spread across his flesh, sending his hair standing on end. A howling wind beat upon the walls of the home, screaming like a thousand banshees at once. He tried sitting up on his haunches, but his body felt weightless and numb. He couldn't move. His body was transfixed in a state of stupor.

He lay flat on the floor with his eyes glaring at the ceiling as it spun about like he'd had one too many drinks. His gut twisted and knotted, sending a wave of nausea riding along his esophagus. He forced with all his might to keep it at bay.

The sudden creak in the floorboards gave his heart a start. Paralyzed and left for dead, Hank forced his eyes to scan the darkened room.

Nothing.

Creeeaaaakkkk!

His heart knocked. Someone's in the house!

Thud! Thud! Thud!

Followed by the tapping sound of long toenails on the hard wood floor.

Oh God!

Thud! Thud! Creeeaaaaakkkkkk! Thud!

Then a long bout of silence.

The wind ceased. The hum stopped.

It was so quiet Hank could hear his own blood pumping through his veins. His heartbeat sounded like it came behind his ears. His breath was quick and short. He struggled to keep from hyperventilating.

Creeeaaaaakkkkkk!

Three dark figures filled his vision and hovered over him, not saying a word.

He slammed his eyes and clinched his jaw.

A bright flash erupted and stung his eyelids. The loud hum returned, followed by gushing wind that ripped at his flesh and hair.

Even with his eyes shut, the light still hurt.

The sound of clicking teeth and slithering tongues pierced his heart. Then he heard what sounded like silverware clanging together. His body began to quiver. The air he pulled into his lungs was like inhaling snowflakes. His teeth chattered without his consent.

It hurt to swallow. Felt like he'd taken on a deadly battle with the flu that no amount of chicken noodle soup could ever soothe.

The stark odor of a disinfectant stung his nostrils. He twitched his nose to relieve the pain and itch.

A strong metallic taste rode along the tip of his tongue as if he'd just licked a cold metal pole.

He took a deep breath and with the pace of a rising sun, he opened his eyelids. His lashes came into view like tiny spider legs trying to tickle his eyeballs. The room was white as a dim light hovered above like one a dentist would use.

The feeling came to his fingers and toes, and he knew then he was lying on a cold metal table with some sort of cloth draped over him.

Was he dead? Was he stored somewhere in a morgue?

The room filled with movement. Coming from every direction.

He slammed his eyes.

The sound of clicking teeth and hissing tongues returned. This time closer and ten times louder. Three distinct voices spoke in what sounded like another language. Going back and forth, hovering just above him.

For the life of him, he dared not open his eyes, but he couldn't not know what he was facing. He had to see.

Hank slid an eye open, the other followed as his eyes were forced wide in shock.

Three black cloaked figures stood hovering over him, with black hoods over their heads and two bright red eyes tucked deep within the hood's realm.

Hank gasped. He sucked in a dose of cold, frosty air which stung his lungs. He tried to squirm but was once again paralyzed except for his eyes and breath.

One of the figures raised a bony black hand and covered Hank's face as if it were just the size of a baseball.

The room went black.

Silence.

Hank's body turned limp and numb like he was floating atop a murky sea. He tried to take one last deep breath, but it was smothered by the creature's hand.

AFTER A WEEK OF SEARCHING and with no sign of Hank Bigsby or Bo Wright, Mr. Joseph Conrad knew they'd never be found. They'd been chosen just like Old Man Starling all those years ago. Why? He'd never know.

As he sat out on the front porch, listening to CCR's *It came out of the sky,* from his old Victrola record player, he looked up at the moon and stared long and hard. He swayed to and fro in a rocking chair while petting a cat in his lap. Stroking the back of his gray Tabby cat, he said, "Some mysteries just ain't never meant to be understood, I don't reckon."

A falling star streaked by.

The record player screeched to a halt.

Mr. Conrad stared at space, not blinking.

The sound of the windchimes caused him to flinch. He jerked his eyes to one of them then started praying.

A loud stir tore through the corn field, rattling the stalks. A howling wind ripped through the air and sent the chimes rattling.

His porch light blinked and stuttered.

His prayers went from a mumbled breath to a declaration. Louder and with more authority.

The cat leapt from his lap and took a defensive position a few feet down, hissing and thrusting a paw at the air.

Louder the old man prayed.

He heard the hum coming, growing in volume.

The porch light dimmed, then winked out before bursting the bulb.

"You need to get on back to hell from whence you came, ya hear! You ain't gonna start all this mess again. I command you in the name of Jesus . . . to leave and never come back!"

A loud shriek blasted through the air from the corn field. Three balls of light exploded just feet above the tops of the stalks, then streaked into the air, leaving a trail of flames and smoke.

The night grew still.

Mr. Conrad drew a deep breath as a small grin twisted his lips.

His cat wandered back and leapt into his lap. He stroked its back and mumbled, "Should've done that long time ago, shouldn't I?"

The corn stalks bowed as a gentle breeze brushed by them. A calming peace entered the air, snuffing out any ounce of fear.

He smirked and returned to his rocking, listening to his cat purr. The crickets sang along with the windchimes.

"Well, I guess sometimes even the darkness itself tries to act like the light. I'm just glad I know who the real Light is. And after all, what's to fear when you know the Light of the World?"

The Vanishing of Thomas Marvin

I started working for the old man back in the summer of 1992. He lived down the hill from us and was only a short bike ride from my house. I had turned thirteen that spring and was thinking of starting a grass cutting business that summer. That was before Thomas Marvin offered me good pay to help him and his wife tend to things around their house. They were both in their early eighties and were having trouble doing the things they used to. I talked to my parents about the old man's offer. They both thought it'd be wise to take the old man up on the job. That simple decision has forever changed my life.

Thomas Marvin owned over one hundred and sixty acres with fifty-three of it being old tobacco fields. He and his wife, Gloria, had made their living for forty years harvesting tobacco in those fields. Together they ran a company which at one point employed about a dozen or more people. The old man was smart with his money and had invested wisely through the years. He understood the pros and cons of debt and interest and learned to use them both in his favor. He respected every penny that was made and was always sure to put it to good use. When he and Gloria retired from the Tobacco business, they leased eighty acres of his land to a local hunting club. The back portion of the land was a mixture of wetlands and hardy pines, which made it perfect hunting grounds. The land was plentiful with ducks, hogs, deer, and bear. The hunting club was happy to pay a premium for the prized land. At one point, they even offered a seven-figure deal to buy it from him outright. The old man refused the offer.

I learned a lot from the old man for the four years I worked for him. He was always telling me tips and secrets about money and investing. Half of the time his words were gibberish as I had trouble understanding his train of thought. As I've gotten older, I've realized just how smart the old rascal really was.

The first summer I worked for him he paid me three bucks an hour plus an extra twenty a week if I read him an hour of the Wall Street Journal each morning. At first, I thought any man who wanted to read or listen to an hour of the Wall Street Journal had to have one foot in the insane asylum, but the more I read of it the less I came to loathe it. After the first month of reading to him for an hour each morning, I actually began understanding some of the things it was talking about. Of course, Tom explained a lot of things along the way. He was Tom to me. He always stressed I just call him Tom. He didn't like for me to call him Mr. Marvin or Thomas. Gloria could call him Thomas, but not me. Tom was what he preferred.

Summer came and went in a flash. My parents were happy I'd found something I enjoyed doing and was able to make some decent money doing it. The way we all figured, another two summers like the first and I could buy my first car soon after I got my license.

The summer of '93 rolled around, and Tom bumped my pay to $3.50 an hour plus an extra $25 a week for reading the Journal to him each morning. He even offered a hundred-dollar bonus at the end of the summer if I helped him finish painting his barn and repair a few slats in his privacy fence beside Pam Rogers, their neighbor.

It was a few weeks before I went back to school for the fall when Tom mentioned the idea he had of buying a few milk cows to graze in a section of the old tobacco field.

He planned to till up the dead plants with his tractor and throw down some grass seed in hopes of making about a two-acre pasture for the cows. He even had plans to build a new barn. He said Gloria had grown up on a farm and had always wanted cows and chickens and such. The way he figured, with the price of milk and eggs the way it was, sounded like a good opportunity to please the wife and save a few bucks while he's at it. I remember he snickered and elbowed me in the ribs when he told me that.

"The way I see it kid, you'll have more work than you know what to do with next summer. If you'll help a feller out with it, I'll be willing to bump ya pay to four an hour plus thirty a week for reading the Journal to me. What'd ya say? Sound square enough for ya?" He said with an outstretched hand.

I didn't even have to think about it. I nodded and shook his hand faster than a rabbit on crack.

It was when he got the cows that things started getting weird. Me, a few of my buddies from school, and an older colored man whom Tom had known since the army, built the barn and redid a section of his tobacco field early that summer. Once we were finished, Tom went to a cattle auction somewhere down in Chester, South Carolina and bought four milk cows. He had them delivered the next day. Gloria had named them Betsy, Bertha, Brenda, and Bonnie. Why they all had to start with a B I never did understand, but that was their names. I remember Charles, the old colored man, laughed and laughed when he heard Gloria rattle off each of the names.

"You folk crack me up. I kid you not." He'd said.

A few weeks after they got the cows, we received a phone call from Tom around two in the morning. My dad was the one who answered it as all we had back then was a landline. I heard him fumble his way into the kitchen, flick the light on, and lift the phone out of its cradle. My dad's voice was thick with gravel, and I could just picture him standing there shirtless in his boxers, rubbing his eyes trying to figure out who in the world was calling at two in the morning.

"You said what now? People are in your field? Who is this?"

By then I had crawled out of bed and was coming down the hall.

"Who? Thomas? Thomas Marvin?"

I entered the kitchen the same time my mother did. She stood in the arch of the hallway tying a knot in her robe. She squinted at my dad and mouthed, *What's wrong?*

Dad shrugged his shoulders.

"Well, what are they doing? What? How many are they? Jesus..."

His voice trailed off. I could hear a voice on the other end but couldn't make out the words. I heard a pop sound and saw my dad flinch before pulling the phone from his ear and staring at it for a short moment.

"What was that?" I asked him.

"It sounded like a gunshot," then into the phone, "Thomas are you alright? Hey. What's going on? Can you hear me?"

I heard two more shots before his voice came back.

I watched as my dad stood there listening and making odd faces.

"Have you called the cops?"

Mom said, "Is he okay? What's going on over there?"

My dad shook his head and held up a hand.

"Yeah. Okay. Well, they shouldn't bother you no more. It sounds like it was probably some teenagers just messing with ya. Me and Derrick will come by tomorrow to check on things with ya. Alright. You be careful now. We'll see ya tomorrow. Alright. Bye."

"Is everything alright? What's going on?" My mom asked as I was about to do the same.

Dad looked at the floor, sighed, and shook his head.

"Lord have mercy. That old fart is losing his mind."

"What is it?"

"He said they were a bunch of lights down in his field where the cows are at. Said he heard them mooing and causing a stir. He got up and said he heard a bunch of voices and saw lights flickering on and off. Said everything disappeared when he fired his shotgun in the air. Tried saying he saw lights in the trees and stuff too." Dad looked at me and said, "Has he ever talked that strange around you before?"

"No. I've never heard him talk like that. Something had to get him stirred up."

"Hmph. I told him we'd come by tomorrow to help him look around. Said he didn't want to call the sheriff. Said he just wanted us to know in case they tried fooling around up here."

Mama added, "That's awfully odd for him to call like that. I hope he's not coming down with dementia or nothing. I know Gloria had told me the other week about how forgetful he's becoming."

"Oh lord. Don't say that." Dad said.

We went back to bed and the next morning, which happened to be a Saturday, my mama cooked a good breakfast of liver mush and eggs before we all headed over to Tom and Gloria's.

We tried knocking on the front door which was opened except for the screen storm door. After not getting an answer, my mama opened the door and poked her head inside. She called out for them, but there was never a returning voice.

I said, "I bet he's in his field."

"He's probably right. C'mon honey, let's look around back," Dad said.

Mama stepped off the porch and joined me and Dad as we rounded the corner of the house. Off in the distance near the back corner of Tom's field, I noticed two people standing there. I could barely make them out, but him and Gloria were looking at something on the ground. There were two large, black mounds resting before them.

"Hank, is that what I think it is?" My mama asked.

Dad grunted and squinted his eyes. He shielded the sun with his hand. He grumbled a curse under his breath.

"Who would do such a thing? Are they dead Hank? I hope they're not dead."

Dad shook his head and said, "I don't know, but those cows sure ain't moving."

As we drew closer, Tom and Gloria spotted us. Tom was holding his straw hat in his hand and waved it in the air when he saw us. Gloria stood next to him with her arms crossed. She wore a long, khaki skirt and a baby blue blouse. Her silver hair was tied into a tight bun.

Tom had his hands to his hips and studied the sight before him. He tightened his lips and peeked up at us as we approached.

"What in the hell happened, Tom?" Dad asked.

The old man shook his head, "I knew I should've came down here to check on em last night. Gloria was afraid one of them people would get me. I told her I liked my chances with the scatter gun." He paused and sighed before adding, "I ain't never seen nothing like this before. I've grown up around cattle most of my life, and I've seen what happens when a coyote or big cat gets ahold of one of them. But this..." His words trailed off as he pointed down at the cow's face.

We were standing behind the animal and couldn't see the face or belly all that good. When we stepped around to see what Tom was talking about, I remember feeling like my heart had taken a shock from a cattle prod. The majority of the flesh around Brenda's face had been stripped away to leave a bloody, grinning skull. I could see her tongue had been cut in half. Her eyes bulged like two ping pong balls. Scanning down the body, I saw her gut had a round hole which had been sliced with prefect precision. Her udder was missing, and her blue, gray intestines lay spewed on the ground. A pungent odor hung in the air. Despite the gore, I couldn't see a drop of blood anywhere.

My mama gasped and covered her mouth before turning away.

"Jesus. What the hell?" Dad said as he scrunched his face at the sight and looked to Tom for answers.

Tom shook his head and pointed his hat to the other cow lying lifeless about ten yards from us.

"Bonnie's the same way. I had to lock Betsy and Bertha in the barn. They kept hanging around and nudging 'em. Those poor things moaned and groaned like people grieving at funeral or somfin."

Gloria sniffled and said, "I told Tom I want to get some cameras set up so we can catch whoever did this. These poor cows didn't deserve this. People are evil nowadays."

Mama came back to us and added, "You need to call the Sheriff so they can file a report."

Tom tightened his lips and grunted, "Sheriff will just laugh at us. That sorry rascal will try saying a bear did it or somfin. Gloria's right, we need camera's so we can have proof of who's messing around."

"Me and Derrick can help you put them up." Dad said.

Tom looked at me and Dad and said, "Really? I'd appreciate that. I don't know the first thing about today's technology."

A few days later, after Tom used his tractor to bury Brenda and Bonnie, me and Dad helped set the cameras up for him. My mom found an eight-camera system at RadioShack that came with the DVR box and monitor. It took us about two hours one evening to get it all set up, but it was worth it. We placed the monitor on a desk next to the living room so the two of them could keep a check on it as they watched their nightly TV shows. We had four cameras stationed at each corner of the house with the other four pointing towards the field, barn, and tool shed.

As much as we thought we were helping at the time, I think those cameras may have been a mistake because that was when the old man's paranoia really began. His late-night calls became a weekly routine after that. He'd call swearing up and down somebody was messing around his house. He'd call cussing up a storm saying he saw lights on the camera and heard people in his field. We'd go over there the next day to run the cameras back but could never find anything more than dust orbs or bugs floating by.

That summer ended without further incident, and I went back to school to start my sophomore year at Clover High. Kids at school had somehow heard about the deaths of Tom's two cows and boy did the rumors spread. My buddies would often greet me in the hallway wearing hats covered in tinfoil. I heard whispers about everything from aliens, the CIA, Bigfoot, a satanic cult, you name it. How people found out about those cows, I never understood. I guess that's the works of living in a small town though. I sometimes wondered if maybe the culprits even attended my school.

I went back to work that summer, and after only a week on Tom's farm, I found Gloria lying in the field, naked, and lifeless. It was at dawn and Tom had driven into town to gather supplies for another fence we were to build. Gloria had fixed breakfast as always and the two enjoyed a meal together before starting the day. Her official cause of death was ruled a heart attack, and despite her nakedness, there was no indication of foul play. As strange as it all was, it looked like she had simply stepped out of the shower and walked into the field before her heart gave out. The bathroom mirror was still damp with moisture and water droplets led from the shower to the back deck. A bath towel was found twenty feet from her body. It appeared something had drawn her out to the field. But what? Had she heard something? When the camera footage was rolled back, it was nothing but gray and white static for two hours surrounding the time it all happened. Still to this day, no one has ever learned the truth behind Gloria's death.

The tragic event only added to Tom's already fragile mental state. The man became a recluse after her death. My parents and I did our best to be there for him, but his behavior became creepy and unpredictable. He talked nonstop about people wandering in his field at night, seeing strange lights again, and hearing voices calling to him late into the night.

I will never forget the night he called and said the people were in his home.

My dad had answered the phone again and was on the brink of cursing. I watched as he gritted his teeth at the annoyance that Tom's midnight calls had become. His anger dissipated quick, and I knew by the look on his face something was wrong. He got real quiet and let the old man talk.

"What is it this time?" Mom asked in a mid yawn.

I watched Dad swallow hard before saying, "Helen, get my pistol from my nightstand and grab my coat."

She squinted her eyes.

"Please. Just do it."

Mom went to their bedroom and came back with the items in hand. She handed dad his coat and he slid into it while still listening to Tom with the phone cradled on his shoulder. He took his .357 revolver, checked the cylinder, then stuffed it into his coat pocket.

"Tom, stay put. I'll be right there."

The phone jingled in its cradle.

He turned to us and wiped the sleep from his face.

"What's going on?" I asked.

"Tom said four people were just in his house. One of them he claimed was Gloria."

"What?" My mom asked in a hoarse whisper.

Dad nodded, "Said it was a big man, a woman, Gloria, and some little girl. Said they came in the front door while he was watching TV and started roaming through his house like they were looking for something."

"Oh my God. Do you want me to call the police?"

Dad shook his head, "No, not yet. It kind of sounded like he had been drinking a bit, so I'm hoping he's just high on the sauce. I'm going to go check on him to be sure."

"You're not going down there by yourself."

Dad ran a hand through his thick hair and sighed, "Well, c'mon. But grab my .38 so you can keep it in the truck with you and Derrick."

Minutes later we were pulling into Tom's driveway. Dad parked the truck and scanned our surroundings. He rolled the windows down and listened. The air felt different here. It had an electric charge to it or something. Like the way it feels during a summer storm just before a lightning strike. It was almost difficult to breathe. I could feel something pressing down on me. It was like the pressure was higher than normal. The night was quiet except for a soft breeze lofting through the trees.

"Alright. Stay here. You see anything odd you blow the horn. Got it?"

Mama nodded.

"Anybody approaches you . . . well that's why you have the .38, right?"

She nodded again and said, "Are you sure we shouldn't call the police, honey?"

"Not yet. Let me have a look around first."

He climbed out of the truck and shut the door. Leaning in through the window he said, "Lock the doors and roll the windows up."

As Dad was finishing his words, the flood light to Tom's back porch came on. We each jerked our attention in time to see Tom, butt naked, walking down the steps of his porch and heading for the field.

Dad cursed and called after him, "Tom! Tom, what the hell are you doing?"

Tom didn't acknowledge him but kept striding to the field.

"Wait here." Dad said before going after him.

We kept the windows down, so I stood up in the cab to lean out and look at them. I watched Dad reach Tom and place his own coat around him. Tom jerked away and said, "Leave me alone. I'm going to see Gloria."

Dad stepped back from him and stared. He tried again to put the coat on him. Tom spun around and back handed my dad across the face. Dad blinked in disbelief. I watched him grit his teeth after rubbing his jaw.

"Hey. Tom, listen to me." Dad said as he took hold of Tom's arm.

Dad shook his shoulders and patted Tom's cheek to wake him from what had to be a dream.

Tom stared at him for a long time before suddenly snapping back to reality. He shook his head and began looking around in a panic.

Dad closed the coat around him, and Tom blushed as he realized his nakedness. He turned and looked at me and Mom with a face of shame and horror. He turned back to Dad, and I heard him say, "What happened? Hank, what happened?"

Dad put his arm around him and soothed him.

"I think you had a little too much to drink, Tom. It's alright. You're fine. C'mon, let's get you back inside, okay?"

"I heard Gloria. I heard her calling for me from the field. I heard her plain as day. She was down there, Hank. I know she was. You have to check. You have to go see."

Dad looked at me and Mama and make a *God help us* face.

"I'll check, Tom. You need to go inside and get to bed."

"I saw those lights right after I saw those people. Those lights were back in the field, and I heard Gloria down there calling for help."

"Tom, I'll look around the house for you before I go to be sure no one's in the field, alright."

"It's not so much the people I'm worried about."

I remember that statement struck me as odd. I have never forgotten the way he said that.

I watched Dad take Tom back inside as he rambled the whole way about the lights and hearing strange noises and such.

After Dad got Tom situated, he came back out, and we rode down into the field to have a look around.

The electric charge I felt in his driveway had multiplied ten-fold when we reached the field. So much so that I could literally feel the hairs on my arms raising as if being pulled by a magnetic force. It reminded me of standing close to a television set and feeling the static charge it gives.

"Do y'all feel that?"

"Feel what?" Mama asked me.

"You don't feel anything?"

She shook her head.

"Dad, do you feel it?"

He thought for a moment, "No. What are you talking about?"

The headlights blinked out when he finished his words.

Mama yelped. I leaned into her and squeezed her arm. Dad cursed and slapped the steering wheel. It wasn't just the lights that went out, the whole truck had died.

I remember how silent everything was. There were no crickets, tree frogs, or cicadas. The field was washed in an eerie stillness. I could literally hear my mama's heartbeat.

The night was overcast and hid the moon. The field was nothing but a black abyss. It was like we had driven into a starless space. A galaxy void of life and light. I swallowed the knot in my throat. My heart pounded against my ribs. My skin crawled as gooseflesh rifled over my entire body.

Dad turned the key and the truck sputtered then made a clicking sound.

"Damn it!"

He tried again but got the same result.

He sat back in his seat with a huff and rested his chin in the cradle of his hand as he stared out the driver's window.

"Do you have your jumper box with you?" Mama asked.

"No, it's in the garage. I forgot to put it back in here after I had to jump the boat battery off the other day."

"Oh my God, Hank. How could you forget to put it back?"

"I just did, alright? Let's give it a few minutes, and I'll try it again."

Those few minutes felt like a few hours as they crept along at the rate of an out-of-date gas pump.

"Do you hear that?" Mama asked as she craned her head.

I didn't hear it at first, but after about ten seconds of listening, I began to hear it too. It was a high-pitched whistle calling from the tree line. Sounded like a high frequency dog training device.

"What in the hell is that?" Dad said as he squinted and grimaced.

The sound was ear piercing and forced us to cover our ears.

Mama began slapping Dad's leg to get him to try the ignition again. He did. The truck fired right up like nothing had ever happened. He threw it into gear and spun grass and dirt to get us out of there. He made a quick stop back at Tom's house to be sure the old man was alright. He raced in and raced out. Said he was asleep in his boxers on the couch.

Nothing else happened the rest of the summer. I went on to help him around the house like I always did. I was making good money by then and was doing good to save for the truck I'd been wanting. It wasn't until the third week of helping him the next summer that things got even stranger.

The big project that summer was going to be a new and bigger chicken coop. Tom had ordered all the material and had it delivered. Me, Dad, and Charles were to build it over the weekend when they were off work. Me and Dad drove over to Tom's a little before seven that Saturday morning. Thursday was the last time we'd talked to him. We got out of the truck and made it onto the front porch. Dad opened the screened door and gave a few good knocks on the window of the main door. He stepped back and sipped on his coffee thermos. How anybody could drink that nasty stuff is beyond me. Maybe one day I'll grow to like it, but I don't know. My tastebuds have an awful lot of growing to do before that day ever comes. We waited there on the porch, but never heard any movement. He'd told dad on Thursday for us to have breakfast with him before we got started. Said he'd have sausage and egg biscuits ready for us.

"The old rascal probably forgot what he told me about those biscuits." Dad said with a grin.

"It wouldn't surprise me." I said as I chuckled and leaned into the window to peer towards the living room. I could see the TV showing a rerun of his favorite show, *Gunsmoke.* I smiled and scanned the rest of the room.

What in the world?

I could see the side of his recliner. There were clothes laid out like someone was sitting there but they had no form to fill them.

I pulled back and looked at Dad.

"Dad, c'mere and have a look at this."

"What now?"

Together we looked in, cupping our hands around the glass.

Dad wrinkled his brow and didn't say anything. He stepped back and went to the door. He tried the handle. It opened without protest. He gave me an odd look before we made our way inside.

"Tom, you up buddy?" He called out.

"Tom?" I added.

Dad did a quick glance around the home as I went to the recliner for a better look.

A shirt, pants, underwear, and socks were all laid out on the recliner like he should be sitting right there in front of me. Even his silver chained watch that he wore on his left wrist was stationed where his hand would be on the arm rest.

I gulped and called for Dad.

"He's not here." He said as he strode up beside me.

I pointed to the watch.

"What in the hell?"

About that time, we heard a car pull into the driveway. I turned and looked out the window to find Charles's truck parking behind ours.

The three of us went on to search the house again before driving down into the field. We never found Tom Marvin that day. The police were called to investigate. They spent the next few days combing over every inch of the property, using search dogs and the whole nine yards. The DNR did a thorough sweep of the woods to be sure he hadn't wandered off anywhere. The only evidence that was ever discovered were his clothes laid out on the recliner. It looked like he had been sitting there watching *Gunsmoke* and simply evaporated out of the room.

He was ruled a missing person and his picture was stapled to every light pole and store window in town. Multiple op eds were printed in the town paper. A handful of independent journalists came to town to investigate once word began to spread of the strange circumstances. More than once, they came to our house for questioning. We never gave them the time of day. Mama and Dad said they'd likely spin things how they needed to suit their story anyway.

With Tom and Gloria never having kids or much other family, the home and all of his assets went into probate. We were able to gain authority to sell Betsy and Bertha to a good home where they could be properly cared for. We did our best to keep his place up, by cutting the grass and keeping the weeds from overgrowing near the house.

It wasn't until a year or so later that we received a letter in the mail from an attorney's office addressed to my name.

Mama had gotten it from the mail while I was at school, and fought every urge to open it, but waited for me and Dad to get home before discovering what it was all about.

I opened it with great suspicion as Mama and Dad watched over my shoulder.

The letter basically said that Tom and Gloria had left the home, land, and all other assets to me who they considered in their will as their adopted grandson. It had a breakdown of the different brokerage accounts they shared together, as well as the amount of gold and silver stored in a safe deposit box at his bank in town. The sum of the estate was worth over $2.2 million. The letter said there would be instructions from Tom within the safe deposit box as to how best preserve and protect the wealth.

Mama dropped the glass she was drinking from, and it shattered on the floor.

Dad stepped away and held a hand to his head, breathing deeply.

Tom was never found, and the majority of the money he left behind for me was left where he had it. Except for $750,000. Five hundred of it was used to start a construction and real estate business which, Dad, Mama and me began operating after I graduated high school. I went on to earn an associate's degree in finance from the local community college.

I followed Tom's instructions to the T. Except for the other $250,000 which I used to create a non-profit investigative entity to look into other strange stories such as Tom's. I bought a thirty-three-foot RV and loaded it down with all of today's best technology to help discover the truth behind the unexplained events around the country. For about three months out of the year, the three of us are on the road researching different stories which have been submitted to our website. We have investigated everything from aliens, Bigfoot, cattle mutilations, missing people, you name it. We've been doing it now for about thirty years, I guess. I even have drones and FLIR technology to scan the woods and stuff.

It's a fun and adventurous gig as you never know what might come through the inbox. I feel that it's a way for us to remember Tom by helping to solve the mysteries of others.

I think it's something he'd be proud of.

At least, I hope so.

The Guest

Legend says our home is haunted. At least that's what the neighborhood kids tell me. I didn't believe them at first, but that all changed after the first few weeks we moved in. I'd be woken in the middle of the night to scratching and clawing on the inside of the walls, strange whispers, and creaking floorboards. I remember feeling something run across my bed one night before thudding to the floor. I wish that was all of it, but that's only the beginning.

I'm Malcom Schroder and this is my story.

WE'VE BEEN HERE for almost a year now and things have only gotten worse. Last night, I felt it get in the bed with me. The mattress gave under its weight and the covers shifted as it covered itself up. I was too afraid to look or move. I just shut my eyes and prayed for the sun to rise. I know it wasn't my little brother Gregory because he doesn't weigh that much. This was a big person. An adult.

"Maryann, did you come into our room last night?" I asked at the kitchen table in between spoonful's of oatmeal. She didn't budge. Her face was glued to her phone with the wires to her ear buds hanging out as if tiny men would repel down them.

I leaned across the table and waved my hand in front of her face. She yanked out her ear buds, clinched them in her hands, and asked, "What?"

"Did you come in our room last night?"

Her face twisted, "No! Why would I do that?"

Of course, it wasn't her. She can hardly stand to be within arm's reach of me, let alone to be sharing covers.

"Just wondering. Someone crawled into bed with me that's all."

"Probably Gregory."

"Too big. I know it wasn't him. Besides he's still in *his* bed."

"Hmm."

My stepmom, Catherine, entered the kitchen. She was dressed in her robe with her brown hair disheveled as she headed for the coffee pot.

"Morning kiddos. Sleep good?"

"Yeah," said Maryann.

"No."

Catherine craned her head before reaching into the cabinet for a coffee cup, "No? Why not?"

"I heard the scratching behind the walls again. Then I woke up in the middle of the night feeling like someone crawled into the bed with me."

"Are you sure it wasn't Gregory?"

"No, it wasn't Gregory. You know what Chris and Will say about this place, right? And what Miss Clancy says?"

Catherine sighed as she closed the cabinet. She said as she poured her a cup of coffee, "I know what people say, honey. And I can promise you it's just a bunch of rumors. We checked into all of that before we bought the place. There were no murders, or deaths, or Indian burial grounds. None of that nonsense. The place is not haunted. We've been here almost a year. We'd know by now, wouldn't we?"

I tightened my lips and nodded then shoveled more brown maple syrup oatmeal and chugged my glass of OJ.

Dad stepped in as Catherine sat at the table. He was dressed for the office and working on locking in his gold wristwatch. He was rushed as always. He leaned down and kissed Catherine on the head as he passed for the fridge before saying good morning to me and Maryann.

"Who keeps drinking all the milk? I swear we're buying a gallon a day now it seems. I just got this on the way home yesterday."

"Well, we do have a teenager now," Catherine said with a smile as she looked to Maryann. She'd turned thirteen a few weeks ago.

"And you don't have much longer. Two more years," Catherine said as she sipped her coffee.

I scoffed and rose to put my bowl and glass in the sink. I took Maryann's too. Although she didn't even acknowledge it. I did it anyway and despite the battle with her raging hormones, she was still my sister and I still loved her. Even though some days I felt like tearing her head off.

Dad grabbed a breakfast bar from the pantry, fixed a mug of coffee and gave Catherine a kiss. He looked at us and said, "Alright, you kids ready?"

I nodded and shimmied into my backpack.

Maryann and I gave Catherine a hug then followed Dad out to the car.

I sat in the back as my sister rode shotgun. I kept thinking to myself on the way to school, that if I could just get proof somehow, then everyone would believe me. Then they'd know for sure that I wasn't dreaming or imagining it.

"Dad?"

He sipped his mug of coffee and looked up in the mirror at me.

"Yeah?"

"I heard the scratching and clawing sounds behind the walls again last night. Then I felt someone crawl into bed with me."

Dad cleared his throat.

"Really? You sure it wasn't uh . . . your brother?"

I nodded, "He was still in his bed asleep when I got up this morning. And I know it wasn't him because it felt like a big person."

"It was probably just a dream or something. Did you eat any junk food before you went to bed? Be honest."

"No. I didn't. I promise."

"Did you feel threatened at all? You know like something bad was in the room with you?"

I gave it some thought then wagged my head.

"Hmm," he said and turned to look at Maryann. She had her legs curled under her as she listened to something on her phone. He nudged her leg, then motioned for her to take the ear buds out.

"What?"

"Did you hear anything odd last night?"

She wagged her head, "No."

"I think we need to get some cameras," I blurted before I even realized it.

Dad craned his head and curled his bottom lip, "Yeah. What the heck. Maybe we can catch us a ghost," he said with a chuckle.

"I'm serious, Dad. Something got in the bed with me last night."

"Well, I could look into getting one of those live cams that connects with the WIFI and our phones. It'd alert us if it picks up anything."

"You seriously don't believe all of this do you?" asked Maryann.

Dad drew a deep breath, "Well, your brother wasn't the only one that heard the noises. I heard them too."

The car grew still.

"And this morning when I got up, it took me forever to find my watch. You both know how particular I am about Grandpa's watch. I always keep in the same box on my nightstand, but this morning I found it in my sock drawer."

Maryann squinted her eyes and tilted her head.

"What?" I asked.

"Yeah. Don't say anything to Catherine just yet. But I've wondered ever since we moved in if something might be going on. I know it's nothing bad because I never feel threatened or anything like I did when I lived in my grandparents' old place. You don't even want to know the kind of stuff that happened there. That was a true haunted house," he said craning his head and emitting a soft whistle, "But I do sometimes wonder if the place may be haunted too, just not in the same way. If that makes any sense."

My sister and I didn't say a word.

The car came to a stop.

"Alright, well you kids have a good day at school. We can talk about this later. I'll see you in a bit. Love you."

Maryann gulped and stared at Dad for a moment.

"Everything's fine. Nothing to worry about. We can talk about it later," Dad said as he patted her leg.

She leaned across and hugged him.

I opened the door and stepped out.

Childish chatter and laughter filled the air as school kids scattered about like disturbed ants.

I reached through the window and gave my dad a hug, then pulled back, "So you believe me?"

He grinned slightly and nodded, "Son, me and you have a gift. We can feel things that others can't. Grandpa was the same way. It's a good gift to have. I'll explain more when you're older. Now, go and learn all you can learn and keep an eye on your sister for me. You have my permission to use a stick to keep the boys away," he said with a wink as Maryann rounded the front of the car.

She scoffed as she passed by.

Dad patted me on the arm, "See you later, love you."

"Love you too."

I stepped back and watched as he drove away.

What is this gift talk all about?

DURING LUNCH I found myself sitting with a few buddies going over what happened last night. I'm sure none of them got much sleep that night after hearing my story.

"Why did you have to tell us that, Malcom? Like seriously. We didn't need to know about some dead person sneaking under the covers with you. That's just plain freaky, man."

"Well, I've got to tell somebody. Until this morning, nobody had ever really believed me. But I think my dad knows a little more than he's letting on. Said he'd get a live footage camera on the way home today."

"He must've seen or heard something."

"Yeah, he knows something," I said tapping my fork on the plate as I glared out the window.

DAD STOPPED AT WALMART on the way home. We got the only live footage camera they had. The cashier said they'd have more in stock in about a week. One camera would be enough for now. Dad said he'd place it in the kitchen, so it'd pick up the living room, dining room, and kitchen all with one shot.

"Maybe we can catch something tonight," Dad said as we left the parking lot and angled for the roadway. As he watched the traffic, his phone began to buzz.

"Hey honey . . . yeah we're coming . . . huh? No, why? . . . What? . . . Really? . . . Okay . . . Yeah . . . Alrght . . . Love you too."

"What is it?" Maryann asked.

"Catherine said we're out of tuna. I just grabbed like half a dozen cans the other day on the way home. Remember?"

"Yeah."

"You didn't eat any did you?"

Maryann wagged her head, "No."

Dad looked in the mirror at me.

"No. You know me. I only eat it in Catherine's sandwiches."

"Yeah, I know. Hmm. Anyway, I got to turn around and get some."

The rest of the day all I could think about was catching whatever or whoever it was that'd slept in my bed last night.

WE MADE IT HOME and enjoyed some of Catherine's famous Tuna melts. Then Maryann and I went to our rooms and spent some time with our homework.

It was just after seven-thirty when I made it back to the living room where Catherine, Dad, and my little brother Gregory sat watching an alien show on the History Channel.

"You all finished?" Catherine asked.

I nodded, then crashed on the sofa next to my brother. By instinct he leapt from where he was sitting and jumped into my lap, ready to wrestle.

"Not now. Hang on, I want to see this. Is this about the aliens and the pyramids or something?" I asked Dad.

"Yeah, I think so. Is your sister about done?"

"Should be."

"Monster Quest comes on after this."

"Oh really? Cool. I haven't seen that show in forever. Oh, did you get the camera set up?"

"Mm hmm. Yup, got it right here," he said retrieving his phone.

I scooted next to him and watched as my side profile appeared on his screen. I tossed up a hand and waved as the little me on the screen did the same. I turned, looking into the kitchen, trying to find it.

"Where is it?"

Dad pointed, "Look on top of the cabinet."

It took me a second. He had it sandwiched in between two boxes.

"Oh yeah."

"You know you two will have a heart attack if you really see something," Catherine said with a half chuckle as she flipped through a clothing magazine beside us, underneath a lamp.

It wasn't long before my sister wandered into the room and crashed next to Catherine.

We watched two episodes of Monster Quest. One about Bigfoot in the Smokey Mountains and the other about a Dog Man in Bolivia. Which isn't too far from us here in Wilmington.

Before we knew it, ten o'clock had come once again. I told everyone good night and glared at the camera in the kitchen as I passed.

Dad had to carry Gregory to my room as he'd conked out on the couch. I watched as he laid him down in his bed next to mine. He tucked him under his buzz lightyear covers and kissed the top of his head. Dad turned out the lamp beside his bed, then stood and crossed to me.

"If you hear anything come get me, okay? The camera's rolling, so maybe we'll get something. Good night, bud. Love you," he said as he messed up my hair and crossed for the door.

"Dad?"

He stopped in the doorframe with one hand on the knob.

"What's this stuff about the *gift*, you were talking about this morning?"

He took a deep breath and rubbed his eyes, "Some other time, okay? Get you some rest."

He began to pull the door shut, snuffing out the remaining light.

"You can leave the door open."

"Oh, okay. Yeah, sure. Good night, buddy, love you."

"Love you too."

And just like that, the night began.

THOUGH IT TOOK ME a bit to fall asleep, once I winked out, I was out. That is until I was awoken to the scratching and clawing sound coming from the walls and the faint sound of a whisper.

Mallll-commmm.

I stirred in my bed and tossed the covers back before forming an L. I blinked and rubbed my eyes, straining to see through the darkness. I reached over and twisted on my lamp to send a wave of light washing away the shadows.

I sat there motionless and listened.

Gregory was in his bed next to mine. He was out like a light and dreaming in some other world as he laid sprawled out in his Spiderman pajamas.

Bam! Creeeeaaaakkkkk!

My heart thumped at the sound of a fist knocking against my wall just behind my bed. It was soon followed by a long fingernail raking along like nails to a chalk board. Long and slow.

My breath quickened.

My pulse soared.

My blood turned cold.

Bam!

This one sent me leaping out of bed.

I stared at the wall just above my headboard where the thud came from.

Bam!

My flesh jumped as I found myself walking backwards in slow steps with my hands feeling for the wall behind me.

Creeeeeaaaaaakkkkkkk!

There was the fingernail again. Gosh, I hate that sound! I'd rather jab ice picks in my ears than to have to listen to that!

I clinched my teeth and covered my ears.

I started to run, but I couldn't leave Gregory by himself, could I? What kind of big brother would do such a thing?

I rushed over and strained to lift him in my arms. I raced with him down the hall towards Dad and Catherine's room. My feet pitter pattering across the hardwood.

I glanced over my shoulder. Peering through the darkness, I caught a glimpse of a dark silhouette streak from mine and Gregory's room to the guest room across the hall. Before I could jerk my head back around, I felt the wind get knocked out of me as I crashed into a wall of muscle. Dad.

I felt his hands on my shoulders as I stumbled backward with my brother. Dad caught me before I took a tumble.

"What is it? Did you see something?"

I was too shaken and winded to say a word. I just bobbed my head up and down.

"Where?"

I pointed behind me.

The hall light flicked on and numbed my eyes. I squinted and turned my head to the floor.

"What's going on?" Catherine's strained voice asked. Sounded like she had a mouth full of sand.

"Says he saw something. My phone alerted me too. Must've got something in the kitchen. Stay here with Catherine," Dad said as he marched to our bedroom.

Gregory squirmed and moaned in my arms.

"C'mon, lay him down in our bed," Catherine said as she led me by the arm.

We entered the room and Catherine flicked on a lamp. I sat him down then explained to her what I'd heard and saw.

She sighed, "Malcom. Are you sure you're not just dreaming? You know . . . like when you are half awake and half asleep, so the dream feels like it's really happening. Something like that maybe?"

"No-no, I know what I heard—"

My words were cut short by the sound of footsteps entering the room. Catherine and I turned, half expecting to see Dad, but it wasn't Dad.

It was my sister. She stood in the door frame, half asleep, and rubbed her eyes.

"Why are you messing with me?"

Everyone went quiet.

"What?" I finally asked.

"Why did you come and get in my bed?"

"What? I didn't get in your bed," I said with a scoff.

"Yes, you did too. I heard and felt you get under the covers. You even placed your arm over me."

My face drained of blood. I wagged my head and gulped.

"I promise you, I didn't."

"Then who did?"

Hey guys!

Dad's voice trailed from mine and Gregory's bedroom.

C'mere!

I looked at Catherine.

"You two go on. I'll stay here with him," she said looking to Gregory.

I rose from the side of the bed and met my sister in the doorway. Together we crept down the hall, clinging to each other's arms.

"You promise you're not trying to scare us?"

"Maryann, I promise you I'm not doing anything. I *promise.*"

I heard her take a deep breath.

We reached the doorframe to mine and Gregory's room. Dad stood in the center of the room, hands to his hips as he glared at the beds. I followed where his eyes were trained.

My bed was bare and missing all the covers.

Just the plain, flower-patterned mattress.

I jerked my head to Gregory's bed. Same as mine. Bare.

Dad spun around. His face twisted in an expression I'd never seen before.

"Did you do this?"

I wagged my head, "No."

Beep-beep! Beep-beep!

Dad fumbled in his pajama pocket, retrieving his phone. He thumbed over the screen then stopped. His eyes grew wide, and I watched him swallow long and hard.

"Judas priest! Something just crawled through the air vent!"

He bolted out of the room and thudded down the hall towards the living room.

"Go to Catherine, now! And don't come out!"

My sister and I dashed into the room, slammed the door behind us, and jumped into the bed next to her.

The sound of Dad's footfalls pounded through the house.

THE SIGHT OF A bony, ashy leg crawling through the air vent next to the couch, before pulling the cover back into place and vanishing had chilled George Schroder to the bone.

He grabbed a knife from the kitchen before streaking to the vent. A knife clinched in his right, phone grasped in his left with the flashlight app switched on, George Schroder took the vent cover off and shined the light through the long, narrow duct tunnel. A small object sat at the end of a T break.

With his palms greased and pulse soaring, George Schroder climbed into the vent and began a steady crawl down the darkened tunnel. His knuckles pressed against the cold metal as he pushed himself onward. Dust particles floated in his phone's light. The sound of metal bending and warping under his weight echoed through the air.

He squinted his eyes and shone his light at the object now just a few feet away. A black box. Grandpa's watch box!

George gulped and rubbed his brow with the back of his hand clinging to the knife.

He reached the T break and shone his light to the left and right, then angled the light to Grandpa's box. He sat the knife down and opened the box. Grandpa's gold watch sparkled back at him.

A fire engulfed George's gut, rising throughout his body, flushing his neck and cheeks. He clinched his teeth, slammed the box shut, and yanked up the knife. He shined his light at the two narrow pathways.

His breath huffed out through tight nostrils. His jaw was set firm. George darted his eyes back and forth, beaming the light to the left, then to the right and back again.

Movement stirred from the left followed by an eerie, childlike laughter too deep an octave to be a kid.

George's heart knocked as he yanked the light to the source of the sound. He caught a glimpse of that bony, ashy leg jutting around the corner at the end of the tunnel.

George steadied himself, stole a deep breath, then charged onward.

THE SOUND OF THAT LAUGHTER was the most unnerving thing I've ever heard. Chills me to the bone just to think about it. I mean jumping Jehoshaphat, I'm getting gooseflesh now as I write this.

I heard them scamper through the vents, the sound of knees and knuckles shuffling and bumping across the metal, drummed through the house.

Then everything went quiet.

"George?" Catherine called out.

Me and Maryann clung to her arms as we sat in bed. Gregory was asleep under the covers next to us.

"George?"

Nothing.

AFTER TRAILING DOWN the vent system, following the narrow tunnel of darkened and dusty duct work, George came to a dead end. Another large vent cover stood before him. The horizontal slits showed signs of a darkened room. George leaned close and peered through. He thought by the track he'd taken, he'd be near Malcom and Gregory's room, but the room wasn't familiar. He strained his eyes and rummaged through the barrage of thoughts flooding his mind.

He pulled away from the vent and lowered his head. He blinked and rubbed his chin, then returned to the vent and pressed his phone's light to the vent slits. Remnants of light filtered in. Nothing he recognized. Just an old, empty, dusty room.

He took a breath and positioned himself feet first to the vent before kicking it. Within three kicks, the vent gave way with a loud clank as it crashed to the floor. George shone his light then proceeded to crawl out and stand to his feet.

Knife gripped in a greasy palm, he raised his other hand and shined the light. His heart knocked at the sight before him. A small wooden table and two chairs sat in the right corner of the room. A white mannequin, dressed in jeans and a white shirt with a feathered and colorful scarf around its neck, sat at one end of the table. It glared at George with soulless eyes. Little green army men laid scattered across the table next to a few vintage action figures. Batman, Superman, and others.

A white plastic fork and a can of tuna rested in front of the mannequin with the lid peeled back, half eaten.

George cursed and stared for the longest time as if he expected the Styrofoam human to stand and confront him. It never did.

George gulped and scanned his light to the left. An empty wall with exposed two by fours and electrical wiring filled his vision. He continued scanning the room. He stopped when he landed on a pile of white covers lying on the dusty floor.

His feet glued in place as if he'd just stepped into a rat trap. The sight of buzz lightyear patterned sheets stole his breath. Just to the mountain of Gregory and Malcom's covers was a horrid attempt of a mattress consisting of blankets and towels. One blanket stood out among the rest. One with horses. The one Catherine lost a few months ago. The one her grandmother had given her before she passed.

George felt his heartbeat thump along his neck.

He was looking at a bedding, complete with covers and pillows made of bunched up towels. Something else Catherine had been complaining of missing lately.

With his heart pounding and sinking lower and lower toward his gut, and his palms drenched with sweat, George continued to scan the room.

His eyes landed on another vent at the bottom of the wall. Small rays of light trickled in through crossway slits. He raced over, dropped to a knee, pressed his cheek against the metal and peered in. His heart dropped at the sight. It was Malcom and Gregory's room.

At that instant a bony hand dug into the pressure point along his shoulder and clavicle to send him cringing and curling to the floor.

"Ahh!"

The hand released, then shoved him against the wall.

George flashed opened his eyes.

He almost wished he hadn't.

The sight of a dirty, malnourished, bearded man with shaggy hair filled his vision.

The man bounced back, bounding up and down on light feet with a twisted smile, giggling like a child.

Dear God!

The man's skin was ashy pale. His eyes were sunken deep in his skull with big black bags dangling below his sockets. His arms were bony but packed with surprising muscle. The fingernails were overgrown and dirty.

The man craned his head at George like a dog. His eyes had a wild, feral look to them. His mouth was wide with a tight grin. He snickered deep within and glared at George.

"Hey. Hey, calm down, okay? We can talk this out. I don't want to hurt you, but I will if I have to." George said with outstretched arms.

The knife and phone rested on the ground at his feet from having been knocked free from the ambush.

The man didn't say a word, but only stared.

George glanced down to check the placement of the knife.

The man grunted.

George jerked his eyes back to him.

"Ssshhh . . . take it easy now. Tell me who you are. Can you talk? Speak?" George said as he patted his lips with his fingers.

The man wagged his head, opened his mouth and gave a "ahh" sound as if being checked by a doctor and pointed to a missing tongue, then smiled big and hard.

George revolted and cursed.

The man grunted at George's words. His smile vanished. His face twisted in an instant to that of rage. He snarled and set his jaw. His cheeks quivered.

"Hang on, we can work this out," George said with his hands extended while he glared once again to the knife lying by his feet.

The man let out a hellish scream and charged like a mad grizzly.

George dropped and grasped for the knife.

The raging man reached him before his hand found the blade. He crashed into him and knocked the breath from his lungs. George wheezed and gasped as he found himself encased in the man's grip. Sharp fingernails dug into his ribs, before balled fist pummeled his side. George grunted with each blow as he searched for breath.

The wild man growled like a rabid dog and foamed at the mouth. His teeth clattered, and saliva slung this way and that.

George sucked in a room full of air as if he'd just surfaced from a deep ocean. A burst of energy sped through his body. He pressed his feet against a two by four and thrust himself into the man's chest, sending them tumbling across the floor.

George got to his feet and braced himself for another rush by the crazed man.

The man staggered to his feet and hunched at the spine. His eyes were wild with a taste for blood. He charged once more, screaming with jumbled syllables.

George side stepped and shoved the man aside, sending him crashing face first into a two by four stud. He collapsed backwards, crumbling to the ground as good as dead.

AND SO THAT WAS THE NIGHT my family finally believed me. All the scratching, clawing, whispers, and bumps in the night were more than just my imagination.

Darryl Childers was arrested that night by the New Hannover County police department. After numerous psychiatric exams and questioning, it was determined that his mental state was parallel to that of a six-year-old child. They shipped him off to a long-term mental health care facility near the Outer Banks. They say he goes days without sleep, pacing the floors, whispering, and humming before having to be doped and forced to bed.

It was determined by substantial evidence that he'd been living in that house for well over thirty years. He'd lived with seven different families counting my own. His single parent mother had left him there all alone as a child during the seventies, dying on the streets from an overdose. The days and weeks leading up to that were the last anyone had seen him. There were numerous reports of having seen him on the street that night with his mother, which led detectives to believe he was taken or must've wandered off during his mother's overdose. They searched the home, but of course they didn't look behind the walls.

As for the gift my dad spoke of? Well, he never got to tell me. He was murdered less than a year after that night by two thugs who decided to rob the convenient store my dad had stopped by one evening on the way home from work. Luckily my sister and I weren't with him when it happened. He'd told Catherine to pick us up at school, because the boss said he may have to work overtime. I think part of the gift that my dad talked about was a sort of *knowing*, if you will.

I hardly slept the night before his death. A wave of dread had washed over me, cloaking me in an inky black blanket. I didn't know what was going to happen, but I knew something wasn't right. I felt it. Now I know. The gift.

But another part of the gift I believe is being able to feel good and evil energy. I can enter a room or pass by someone on the street and immediately be overtaken with a sense of darkness. Like the oxygen had turned to a thick black smoke. Then there's other times when the opposite is true. I enter a room or meet someone and it's like the atmosphere is buzzing with a radiant light unseen to the natural eye.

I think the reason Dad was confused about the whole deal with Darryl Childers living in our walls was because he never felt threatened by a negative energy like he had growing up in the haunted house where he lived with his grandma and grandpa by the cemetery. Catherine has told me and Maryann things through the years that I truly wish I never heard.

Like the night my dad was woken to the feeling of being watched only to find someone standing in the corner of his room who then walked to the base of his bed, grabbed his foot, twisted, and squeezed until the big toe snapped like a twig. He called him the shadow man. After speaking to his grandma and grandpa about the man he saw, he learned that it was the spirit of Gerald Larue, the man who owned and died in the home a half century prior.

I think my dad didn't really believe our home was haunted because he couldn't feel anything. That's why he asked me that day in the car if I felt threatened. He probably never imagined the noises were coming from a living being.

So, it was true after all. Our home was sort of haunted. Not by the dead of course . . . but by the living.

A Native Tale

1589

Deep in the Mountains of North Carolina

A gentle breeze rustled the browning leaves in the tall oaks. Wispy clouds streaked past the full moon hanging high in the Eastern sky. A pack of coyotes cackled in the distance as they chased their evening meal. A lone cricket did his magic under the crevice of a nearby rock, sending his song into the wind. The rich aroma of piped tobacco lingered lazily through the air. The crackle of the flame and its wave of heat was a welcome sensation as I remember cuddling closer to my mother's side. I looked at the tribal elders seated with us around the fire. They were each dressed in full Native Regalia. Tanned leather long sleeved jackets with matching trousers, decorated with more feathers, beads, colorful ribbons, and jewels than I could possibly count at such a young age. Each wore different headdresses made from coyote, bobcat, or bear hide. Some were made of Eagle feathers. I remember not particularly liking it much when the headdresses went on. It can be scary for a seven-year-old to be seated around a fire at night with a bunch of strange-looking creatures. But my parents had taught me the traditions, and I'd learned enough from the elders over time that I was slowly growing accustomed to it. Our tribe had taken a big hit from the previous year's sickness and war. We went from being about two hundred strong down to just over fifty counting the elders and my family. Just a third of that number consisted of strong warriors. To say we were in desperate times would be a vast understatement. Then when the wood devil appeared, our elders said we were cursed by an omen who'd come to finish us off. I didn't fully understand the danger we were in until I saw it take my brother. That's when I came to the realization that I may not live to see my eighth birthday.

I remember the words of our chief elder from that night by the fire, "Tsul 'Kalu . . . the slant eyed giant of Tsunegun'yi has visited us. He has been sent by the devil to ravage all that we hold dear . . . our children, our crops, our land . . . but he will not succeed in taking our spirits!"

As our tribe gathered around the fire, we nodded and cheered as our chief elder sat before us, speaking in soft but authoritative tones. He wore a golden eagle headdress which is given only to those of highest honor. He had black, white, and red paint smeared across his copper and chiseled face with a jaw line sharper than most arrowheads.

He raised a finger to the moon, "Our Great Creator is watching. He will not let us come to ruin. No matter how hard this gets, we are never out matched for the battle," he said before lowering his hand and picking up a bundle of sage wrapped tightly with a cord of tall grass. He leaned forward and stuck the sage bundle into the flame. It lit to send smoke and a savory aroma to the heavens.

Our elder chief, White Crow, raised his vision to the Great Creator and shut his eyes. His lips entered a chant in our Native tongue as he asked for wisdom and protection.

He-agh, He-aghhhh, ya, yeh, oh waaaa.

A soft drumbeat began, followed by the jingle of a handheld bone rattle, along with a melodic tune of a wooden flute. Our chief elder continued his chant, keeping cadence with the instruments as the drum kept rhythm with my beating heart.

He-agh, He-aghhhh, ya, yeh, oh waaaa.

His chant was accompanied by the high pitch wail of an elder lady. Sings with the Sun was her name.

Then the other three elders dressed in their regalia, rose to their feet, and began to march around us, dancing as the chant and music continued.

He-agh, He-aghhhh, ya, yeh, oh waaaa.

The dancers tilted their shoulders to the earth as they each clinched large golden eagle feathers. They made wide swooping arc motions, going from the earth up to the heavens as they bounced rhythmically on their feet, keeping in step with the beat of the drum.

The flame crackled, sending bright embers dancing skyward. The pack of coyotes in the distance rose in pitch to meet that of Sings with the Sun. The wind picked up its pace, tickling the limbs and leaves surrounding our village. As loud as everything was, it all went silent the moment that ear-piercing, bone-chilling, half shriek, half roar ripped through the night. I remember the look on everyone's faces as their eyes grew wide and their faces twisted in utter terror. I buried myself deeper into my mother's side, clinching with all my might to her warm bosom.

My eyes found our chief elder. He was unfazed, unmoving, and strong as an ancient mountain. A slow grin stretched his lips, "Do not fear. The Great Creator has heard our pleas. This evil will be vanquished for the time being, but when I am passed to the other world, it will be up to *you*," he said extending a finger and scanning it about us, "to see that this beast be not allowed to enter our village again. *You* must keep to the traditions and remember what you have seen tonight, burn it in your heart. Never forget."

But it wasn't long after our elder chief passed, we did forget, and that god-awful creature . . . returned.

1602

IT WAS THIRTEEN YEARS LATER, in the time of my twentieth year on earth and six years after our elder chief's death, when I saw the creature for the first time since I watched it take my little brother.

Our village was once again ravaged with death, sickness, and war. Causing many of the faithful to fall from our traditions and beliefs. We'd ceased having our weekly gatherings as many had lost respect for our ancestors, not holding their values dear as in times past. It wasn't long afterwards that the Slant Eyed Giant appeared.

It started late one night while the village was resting and wandering in dream worlds. I was awakened to the piercing wail of a devasted mother. A cry so strong, that the whole earth was forced to stop and listen.

I jolted from my bedding. By the time I stood to my feet, the cry was silent. I stood listening, daring not to move or make a sound. Commotion came to life outside my tipi, the sound of trampling feet and quick chatter filled my ears, followed by another long, heart wrenching wail of a mother in distress.

My heart knocked against my chest to send blood racing through my veins like a million shooting stars streaking across the galaxy. I dropped to a crouch and snatched up my tomahawk and spear next to my bed. I grabbed my moccasins and made my way out of the tent. I planted my feet to the ground and sent my eyes darting about the village in search of the lurking danger.

People raced toward the mother's cry emitting from the edge of the woods. I rushed to join a group of men, Walks by Night, Watches from the Wind, and Strikes without Sound, as they ran with long, galloping strides to the action. Tomahawks, bows, clubs, and knives clinched tight in their strong calloused hands. One of them carried a small torch.

At that point, due to my youth, I'd yet to gain their respect. But that night and the coming days would change everything. Because it was that night that I became a man, a trusted warrior, and a faithful member of the village. I must say though, I didn't think I would live to see another day, not after seeing what I did.

AS I CAUGHT up to the men, I noticed their searing glares in mid-run, but I paid them no mind. Our village had been attacked and all that mattered was that we were fighting the same enemy. Whatever that enemy was.

We tore through a crowd of bystanders which consisted of women, children, and the elderly. They stood watching with their faces twisted in fear of what lurked beyond the shadows of the night. A few men of fighting age were mingled about them. They joined us as we plowed forward toward the wood line where the mother's cry was still in mid chorus. We pounded ahead, tearing into the thick patch of woods, consisting of oaks, hemlock, tulip poplar, and maple, among a few bushes and briar patches scattered here and there.

The mother's frantic cry ripped through the air once again, stinging our hearts and minds. Leaving the imagination to wonder what was lurking within the dark woods. The thought crossed my mind, but I was quick to take it captive before it took root to prosper . . . the Slant Eyed Giant.

No! God no! Not again!

Our elder chief said it'd return if we forgot that night, and I was among only a few who still remembered.

Oh God, help us!

The screechy wail grew louder as we zig zagged our way closer to its source. We entered the clearing. A long but narrow path used for hunting came into view. We stopped to listen. Our breaths huffed out and steamed into the night air. Strikes without Sound aimed the torch down one lane of the long path, sending the light licking away the shadows. Nothing but empty blackness and dead leaves returned our glares.

We all jumped at the loud blast from the mother's lungs. She couldn't have been any farther than a stone's toss away.

A soft rustle of leaves stirred from the opposite direction of the path. We each yanked our attention to the source. Strikes without Sound spun and pushed the flame onward. The silhouette of a lady filled our vision. She was sitting on her haunches as her tan hide dress sprawled across the ground. Her head full of black braided hair dangled to her knees. She cried behind her hands.

We regained our spirits and in quick unison, crossed to her, offering soothing words as to not send her running mad, deeper into the forest.

As we neared, I noticed a shredded cloth resting in her lap. It was covered in blood. She rocked to and fro, sobbing from deep, inner heart ache. Sounds no human should ever be forced to make, spewed from her torn soul.

"He took him. He took my baby," she managed to mumble with a broken and shaken voice.

Strikes without Sound lowered himself to a crouch and gently touched the mother's arm. She flinched and shot her head upward, locking eyes with him as she scooted across the earth, kicking her feet and grasping at the dirt with her hands. She had a wild look in her eye.

As Strikes without Sound tried to soothe her, my heart fell to the pit of my gut as every hair on my body stiffened at the sound of that high-pitched scream ripping through the air from a deep gravelly throat created by the devil himself. It seemed to come from behind us yet circled us like a howling wind. It was everywhere, yet nowhere at once. A dark heavy presence filled the air, pulling my heart and soul to the grave, weighing it down with fear unlike any I'd ever known. Flashes of that monster sized, hair covered arm reaching out to wrap around my brother, stealing him away into the night, filled my mind's eye.

Whether I said it aloud or only in my soul, I can't say, but the words formed without my consent, *Tsul 'Kalu…the Slant-Eyed Giant.*

The sound of a thousand trees crashing to earth at once boomed through the air, rattling my innards, shaking my very soul to its core. My heart was flooded with a wave of terror. Heavy feet pounded against the earth floor and rushed towards us.

The men I was with found themselves stumbling backwards with eyes frozen to the patch of forest ahead. A loud roar, deeper, yet higher pitched than anything I've ever heard exploded in a blast of air that trailed on for all eternity.

I clinched my jaw, planted my feet firm into the ground, steadied my grip on the tomahawk, and pushed away the fear ravaging my body like a quick spreading disease. I lowered my gaze and prepared my heart to meet the devil.

I screamed to the limit of my lung's capacity with every muscle stretched taut as the beast tore closer. My war cry was single at first but was quickly joined by the hearts of the others as we braced ourselves to meet a quickly approaching death. One of two things would happen: either we'd all die in the next few seconds or the beast would be sent back to hell. But one thing was for certain, there could only be one victor in this fight.

Then the thought hit me like an arrow, the words of elder chief pouring into my mind, "Never forget the power of the Creator within you. You can't fight darkness in the dark. You must open the window and allow the light to flood in to push away the darkness. Speak light and the darkness will hide."

Elder chief's chant from that night long ago pounded at my ear drums. Along with the booming foot falls and crashing trees of my approaching death.

He-agh, He-aghhhh, ya, yeh, oh waaaa!!

I belted to the top of my lungs. My whole body filled with a fire originating from the deep parts of my inward man. Heat instantly dispersed throughout every member of my body.

He-agh, He-aghhhh, ya, yeh, oh waaaa!

Louder I screamed.

Out of nowhere the deafening crackle of lightning pierced the air. It streaked across the night sky and spread out like fingers above the canopy of trees and limbs.

We flinched at the sudden roar of mother nature as the Creator responded to the chant and prayers sent forth from members of His creation.

The white flash of lightning vanished, disappearing among countless sparkles of light from a million stars.

An eerie silence confronted us.

I stood next to the pack of men as the mother rested on her haunches behind me. The silence didn't last, as the sound of crunching leaves and twigs slowly edged toward us.

I gulped and stole a deep breath, setting my jaw and clinching my grip around the tomahawk.

Thud! Thud!

We were all gasping for air at this point as our breaths ghosted out and combined into one cloud-like apparition hovering in the cold air.

Thud!

Strikes without Sound shifted the torch in the direction of the commotion. My heart got a start at the sight just on the other end of the light. It stepped out of the mixed grove of trees. A brown, hair covered leg as big as most pine trees stepped into view, before being joined by another of equal size. Long, muscle chiseled arms covered in the same thick wavy brown hair dangled past the knees of this monstrous beast. Another flash of my brother's taking struck my mind like the recent lightning. I've seen those arms before. The same creature that stole my brother now stood before me, not saying a word.

I raised my vision to meet its face. An icy chill shot down my spine at the striking similarities it had to that of a human face. This monster was almost identical to you and me, except for its size and hair.

For the longest time, we all just stood there in awe of this creature. Our eyes were locked in wonder at its majestic size and daunting presence. I watched as its deep sunken black eyes on either side of its wide flat nose, seared into my soul at a razor-sharp angle. Its lips parted in a slow, hair-raising fashion. Big square, yellow teeth like yours and mine, filled the cavity of its orifice. It raised one end of its lip into a snarl and let out a low rumble and growl that rattled the cage of my heart.

This was the Tsul 'Kalu from Tsunegun'yi. The Slant-Eyed-Giant and here it stood glaring at me with slanted eyes.

My trembling fear was met with a crash of unwavering courage as heat once again flowed through my body, building in my gut, then traveling and flowing out of my mouth to begin our elder chief's trademark chant.

He-agh, He-aghhhh, ya, yeh, oh waaaa!!

I began soft and slow before gaining traction and volume.

The beast jerked its head, craned, and watched me with curious, prodding eyes.

Again, I chanted, *He-agh, He-aghhhh, ya, yeh, oh waaaa!!*

Only this time I was joined by the others.

The creature's breath quickened as it grew timid, weary of our words and authority.

Unfazed, we continued chanting. We picked up speed as our voices joined in harmony to reverberate off the trees, echoing through the dense forest.

The creature drew a deep breath and huffed it out, then turned and in one fell swoop, disappeared into the woods.

We heard the thudding of its huge feet as it ebbed away deeper into the forest before it was eventually too distant to hear.

I turned in a slow sweep to my right to see two of the men staring into the forest with blank faces. I turned to my left and saw Strikes without Sound staring at me with a face that'd been drained of blood but was slowly regaining its color. He swallowed hard, then gave me a small dip of his head. The first that any of the three warriors had ever done such a thing. Gaining these men's respect meant everything in the hierarchy of our tribe. If they'd welcome me into their war party and if I could survive long enough to establish myself as a proven warrior, then I'd have the chance to one day become elder chief.

My thoughts were pushed aside at the piercing cry of a baby.

Us men stirred as the disturbed mother bolted to her feet and rushed for the sound, vanishing into the woods not far from where the creature had just entered.

We immediately stole after her. Once again tearing through the thick trees and bushes, pushing past the briars and limbs slapping against our faces.

We stopped when we reached the mother with her back toward us. She was hunched at the spine. Our breaths gasped in unison as it rose like smoke to the Eastern sky.

Strikes without Sound stretched forth the torch to encompass the distressed mother. She turned in a slow sweep with her arms clinched tight to her breast, clutching her baby. Other than two superficial cuts that were angled across his cheek and forehead, the child was unharmed. His clothes were torn as if caught in a briar, hence the reason for the bloody patch of cloth the mother had clung to earlier.

Thanks to the Great Creator, the child had not become another victim of the Slant-Eyed-Giant.

Fifty years later

AS I MENTIONED that night changed everything for me. As the prized warriors got a firsthand glimpse of my courage and wisdom, they openly welcomed me into their war party. In which I would go on to fight in many battles against the evil possessed tribes of the North. I collected a vast array of feathers in my day, all a direct showcase of my fearlessness and success in battle.

I killed many men during that time, which earned me the name *Strikes Like Lightning*. My name also serves as a reminder to myself and those around me of that night when Tsul 'Kalu was brought into submission. The Great Creator has been good to us as our village has been blessed with fruitful crops, good rains, and an influx of strong, healthy children to rise up and continue our ancestors' traditions.

From that night on, we returned to our values, holding our weekly gatherings, offering dances, praises, and prayer to the Great Creator. In return for our faithfulness, the Tsul 'Kalu has been forced to stay at bay. Not to say we haven't heard him or found footprints. Some have even claimed to have seen him a time or two along the ridges of the mountain, but he has yet to return to our village. He has learned to respect us, just as we have him.

Other tribes, not so much. He tends to have his way with those who've forsaken the elder's traditions.

That's why every week since my succession as elder chief, I hold a gathering just as our former chief did when I was only a child. We bring out the drums, flutes, and bone rattles as we sit around the fire before entering song and dance, asking the Great Creator for protection from the Tsul 'Kalu. As long as we keep this practice and continue to honor the Great Creator with our hearts, we need not fear the Slant Eyed-Giant.

His presence still lingers, but it's only like a shadow in a dim room. As long as we keep the light on, we cannot be threatened.

Timmy

Supply, North Carolina
Friday
October 24th, 1988

The seasons have changed as the leaves have turned and sea sawed down to blanket the earth. The air has lost its humidity. The wind has added its icy touch that turns cheeks red and causes noses to drain with snot. Hurricanes have decided the Coast has taken enough beatings for the year and chosen to remain at sea, plotting its evil schemes for next year. Peanut Butter Spiders have emerged from hiding, spinning webs here and there. Most cornfields have been harvested, and pumpkins are sold at every corner. All the stores in town have stocked their shelves with Halloween decorations and costumes. Kids of all ages eagerly await the coveted holiday which is sure to deliver its fair share of cavities over the coming months.

For the kids of Mount Pisgah Road, that means the annual fall get togethers are in full swing. A tradition that began when the grownups were children. The adults build a fire so the kids can roast weenies and marshmallows while the parents pass around coffee thermoses and flasks. The kids stoke the fire or play hide-n-go-seek once their bellies are filled. Then, before the night is over, one of the adults will begin telling campfire stories. Everything from the man with the golden arm, to sleepy hollow, the bride with the ribbon around her neck, bigfoot stories, ghost stories, and the like.

And of course, before October comes to an end, there's always a snipe hunt to play on the newbie. With this being the last Friday night before Halloween, the group decided the snipe hunt would be tonight. The newbie to be pranked happens to be Aaron Parker. The ten-year old who'd moved from Ohio with his recently divorced mother.

With the stars and crescent moon hiding behind wispy gray clouds, a chill mist begins to fall and sends with it a sinking fog. Crickets sing into the night as coyotes cackle in the distance. If you listen closely, you'll hear two owls arguing back and forth. They sound like chattering monkeys. The fire hisses and cracks as a log settles deeper into the flames. Orange embers rush heavenward.

"C'mon man. It's not that bad. It'll be fun, you'll see." Scottie Holland says to Aaron Parker.

Aaron and his mother had moved to Mount Pisgah Road at the first of the year. Aaron and Scottie were in the same grade at Robinson Middle School. Aaron could recall more than once when Scottie had stuck up for him at school and warded off the class bullies. Having seen his mother recently divorce his narcissistic father, Aaron appreciated Scottie ending the bully's harassment. On numerous nights, Aaron had cried himself to sleep while asking why his dad couldn't be more like Scottie's dad. He often wondered what it'd be like to have a father. A real father. A good father.

Sitting upon a log by the fire and unconsciously stabbing at the hot coals with a flimsy stick that'd make a good switch, Aaron takes a deep breath and allows the decision to sway back and forth between his ears. About seven or eight adults and half that many children encircle the flame and await the newbie's response. Feeling their glares, Aaron raises his vision and looks sideways to Scottie, "Alright. Sure. What the heck is a snipe anyway? I never heard of one when I was in Ohio."

That sent a chuckle passing through the group.

"Yeah, I reckon it must be a southern type of thing." One of the dads says as he elbows Bill Holland sitting next to him.

Bill Holland, Scottie's dad, smirks and says, "I guess so, huh?"

Scottie's mom, Brenda, says with squinted brows as she's wrapped tight in a blanket, "Oh for goodness's sake, will you behave yourself? He's just a boy, Bill. Keep a lid on things out there will ya?"

"Oh, don't worry. We'll be fine. Every boy has to go snipe huntin' at least once in his life. It'll be fun. Now c'mon, let's get out there before the big one shows up."

"The big one?" asks Aaron.

"Yeah, the big one." Bill says as he demonstrates with his arms. "It's kind of a legend around here. You'll know if you see him. He's real big and, and . . . ugly. Goodness gracious is he ugly." Bill says with a grin towards Greg Alison who sits across from him.

All the kids giggle and nudge one another. Greg is a beer bellied, ball headed, hot dog eating lump of flesh that doesn't have to wear a mask in order to play a snipe. It's rumored among the kids that the man is so hairy he doesn't even use a blanket at night. They say he could survive in the arctic with no clothes. Greg takes a sip from his cup, belches, and says, "I hear ya. Well, I reckon

I'm goin' turn in for the night. You're staying with Scottie tonight, right Joey?"

His eleven-year-old, red haired, freckled face son says, "Yeah."

"Alright then, you bunch of goons have fun out there and let me know if you find a good one. But be careful, some of them can be a little feisty. You better get going. They get meaner as the night wears on."

"Yeah, he's right kids. We best get moving," says Bill. He stands from a log and in unison, Jason Williams, Phil Baylor, and Lance Dudley along with their kids each do the same. Scottie Holland, Aaron Parker, Joey Alison, Frankie Williams, Bobby Baylor (who the kids call BB), and Josh Dudley, angle close to the adult's sides.

The moms hang by the fire, bundled in blankets, sipping spiked coffee, and gossiping about the local buzz. Meanwhile, big and hairy Greg Alison slips off into the woods.

Bill and the men cross towards the wood line. "Alright boys, each of ya find you something to whack these things with. Some rocks if you got a good arm, a good-sized log that you can swing pretty good . . . you know, something like that."

The boys take a few minutes to gather their weapons. The whole time, Aaron stays tight to Scottie's side.

With the fire blazing and crackling behind them, a chilly breeze brings in more fog. It snakes in and out of the trees like ghosts marching to the beat of their own tune.

Clutching a club with cold, trembling hands, Aaron says, "What if there's a Sasquatch in these woods?"

That sends another chuckle among the group. Even the moms back at the fire must've heard because Aaron could hear them cackle too. Aaron felt as if he'd shrunk four inches. It suddenly felt like everyone was looking down on him while they laughed at his words. He knew the feeling well. Aaron was small for his age to begin with, so these shrinking feelings were never a pleasant experience.

"Hey, c'mon now. He's right. What if there is a Squatch out there? You know, like the one Greg was telling us about?" says Scottie.

"Son, Greg didn't see no Squatch. I think he just happened to see himself in the mirror one morning and the image left a burnt spot on his mind."

Another round of belly laughter.

Phil Baylor cranes at the waist and slaps his knee.

Lance Dudley says "Hey, that's a good one Bill," while he wipes tears from his eyes.

Bill finishes his chuckles and then walks over to Aaron Parker. He squats down to come eye to eye with him.

"Listen son . . ." Aaron always liked it when he said it like that. "That feeling you got swirling around in there," Bill poked at Aaron's gut, "That's called fear. Now you can either give in to it and let it control you, give you the shakes and tremors, send a million worries flying around your head . . . or you can stand up to it and say, 'Hey, listen here you old good for nothin' big headed baby huey looking thing, I don't have time for all your nagging. You back up, shut up, and get going.' Sometimes you got to stand strong and fight that ole feeling of fear. You got to rule over it. Don't let it control ya, you hear?"

Aaron heard. Loud and clear. He nodded.

Bill smiles, stands to his feet, and pats Aaron on the shoulder. "Good. Now c'mon. Let's go get us a snipe, huh?"

With that, the group sets off into the woods.

"Be careful." Comes a voice from one of the moms by the fire.

The men and boys fall in line behind Bill Holland. Bill has the only flashlight. They begin stepping over sticks, logs, and branches. Aaron, Scottie, BB, and Phil Baylor bring up the rear.

Crickets whirr amidst a howling wind as distant chatter lingers from the moms.

As Aaron takes a step, he looks up past the black, finger-like tree branches towards the sky and sees a glimmer of moonlight peeking out from a cloud. A coyote howls in a distant land. Aaron can smell smoke coming from his clothes. Aaron lowers his head and repeats the words Scottie's dad had told him before they entered the woods.

More stepping over logs and breaking branches.

Bill stops and the train behind him puts on its brakes.

He turns around to face them. He holds the flashlight to his face and raises a finger to his lips. The boys begin whispering to one another. Josh and Frankie giggle. Bill taps his finger in the air towards the right of them. A twig snaps in that direction. Aaron watches as everyone tightens the grip on their logs and rocks. *This must be it. This is snipe hunting, and I'm really doing it.* Aaron thinks to himself.

He watches as Scottie's dad takes small, quiet steps towards the source of the rustling in the leaves. The rest of them follow.

They come to an open patch of woods where the moonlight is finally able to break through the clouds and trees. It's now that Aaron notices two distinct trails forking off to the far right of them.

It's down one of these trails that something catches his eye. He thought he may be seeing things, so he blinked hard and tried again. No, it's still there. He can hear the others continuing to make their way toward the snapping twigs, but Aaron is captivated by what he sees. He looks back at the group and counts the other boys. They are all there. Then who is that?

Almost as if hearing his question, Scottie stops and turns around. "What are you doing? We're about to get us a snipe?"

Aaron doesn't answer but only points a finger down one of the forked trails.

"What? What is it?"

"Who is that Scottie?"

"Huh?"

"Look."

Scottie cranes his head a little and squints at the moon lit path. "What in the world? Looks like a little kid lying on the ground or something. C'mon, let's go check it out."

"Huh uh. Are you crazy?"

They could hear the others going on without them. They thought they heard one of the men call out for them, but they weren't sure. The sight of this kid lying face down on the trail held their attention.

Scottie sighed and looked back to Aaron, "Oh c'mon, remember what my dad told you earlier. You got to stand up to that fear. What if this kid needs our help?"

Aaron bites his lip then drops and shakes his head. "Okay. Alright. Let's go."

Together they take timid steps toward the kid on the path. Which, by now, has begun to hide in a shadow as the moon is covered again by a cloud. The silhouette grows closer as they take three more steps.

"Who could this be?" asks Aaron.

"I don't know, but we—" Scottie's answer is cut short by the sound of loud growling, followed by laughter and giggles in the distance.

Aaron stops and braces at the knees. "What the heck was that?"

Scottie smirks, "I think they found their snipe."

Aaron swallows hard and turns his eyes back to the kid lying on the path.

"Hey? Are you okay? Can you hear us?" Scottie says.

No answer.

They begin to hear their names being called out behind them.

"Hey, come over here. We need you." Scottie calls back to who sounded like his dad.

The two continue to step closer, now only a few yards away. The complete outcropping of a child's body is becoming visible and so are the details. The body is stiff. Unmoving. Not breathing. Dead.

Aaron looks hard. The arms and hands are barely touching the ground as they're straight out by the legs.

"Wait a second . . . what in the world? Oh man. Look at that. It's no kid. It's a stinking doll. My goodness," says Scottie.

Aaron looks hard again at the plank like arms and hands. He feels a knot of tension and fear loosen in his gut. His throat expands to allow his breath to flow again. His heart takes slow, but deep and painful beats.

"Whew. Yeah, I think you're right." Aaron says as the two come close enough to stand over it. Scottie nudges it with his shoe. It rolls with his prodding then returns to its place. It's dressed in what looks like blue jeans and some type of blue raincoat maybe.

Loud footsteps can be heard crunching over leaves and branches behind them. Their names are called out into the night.

Aaron crouches into a squat and reaches out to roll the doll over onto its back.

"Oh gosh. What in the world?" says Scottie. Aaron pays him no mind as he's struck by the big, googly eyes with true boyish like features. It has brown, messy hair like his own and wears a tight grin that stretches from ear to ear. His color is pale pink like pigskin. The blue rain jacket is left unbuttoned to the middle of his chest to reveal a white tee shirt underneath. On the left breast, written in blue letters on a white patch, is the name . . . *Timmy.*

DESPITE EVERYONE SPEAKING of the ugliness and creepiness of the thing, Aaron couldn't be happier to bring Timmy home to Mama.

Aaron was supposed to spend the night with Scottie and the boys but insisted on going home instead. So, not without prodding him to stay, Bill and the boys loaded Aaron and Timmy in the pick-up truck and took them home.

"Alright now, you sure you don't want to stay the night?" Bill asks as he turns into Aaron's driveway. The tires crunch over gravel along the way.

"Yes sir, I'm sure. Thank you for the ride," Aaron says while looking to Timmy sitting on his lap. Aaron opens the door and hops out. Scottie slides over from the middle seat and onto the passenger side. Josh and Joey sit in the back seats.

"Where do you think he may have come from?" asks Scottie as he crosses his forearms along the window seal.

Aaron shrugs his shoulders.

"You don't think it's sort of creepy and all?"

Aaron tightens his lips and shakes his head saying, "I don't know. I mean, it's just a doll, right?"

"Yeah, you're right. It's just a doll."

Aaron tells them bye and makes his way up the porch steps. He wonders what time it is and if his mama is still up. He guesses it'll depend on if Johnny Carson is on or not. His mother never goes to bed without watching him. Either way, he's careful with the door so as not to wake her in case she's asleep.

He makes his way through the foyer and kitchen and can hear the tv talking in his mother's room. Sounds like Carson is on, so she should still be—

"Honey, is that you?" her voice comes soft and mellow.

"Yeah, it's me," he says carrying Timmy on his hip like a toddler as he goes down the hall to her room.

"What happened? I thought you were going to stay with Scottie and the boys?"

"Yeah . . ." he says coming to her door frame. "But I found this."

His mother gasps and jolts up in bed.

"Dear God. What in the world? Geeze Aaron, I thought you were carrying a kid." She adjusts and scoots up against the headboard. The glow of the television flashes across her covers as Johnny Carson and his audience erupt into laughter. Looks like he has one of those singers or actors on again. A strong floral aroma of Jergen's lotion hangs in the air.

"My goodness. Where on earth did you find that ugly thing?"

Aaron giggles and says, "In the woods while we were snipe hunting."

"Snipe hunting? Oh goodness. Well bring him over here and let me look at him." She says as she reaches over and flicks on a bed lamp.

She looks him up and down and tests his cotton.

"Timmy, huh?"

"Uh-uh. What do you think? Can I keep it?"

She looks into its big eyes and rubs a finger over one of its freckles.

"I don't know, Aaron. This thing looks sort of expensive. Some child is probably really missing him." She takes a deep breath to consider the matter.

"I tell you what . . . we'll keep our ears open about any missing doll. Maybe we should ask a few locals with young children if they're missing a doll. After a few days if no one comes forth, then you can keep it."

Aaron takes Timmy back from his mama and says, "Thank you. Thank you. Thank you," as he gives her a tight hug.

"Don't you think it's kind of odd though for it to be out there in the woods? That's really strange. Huh. Well, go get you some sleep. We can talk more about it in the morning, sweetie."

He hugs his mother and tells her he loves her, then heads off for his room.

A light rain had begun to fall and ting upon the roof. Aaron goes to the corner of his room and places Timmy in the wicker rocking chair his grandmother in Ohio had made for him. Aaron watches him while he changes into bedclothes, and Timmy watches him back with those big, googly eyes.

Aaron tosses his dirty clothes to the floor, undies and all, then jumps into bed and crawls beneath the covers. With Timmy watching from the corner, Aaron reaches over and turns out the light.

HE SWAM IN darkness as he could hear and feel wind rush past him, bristling the hairs on his arms. His stomach was taken with the feeling of falling. With much effort, he forced open his eyes. The wind subsided. He's in his bedroom. It's dark and very quiet.

Too quiet.

His ears begin to hurt and pop the way they do when he swims to the bottom of a deep swimming pool. He rolls onto his back and looks up at the ceiling. He blinks his eyes and moves his jaw side to side. He sticks a finger into his right ear and feels around. He's suddenly taken with the feeling of being watched. He angles his chin to his chest and peers through the darkness.

His door holds a slight crack in it which allows a faint golden hue of light to trickle in from the living room lamp his mother always leaves on. His heart knocks hard against his ribs. Standing in this angle of light is a big, bulky shadow. He can make out the silhouette of a man. The arms, the legs, the neck, the head.

Aaron goes to scream, but he can't. There's no sound. Then faintly and barely there, he begins to hear whispers. Not just one voice, but many. He slams his eyes shut and clamps his jaw. He grabs the covers and hides beneath them, hoping their magic will shield him from the boogeyman.

That familiar feeling returns to his gut, swimming and sloshing around, beginning to steal his breath. He began to pant when he remembered Scottie's dad's words about fear. *Or you can stand up to it.* He'd said. Yeah, stand up to it. At that moment, as he regained some resolve, sound slowly returned. It returned by way of a woman shrieking as if being murdered.

Mama!

Aaron throws the covers back and leaps off the bed. The big shadow had disappeared.

Aaron rushes for the door, slings it open and pounds his way to his mother's room. Her voice is still loud and shrill as if she's struggling for her life. He even heard some of the dogs barking outside. He makes it to her room and fumbles for the light switch. The overhead fan kicks on with the light, and Aaron finds his mother fighting the bed sheets as if they were possessed by an evil spirit. Taken by the horrible sight of his mother fighting this invisible monster, Aaron rushes to her bedside and attempts to calm her.

After some soothing words, she opens her eyes and begins to settle. Though she's still distraught as tears rush down her cheeks. She gasps for breath as she reaches out and takes Aaron in her arms. He feels the fear in her grip. Her hands tremble and her heart pounds hard against his chest.

She begins to speak. "Aaron . . . Aaron, we—" Her voice is hoarse as if she'd just been rescued from a dry dessert. "We have to get that thing out of here. It can't be here. It's cursed."

"What? What are you talking about? What happened?"

"The doll. It was in here. I saw it."

Aaron felt his flesh tense up and tiny chill bumps spread across his body.

He pulls back from her. He's never seen such fear in his mother's eyes before, not even when she'd confront his drunken father.

"I heard you calling for me. It was your voice, Aaron. Then I saw what looked like you, come to my door. I went to ask what was wrong, and that's when it ran and jumped in my bed. It wasn't you . . . it was that doll." The last words were hard for her to finish without her voice breaking off.

She sniffles and says, "We have to do something with it. It can't stay here."

Aaron swallows hard and bobs his head.

His mother gets out of bed and together they make their way towards his room.

Other than the lamp light filtering in from the living room, the home is dark and full of shadows. Each which may very well contain the unnerving human-like doll named Timmy. Aaron found himself clutching tight to his mother each time they passed a potential place for Timmy to emerge.

Who had he seen standing by his bedside? Just standing there, watching. Was it Timmy? Had he grown up? Was it Timmy's owner? And what in the world had shaken up his mother so much? Did she really see Timmy run and jump in the bed with her? No way. This is crazy. They're both going to feel really stupid when they enter Aaron's room only to find Timmy sitting obediently in the rocker by the corner. At least that's where Timmy should be.

Together Aaron and his mother creep along closer to his bedroom. Their feet travel softly over the hardwood with tension pulsing through their heels. Tighter and tighter Aaron clings to his mother's side, squeezing the blood from her arm and wrist. The floor creaks beneath their weight. The creaks are loud and take their time resounding amongst the home.

Finally, they reach the doorway to Aaron's room. The door stands wide to reveal an empty, dark void. Like a gateway into the abyss. Is that man still lurking in there? Standing in the corner? Rocking in Aaron's rocker? Aaron feels the back of his neck go cold and prickly as the hairs begin to straighten.

They come to the door frame, and Aaron's mother bends down to whisper to him.

"Now, you stay right here while I check your room, okay? Stay in the frame where I can see you."

"No, Mama. Please. Don't go in there. Don't leave me," Aaron says pulling back on her arm as he feels her weight tugging for the darkness.

"I have to. I have to check. I'll make it quick. I promise."

Aaron whimpers as she gently pulls free from his grip. He feels his lips quiver as tears burn his eyes and begin to leak out. He watches as she steps into his room, blending with the shadows and turning into a human silhouette.

He spins around and checks behind him. He has a terrible feeling that someone is watching, even crouching up behind him perhaps. He hugs himself tight and rocks side to side on fidgety feet. His eyes dart about his room and then the hallway behind him as he constantly checks over each shoulder.

In all of his frantic checking, he begins to notice how quiet his mother is.

"Mama?"

He hears his lamp switch flick a couple times before the bulb hums and kicks on. He watches as his room lights up and licks away the shadows.

He hears his mother gasp. He hears footsteps.

"Mama?" Aaron says this time with a hint of whimper.

Aaron gathers enough courage to take a step into his room. His vision is blocked by the back of his mother as she slowly backs her way out. Visibly shaken, she has both hands to her mouth and her eyes are glassed with tears. He watches as she removes her hands and begins to prod him out into the hall. The whole time she never takes her eyes off his room. He feels her soft, delicate hands tremble upon his chest.

"What is it? Mama, you're scaring me."

Sounds begin to emerge as her words struggle to find their place.

"It-it-it's go-gone. It's n-not-not there."

Her words were like a cinder block to his heart as he felt them send it sinking quick and hard, crashing deep into his quaking gut.

Now with their backs against the wall, his mother manages to say, "Get som-some clothes. We're lea-leaving."

Within a few minutes the two had packed their essentials and were heading out the door for his mother's station wagon. They found shelter with his mother's friend and never again returned to their home on Mount

Pisgah Road. Not even to return for their belongings. His mother spent a week's worth of pay to hire a moving company to load things up. His mother rarely if ever spoke of that night. She did her best to pretend it never happened or was just a figment of their imagination which stemmed from too many tv shows and what have you.

But Aaron knew deep down it was more than that. He would never forget that night or the fear he felt. The image of his mother fighting the invisible monster and the image of that large, bulky shadow standing by his bed will forever be ingrained in his mind's eye.

Of course, he'd also never forget Timmy or his realistic, boyish features. Or the creepy circumstances of how he found Timmy. He'd be reminded of them every time he ventured into the woods, especially at night. These things he knew would live with him for the rest of his life, no matter how much his mother suggested they wouldn't. Despite Timmy disappearing, Aaron Parker knew the memory of him wouldn't.

October 15th, 2020

Georgetown, South Carolina

AARON PARKER HAD grown up to do quite well for himself since his experience that night. Though he still isn't too fond of the woods or dolls, that hasn't slowed him down. He excelled in school, despite his encounters with bullies, and managed to earn a few scholarships to Chapel Hill where he'd go on to earn his MBA. He married a sweet girl who he met during his junior year at UNC. He and his wife have two young children, a seven-year-old and a nine-year-old. Boy and girl.

Since graduation, Aaron has become a successful real estate broker. Along with the help of his wife Karissa, who has a Master's in accounting, they have both been in business serving the Georgetown and surrounding areas for the past twelve years.

Travelling along highway 17 en route for Georgetown Elementary, Aaron Parker navigates traffic while retrieving his cell. He manages to answer on the third ring.

"This is Aaron with Parker Real Estate."

"Hello, my name is TJ. I'm interested in the home you have listed over on Greenwich Drive. The two-bedroom, two bath near the marsh."

Aaron clears his throat and checks over his left shoulder to switch lanes. He clicks off his turn signal and says, "Uh, yes okay. Give me one moment here."

"Sure thing."

"Now are you looking to make a move in the next few months or?"

"Um yes, actually I am."

"Okay, cool deal. And do you have a realtor helping you?"

"No, I do not. I thought I would just use the listing agent."

Aaron snickers a little at that and thinks *No skin off my back if you want to be an idiot. More money for me.*

It always amazes Aaron how so many people get caught up in thinking they are somehow saving money by just using the listing agent. What people don't realize is the money that would be going to a buyer's agent ends up going to listing brokerage, so they get to keep the full 6% commission and the buyer ends up without a representative to negotiate on their behalf. It's sort of like using the same divorce attorney as your angry spouse when you stop and think of it. A buyer's agent is free because the seller pays their commission. It's really a no brainer, but for some that just isn't the case.

"Okay, well no worries. When would you like to view the property?"

"Um, yes. I was wondering if you could meet me within the hour. I'm actually from North Carolina but was just passing through the area and happened to stumble across the place. I'm here now in the driveway."

"Oh. Oh, okay." Aaron looks at his watch. "Yeah, I'm on my way to pick my kids up from school. I could meet you around . . . say 3:15? Would that work?"

"Perfect. I'll be waiting."

"Sounds great, TJ. I'll see you shortly."

"Thank you. Bye bye."

Aaron squints his eyes and pulls the phone from his ear. A burst of static interrupted the man's last words and were followed by the beep to end the call.

Aaron shakes his head and continues to Georgetown Elementary. He crosses the bridge over the Sampit River. Winyah Bay sits off to the right. Sailboats, fishing boats, and a large barge angles down the river. The water ripples and creates snake-like lines here and there as it's driven by the winds. The sun peeks out from a cloud and sends a ray glistening off the navy and emerald colored water. Gulls fill the air, crying out to one another.

On the left-hand side stands a tall cylinder structure with various other pieces of machinery. A cloud of smoke billows out and lingers atop the town, casting a shadow over it. The odor of pig manure and burnt pinto beans becomes evident. The papermill is in full swing, harvesting trees and stripping them of their hardiness before sending them down the line to be slaughtered and processed. The chemical reaction fills the air and screams loud and clear, "Welcome to Georgetown."

Aaron comes into town and with his mind fumbling over numbers, he thumbs the radio up with the button on the wheel. A classic rock station, which he'd programmed into the system, picks up with a tune from Bob Seger. Aaron takes a deep breath, rests his left elbow upon the window seal, and combs his fingers through his hair. Along with the numbers, his mind is occupied with the thought of this new client named TJ. Something about the man felt . . . well . . . odd.

Beeeeeeeeep!

Aaron swerves to the left to avoid a car in the right lane who'd swerved from a car which had just pulled out into traffic.

"Geeze, lady!" Aaron says as he zooms by. "People these days." He says to himself as Mr. Seger's booming voice continues to fill the air.

Aaron makes his way to the school and proceeds to enter the pickup line. Half-way through his wait, he decides to call Karissa and tell her about the new buyer.

"Yeah, I hope so. It'd be nice to mark this one off the list. I know the Owen's would sure appreciate it."

Aaron pulls up next to where Samantha and Carter stand with their book bags strapped to their backs. Aaron unlocks the door and offers a friendly wave and smile to the teacher. He noticed that Carter's bag looked tight like it could barely hold the zipper in place. The door opens and the two crawl inside.

"Hola amigos. Que pasa?" Aaron says with a grin as he shifts to drive.

Samantha buckles her seat belt while saying, "Oh dad, stop it. You're not a Mexican."

He smiles and picks back up with Karissa. "Should I grab something out for tonight?"

"No. I've made plans for some new recipes I want to try."

As Aaron is busy speaking with his wife, he notices in the rear-view mirror that his son Carter is working to unzip his backpack. After numerous tries of tugging on the zipper and even passing it over to Samantha to try, the two finally give up. He hears Carter say, "Don't worry about it. I'll have to get Dad to open it."

"What is it, anyway?" Samantha asks.

Carter only smiles and says, "A surprise."

IT WAS TEN minutes of three when Aaron pulled into the driveway of the home off Greenwich. Aaron takes notice of the older model ford pick-up and begins speculating on the type of budget this TJ fellow may have. Aaron shifts to park and turns to look at Samantha and Carter in the backseats. With his right hand on the back of the passenger headrest, he says, "Okay, kiddos, this shouldn't take too long. An hour tops. Behave like you always do and be mindful of your manners for me. Okay?"

They both nod absently as they stare out of their windows.

Carter looks to his daddy and holds out his backpack, "Can you open this for me? I think the zipper is stuck."

Aaron takes the bag and feels how tight it is. He cranes his eyebrows and says, "What do you have in here? A body?"

Carter smiles and shrugs his shoulders.

Aaron fiddles and tugs on the zipper, but it holds its ground. Frustrated, Aaron turns and looks at Carter, "What did you stuff in here? Sam, do you know?"

"I don't know. He wouldn't tell me. He just said it's a surprise."

Aaron sighs and says, "Son, if I have to end up cutting this thing, you're going to wish you hadn't have done this. Your mother and I paid good money for this bag."

Just as Aaron finishes his words, his heart gets a start at the sharp knuckle raps upon the window. Aaron spins around to see a man, dressed in a black t-shirt and dark jeans, standing outside his car door. The man steps back to reveal his face.

Aaron's head swims with a dose of déjà vu. His mind suddenly becomes fogged and his gut twists with nausea. He blinks hard and takes a long swallow. This man, whom Aaron assumes is TJ, continues to stand in the driveway and looks at Aaron with big, far reaching eyes while wearing a tight grin. The man gives a gentle wave. Aaron dips his head and passes Carter's book bag back to him. He undoes his seatbelt and opens the door. The kids do the same and join their daddy.

"TJ?"

"Yes sir, pleased to meet you."

The two shake hands.

"TJ, this is Samantha and Carter."

TJ squats down upon his calves and extends a hand to each of them. He stands to his feet and says, "Fine kids you have here, Aaron. You done well raising them."

Aaron tilts his head and angles his brows, "Well thank you. Uh, shall I show you inside?"

"Of course."

With that, they march on toward the steps of the porch and Aaron begins to produce the details of the home as he has done for countless others in the past. The kids follow along, picking and teasing at one another. Aaron only had to give them *the look* once.

Twenty minutes pass, and they now make their way back into the kitchen.

"So, is it just you, or?" Aaron asks.

TJ nods and looks down at the floor while beginning to chew on the inside of his lip.

Aaron senses there may be more there than TJ is willing to reveal, so he says, "No worries, you don't have to say."

"No, I totally understand, Aaron." TJ continues to stare at the floor. Aaron can see the wheels spinning as if TJ is in deep thought. Aaron takes a breath and begins to speak but is cut short.

"What I don't understand is why your mother found me so hideous. I know deep down you felt the same way. You felt sorry for me, didn't you? That's why you took up with me the way you did. You knew what it was like to feel ugly, to feel insecure, to feel less than. You thought that by taking me in you could soothe your loneliness and that you could use me to help you cope." TJ slowly raises his head and looks deep into Aaron's eyes, "Didn't you, Aaron?"

"Daddy, what is he talking about?" Samantha asks with a shake in her voice.

Aaron felt his jaws begin to quiver and noticed that his fists were clinching tight by his sides. Samantha and Carter draw close to him. Aaron begins to breath hard in and out of his nostrils as he feels them flare. A hot dose of blood rushes around his eyes and face. His heart pounds with deep, heavy beats.

TJ's eyes widen, and his lips stretch into a tight grin.

Aaron's mind flashes back to the night which he had buried deep within his memory bank. His flesh turns cold as the memories resurface. He was squeezing his fists so hard he began to feel his nails dig into his palms.

With a quiver in his voice, Aaron says, "Who put you up to this? Huh? Did Scottie do this?"

TJ shakes his head and keeps that wide-eyed, tight-lipped grin on his face.

Aaron takes a step closer, then stops himself. He stares into those big, wide eyes.

"I thought you were the one, Aaron. I thought you'd be the one to set me free. It turns out you weren't any different than the others."

"What are you talking about?"

"I think you know, Aaron."

"It's time for you to leave. I don't know who put you up to this, but this isn't funny. Get out before I call the police." Aaron says while retrieving his phone.

TJ eases away the grin and walks out of the kitchen without saying another word. Aaron watches the man open the front door and proceed to climb into his blue ford. The blank expression never leaves his face, he backs out of the driveway and disappears.

Aaron makes sure the place is locked up and then takes the kids outside. As he inserts the key to lock the deadbolt on the front door, he holds his phone to his ear. It was on the fourth ring for Scottie Holland.

Aaron sends the deadbolt home and angles down the steps. Now on the fifth ring and about to go to voicemail, Aaron feels his face flush as his blood pressure continues to rise. Now opening his car door, Scottie answers.

"Hey man, what are y—"

"Save it. I don't know what the heck you think you're doing, but this has crossed the line, Scottie. That wasn't funny."

Scottie gives a confusing chuckle, "What? Aaron, are you alright man? What happened?"

"Oh don't play that crap with me, alright? I know you did it. I know you set me up."

"Aaron, chill man. I honest to God have no idea what you're talking about. Take it easy for a second, okay. Geeze, man."

Aaron rubs his face as he proceeds to back out of the driveway. He takes a deep breath and says, "Scottie, I just met a man who called himself TJ. He knew about the doll you and me found back when we lived off Mount Pisgah."

Scottie gets quiet on the other end.

"Did you have anything to do with that?"

Scottie still doesn't say a word.

"Hey. Did you have anything—"

"He came to me too, Aaron."

Aaron feels his heart sink into the pit of his gut. He didn't hear him right. He couldn't have.

"Was he dressed in dark clothes and driving an old blue ford pickup?" Scottie asks.

Aaron glances in the mirror to check on his kids and also to be sure a third person wasn't staring back at him as he'd suddenly felt like he was being watched. Much the way he felt that night he found the doll lying on that darkened path in the woods.

"Yeah. What did he say to you?"

"Well, that's the thing, he didn't say anything. I saw him in a dream. He was driving the ford down a dark path in the woods. It was like I was sitting in the passenger seat watching him or something. I remember the truck came to a stop, he got out, then walked around the front, passing through the headlights, and got me out on the passenger side. I didn't fight or anything, it was like I was asleep or unconscious or something, I guess. But I remember being placed down on the ground—"

"Christ, are you serious?"

"As God as my witness, man."

Aaron changed lanes as he entered into traffic. "Well go on, what happened?"

"So, I remember hearing a shovel digging through dirt. I never saw it, but I heard it. My eyes were fixed up at the tops of the trees as if I were lying on my back. The stars were out and the branches on the trees rattled with the breeze. Then the shoveling stopped and my vision went black. I thought I was going to wake up, but I didn't. When I opened my eyes, I saw the path lit up by the taillights and in the distance, I could make out what looked like that doll me and you found. And that's when I woke up."

"My God. When was this?"

"A week ago."

"And you didn't think to call me?"

"I mean, I didn't think much of it at the time. I thought it was just a crazy nightmare, you know. But now that you've called, it's kind of creeping me out, man."

Aaron feels goosebumps spread across his arms as he once again glances in the rear-view mirror to check on the kids.

"Listen, I think—how old was the guy in your dream?"

"I don't know, thirties or forties maybe. What about your guy?"

"Yeah, about the same. What the heck, man. And you swear you're not pulling my leg?"

"Aaron, I promise you. I didn't do anything. And I'm not lying about the dream."

"What in the world? Do you think some kid was murdered out there or something? Like you had a vision of the killer?"

"But why would the killer show himself to you?"

"Maybe that wasn't the killer. Maybe it was the kid disguised as the killer, so we'd know who it was. Geeze man listen to us. This is crazy." Aaron says.

"Should we file a police report, you think?"

Aaron gives a half laugh and says, "Yeah, if we want to be put away in a looney bin. Man, they'd think we were nuts."

"Yeah. Well, what should we do?"

Aaron sighs deep, "I say we go back out there and start digging around where we think we found the doll. See what we find."

"Yeah, and maybe it wouldn't hurt to search and see if there are any cold cases from around the area. I don't remember anything growing up, do you?"

"No, but it may have happened a long time ago, so it wasn't that fresh on anyone's minds. And the kid may not be from around there anyway. That could have just been the dumping grounds."

"Goodness. When do you think you can meet me out there?"

"How about tonight?"

"Tonight?"

"Yeah, let's get to the bottom of this, I won't be able to sleep if we don't. You're still in Shallotte, right?"

"Yeah, I can be at Mount Pisgah Road in about twenty minutes."

"Okay. Well, if I can smooth things over with Karissa, we'll plan to see you around eight o'clock. Will that work?"

"Yeah, sure. Jumping Joseph, this is crazy."

"I'll call you back on the way up."

"PLEASE, HONEY. I know it sounds crazy, but you have to trust me."

Karissa stands in the kitchen with her arms crossed and looks at her husband oddly as if checking to be sure he hasn't lost his marbles.

"Why didn't you ever tell me about this?"

"Because I know how crazy it sounds. I promise you though it's the truth. If my mother were still here, she could tell you herself. If she could stomach recalling that night. She had nightmares for years after that. It wasn't until I met you that she was finally getting over it."

Carter walks in from the living room carrying his tight backpack. "Daddy, can you open this for me?"

"Yeah, just a second, okay?"

"I really need you to open it. Now."

Aaron and Karissa both notice his strange emphasis at the end.

Aaron looks to his wife with squinted brows, then looks back to Carter. "What do you have in here that's so important, huh?"

"Like I said, it's a surprise, but you really need to see it now."

Aaron rubs a hand over his forehead and clears his throat. He pinches his tear ducts then takes the bag from his son. He sets the bag on the kitchen counter and picks Carter up to sit him next to it.

"What in the world do you have in there? Why is it so tight like that?" asks Karissa.

Aaron begins tugging on the zipper, but to no avail.

"Honey, can you get some olive oil spray from the pantry? Got to see if I can loosen this thing up. I may need a fork too. I think the flap is caught in the teeth of the zipper." Aaron grunts and says, "Boy, you really packed this joker tight, didn't you?"

Karissa passes him the spray and a silver fork.

Aaron continues to pry and tug.

Carter finally says, "I found it on the playground during recess."

The zipper gives way and jerks open three inches. Carter continues, "It was laying under the big slide."

Those words coupled with what Aaron's eyes were showing him as he further unzipped the bag was enough to send his heart leaping through the ceiling. Aaron jolts back and slings the bag off the counter. The half open backpack lands in the kitchen floor. A stiff, cotton filled arm dangles out like a pedestrian lying in the road after being struck by a car.

"Honey . . . what is this?" Karissa asks.

Aaron can't speak. He's frozen in place with his heart banging like a drum, causing his chest to ache. He feels cold fingers walk up and down his flesh. His breath comes in short gasps.

Carter hops down from the counter and stands over the bag. "His name is Timmy."

THE RIDE UP seemed to go a lot quicker than Aaron imagined it would. The whole way, he, his wife, and the kids talked about the doll (which they managed to stuff back into Carter's bag before tossing it into the trunk of their Mercedes) and the strange man from earlier. Aaron had talked to Scottie numerous times over the phone to discuss potential cold cases which may be linked.

It's scary when you realize how many missing kids and people there are out there. It's as if the earth just has a way of opening up and swallowing them . . . or something is plucking them up from the sky like a hawk taking a field rat.

Either thought brings chills to Aaron's spine. Karissa combed through Google searches on her phone and of the more than two dozen cold cases, none really seemed like a true connection. It was all guess work.

"But if there's a body out here, I mean we'll have all the evidence we need. As long as it has teeth and is still intact, the coroner can probably figure out who it is."

"It depends." Aaron says to Karissa.

"On what?"

"How long the body's been there. What if this is an old case? Like prior to World War Two or something. I doubt there'll be any dental records to compare with. It'll be tough to identify them if it's an old case. Unless there's other evidence to go on."

It was a quarter to eight and the sun had set. Darkness had covered the earth. Travelling along highway 17, Aaron takes a right onto Mount Pisgah Road. A swell of memories crashes over Aaron, and he immediately goes back to that night of the snipe hunt. He can hear the laughter, the crackling fire, along with the smell of roasted weenies and marshmallows. He can hear the wind sing as it tickles the leaves. He can hear the coyotes howling at the moon, and he can see the doll lying stiff upon the moon lit path.

With their headlamps lighting the way, cutting through the sinking fog, the Parker's amble on, pushing for the place where Scottie awaits.

Ten minutes pass before Aaron begins recognizing any houses or street names.

"I think this is it." Aaron says as he bumps his turn signal up. A green street sign, with the name *Young Blood Dr*, comes into view as the headlights shine upon it.

The road is dark and quiet with tall oaks on either side. Corn fields pick up where the trees leave off, before giving way to more trees again. Not many homes remain out here. The ones that do seem vacant and left to rot.

Aaron turns the radio off and leans up on the wheel. The double yellow line becomes harder to see through the fog. He looks off to his left and sees the big oak which all the neighborhood kids used to climb. "We're getting close."

Next comes the home the Allison's once lived in. It's a white home the size of a cracker box which looks to be missing most of its windows. Grass and weeds seem to be the only occupants. Of course, there's sure to be plenty of varmints laying claim as well.

Aaron keeps moving. Up ahead, a half dozen homes come into view. The two furthest in the distance, at the edge of vision upon the grassy knoll, are the only ones with any lights on. One of them is the home Aaron and his mother lived in. He wondered if anyone lived there or that was just his mother keeping the lights on for him. He tried his best to push aside the creepy thought, but for the life of him he couldn't get the image of his mother in her rocking chair in the corner of the living room, knitting on something and waiting for him to come through the door. Her flesh had turned gray, and her hair was stringy from years of decay. When she smiled at him, a rotten tooth tumbled onto her frail frame. Her hands and fingers were nothing but bones wrapped in tight flesh that looked like rawhide. Aaron blinks hard to rid the image. The other homes sit empty and dead like cemetery stones giving notice of something that once was. A corn field and patch of woods sits to the left. Within that patch of woods is where Timmy once laid.

Scottie's white GMC Sierra truck comes into view as he sits off the side of the road, his red reflectors refracting the light of the Parker's Mercedes.

"Okay. So, Scottie's wife and son are going to stay with you in his truck. We won't be gone long. We'll have our phones on us, so we can keep check on each other. You'll be okay. Scottie's son is going into the Army next year, so you'll be safe, okay?"

Aaron pulls into the driveway of the home across the street from Scottie. The home where Phil Baylor and his family had once lived. Aaron kills the engine and steps out. Karissa and the kids follow close behind him as they cross the street to Scottie and his family.

"It's good to see you Aaron, but boy I sure wish it wasn't for something like this. Have we lost our friggin' minds or what? For goodness sake man, what if we really find something out there? Do you think the cops will believe us?"

"There's only one way to find out."

"Jumping Joseph," Scottie says as he lowers and shakes his head while pulling one last drag on his cigarette. The orange glow grows brighter like a hungry furnace.

Scottie drops the remains to the ground and rubs the embers out with his toe. He blows the smoke high into the air, away from Aaron and his family.

"Nice looking family you got here, Aaron. Your mama would sure be proud of you."

"Thank you, Scottie." Aaron says before introducing them.

The back window to Scottie's truck rolls down and his wife Melanie leans out. "Come on inside where it's warm. Get yourselves out of the cold weather."

Karissa and the kids angle over and climb inside. Not before saying their goodbyes to Aaron though.

Scottie takes Aaron to the back of his truck and opens the lid and tailgate. Scottie shines a flashlight inside and pulls back a blanket. Beneath it was two spade shovels and a metal post to hold the electric lantern with. That way they'd have something to light their way as they dig for bones.

Aaron sighs and says, "You remember how to get there?"

Scottie bobs his head, "I think so. Do you?"

Aaron holds out his hand and twist it side to side, "Sort of."

"Well, let's hurry up before someone calls the cops or the big snipes come out."

Aaron chuckles mildly, "Yeah, like the big ugly one named Greg Alison?"

"Especially that one."

The two set off into the woods, just like they did thirty-two years ago, only this time looking like they're ready to bury a body or rob a grave. They disappear into the woods and begin to step over logs, crack branches, and crunch leaves.

The smell of chimney smoke hangs heavy in the air. At least someone is warm, cozy, and safe. The crickets sing loud, and the wind plays among the leaves. Every so often you'd hear a cicada join the assembly with its long screechy wail.

Together, Aaron and Scottie make their way deeper into the woods where the trees drew tighter together, and the fog grew thicker.

"Were we this deep in the woods?" Aaron asks as he follows behind Scottie who totes a Maglite and one of the shovels. Aaron carries the other shovel, the metal post, and lantern.

"Yeah, I think so. This feels right to me. The big cedar tree should be up here just a little further. You remember how we used to play on it, right? Remember we tried to build a tree house that one time?"

"Yeah. The one with all the forks on it? It was like two cedars combined into one. We called it the Siamese twin." Aaron says.

"Yeah. The Siamese twin. Man, why did we ever grow up. Life was so much simpler when we were kids," Scottie giggles as he hops over a log with a grunt.

Aaron follows suit. "You got that right."

They come to the Siamese twin and break off towards the right.

"It should be up here, shouldn't it?" asks Aaron.

"Yeah, I think so."

The two come into the small opening where the sky reveals itself through the canopy of trees. Aaron remembers looking up in this same spot all those years ago and seeing the moon peak out from the passing clouds, joined by a million stars. Aaron lowers his eyes and looks to the left of him. Scottie shines the light where Aaron is fixed, and the forked path reveals itself. A stone's cast away, down the one path is where they found Timmy. The same Timmy that now rests in the back of Aaron's trunk like a dead body.

For a moment, Aaron can recall seeing that stiff, plank-like body as it laid helplessly upon the dirt. He can remember the fear he felt when he imagined it to be a child left all alone.

"I think that's where we found him, wasn't it?" asks Scottie.

Aaron nods and takes a deep breath to fight that familiar feeling of fear rising in his gut, taunting him like a school yard bully. Aaron takes another breath and shoves the bully aside. "Yeah. C'mon."

Together, Aaron and Scottie walk over to the spot.

"This feels about right, don't you think?" asks Scottie.

"Yeah, I think so. Why don't you start on that side, and I'll start on this side? Try to dig like a ten-by-ten square in line with where we found him. If there is anything here, it must be just off this path."

"Right." Scottie nods and then mumbles to himself, "Jumping Joseph."

They go on to spend the next half hour digging shallow graves along the path. Tossing fresh soil and wet leaves this way and that. Tearing through roots, pinging off rocks, but never finding any bones.

That is until Aaron hit something that felt like rock but didn't ping. He felt a vibration travel up the shovel and disperse through his hands. It was like being tickled by a ghost. Aaron stopped and called out to Scottie who was now working further off the path than when they first begun.

"Yeah?"

"I think I may have something."

Scottie wipes his brow with the arm of his camo jacket and ambles over.

"What is it?" he asks.

"That didn't feel right. I hit something down there."

"Really?" Scottie asks.

"Yeah. Let's dig around this spot, you know, make a big circle and see what we get."

"Right."

A few minutes pass before they hit anything again. This time Scottie has that weird vibration travel across his hands and forearms. They dig a little deeper. Aaron fixes the lantern. Light filters into the dark hole which is now about five-foot wide by six-foot long and three-foot deep. Lines of white appear like fossils. Slowly, the outline of a small skeleton begins to surface. Remnants of blue cloth are matted to the bones. Aaron and Scottie stop and step back from the hole.

Scottie curses as he walks in circles with a palm to his beanie covered forehead. Aaron is bent at the waist a few yards away with his back to the grave.

"For heaven's sake man, this is a friggin' crime scene. That's somebody's kid down there." Scottie says before cursing again.

Aaron gathers himself and straightens his spine. He sniffles and wipes his nose with the back of his hand. He turns around and pulls out his phone.

"What are you doing?" asks Scottie.

"I'm calling to tell Karissa to check our trunk."

Scottie looks at him with narrow, questioning eyes.

"I'm going to see if the doll is still there," Aaron rubs the back of his neck and adds, "Then I'm calling the police."

"Geeze, man. What if they don't believe us?"

"Well, we know this must've happened sometime when we were kids or even before that. I think we'll be good. We'll tell them the truth. That's all we can do. No matter what, we have to be honest. We have to trust that the truth will defend us."

Karissa answers.

"Honey. I need you to do me a favor. I need you to go out and get Carter's backpack from the trunk."

She's quiet for a moment, then, "Why?"

"Just trust me, okay. Go get the backpack."

He hears her get out of the truck. He hears two doors slam. It sounds like Scottie's son is with her. The Mercedes beeps as she unlocks it.

"Okay, I'm getting—" her voice stops in mid-sentence.

"What is it, honey?"

With a tremble in her voice she says, "The bag is empty. The doll's gone."

Aaron draws a deep breath and says, "I thought so."

IT WASN'T UNTIL A year into the investigation that detectives were able to begin piecing the puzzle together. The skeletal remains belonged to an eleven-year-old boy by the name of Timothy William Johnson. He'd been missing from a small town in southern Georgia since the nineteen sixties, and his case had been cold ever since.

He disappeared one night after never returning home from trick-or-treating. They found his bicycle mangled and dumped off the side of a deserted road two towns over from where he disappeared. It appears he was victim of a tragic hit and run, and though detectives still do not know who the driver was, with all of the other evidence which Aaron and Scottie provided, they have no other choice than to believe the man responsible must be who Aaron and Scottie each encountered in their own mysterious ways.

So, now every time Aaron and Scottie pass a stranger on the street or in their local supermarket who resembles an older version of the ghost man, they find themselves drawn to stare until the person notices and pushes away their glares. The two keep in contact and often collaborate with detectives in the case. Neither of them has had any encounters of the ghost man or doll since.

The remains of Timothy Johnson were cremated as wished by the remaining family who happened to be his widow mother in Atlanta and brother and sister there in the neighboring DeKalb County. Despite having not caught the man responsible, the family has found comfort in learning of what likely happened to their beloved Timmy.

Aaron remembers the many questions that surfaced after their discovery that night, one being which he asked Scottie himself, "Why did the kid show up like that? You know, why show up like the man who ran him over, and the whole deal with the doll?"

The answer which Scottie gave was simple, yet profound, "It got our attention, didn't it? I mean after all, that's what this kid and his case needed wasn't it?"

It was. It was indeed.

Though his killer has yet to be found, Aaron and Scottie find it easier to sleep at night knowing the boy is at rest.

Timmy has found his way home,

The Hunted

The sun had begun to set as Matthew Johnson and his nine-year-old son, Easton, sat in their tree stand. They had been there since two-thirty and as the clock rolled closer to five, Matthew leaned in and whispered to Easton.

"We'll give it another ten minutes or so then we need to get going, okay?"

His son nodded. His black and green war paint was smeared as he'd wiped sweat and swatted mosquitoes all evening.

Matthew adjusted in his seat to relieve his aching buttocks. He watched as a squirrel in a nearby tree barked and flicked his tail at them. A crow lit on a branch and cawed. Another crow landed in the top of the tree. It craned its head and eyed them carefully.

A foul odor wafted through the air. Matthew crinkled his nose and looked down at Easton. His son snarled and looked up at him. They both were asking the same question with their eyes, *Did you do that?*

Matthew made a shew wee face and shook his head. Easton let out a faint chuckle but was quick to hide it behind his hand.

A twig snapped behind them.

Easton's eyes grew wide.

Matthew gripped the rifle and began to steady his breathing. Another stick cracked. Matthew straightened his back and gestured for Easton to remain calm.

Pop!

To their left this time. He could hear leaves crunching beneath heavy feet. *How did it get over there so quick? Must be two of them?* He thought. As he listened closer to the sound of it walking, something stood out and struck him as strange. He had a hard time making out the chi chi sound a deer makes as it trudges through the forest. It sounded more like it was on two legs rather than four. He squinted his eyes and listened again.

Two heavy thumps hit the earth as leaves crunched and branches broke. He cursed under his breath and began running a list of names of who he'd guess might be passing through the woods. If he had to bet, he figured it'd be Ben Michaels, the neighbor down the road from him. The sorry rascal always seemed to know exactly where Matthew's hunting spot was, and it never failed at least once a season for him to walk up on him and Easton in mid hunt. They had argued two seasons ago, but that didn't stop him from doing it again last year. Matthew had made up his mind, if it happens again, the man would be in desperate need of a nose straightener.

Matthew looked down to his left and peered into the thick growth. Whatever it was had stopped. The forest went eerily still. The birds quieted. The squirrels hid. Only the wind dared make a sound as it whispered among the pines.

Matthew had a cold chill come over him as he felt the hairs on his neck stiffen. The sun sank behind the trees and an enveloping shadow passed across the land. A coolness entered the air. Matthew stared at the woods, trying to see whoever was making the sounds. He grinded his teeth before finally calling out, "Ben, is that you?"

Easton huffed and snapped his head at him, "I thought we were supposed to be quiet?"

"We are, but I don't think that was a deer."

"What? What do you mean?" A dawning realization covered Easton's face and Matthew watched his brow furrow. He turned back to where the noise came from and said, "Ben, that better not be you. My daddy will whoop your tail."

Matthew elbowed Easton in the ribs and said, "Hush boy."

"Well, I'm just repeating what you said you'd do."

Matthew started to say something but thought better of it and tightened his lips. They waited for a few minutes, but never heard any more movement. The forest was still captivated in an eerie hush. It was so quiet he could hear the hum of a mosquito as it landed on the tip of his nose and dug a jack hammer into his flesh. He swatted it away, but the tip of his nose took on an instant itch.

"C'mon boy, we need to get going. It's getting dark."

"What about whoever that is walking around down there?"

"I'm sure it's nothing to worry about. Maybe it was a deer and it had a limp or something. C'mon let's get going. Your mama's going to be getting worried here soon. She's probably already got supper waiting on us."

"That was weird though don't you think?"

Matthew nodded as he slipped the rifle strap over his shoulder and moved to the ladder.

"I'll go down first. Wait until I'm at the bottom before you start coming down, alright?"

"Why?"

"Just do as I say, okay?"

"Okay."

Matthew took hold of the ladder and began the descent. He glanced up and saw Easton's paint covered face looking at him. He reached the bottom and unslung his rifle to hold it near his waist. He scanned the darkened forest and listened for any movement. Easton was making his way down when a small pebble whizzed by Matthew's head and tumbled across the ground in front of him. Matthew cursed and spun around, gripping his rifle tight.

"Alright, who's out there? What's your problem."

The woods were silent and dark.

"Easton, hurry up. Get down here."

"What was that?"

He reached the bottom and crowded close to Matthew's side. He could feel his heart pumping hard as it sped blood through his veins. The rifle was slick in his hands. He wiped a palm on the side of his pants. He searched the woods again. Nothing.

He took hold of Easton's hand and said, "We got to get out of here."

They began a brisk walk towards the trail they'd come in on. The long trail was an old logging road which became overgrown when the company went out of business some thirty years ago. Trees stretched over it to make a tunnel of branches. It wasn't for another fifty yards until the road began to snake and wind its way to a dried creek bed where Matthew's truck was parked. It would be another hundred yards from there to the main road. The distance between was nothing but a skinny trail which zigged and zagged the whole way.

They hadn't taken but a few steps along the old logging road when Matthew was hit in the back with a rock. This one almost knocked the breath out of him. He stumbled forward and found the rock rolling into the ditch. It was the size of a baseball. He grinded his teeth and snickered with anger. He looked down the trail and studied the darkness. The outcropping of a man came into view. Matthew pulled a flashlight from his back pocket and clicked it on as he said, "I don't know what the heck your problem is man, but you are—"

His words were cut short when his light beamed upon the hulking creature standing less than thirty yards from him and his son. Easton let out a blood curdling scream.

The creature turned the instant the light hit it and jutted for the tree line. Matthew could see long strands of hair float in the breeze as it strode away with an awkward gait. He felt an iron clad hand squeeze his heart and all his blood turned to ice. He could hear trees crash to the ground as the creature tore through the woods like a tank.

Easton gripped his arm until it hurt. Matthew blinked his eyes and shook his head. He slung the rifle over his shoulder and took Easton into his arms before bolting up the trail towards his truck. He dropped his flashlight and something else but didn't stop to pick it up. Easton adjusted and wrapped his arms around Matthew's neck with his legs interlocked around his waist. Easton was crying and panting for breath. Matthew ran with all he had and thought his lungs would burst any minute now.

As he raced up the trail, he began to hear heavy footsteps pounding the earth behind him. The creature let out a deep roar as it tore after them. He could hear it grunting and breathing from a phlegm-filled throat.

"Oh Jesus."

Easton shrieked and clung tighter to his neck. He had to pat him on the back to have him loosen his grip or he'd choke.

Matthew gasped for air. His legs were like bags of wet concrete. His muscles burned and screamed with every step. He stepped on an unseen rock, and it jabbed the arch of his foot. He grimaced but kept moving forward.

He had to make it to the truck. He was almost there. He has to keep moving.

The creature let out a bone chilling wail that echoed among the forest. It was so loud Matthew felt his insides rumble. Matthew and Easton pressed onward.

The creek bed was just ahead. If he looked hard enough, he could almost make out the silhouette of his truck on the other side.

The creature growled and grunted just behind his heels. Easton screamed and dug his fingers into Matthew's back.

Matthew reached into his pocket and felt for the keys.

He reached the creek bed and padded through it to reach his truck. He sat Easton on the ground and fumbled his key into the door. The lock popped and he slung the door open. Matthew could hear the creature still breathing and chasing after them. He grabbed Easton and shoved him into the truck. He shouldered his rifle and spun on his heels, pressing his back against the door of the truck.

Matthew swept the rifle side to side.

His breath came in short gasps. His eyes twitched and darted this way and that. The creature was nowhere to be found. The air was still and void of any sound. He reached behind himself and took hold of the door handle. Once inside, he turned over the ignition and shifted the truck into gear. The old Chevy pickup lurched forward, and Matthew angled for the narrow path leading to the main road.

After navigating the trail for a few minutes and catching his breath, he glanced over at Easton. The boy sat at the edge of the seat hugging himself. Matthew placed a hand on his arm and said, "Hey. You okay?"

Easton didn't answer. He only sat there gazing out the windshield. His whole body trembled.

Matthew turned his eyes to the trail only to find a black, hairy mass blocking the roadway. Matthew yanked the wheel to avoid hitting the creature. The truck skidded off the path and smacked sideways into a pine tree. The truck jarred and tossed Matthew and Easton around like rags in a washing machine. He smacked his head against the window and had stars flash before him. The back right tire blew in the process.

Dazed and shaken, Matthew could feel something warm snaking down the bridge of his nose. A searing flash of pain spread across his forehead. He touched it with the back of his fingers and winced. He could feel a gaping wound as the flesh had split from the impact he had with the window.

He reached across the seat and felt for Easton. When he couldn't feel him, he removed his fingers from his head and turned to look. Easton was lying on his back on the floorboard, moaning.

"You alright, Son? Hey. Talk to me."

"It hurts. Oh, it hurts Daddy."

Matthew noticed the passenger window was shattered and saw glass scattered in the seat and floor.

"What does? What hurts?"

"My leg. Oh. It burns."

He looked and could see a chunk of glass protruding from his pants leg. Blood was pooled around it.

He bent over to help Easton off the floor when his ears were flooded with the guttural wail of the creature. The sound blasted forth with unbelievable power and tone. The cab of the truck vibrated as the wail pierced the air. He thought it would never run out of breath. The screech went on and on and on. When it did stop, the truck jolted as the creature took hold of the hood. Its sharp nails dug and scratched into the metal. The noise raked through the air, sending every fiber of Matthew to tense with irritation. It rocked the truck once more and wailed long into the night. Easton covered his ears and whimpered. Matthew watched as the bulky creature swung back a lanky arm before crashing its hand into the front windshield. Matthew pulled Easton close and covered him with his body. Glass shards exploded every which way. The creature roared and beat upon the hood of the truck.

Easton screamed and buried himself deeper within Matthew's arms. Matthew watched the creature as it continued beating its fists upon the truck. The creature paused for a moment to gather its breath. It huffed then snapped its head around and glared at Matthew. Its eyes were like two billiards eight balls. It peeled back its rubbery lips to show rows upon rows of teeth. Its entire body was covered in thick, matted hair except for its face. The face was bare and looked like worn-out leather. Deep set wrinkles and scars snaked their way from its forehead down to its chin. Matthew was frozen as he'd locked eyes with the creature. It stared deep within his soul, searching and prodding. Its humongous nostrils flared, and its brows angled at him. A horrible stench entered the air. It was a mixture of raw sewage and soured milk. Matthew's gag reflex kicked in and he thought he would vomit right there in the truck.

The creature stood straight and beat its chest before letting out another roar. Matthew watched as it turned its back and marched into the dark woods.

Matthew let out a breath for what seemed like the first time in twenty years. Phone. He has to call Jessica. Then he'll call 911.

He patted his pocket for the phone but came up empty.

It must've jarred loose and flung out during the wreck. It's probably under the seat or something.

He searched the entire cab and felt his pulse quicken again when he didn't find it. Then it hit him. He didn't just lose the flashlight back there. There was something else he'd dropped along the road.

Please God, no. Don't tell me I dropped my phone back there.

He had to because it's not here.

"Dang it!" Matthew growled and smacked the steering wheel.

They could never make it to the main road with his truck in the shape it's in. They'd have to walk it.

His head throbbed and he touched the wound. He grimaced and wiped the fresh blood with his shirt. He turned to Easton.

"Hey. Hey, listen up. I have to carry you out of here. We won't make it in the truck. C'mon."

"No. No. Huh uh. No way. I'm not going out there. Noooo."

"Easton. We have to. C'mon." Matthew said as he tugged on his arm.

Judging by how far they'd made it along the trail, the road had to be only about seventy yards or so from where they are now. He could make a hard dash for it and flag someone down once he got there. It was either that or wait in the truck until dawn. He couldn't bear the thought of having to witness another rage fit by the creature. He couldn't put Easton through that again.

He climbed out of the truck, shouldered his rifle, and reached back for Easton.

"C'mon buddy. I got you. The road is just up there. It's not far."

Easton eyed him with suspicion and finally gave in.

With Easton wrapped around his neck again, Matthew shut the truck door, drew a breath and said, "Hang on tight, okay? We'll be there before you know it."

"I'm scared, Daddy."

"Hey. I know you are. But I'm here. I won't let nothing happen to us. I have my rifle right here. We'll be fine, alright. Now, hang on."

With that, Matthew made a dash for it.

He pounded along the jagged and crisscrossed trail. Trees and brush whipped passed them. He could hear cars driving by in the distance. Not much further.

Something stirred in the woods next to them. Trees began crashing to the ground as the monster made a break for them. He could hear it grunting and growling again as it hunted them down. Matthew pushed forward. His legs ached and his lungs were like fire, but he kept moving. He could hear the creature gaining ground. He saw the headlights of a car shine through the trees as it passed.

Easton squeezed his neck and screamed, "Shoot it! DAD! SHOOT IT!"

Matthew took hold of the rifle and set it to his hip. He spun around and back peddled. The outcropping of the creature loomed over them. Matthew squeezed the trigger. Fire blasted from the barrel and lit up the night for a mere second, but that second was enough to show the creature in all its glory. The gun blast rung his ears but he could still hear the thing when it let out another ear-piercing shriek before bolting out of sight. Matthew chambered a round and aimed in its direction. He could hear it crashing through the undergrowth and tearing away anything standing in its way. Matthew turned back for the road and raced onward. He could hear a car coming around the bend. Its lights angled with the curve and lined the woods.

Matthew began to holler.

The car passed.

"Dang it!"

He emitted out of the woods and strode to the black top. He stood at the side of the road to catch his breath. He heard the creature scream into the night. Matthew looked up into the dark sky and saw heat lightning flash in the distance. At the same moment something dug into his gut as a cramp spread under his rib cage. He winced and clutched his side, still trying to find his breath. Not seeing or hearing any cars, he began stepping down the road. The whole while he kept his eyes on the wood line. A car eventually did come along. An older man picked them up and took them to the police department, who in return, took them to the DNR's office to file a report of a bear encounter. Matthew didn't argue so as not to risk being thrown in the looney bin. He knew beyond a shadow of a doubt it was no bear but figured it would cause less of a scene if he agreed it was.

MATTHEW QUIT DEER HUNTING after that. He quit going in the woods at all for that matter. Easton didn't return to the woods until he was well in his late twenties or so. His father never liked to talk much about that night, and always agreed with the DNR report of it being a bear they encountered that night. Easton knew in his gut his father didn't really believe it, but he was too stubborn to admit anything else. It wasn't until Easton was hunting with his son some thirty years later that he knew without a shadow of a doubt what it was that had ran him and his father from the woods that night.

As Easton climbed the ladder to a hunting blind out in a field behind their house, he stopped near the top and shouldered his rifle to scan the wood line. His son, Matt, stood on the ground below him.

Easton looked through the scope and eyed the tree line. As he swiped to his right, something caught his eye. It was a dark spot among the trees that seemed out of place. It was blurry at first and Easton had to adjust his scope to bring it into focus. When the lens was righted, his heart sank into the pit of his gut. Staring back at him was a huge, bipedal ape-like creature covered from head to toe in stringy, mangy hair. Its head was rounded at the crown, and it had no neck. Its shoulders were massive and sculpted like an NFL linebacker. Easton watched it for what must've been ten seconds or more before it turned and disappeared deeper into the woods.

Easton put the rifle down and looked at his son below him.

"Hurry, get up here."

He never told anyone of what he saw.

He'd do anything if his dad were still here. He'd been the only one he would've told.

After seeing the creature watching them in the field, Easton quit deer hunting. The memories of that night with his father became all too real. From then on, he was mindful and extra careful with the kids playing outside. He forbade them from venturing into the woods and made it mandatory for them to never be alone outside after dark.

That day in the field made him wonder how many times he'd been watched like that without him ever knowing. How many times have those creatures had him within their sights?

The questions sent shivers down his spine.

He never did step back into the woods, and he never spoke of the reason why either. Like so many men before him, he carried the secret to his grave.

The eBay Killer

Jeffrey Alan Edwards, known to his boss and co-workers simply as Jeff, spends his free time operating two eBay stores named *Jeffrey's Collections* and *Jake's Treasures*. He spends most every weekend combing through yard sale tables, Goodwill shelves, and flea market booths. On occasion he takes items from victims' homes and lists them for sale on his eBay stores. Those are the sales that really get his juices flowing.

Having just sold a pair of women's Nike sneakers size six and a half, Jeff slips a pair of latex gloves on to prepare the packaging. He also wears a hair net and surgeon's mask to prevent any chance of DNA samples being discovered. Jeff began his hobby over a decade ago and so far, detectives have yet to connect anything to his eBay stores. Jeff plans for things to stay that way.

The sneakers he just sold belonged to his last victim. She was a forty-four-year-old middle school teacher from Connecticut. Of course, he had done his due diligence well in advance before choosing her as a victim. He googled her address as soon as her order came through to get an idea of the layout of her property. Liking what he saw, he then went to Facebook and found her page. She lived alone in a small town and made for an easy target. He monitored her Facebook posts for a month before making the trip up to Connecticut. He had snuck in through the back door and entered her bedroom without her ever knowing. She was quite the screamer that one.

Having finished his deed, he searched her closet for something to sell. When his eyes fell across the pair of pink Nike sneakers, he knew he'd found what he'd come for. They would make a quick sell and would lead him to his next victim.

Jeff finishes packing the shoes. The return address is to a PO Box in Florida. He would take the package to a post office in South Carolina tomorrow morning. He would be disguised as an elderly woman. He had purchased the mask from a Halloween store a few years back. He'd paid with cash as always. At the time he also bought a bald-headed man mask with a mustache. This is the one he often wears upon entering a victim's home. Although sometimes he likes to mix it up and wear another mask which he's owned for well over a decade now. The mask has big bushy eyebrows, a thick white beard and long white hair. It reminds him of Gandalf from Lord of the Rings or what he imagines Moses or God to look like. He often wears a black cowboy hat and a long trench coat when he chooses this particular mask.

He places the package on his computer desk, powers down the laptop, and crosses for his twin sized bed. No need for wasted space or resources. A twin bed suits him just fine. It also gives him more room to store his inventory. He has boxes and totes stacked four high around the bedroom. He removes his clothes and climbs beneath the silk, black sheets, fully nude. He turns on his sound machine. Tonight, he chooses the ocean. Even with the lamp lit, the room is already dark with the black painted walls and ceiling. When he reaches to turn the lamp off, the darkness consumes him. He rolls onto his back and interlocks his fingers by his naval. He awoke eight hours later in this exact position. He needs no alarm because his internal clock works just fine.

He rises and crosses to the closet. He retrieves the old woman mask and clothes. He takes a deep breath then enters the skin and character of the old lady. Afterwards, he packs a suitcase. He goes to a floor mounted safe and retrieves an envelope full of five thousand in cash, and a soft case which houses his .380. He has no intention of using it, but always brings it along in case the victim is rowdier than expected.

A few hours later after delivering the package to the post office, he's heading towards Charlotte where the package would be arriving within the next forty-eight hours. He would spend two weeks in a hotel located fifteen minutes from the victim's home. He would use the two weeks to monitor her, and her family's every move. After he received the intel he needed, he would strike.

Fast, ruthless, and precise.

T wo weeks later

Near Hartford, CT

DON JAMES, LEAD DETECTIVE of the Broad Brook Police Department, sipped his coffee while strolling through a list of potential murder suspects. Bethany Henderson was murdered mercilessly in her home two weeks ago. This case has been unlike anything Don James has ever seen in all of his thirty years of working homicide. That is saying a lot considering the gory and downright evil cases he has been cursed to investigate over the years. The victim had been bound to the bed posts with each limb stretched tight by thick rope. The killer had cut off her lips and eye lids, so it looked as if she were a wild-eyed clown. He had also gutted her and left her entrails in a bag within her stomach like a coroner would do after an autopsy. The cause of death was cardiac arrest which told the medical examiner that she was most likely alive while she was cut on, meaning she either died from blood loss or terror. Either way, it sent chills down Don James's spine.

There was no sign of forced entry and nothing of value had been stolen. The victim was obviously targeted, but for what reason, Don had yet to discover. The knuckle wrap on his office door pulls him away from the computer screen. He spins around in his chair and lowers his eyeglasses to the bridge of his nose.

"You got a minute?"

Don nods and says, "Sure. What cha got?"

Steve Shilling, Don's partner, places a folder onto the desk.

"The CTV footage came back from forensics. They were able to pull about a minute clip off the DVR system. The rest was trashed," Steve said as he opens the folder. "Here are some still shots. Wendy will be emailing the complete footage over to us shortly, but here is what we have so far."

Don pushed his glasses back on and leaned close. A ghostly hand caresses his spine as he feels a chill travel down it. The image was from the camera in the living room shining past the kitchen towards the foyer. The killer was caught walking through the foyer after having stepped through the front door.

"Geez. No wonder the coroner said she may have died from being scared to death. With the creep being dressed like that, I'd of shit myself. He looks like Moses if he'd have been around to join Jesse James's gang. There's no telling what he hid in that trench coat."

"Then there's this one." Steve places another eight by eleven image next to the first. "Look at the time stamp."

"Three o four. That's thirty minutes after he entered. That's quick considering what he did. The sorry bastard is just standing there, rubbing it in our faces." Don said as he stared at the picture of the masked killer standing in the backyard looking up at the camera while offering a friendly wave.

"Take some deputies with you and go back out there today. I want you to canvas the neighborhood and show everyone this picture. See if anyone recognizes the mask or trench coat."

"Sir, we've already spoke to all the neighbors."

"Then do it again."

Steve returned the images to his folder and said, "Whoever this is has done this before. This isn't his first rodeo. I hate dealing with the feds as much as anybody, but Don, I think it might be time to consider—"

"I already made the call. I'm waiting for the bureau to call me back as we speak." Don said as he leaned forward, propped an elbow on a knee and rubbed his tear ducts. He could feel a migraine working its way home.

Steve's surprise betrayed his face and he said, "Oh, well that's good. Maybe they can get things rolling."

As Steve was finishing his words, Don's phone began to ring.

Don sighed then motioned for Steve to leave the room. He told him to shut the door on the way out. Don picked up with a less than jubilant tone, "Detective James. Broad Brook Police Department."

"Detective James, I'm Special Agent Clark Gibson."

Don raised his head and straightened his spine.

"I received your message. I believe I may have a connection."

ANNE DECARR WASHED dishes while her husband, Daniel, was busy finding the girls a movie to watch in the living room. Anne had made homemade lasagna from her late grandmother's recipe. She heard the girls calling out different movie names as Daniel flipped through Netflix.

"I want to watch something *scary* this time," Claire had said.

"No. I'm not watching nothing scary. I want to watch a funny movie. Ooh. Stop. Go back. Yeah, the Smurf's. Let's watch that one."

"Emily, you're such a baby. You always want to watch kiddie movies."

"Hush. I am not."

Anne heard Claire make a loud fart sound with her tongue and could picture her making a face at her sister.

"Alright. Knock it off. How about the Smurf's for now, then later we can find a movie we'll all want to watch that's a little spooky. Huh, sound like a deal?" Daniel said.

"Sure. Whatever," Claire said.

"Yay. The Smurf's. Their so cute."

Daniel came back to the kitchen to help with the dishes. He rinsed while Anne dried.

"That was smooth," Anne said with a grin.

"Yeah? Kind of like when I asked you out for the first time, huh?"

"Pssh. Please, not even close. You were still a rookie back then. You're lucky I overlooked your corniness."

"Oh c'mon, cut me some slack babe," Daniel said in her ear before he kissed her cheek.

Anne smiled and continued drying.

SQUATTED IN THE BUSHES, Jefferey Alan Edwards watched Anne DeCarr through the kitchen window. She was prettier than her Facebook pictures. Which he found as odd. Usually, it's the other way around.

A mosquito buzzed in his ear. He swatted it away. A bead of sweat trickled down his forehead and landed in his mouth. He licked his lips and tasted its saltiness. He felt his heart quicken as adrenaline surged through him in anticipation of what was to come. He could feel the dopamine popping off like firecrackers in his brain. His hands and feet felt light as blood concentrated around his heart and brain. He swallowed and drew a deep breath to steady himself. He felt in his pocket and grasped the box cutter. He extended its blade then retracted it. A crooked grin twisted his face.

He adjusted his mask to better see through the slits. Anne and her Husband, Daniel, were embracing by the sink. She had her arms over his shoulders as she stared up into his eyes. He bent down and kissed her.

Jeff moved into position.

He checked his watch. It's a quarter of seven o'clock.

He waited patiently for five hours until standing and emerging from the tree line. He crept to the back door and retrieved his lock pick. Moments later it gave away and he was inside the DeCarr's home.

DON JAMES AND STEVE SHILLING were hidden in the shadows of the street, parked beneath a large oak tree. Don sipped on his third cup of coffee and was fighting the urge to pee. Special Agent Gibson and an Horry County Detective were parked three blocks behind them. Their eyes were focused on the home in the cul-de-sac.

The crackle of the radio broke the silence and gave Don a start. He almost spilt his coffee. The static clawed at his ears, and he squinted before picking up the receiver. The dispatcher said there was a body found on a street corner believed to be a byproduct of drug crime. Don cursed. As he was speaking back to the dispatcher, something caught his eye up ahead. Steve must've saw it too because he leaned closer to the windshield. Don dropped the receiver and reached for the door handle.

A man in a hood came running from around the back of the house and crossed the front yard.

Don and Steve exited their vehicles and rushed towards the home. The FBI agent and detective behind them did the same.

A gust of wind whispered through the trees. Don drew his gun and fell behind the other three. Despite being in great shape for his age, his seventy-two-year-old heart betrayed him. Not to mention the bum knee he adopted after a scuffle with a wanted fugitive a decade before. He panted for breath and trained his eyes on the subject bounding across the front yard of the home. He kept his head on a swivel, looking for any accomplice and watching the men's backs.

Detective Shilling and Agent Gibson yelled out together, "Freeze!"

The man obeyed. He nearly jumped out of his skin when the four of them surrounded him.

"Lower the hood then keep your hands where we can see them," Detective Shilling yelled.

Don watched as a teenager with a pepperoni face stared back at them. He was scared shitless.

Don cursed and lowered his weapon. The other men did the same.

"What did I do? What did I do?" the boy asked with his voice cracking.

"What's your name, son?" Don asked.

"Uh. Uh. Jacob."

"Jacob what?"

"Hunter. Jacob Hunter."

"Do you live here?"

Jacob nodded.

"How long have you lived here? You can put your hands down, just keep them out of your pockets."

"We just moved in two weeks ago."

"Where are you going this late at night?" Don asked.

Jacob licked his lips and swallowed.

Don lowered his gaze and shined his light in Jacob's face.

"A friend was coming to pick me up."

"Sneaking out of the house, huh?"

Jacob looked at the ground before asking, "What is this about? Am I in some sort of trouble or something?"

"No son, but whoever used to live here is."

Don drew a breath and turned to watch the wind rattle the lives in an old oak tree. A dog barked from the home next door. Don saw a porch light flick on followed by three others further up the street.

Agent Gibson cleared his throat and asked, "Did you ever see the man who lived here?"

Jacob shook his head, "No, he was a renter just like us. All I know is he left in a hurry. Landlord said he paid the remaining three months left on the lease in cash and had a Uhaul parked outside that same day. The neighbors said he left in the middle of the night. I've heard he was strange. What did he do?"

No one answered.

"Did he kill somebody or something?"

Again, no one answered.

"Shit, he did didn't he?"

"Go back inside kid before you get in trouble with your parents. We'll talk to everyone in the morning."

"Holy cow, this is like one of those ID shows or something. Or uh, shit, what's that other show that's always doing murder cases and stuff?"

"Forensic Files?" Steve asked.

Jacob snapped a finger at Steve and smiled, "Yeah, that one. Shit this is crazy. Dude, what if there's a body buried in the back yard? Or a skeleton hidden behind the wall?"

Don waved a hand in the air and said, "Alright. That's enough, kid. Go on now."

Jacob laughed with wild eyes and said, "This shit is crazy. I can't believe this."

As he headed back to his home, Agent Gibson looked at Don and said, "I think we're on the right track. These neighbors might know something."

Don nodded and ran his tongue along the back of his teeth. He spit to the side and said, "I want to speak with the landlord too." Don looked at the Horry County Detective and said, "And it might not be a bad idea to get the cadaver dogs here."

The detective craned his head, "Why's that?"

"In case there's a body in the back yard like the kid said."

THE NEXT MORNING WAS a Friday and the girls had slept through the shaking of their mother. Their alarm clock never did the trick. It was always Anne who was left with the task of jostling them awake. It was a little past eight thirty when Emily awoke after a bad dream. She said she dreamed she was in an old cornfield all alone and heard something rustle beside her. She screamed and began to run. The unseen being chased after her while laughing with a voice that resembled a clown. Her dream then flashed to the inside of a church where she was walking down the aisle towards a coffin. The church was empty and still. The coffin was a long way away, but she could see there was an arm draped over the side of it. As she stared and tried to make sense of who may be in the coffin, the table it was sitting on collapsed. The coffin landed at an angle and a body came rolling out to flop onto the floor. She never saw who it was. She awoke screaming.

It had caused Claire to jolt awake.

She climbed out of bed and rushed to console her sister. After getting her settled down, Emily hugged and squeezed her back before telling of the dream.

Claire felt goosebumps scatter across her flesh and for a change, she was the sister being scared. She rubbed her eyes and looked at the digital clock on their nightstand.

"It's eight-thirty-two. What in the world are we doing home? I should be taking a science test right now."

"Yeah, and I have my reading quiz this morning."

Claire put a finger to her lips and said, "Sshh. Listen."

"What is it?"

"It's quiet. Too quiet. Mom or Dad should be up by now. We should hear the coffee maker or something."

Emily drew close to her big sister and clung to her arm as the two of them crossed for their bedroom door. Claire leaned her ear against it and listened. A moment passed before she opened it. They stepped out into the hallway and listened again. Claire narrowed her gaze and wrinkled her brow at her sister. Emily gulped.

The girls crept towards their parents' room at the end of the hall. The door was shut.

Claire knocked and said, "Mom? Dad?"

No answer.

She twisted the doorknob and was frozen in place at the scene before them. Emily let out an ear-piercing wail before bolting away. Claire couldn't move. She felt a wave of nausea billow from her gut as the room was filled with a sharp copper smell. She could almost taste it in the air.

Tears welled in her eyes as she said with trembling lips, "Mom? Dad?"

They didn't answer.

THE MECKLENBERG POLICE DEPARTMENT received a call just before nine o'clock from an eighty-three-year-old widow named Elizabeth Sessions. She gave her address and said she was afraid "Somfin bad has happen" at her neighbor's house. The dispatcher could hear what sounded like two young girls crying in the background.

Authorities arrived ten minutes later to find Mr. and Mrs. DeCarr slain in their bed. From the looks of it, they were bludgeoned by a blunt force object. The room was doused in blood as if someone had taken turns splashing red paint about the room. Both victims had large Xs carved into their chests from a razor like blade.

Detective Jason Peacock spent half an hour looking over the gruesome scene before retreating outside to speak with Mrs. Sessions. She sat at the back of an ambulance wrapped in a blanket. The DeCarr girls did the same at another ambulance some thirty yards away. A female detective was squatted down in front of them asking questions as she took turns rubbing their shoulders.

Detective Peacock sighed and returned his attention to Mrs. Sessions.

"Tha girls come running and screaming up ta my door, saying they needed help. It nearly scared me ta death. I spilt my coffee and everything. I open tha door and they both come rushing in, grabbing hold of me saying I needs to call the police."

Detective Peacock nodded and scribbled notes.

"So, I took the girls over to Miss Irene's and told her to keep watch of em. I knows she keeps that shotgun of hers in the corner of her bedroom in case of a emergency. I tolds her this was one of them times. On the way to her house, I calls 911 and asks for help. Then I go back to the DeCarr's place to see for myself. The dispatcher stayed on the line with me as I entered the home. I could smell the blood as soon as I stepped through the front door. See I was an ER nurse back in my day. I knew when I smelt that there was somfin bad wrong. I had a cold chill crawl over me when I smelt it. I's go on towards the hall where the bedrooms are and the smell grow stronger. That's when I find them in theys bed all bashed up like they were."

"I see. Anybody come to mind who may have had something against the DeCarr's? Do you know if they had any enemies?"

"Lawds no. The DeCarr's was fine folks. Fine folks indeed. I's can't think of anybody who'd want to do such a terrible thing." She sniffled and looked over at the ambulance where the girls were.

"Have you noticed anything unusual within the past few days or weeks? Any strange activity? Odd cars? That sort of thing?"

She removed her glasses and pinched the bridge of her nose as she gave it some thought. Her eyes flashed wide and she looked up at Detective Peacock.

"There was a van."

"A van?"

"Yes. Lawd have mercy. I told Irene about it just last week. It was a white construction van with a ladder on the roof. It had some type of writing on the sides, but I couldn't make it out. It sat right out there in the road on two separate occasions. Acted like they was doing work or somfin, except I don't know of any neighbors having any work done. I found it strange and kept an eye on it. I couldn't much see inside except for someone moving around like they was eating lunch or somfin. I told Irene it looked like they was scoping somfin out, but she said I was just being too nosey and paranoid. I felt in my gut they was just somefin off about it. I should've listened to my instinct and had one of you to check into it." Tears filled her eyes and she swept a feeble hand towards the DeCarr's home, "Lawd I could've stopped all this. Why didn't I do somfin?"

"Sshh. Now, don't go talking like that." Detective Peacock said as he stepped forward and patted her shoulder.

She sniffled and he dug into his coat pocket to retrieve a Kleenex. He stepped back and jotted down more notes.

"Those poor youngins. Those poor poor youngins. They's too young to be without they parents. What sort of person could do such a thing?"

"An evil and sick one."

Peacock followed the lead on the white construction van, but it turned out to just be a handy man who was doing some work on a house a few streets over from the DeCarr's. The street he was working on was lacking for shade trees and the DeCarr's street was where he settled for lunch breaks the two days he was on the job.

No other lead was present. There were no prints, DNA, boot tracks, nothing. It was as if the crime was committed by a ghost or by someone well versed and experienced. Either scenario made Detective Peacock's skin crawl.

LATER THAT DAY AS Detective Don James and Special Agent Clark Gibson had spent most of their time speaking with local Uhaul owners and putting out an APB, Jeff Edwards was settling into his hotel room. He'd paid with cash of course and had used a fake name to match that of the mask he wore. The sun had set, and Jeff sat at the desk with his laptop opened. Lying next to the laptop was a red and black Craftsman hammer. He had taken his time cleaning away the blood and tissue. He was also sure to scratch out Mr. DeCarr's initials which were carved into the metal. Jeff flicked on the lamp light and took a half dozen pictures before adding them to his eBay account. He wrote out a generic description but added at the end *"Could even be used as a weapon if the need arose. Could certainly crush through bone or skull if needed."*

Jeff snickered as he typed it out. He was still smiling while he sipped his coffee. He moved onto the price and was sure to list it for an offer the right man couldn't refuse. The listing went live.

Jeff chuckled as a sly grin stretched his lips. He shook his head and closed the laptop. He shimmied out of his clothes like a snake shedding its skin, turned out all the lights and crawled beneath the covers. He was still grinning when he drifted to sleep.

One Week Later

AT EIGHT O'FIVE that morning, Jeff was called into his Bossman's office. His reason for having missed so much work in recent months was his mother's poor health. He claimed she lived with him, and he was the primary care giver. Jeff had created an elaborate story of how she had come down with some autoimmune disease that had doctors baffled and was constantly fending off pneumonia, colds, and stomach bugs. The truth was his mother had been dead for years. He had taken care of that issue long ago. She was always the nagging type anyhow, and after coming home late from doing a dirty deed, her nagging had pushed him over the edge. Long story short, she's now peacefully buried in the basement under five hundred pounds of concrete.

"Jeff. Jeff. Hey, are you with me?" His boss said as he waved a hand in front of Jeff's face.

Jeff cleared his throat and scratched his forehead.

"Uh, yeah. Sorry. You were saying?"

His boss sighed and shook his head.

"What am I going to do with you?"

Jeff massaged the wooden arms of the chair and glared at the short ball headed man with a pudgy gut. He reminded him of George Constanza from Seinfeld. He watched as the man stood from his chair and crossed to a window looking out to the work floor. Machines wined and hummed as men moved about the building like ants.

Jeff's eyes began to wander about the room, searching for something heavy enough to crack through skull. The boss continued talking, but Jeff wasn't listening. He was too busy searching. He settled on a marble bookend carving of a grizzly bear. The thing had to have some weight to it. He had watched the Bossman maneuver it along the bookshelf before and noticed how it seemed to sit heavy in his chubby hand. He could pounce and be on the man before he ever knew what hit him.

The Bossman stopped talking and turned around to face him. Jeff diverted his eyes from the marble sculpture and refocused his attention.

"Well?"

"I'm sorry, what was the question?"

The Bossman glared at him and began to grind his molars.

The air grew thick between them. The room suddenly became muggy and humid.

"I'm going to say this once, and I will not be repeating myself. You have thirty days to clean up your act or you will be replaced. Is that understood, Jeff? Do I make myself clear?"

Jeff tightened his jaw and nodded.

"Good. Now get out of my office."

As Jeff stood from the chair, his phone pinged with a notification. He exited the room and retrieved his cell. He swiped down and felt a surge of adrenaline rush through him. His muscles quivered with excitement.

The hammer had sold.

He swallowed hard and felt his breath quicken. He clicked on the details and scrolled down to see where the buyer was located.

Beaumont, Texas. Henry Janson.

Jeff smiled as a sense of giddiness washed over him. He pocketed his phone, inserted his ear buds, and returned to the work floor. He could hardly wait to get home and package the item. He'd spend most of the night researching Henry Janson and the layout of his home. If he shipped the hammer out first thing in the morning, the man should have it by Wednesday or Thursday. That would allow Jeff to leave Friday after work and if he drove it straight through, he could be in Beaumont by Saturday afternoon. He could grab a bite to eat, take a quick nap at a truck stop, do the deed that night and be back by late Sunday in time for work on Monday.

Sure, it would be a quicker process compared to what he'd much prefer, but with the Bossman cracking down on him, he could not afford to miss any more work or he would be at risk of raising suspicions. He could continue to do his side hustle, but it would require less time for research and stalking. As long as he kept every scene different without leaving clues, signatures, or MOs, no one would ever catch on to him.

Would it be riskier this way?

Of course.

The added risk added to the thrill of it all, and that was what made his side hustle so fulfilling.

HENRY JANSON IS A retired long haul truck driver of twenty-three years according to his Facebook profile. He had his seventieth birthday just last month. Jeff counted over two dozen birthday wishes on his Facebook page. Little did all those friends and relatives of his know that that would be his last. The reaper had come bearing his scythe, and tonight Henry's soul was Jeff's to take. Jeff smiled at the thought as he hid behind a tree in the old man's backyard. It was a quarter past midnight, and Jeff had been watching since dusk. The old man lived alone. At least it seemed that way. There was no lady friend on his Facebook and by the looks of it, his wife had died some years back. There was one vehicle in the driveway. A silver Honda Civic. Jeff had watched Henry let the small, terrier looking dog out to pee two hours earlier before turning out all the lights.

Despite the man's age, he would be a challenge. Henry Janson was much larger than Jeff himself. He was a thick, barrel-chested man and had Popeye like forearms. Jeff reached a hand into his pocket and touched his .380 pistol. He had no intention of using it on the man, but should the need arise, Jeff took comfort in knowing it was there.

He draws a deep breath, shuts his eyes, raises his face to the full moon, and exhales slowly. He feels the dopamine surge through him in anticipation of what is to come. He stands and bounds on the balls of his feet like an octagon fighter. He cranes his neck side to side, and it gives off a sick crack. A wry smile stretches his lips, and Jeff emerges from the wood line.

THE JEFFERSON COUNTY Police Department received a well fare call for Henry Janson five days later. His daughter in Washington State had been unable to reach him for the past few days. Due to their close relationship, she knew something was wrong when her father had failed to respond to her calls and texts.

A sheriff deputy responded to the home around nine that morning. He knocked on the door and cupped his hands on the windows. He saw and heard no movement despite Mr. Janson's car being in the driveway. The officer did notice a foul odor and considering the circumstances it was enough for him to make his way inside. The odor grew louder as he made his way towards the back bedroom. With his gun drawn, the deputy placed his back to the wall and slid down the hall. He noticed blotches on the carpet near the doorway of the bedroom. The tan carpet looked to have been bleached in several places.

The deputy trained his pistol and entered the bedroom. He felt his heart thud when his eyes took in the outcropping of a body lying in bed. Blood spatter was everywhere. The deputy tucked his nose beneath his shirt and swallowed hard to keep the vomit at bay. The decomposed body of Mr. Janson lied atop the comforter with his arms crossed over his chest as if his killer had prepared him for burial. The deputy felt a cold hand sliver down his spine at the thought. Tilting his head against his shoulder and speaking through his shirt, the deputy called it into dispatch. Within minutes, back up arrived. Half an hour later detectives and CSI were on scene.

ONE CSI WORKER, Melissa Shelby, had been an investigator for Jefferson County for the past twelve years. Prior to her time in Jefferson County, Melissa was a part of the CSI crew in Broad Brook, CT. She had often worked alongside Don James and the two had become good friends through the years. They even dated for a short while at one point.

The two still kept in touch and had actually spoke just last week when Don had called to tell her about his struggle in tracking the ruthless killer of a lady there in Broad Brook. The two had talked about the crime scene for an hour that night. Don often called her when he had trouble piecing things together. One thing he had told her that stood out was the way the killer had *gutted* the lady as if preparing her for the coroner. The way Don described it and the way he worded it, had really stood out to her. With that in mind, when Melissa Shelby walked into Mr. Janson's bedroom and found him lying there with his arms crossed like he'd been prepared for his funeral, she couldn't help but go back to her and Don's conversation.

Could this be the same guy? There's no way. Has to just be a coincidence.

These thoughts played through her head as she combed over the scene. In the far corners of her mind, she kept repeating a phrase she had heard Don say over and over during her time at Broad Brook, *There are no such things as coincidences. Two plus two will always equal four.*

As she examined Mr. Janson's body, she noticed the ligature marks around his neck. It was obvious he had been strangled with some type of cord. She pulled away from the body and did a slow scan of the room. One thing that immediately grabbed her attention was the lack of a bedside lamp next to where Mr. Janson was laying. The nightstand on the other side had one. Melissa angled around the bed and went to examine the lamp. It wasn't an ordinary lamp. It appeared to be an antique. It had a cherry wood base and from that base rose a fly rod that bent over like a question mark. A wooden rainbow trout hung from the tip of the rod. On top of the bent rod was an extension where the bulb and shade were. A long black cord ran from the base and went behind the bed. Had the killer used the other lamp and discarded it? If he used the lamp to kill him, why stab him so many times? Had he tied the man up prior to killing him? As Melissa ran these questions through her mind, she went back to the doorway and spoke to another CSI worker who was busy taking samples from the bleached carpet. It appeared the killer must've cut himself as so many do in such violent attacks. In a frantic attempt to clean things up, he doused bleach where there must've been blood droplets. If they're lucky, there may be a trace amount of DNA left.

"He did a pretty good job with the cleanup, didn't he?"

"Yeah, but I'm hoping there's enough down deep in the fibers for us to pull from." The CSI worker told Melissa.

"Good. Put a rush on that, will you? I think I may be on to something. I need to make a call."

The CSI worker paused her work and looked up at Melissa from a squatted position. "Really? Whacha got?"

"Let me call my friend in Connecticut first. I'll fill you in when I get off the phone. Do your best to pull DNA from that sample." Melissa finished as she made her way down the hall and out the front door.

AROUND TEN O'CLOCK, Don James was seated at his desk when Melissa's call came through. He smiled when he saw the name light up on his phone.

"Tell me something good, girl. I need some good news for once."

"I think I can do that."

Don chuckled, "What are you up to?"

"I'm investigating a homicide."

Don sipped his coffee and watched the wind rustle the leaves outside.

"Go on."

"No sign of forced entry. Not a robbery. Seems to be personal or ritualistic."

Don leaned forward in his chair and sat his coffee down.

"What do you mean *ritualistic*?"

"It reminds me of what you said about your lady there in Broad Brook."

Don gulped and blinked his eyes.

"I'm listening."

"Our victim was found in bed with his arms folded over his chest as if *prepared* for burial."

That word *prepared* reverberated through his mind like a pinball.

"He has deep ligature marks around his neck which could have very likely been enough to crush his windpipe and block any airflow, but he was also stabbed twenty-seven times."

Don cursed on the other end.

"It appears our perp may have cut himself in the process. We are working to extract blood samples from the carpet, but the damn bastard used bleach where he leaked out."

The line grew quiet for a moment.

"Something else that grabbed my attention was a missing lamp by the bedside. The one that's there appears to be an antique of sorts. I remember you mentioning that your victim was big into antiques. Didn't you tell me that?"

"Did I? I don't recall that I did."

"Yeah, remember you talked about the old pictures and artifacts. You said she had good taste."

"Yeah, she did."

"I know it may seem like a stretch to connect this, but like you've always said, two plus—"

"Two will always equal four. Yeah, guilty as charged."

"There are no coincidences. If these cases are connected somehow, the victim's love for antiques may be the link."

"Where do antique lovers like to shop?" Don wondered aloud.

"Well, yard sales for one. Flea markets. Facebook marketplace. Craigslist. eBay. I'm no antique expert, but besides looking around at the antique stores I think these are places they would all have in common."

"Most of those places you just mentioned would be bound to a local area. If a murder in Connecticut is going to be connected to a murder in Texas, there must be a thread online somewhere."

"Yeah, you're right. eBay then."

"It sounds like a long shot, but I think it'd be worth looking into. We could pull their bank records to see if either of them had purchased anything from eBay recently and try to see if there is a related account they bought from." Don said.

"Sounds like a bread trail worthy of following."

"Thank you, Melissa. I'm sending Agent Gibson a message now. Keep me apprised of the situation there in Beaumont, and I'll do the same here."

"10-4."

JUST BEFORE MIDNIGHT, Jeff was busy showering and preparing for bed. He did his best to keep his cut hand away from the water. On a few occasions water snaked down his arm and stung him on the raw meat. He cursed and gritted his teeth each time. Stepping out of the shower, Jeff wrapped a towel around his waist, wiped condensation from the mirror, and sat upon the sink counter. He opened a bottle of rubbing alcohol with his teeth, took a deep breath, and poured it over the wound. His jowls quivered and beads of sweat broke out on his forehead. Jeff groaned and continued pouring. He finished, balled his hand into a fist, and cursed again through clinched teeth. Jeff retrieved a bandage and a roll of white gauze tape from his first aid kit. He wrapped his hand then headed for the bedroom where his laptop waited for him on the desk.

Still wrapped in the towel, Jeff took a seat at the desk and booted up the laptop. He connected to the motel's WIFI and logged into his eBay account. He had all the pictures of Mr. Janson's lamp already downloaded. He uploaded nine of them and wrote out a brief description of the item. He ended the description by saying, *The cord is long enough you could probably strangle your mother-in-law with it. Just kidding. It is a really long cord though.*

Jeff snickered as he clicked the button to list it. The item went live, and he couldn't help but smile. His next victim would surely be coming along soon. It was a fine lamp, and it did indeed have a really long cord. Jeff chuckled and stood from the desk. He powered down the laptop, dropped his towel, and slithered beneath the covers. He fell asleep smiling and thinking of how that cord felt in his hands as Mr. Janson struggled for his life. He may just have to use that lamp twice. At least once more then he'd move on to something else. He could hardly wait for a buyer. Something about the cord on that lamp had stirred a craving in him. He liked the way he could feel his victim struggling and fighting for life. It had sent a thrill and extra dose of dopamine through him unlike anything else. He couldn't wait to do it again on the next buyer.

DON JAMES AND AGENT GIBSON had spent the last few days working with both the bureau and Broad Brook Police Department on combing through the victim's bank records for any purchases made from eBay. It hadn't taken long to find it in the statements. Both victims had bought items from eBay shortly before their murders. The first victim had purchased an antique painting from eBay one month prior to her murder. The victim in Texas had bought a craftsman hammer from eBay only days before his murder. A few hours after making the discovery on the bank records, the IT and Cyber Security team was able to log into both victims' eBay accounts and discovered they had both made their purchases from a store called *Jeff's Collections*. Melissa was right. Two plus two does equal four. After sorting out the account's listed items, the most recent item listed was an antique lamp. Don snapped a picture of it and sent it to Melissa. She confirmed it as the mate to the one found in Mr. Janson's home.

"The sorry bastard is taking items from his victim's homes and reselling it to new victims. And look at what he says in the damn description. Did you read that?" Don asks.

Agent Gibson stands behind the IT worker's chair with his arms crossed and a finger over his lips. "Yeah, I see that. He rubs it right in our faces."

"So instead of hunting his victims, he's luring them to himself. He's like a damn snapping turtle."

Agent Gibson wrinkles his brow, "Like a what?"

"I said he's like a snapping turtle. Growing up poor in the south, I've had my fair share of cooter stew. I remember one day when I was watching my daddy butcher and prepare one for supper, I noticed it had this worm looking thing in the bottom of its mouth. I asked my daddy what it was and he said it was what the turtle used to lure the fish into its mouth. He said that turtle would find a nice spot on the bottom of the lake, open his mouth wide, and wiggle that little piece of meat so it looked like a worm. A little ole fish would come along thinking he had himself an easy meal but before he even knew what happened, that turtle had done clamped his jaws down on it. That's what our killer has been doing to these people. Instead of going out on the hunt like most killers, he used this eBay store to lure his victims to himself."

The room went quiet.

Don could see Agent Gibson was thinking.

Their eyes met. They were thinking the same thing. Two can play this game.

JEFF DIDN'T HAVE TO WAIT long. Three days after listing the lamp, he got the notification on his phone that the lamp had sold. While on his lunch break, he checked to see who bought it and where they were located. Melody Stensland from Ohio was the buyer. He did a quick glance at her Facebook and was happy to see she was another middle aged, single lady. Certainly makes his job a little easier. He googled the address and switched to the street view. It was a decent single-family home. Probably thirteen hundred or so square feet. It wouldn't give her much room to run, which once again, would make things a little easier.

After going back to work from his break, the rest of the day his mind was focused on completing his new task. He ran scenarios through his head, plotted out a step-by-step plan, and estimated the hours and miles it would take to drive there and back. If he went home and packaged the item so he could ship it out first thing in the morning, the lady should receive it by Tuesday of next week. That would give him a few more days to do his research. He thought about doing like he did with the Janson murder and do the deed over the weekend, but he was afraid of creating a pattern. He decided it would be best to make the nine-hour drive Wednesday right after work. He would call in sick Thursday before making the drive back into town after having done the deed early that morning, likely sometime around two or three am.

Jeff could hardly wait to get home so he could pack the lamp for his new victim.

FROM THE MOMENT Don and the investigators purchased the lamp, using the account of a friend of a woman at the department, they positioned FBI agents and local police to watch the place over the following days and weeks. However long it took for the killer to arrive, they were prepared to wait it out. Don and Agent Gibson were on scene and communicated through radio. The lamp had arrived at the woman's home yesterday afternoon. The past five days since the item was purchased had preceded without any sign of their killer. However, since the lamp was delivered, everyone's senses were on high alert.

It was just after nine o'clock on Wednesday night when Don radioed into Agent Gibson.

"Anything?"

A moment passed before Gibson's gruff voice came back through the static, "Nothing yet. Keeping our eyes peeled on the south entrance. My gut says that's the way he'll approach."

"10-4."

AN HOUR LATER and Jeff had reached his position. He squatted in the shrubbery and peered past the branches to peek through the kitchen window. Most of the lights were still on and he had caught a glimpse of Melody filling a glass of water by the sink. She had long blonde hair that rested over the shoulder of her white robe. The room was dimly lit and cast a shadow over her face. He could only see her from the shoulders to her waist. He grinned and breathed deeply through his nose. The dopamine surged through his veins and caused every muscle to quiver. He felt electric. Like there should be sparks emitted from his fingertips. The rush and thrill of it all was settling over him and he knew it wouldn't be long before the deed would be performed. He checked his watch, *10:41*. He would wait until after one to enter. As long as he was back on the road by two, he'd have plenty of time to get back to South Carolina by tomorrow morning. He had to control his breathing as the excitement was overwhelming him.

Stay calm. You got this. Breathe Jeff. Breathe, he told himself.

A mosquito dug into his neck, and he slapped his flesh. It gave off a loud smack. He heard a dog bark in the distance. A cricket whirred next to him. He grinded his molars and stared in its direction, wishing it were dead. He narrowed his brows and felt hot breath steam from his nostrils. The cricket must've felt his energy because it suddenly went quiet. Jeff smiled and began to chuckle. He turned his attention back to the Stensland home and waited.

AT ONE O'SEVEN Jeff made his way in through a side door. He removed his boots like a gentleman and walked with socked feet to keep the noise down. The house was pitch black and silent. Jeff knew by her Facebook account she was single with no kids. Again, things that only made his job easier. A part of him felt guilty for doing something so easy. He sort of wished this one would have put up more of a challenge. At least he could re-use the lamp again. That would make it all worth it. Maybe his next victim will present greater difficulty and require him to up his game.

He kept his eyes peeled for potential items he could use in the future as he crept through the darkened home. He was sure to walk along the walls to avoid the floor from creaking. The master bedroom was adjacent to the living area. Jeff watched his black shadow pass across the television screen. As he neared the bedroom door, he reached back instinctively to feel for his .380. He had no plans of using it tonight, but as always, it was reassuring to know it was there if needed. He then slid his hand to the buck knife on his hip. The plan was to take her life with the lamp cord if it were next to the bed like he'd hoped. If it weren't, he'd hold her at gunpoint until she showed him where it was. The idea of using the knife to take a finger or ear had crossed his mind also. He figured it'd be something else to add to the mix to keep things different.

He reached the bedroom door and pressed his back to the wall. The door was cracked halfway and open enough for him to slither through. He slid his feet across the hardwood and stood just inside the door frame. There she was lying in bed with the covers clinched tight around her face. The room was too dark to really see her features, but he could see the outcropping of her disheveled hair. Jeff felt his heart knock hard against his ribs. He licked his lips and swallowed hard. He diverted his eyes to the nightstands and felt a surge of adrenaline when he saw it. There it is. Waiting for him. Waiting for him to wrap the cord around her neck like a snake and squeeze the life from her.

His pulse began to soar.

His breathing quickened.

He stepped forward.

There was movement. The bed stirred.

The covers flew back in such a flash his mind had no time to process what was happening. A bright ball of fire filled the room followed by three rapid explosions.

He dove to the floor at the foot of the bed. His shoulder slammed into the hardwood. A flash of hot searing pain stung him in the side of his gut.

The dumb witch shot me. I'll be damned.

He placed a hand to his side and felt warm blood slip between the webbing of his fingers. He heard her stand from the bed. Jeff squirmed backwards across the floor while reaching for his .380 with the other. Voices could be heard outside. Static from a radio crackled somewhere. He reached the wall and had just found purchase of his weapon when the person who shot him stepped around the corner of the bed and yelled, "Hands. Let me see your hands."

Jeff didn't move. He stared through the darkness. His mind tried to process what was taking place. The voice was that of a man. An older man at that.

What the hell?

He'd been set up.

"Show me your damn hands, now!"

Jeff began to chuckle. He watched as the man removed the wig and tossed it to the floor. Jeff released the grip on his .380 and raised both hands in a defenseless gesture.

"You piece of shit. Why I ought to end your worthless life right now. You're a waste of air you know that?"

"I wish you would. Just get it over with. I'll even reach behind my back so you'll have justification for your actions. What do you say? Want to see who's got the faster draw? Hell, I'm even giving you a head start."

"You move a damn inch, and I'm emptying this magazine right into your friggin face. Don't test me."

Jeff grinned big enough to show his teeth. He stared at the man long and hard. Another voice crackled over the radio. Footsteps could be heard pounding closer outside. Jeff made a break for it. Instead of going for the pistol on his right side, he went to the knife on his left. The man began firing on him. He had only gotten off two shots before Jeff managed to retrieve the blade and flick his wrist to send it sinking into the man's hip. The man yelped but kept firing. Jeff took two rounds. One to his right shoulder and one to his left elbow. He felt the bones shatter and fragment. Jeff dove to his right to hide on the other side of the bed. He reached behind him and gripped his pistol. He stood from his crouched position and took aim of the man. The man was doing the same to him. They both began to fire.

The room lit up in bright flashes.
The shots reverberated off the walls.

AGENT GIBSON POUNDED through the home, racing towards the bedroom. The SWAT team was just ahead of him. He heard the shots and seen the bedroom window light up as he rushed for the front door. The home was silent when they entered except for the booming voices and charging feet of the SWAT team and other officers.

They barged through the bedroom. Smoke hung in the air and the smell of gunpowder was so thick you could taste it. Someone flicked on the light. Blood spatter littered the walls. Gargled breathing came from the right. Agent Gibson looked down to find Detective Don James lying on his back with blood bubbling from his mouth. The SWAT team rushed past them and focused their attention on the other side of the bed where the suspect lay in his own pool of blood. After hearing them bark out commands, Agent Gibson heard one of the officers finally announce there was no pulse.

Gibson applied pressure to the wound in Don's chest and tried to soothe him as he called the others for help. Don locked eyes with Gibson and started trying to talk. Gibson leaned close.

"He's not...not..." more heavy and gargled breathing. "He's not...alone. Someone...someone...else."

Gibson pulled back and yelled out, "Secure the perimeter. Clear the house. Now!"

He felt Don clinch his arm. He looked back to the dying man. Don shook his head. Gibson squinted his eyes.

"Not here. An acq...uain...tance."

Gibson felt his heart drop at the word. How did Don know. Had the killer revealed something in his final moments?

Gibson watched the life fade from Don's eyes and felt him release the grip on his shirt. Don's labored breathing ceased, and he rested his head against the floor. His glazed eyes glared at the ceiling. Clotted blood leaked from his mouth.

Gibson cursed and rubbed a hand over his face before standing to his feet. It should have been him used as bait. He should never have listened to Don and let him take on such a risky mission at his age. Don had told Gibson he had less to lose. Gibson was the one with a wife and kids. Don was divorced with no kids. If one of the men were to die in this fight, Don had refused for it to be Gibson. He was proud to take on such a duty and absolutely refused the offer of anyone else. This was Don's job. He was the one who had brought them all into this and if anyone were to be taken out, it was going to be him.

Gibson shook his head as he recalled Don's words during the briefing only days before.

Paramedics rushed into the room and Gibson stood over them and watched as they tried to resuscitate the man. Gibson followed them out as they rushed Don away on a gurney with an oxygen bag over his bloodied face. Gibson road with him in the back of the ambulance. Don was pronounced dead before they even reached the hospital.

Gibson couldn't shake the last of Don's words.

Why did he think there was someone else?

What had the killer said to make him think that?

Three Months Later

INSIDE THE HOME where Jeffery Alan Edwards once lived, Jacob Hunter sits at a desk in the dark. His laptop is booted up and glows upon his face. It's just after two in the morning and he had one more item to list before calling it a night. He uploads the pictures, writes the description, and gives it a price. The item goes live. Jacob logs out of *Jake's Treasures* and turns off his laptop. He undresses and crawls beneath the covers fully nude. The pair of running shoes shouldn't take long to sell. He could hardly wait to get started. If he listened closely, he thought he could hear the spirit of Jeff's mother calling out from the basement, begging him not to pick up where Jeff had left off. Too late for that because things had already been put into motion. Jeff's contingency plan was laid out with perfect directions and Jacob was determined to follow them to the tee. He grinned at the thought.

An hour later, he heard his phone ping. He rolled over and checked it. The shoes had already sold. Some lady from Arkansas. Yes, the plan had been put into action and the universe was rewarding him for following Jeff's orders. He'd do his research in the morning. He'd never been to Arkansas. But there's a first for everything, right? He snickered and fell back to sleep with a long grin stretched across his face.

Somethings out There

As I grow older, I find myself questioning things I used not think twice about. Such as why dogs tend to only live for a dozen or so years, yet a dang turtle can live upwards of a dozen decades. I mean what the hell is up with that? I also have begun to wonder what this world will be like when my kids are grown. It's scary to think of, and I try not to but sometimes, damn it, I just can't help it. Kind of like I how I can't stop thinking of what happened to me and my cousin once when we were young. I've never really told anyone about it before, so I figured I'd write it all down and let you the reader decide for yourself. I've always been better at expressing myself through written words anyhow. I hope one day, when my children are grown and the world isn't quite what it used to be, that maybe they can come back to this story and get lost in a world that once was.

"MAKE SURE TO BRING your glove with you. I've been practicing my two seamer. You won't believe how much it moves now."

My cousin Matt had said over the phone.

We had both started playing baseball the year before. I mostly played second base or left field when I wasn't pitching. Matt was our short-stop and star pitcher. He was a hard throwing righty that kept hitters on their toes. I remember watching this one poor kid with tears running down his cheeks as he had trouble gripping the bat with his trembling hands. He struck out on three pitches of course. He swung at everything Matt threw and if he was lucky, he may have come within a foot of putting the barrel on the ball. I think he struck out on purpose just to get the at bat over with.

Me and Matt were more like brothers than cousins. We played baseball and basketball together and spent pretty much every weekend at one or another's house. We never once argued or fought. That's the Gods honest truth.

This one weekend though, I'll never forget.

It was my turn to spend the night at his house. I remember I couldn't wait to get home from school that Friday so I could pack and have my mom drive me over to Matt's place. We talked about our plans all week at school. We shared second and third period together and always sat with each other for lunch. We made plans to camp out in his backyard and tell ghost stories by the fire. Ride the four-wheeler in the field behind his house before going fishing at Mr. Gann's pond. It was stocked with bass and catfish the old man caught from the lake. We also talked about what scary movies we wanted to watch on the night we didn't sleep in the tent. We loved thrasher movies and creepy mysteries. Our favorites were Jeepers Creepers, The Mummy, Texas Chainsaw Massacre, and the like. I bet we watched those films over a dozen times a piece, but still got a start at each jump scare. We also loved watching Dumb and Dumber and The Nutty Professor. Our favorites were always the scary movies though.

As soon as my mom pulled in our driveway, I bolted out and raced to my room to finish packing. I had packed most of my stuff a few days before hand. I just had to add some fresh underwear, socks, and be sure I had my ball glove and that my tackle box was ready to go.

I made it over to my cousin's house late that afternoon and the first thing we did was throw the baseball. I remember it was early October some time because the leaves were just beginning to change colors and the fall weather was settling in. The days were mild and sometimes warm without a fall breeze, but the mornings and nights would often get down to low fifties or high forties.

As we tossed the ball back and forth, the leaves fluttered in the trees with a handful losing their grip and drifting in the wind. Birds sang over us, and two crows cawed from the ridge of the house.

"Hey, did I tell you about Jenna laughing at my joke the other day?" Matt asked as he caught my throw near his chest.

I shook my head, "No, but please tell me you didn't tell her the one about the looneys chanting numbers over the fence."

He smiled and threw back a two seamer that popped me right in the palm. I winced and shook away the sting.

"That's such a lame joke, dude. You can do better than that." I said as I returned the favor with a two seamer of my own. It didn't move as much as his, but he caught it in a bad spot too.

"What's wrong with it? You laughed when I told it to you?"

"I mean yeah, it's funny and all, but I thought you would have done better than that."

He started laughing at a thought I could see him channeling. He looked at the ball and fiddled with a grip before throwing one back near my ankles.

"What are you laughing at?"

"I'm just picturing the poor dude getting poked in the eyeball for being too nosey. I think there might be a life lesson in there somewhere."

I chuckled and said, "Yeah, don't stick your eyeball to a hole in a fence belonging to the insane asylum. Maybe you can do a speech when we graduate high school."

We both laughed and continued throwing the ball.

A half hour later, my aunt called us in for supper.

She had made Sloppy Joes and we licked our plates clean.

After supper we retreated to Matt's room and played a few games on the PlayStation. We liked football, baseball, and army games. After a few rounds of that we settled for popcorn and a scary movie. We started with Jeepers Creepers then switched to Chainsaw Massacre. It was probably halfway through the second movie that we both began drifting to sleep. We turned in for the night sometime around one o'clock. I remember hearing my uncle come home from second shift about an hour before falling asleep.

We woke up the next morning around seven-thirty to the tune of Matt's alarm. He had downloaded a whistling bomb sound effect without telling me and it nearly gave me a heart attack. I thought we had been nuked or something. He got a good belly laugh when I nearly scrambled out of bed. I gave him a frog on his arm for compensation.

The savory aroma of bacon and eggs hung in the air, and I could hear voices in the kitchen. My uncle loved to cook and always made the best bacon and egg sandwiches.

"What cha want to do today? Still want to ride the wheeler in the field? I can hook up the old canoe to it like last time." Matt said as he changed shirts.

I nodded, "Yeah that sounds fun. Maybe we could fish after that."

"Yeah, I got a new spinner bait I picked up last week when me and Dad went to Bass Pro. I've been dying to try it out ever since. I want to try that pond in the woods out there. Dad don't want us venturing that far, but I would bet my left nut there's some monster's over there."

"Boy, you crazy." I laughed before adding, "Why don't he want us over there? That's still part of Mr. Gann's land, isn't it?"

"I don't think so. I kind of think it might still belong to whoever lived in that old house on the hill over there."

"Oh. Well, who did live there?"

"I think it was Mr. Gann's Mama and Daddy's place, but I think his sister sold it after they died. That's why Mr. Gann hates his sister so much. Somehow, he says she sold it without his permission or something. Whoever bought it just sat on it and ended up letting it rot. I heard there was a hermit living in it at one time. That's why Dad don't want us over there, I guess. But I mean, he'd never know if we ventured over there, right?"

I tightened my lips and craned my head.

"We'll think about it then, won't we?"

"Yeah. Sure." I said.

After changing clothes with our backs to each other we made our way into the kitchen. Aunt Amy was leaning against the counter while flipping through a home décor magazine and talking about paint colors. Uncle Trace was busy scrambling eggs over the stove.

Aunt Amy looked up from the magazine as we came into view. She smiled and said, "Morning night owls. Y'all sleep good?"

I smiled and nodded.

Uncle Trace turned around and said, "Hey boy."

"Hey Uncle Trace."

"Figured y'all could use one of my bacon and egg sandwiches to start your day." He said with a big grin. His short black hair was spiked in the front as always. He wore a silver chain beneath his white t-shirt with a blue and white flannel long sleeve over that. It was tucked into his khaki cargo pants.

I always had such a good time over at Trace and Amy's. Me and Matt were always finding something to do. If by chance we ever got bored, Uncle Trace would often take us to the flea market or to Chimney Rock to look for arrowheads and try our luck at trout fishing. There was always something fun to do. It was never a dull moment when we were all together.

"Matt, we need to make sure you take your Lantus before y'all start playing. Probably need to go ahead and give it to you. Breakfast is almost ready anyway," Aunt Amy said to him as she sat the magazine down and reached into the fridge for a vile of liquid. A box of needles rested next to the fridge.

I remember we were at the flea market when Matt found out he was a juvenile diabetic. Uncle Trace is a bad diabetic himself, so when Matt couldn't stop going to the bathroom every fifteen minutes or so, Uncle Trace got suspicious. We first thought it was the Sundrops he'd drunk earlier that morning and quickly blamed it on those, but after Matt's fourth trip to the men's room in less than an hour, Uncle Trace knew something was wrong. We came home early that day and Uncle Trace brought out his sugar checker. He pricked Matt's finger, and the darned reader wouldn't read his sugar. They tried it again with another checker and got the same result. Aunt Amy hopped on the phone to call the doctor. The doc said they needed to get Matt to the hospital asap.

Once there, the doctors checked his sugar and found out it was in the low five hundreds and climbing. That was two years ago.

Amy finished giving him the shot. He rubbed his belly and stuck his tongue out at me when saw me watching. I laughed and turned to look out the sliding glass doors. Outside was a large back deck overlooking an in-ground pool and a fenced in yard. Beyond the fence was a thick grove of pines followed by cut fields. Four-wheeler trails snaked their way here and there, leading to the fields and fishing ponds of Mr. Gann's

I remember I still had a bad case of a poison oak rash behind my right knee. I caught myself scratching at it as I stared out the window at the woods. My mom had sent my prescription of prednisone with me, and I was to take it twice a day with a meal. I figured I'd take it with breakfast, then take it again with supper.

"How's your poison oak doing, James?" Aunt Amy had asked me as she noticed me scratching.

I'd popped a few crusty bumps and would later regret it. I looked up at her and said, "It's getting a little better. Still aggravates the snot out of me but not as bad as it did."

"That's good. Just try not to scratch it. I know it's easier said than done, but you'll only make it spread the more you scratch at it."

"I know. That's what Mama told me. I try not to, but sometimes I forget and just start going to town on it."

Matt said, "I told him if he had a dollar for every time he catches that stuff, he could retire before he finished high school."

We all shared a laugh at that. It was true though. All I had to do was look at a leaf of it and I'd catch it. Hell, sometimes all I had to do was think about it and it'd somehow start. I'm allergic to it now as an adult, but not near as bad.

"Alright folks, get it while it's hot." Uncle Trace announced as he shoveled the eggs onto a big plate. We each made our own bacon and eggs sandwiches. A rerun of Andy Griffith played over the small TV in the corner above the dining room table. We laughed and downed the delicious sandwiches.

"What you boys got planned for the day?" Aunt Amy asked as she tossed a braid of her blonde hair over a shoulder.

Me and Matt looked at each other.

Matt turned to her and said, "We'll probably ride the four-wheeler for a bit in the field. Might pull James around in the old canoe for a bit. Then I think we might fish some in Mr. Gann's pond."

Uncle Trace finished chewing, took a sip of coffee, cleared his throat, and said, "Just remember what I said now. I don't want you boys near that old house or the pond in the woods over there. Alright?"

We both nodded.

I wanted to ask why, but the way Uncle Traced had said it, I chose not to.

Shortly after breakfast, we were out in the building gassing up the four-wheeler. We spent the next three hours riding around in the field and taking turns pulling each other in the canoe. It was an old boat that Uncle Trace had got from a buddy years ago. We fished out of it for a while until Uncle Trace got the Jon boat. By then the canoe had gotten a big hole near the back of it, so me and Matt had the idea of cutting the back half off and using it as a makeshift sled during the last great snowstorm we had two years ago. We talked Uncle Trace into doing it, and we played with that thing ever since. We didn't need no snowstorm. We just tied it up to the back of the four-wheeler and drug each around the field with it.

I remember it was my turn to ride, and Matt had been pulling me around the field for a few minutes when he returned to the muddy trail for a stretch. I watched as he stood up and peered out ahead like he saw something. He slowed to a stop.

"What is it?" I asked but he didn't answer.

He eased up a little bit then started looking at something on the ground next to him.

"What is it?" I said again.

He didn't say anything, but only pointed at the ground.

I rose from having my legs crossed Indian style in the canoe and strode over for a better look.

In the mud before us were two footprints. Each had four toes and were at least two maybe three times the size of my own foot when I placed my boot next to them. I remember the hairs on my neck standing up and a sliver of goosebumps spreading over my flesh. I gulped and looked at Matt who only stared with wide eyes, not saying a word.

I glanced around the field as I had the sudden feeling we were being watched. By who or what I had no idea, but I could feel their eyes glaring into my soul.

Finally, Matt said something. "Oh, it's probably just that half retarded man staying out there in that old house."

"Don't say that."

"Why? Are you half retarded or something?"

I snickered and said, "No, but I think you are."

He made a funny face and crossed his eyes at me.

I shook my head and squatted down for a better look of the prints.

"I'll bet it's the old man. I heard he looks like the giant off the Goonies. I'll just bet that ole sucker only has four toes. He probably comes out here butt naked at midnight and chases the deer around."

I chuckled and said, "Shut up. You're crazy, you know that?"

"I'll bet my right nut it's the truth."

"You keep betting like that and pretty soon you ain't going to have no nuts."

We both got the giggles at that.

We brushed off the footprints and went back to what we were doing. An hour later we were ready to go fishing, so we headed back to the house for a quick lunch before packing our gear.

We loaded our rods and tackle boxes onto the four-wheeler and strapped down a cooler full of diet Sundrop and Cheerwine like we were real rednecks ready to raise hell. They were diet because regular soda would raise Matt's sugar too much. We also had to pack plenty of snacks in case his sugar decided to go the opposite direction and leave him feeling like a sack of taters. I always knew when his sugar wasn't right because he'd start acting funny. If it was high, he'd get all hyper and start talking crazy like some crack head outside a convenient store late at night. If it was low, like I said, he'd go limp like a sack of taters. He'd start acting tired and sleepy, and I'd know he needed a snack or something sweet to give him for the boost he needed.

After packing the four-wheeler, we went into Uncle Trace's building in search of a can to put worms in. Matt found an old Folger's Coffee can that only had a few screws and bolts in it. He dumped it out, and off we went to the chicken pen. That was always the best place to dig for worms. They had about a dozen chickens of all different kinds. Everything from Road Island Reds, Domineckers, and whatever the solid white ones are called.

We gathered our worms and headed back to the four-wheeler. Matt crunk it up, and we were on our way. We trudged along the trail through the pines before coming out to the field. He followed the path along the wood line, and within ten minutes we were at Mr. Gann's pond.

Matt tied on his new black skirted spinner bait while I tried my luck with a white floating worm. Within half an hour we had both caught two pretty good size bass a piece. We spent another hour without either of us getting a bite.

"I might try catfishing for a bit," Matt said as he walked down the bank towards me.

"Yeah, I think I'll do the same."

We fished for another hour or so, waiting for a big cat to strike but that moment never came.

Me and Matt sat on the bank with our fishing rods resting in y shaped branches we had jammed into the dirt. Mr. Gann's house sat in the distance behind us up on the hill. We were in the middle of talking about the hottest girls at school when we heard the man's tractor rev up. We turned around to see him backing out from beneath the lean to next to his barn. He spotted us and tipped his straw hat. We both smiled and waved back.

"I've always liked old Mr. Gann. He's a good feller." Matt said. "He showed me and my dad his gun collection once after he'd invited us over for oyster stew. Whew. You wouldn't believe the kind of guns that man has."

"Really? Like what?"

"Shoot. He's got everything from Civil War muskets, to single shot rifles from World War One to Garands and

Tommy Guns from the second World War. He has a whole room full of safes slap full of stuff."

"Wow, that's crazy."

"Yeah, it's wild. He promised to leave me and Dad a Garand and Wilson when he's gone. He also mentioned he'd leave us both a 1911 pistol."

"That's aweso—"

My words were cut short by the sound of something walking in the woods across the pond. Me and Matt both went silent and glared at the woods. Whatever it was, must've known we were watching because it never moved after that. I had the eerie feeling that even though I couldn't see it, it could see me. My mind flashed back to the footprints we found in the field.

"Aww it ain't nothing. Probably a deer." Matt said without much confidence in his voice.

"Right. Yeah, just a deer probably." I added while trying to sound tough.

"Fish ain't biting, you won't to call it day and head back before it gets much later?" Matt asks.

I nodded, "Yeah, sounds good."

We loaded up the four-wheeler and made it home just in time for supper. The whole ride back I struggled to rid the feeling we were being watched. I kept looking back behind us as I held onto the metal bars while Matt steered us home. I kept imagining something stepping out of the wood line and bolting after us. I told myself I had watched too many horror flicks and that things like that only happened in movies.

After supper, me and Matt went to Uncle Trace's building and dug out the tent. We made camp on the other side of the backyard fence. After setting the tent up, we gathered sticks and branches for our fire. Uncle Trace let us use some of the firewood he and Matt had stacked a week ago. We just needed some kindling to get things going. Aunt Amy gave us a bag of marshmallows.

As the sun set and darkness covered the earth, we found ourselves seated around the fire taking turns seeing who had the scariest ghost story.

I listened to Matt give his rendition of the man with a golden arm. He was in the middle of crying out in hoarse voice, "Where's my golden arm? Where's my golden arm?" when a branch snapped in the woods behind us. We both yelped and spun around.

The crickets got quiet and so did the cicadas singing from the trees. A gentle breeze whispered over the leaves. The clear sky gave way for the full moon's light. We stared at the wood line and did not dare make a sound. Slowly, the crickets and cicadas returned to their song. Me and Matt looked at each other for a moment. He smiled and said, "I'm telling you it's that crazy hermit that lives out there in Mr. Gann's old house. I heard he's even feral or something."

"But for real. What do you think those footprints belong to?"

"You mean *who* do they belong to? Not *what* do they belong to."

"You know what I meant."

"I don't know. That was weird. I mean who in the world would be out walking in a field barefoot like that?"

"Right. That's what I'm saying."

Matt tightened his lips and poked a stick around in the fire, sending embers heavenward.

"Dad's been acting kind of weird lately about not wanting us around that other pond. It's like he knows something."

I shifted on the log I was sitting on to give my left butt cheek a rest. I leaned forward and said, "What do you mean?"

"I don't know. It's just that over the last few weeks or so, he keeps pounding it into my brain not to go near that other pond and to stay away from the abandoned house."

"Do you think Mr. Gann may have told him to keep us away?"

Matt shrugged his shoulders, "Maybe. I don't know." He tossed the stick into the fire and stood to cross to the pile of logs. I watched him pick one up and place it on the fire as he said, "I kind of want to go over there to see what all the fuss is about."

"No. We can't do that. We'd get in trouble."

"Not if no one ever knew but us." Matt looked up at me and added, "I mean come on, how would anyone know if we never got caught?"

I looked down to find a rolly polly ambling around near my boot. I picked it up and watched it ball up in my palm.

Matt came over to me and took it out of my hand. He talked as he did so, "We sneak over there on the four-wheeler, have a quick look around, then head back the way we came." I watched as he took the last swig from his can of diet Sundrop before dropping the rolly polly inside.

"What are you doing?"

He didn't answer but just kept talking about the plot to sneak over to the pond. He placed the can at the side of the fire and squished it into the coals.

"There's a trail that goes in and out of there. We don't even have to go through the field. Less chance of being seen that way."

"How do you know about the trail?"

"I saw it with my dad one time when we were deer hunting out there. He warned me too not to go over there."

"I mean if he's warned you that much about it, there must be a good reason."

"Yeah, maybe that's where the old man stores his werewolf skins." Matt said and laughed.

"Like on that one Goosebumps episode?"

"Yeah, were the kid stays with his Aunt and Uncle and finds out they're werewolves."

Matt laughed, but I didn't.

"What are you doing with that can anyway?"

"You'll see. It should be about done."

Matt took hold of the top part of the can then dumped it out into his palm. A fried rolly polly tumbled out. Matt looked at me with a crooked grin before tossing the bug into his mouth. He pealed his lips back and made obnoxious crunching sounds as he stared at me with big, wild eyes.

"Hmm. Mmm. Nothing like a fresh fried rolly polly."

"You are a nut. You know that?"

We stayed up for another hour before our tired eyes betrayed us. After Matt peed on the fire, we crawled into the tent and snuggled into our sleeping bags.

I woke up in the middle of the night to the sound of crunching leaves. I jolted out of my bag and formed an L. Everything was still again. Other than Matt's snoring, it was eerily quiet. I listened for a good while, but never heard anything else move in the woods. The sounds of night returned, and I went back to sleep.

The next morning, we went inside and ate leftover bacon and eggs. Uncle Trace and Aunt Amy were still in the bed, so we did our best to be quiet. Being serious and quiet was hard for us because all we had to do was look at one another the wrong way and we'd enter a giggling fit. After a quick breakfast we went back outside and shot Matt's bow a few times. We practiced on a Styrofoam deer Uncle Trace had set up in the back yard. One of its antlers had fallen off to make it look like the dog from the Grinch.

After sending a dozen or more arrows down range, we grew bored and tried our luck at making a human sling shot. We took two big tree limbs, dropped them into holes we'd dug with Uncle Trace's posthole diggers, then took a bicycle inner tube and tied it on each pole. I think we may have gotten the idea from that Jackass show or something, but I can't rightly recall. We both tried it, but other than it giving us a good running start, neither of us took flight.

"You ready to go fishing?" I asked.

"Yeah. Let's go. I'm going to go tell Mom and Dad what we're doing. You can go ahead and gather some worms if you want to."

"Yeah, good idea. Do you remember what you did with the worm can?"

"Should be on the second shelf on the right in Dad's building."

"Cool."

I made my way into Uncle Trace's building and tried flicking a light on but had no luck. The bulb must've burned out or something. As I was combing through the darkness in search of the worm can I knocked something off a shelf. It fell onto the work bench with a loud clatter. It looked like a foot.

"What in the world?" I said as I leaned close for a better look.

It was a thick, white foot.

My eyes grew wide at the realization of what it was. I had seen one before on an episode of Monster Quest. It was a plaster cast of a footprint. It was way too big to be a man's. This thing would be almost twice the size of my dad's foot and he wore like a size twelve or something.

I heard Matt step inside as I turned the cast over in my hands and studied it.

"You find the worm can?" He called to me.

I answered with a question of my own.

"What the heck is this?"

I watched his jaw drop as he froze into place. He tried to say something but only stuttered.

"He must've hidden it behind something on the shelf. I knocked it down while looking for the worm can. Is this what I think it is?"

"Dude. No way."

"Maybe this is why your dad doesn't want us near that other pond."

"No. It's probably just something he bought off eBay. You know how he likes to buy odd things and antiques off there."

"But why was it hidden?"

"I don't know. Did you find the worm can?"

"Yeah, I got it right here."

"Alright, well let's get going. Dad said he might take us to the flea market later. And make sure you put that back where it was."

"Yeah, I'll try to."

I looked the cast over once more before returning it to the shelf. I thought about that thing the whole way to Mr. Gann's pond. Why did Uncle Trace have it in his building? Why was it hidden the way it was?

Matt parked the four-wheeler and hopped off.

"Hey, you alright? Space to ground patrol come in. Where you at dude?"

I shook my head and returned from my daze.

"Sorry, I was thinking."

Matt snickered and wagged his head, "I noticed."

I climbed off the wheeler and took up my fishing pole and tackle box.

"I can't stop thinking about your dad having that cast in his building like that. It's weird, isn't it?"

"Yeah, but so are your big ears."

"Oh hush. I'm being serious."

"Me too."

I punched his arm, and we made our way to the water's edge.

"What is it about that other pond? Is there something over there they don't want us to know about?" I said as I made a cast.

"Like what? A wild man with a big foot and humongous wiener?"

"I'm being for real. What if there's like a family of Sasquatches over there or something?"

"That'd be so cool. Like on Harry and the Henderson's?"

"Yeah. Something like that."

"Well let's head over and see then."

"What, right now?"

"Why not? You chicken?"

"No. I mean I just don't want to get in trouble that's all."

Matt hooked his spinner bait onto the middle eye of his rod and smiled, "How are we going to get in trouble if no one ever knows we're over there?"

I felt my heart pound hard behind my ribs as Matt drove the wheeler up and over a steep hill before aiming for the trail he'd talked about. In the far distance to my left, I could see the abandoned house sitting atop the hill. It glared down at us with its crooked shutters and flaking paint. I could see that part of the roof had caved in. There's no way anyone lived there. Matt had to just be pulling my leg. The house reminded me of something from the Chainsaw Massacre, and I half expected to see Leather Face himself come charging down the hill after us wielding a chain saw over his head. I shook the image away and tightened my grip on the metal bars. We disappeared into a thick grove of pines and snaked our way deeper into the woods. It got super dark as the sun was blocked out from all the growth. Pine needles littered our path as we crunched over pine combs and swatted away spider webs. Matt jerked the four-wheeler to a sudden halt and climbed off.

"What are you doing?" I asked as I watched him dart away as if searching for something.

He grabbed a branch and rushed back.

"This ought to do the trick." He said as he jammed the branch in place at the front of the four-wheeler. "You know how much I friggin hate spiders."

We continued onward. I had to adjust the fishing rods as my lure almost got caught on a limb. Matt hit a big stump that rattled us pretty good.

I heard him groan and grab his crotch, "Oh that didn't feel too good. I think I might be sterile for now on."

I laughed and shook my head.

As we traversed the narrow path, I kept my eyes peeled. I hadn't gotten the feeling of being watched yet, but the way this place looked, I knew it wouldn't be long before I did.

I could see the pond up ahead behind all the limbs. The trail finally opened up, and I watched a big Blue Heron walk along the bank before taking to the air. Matt turned the engine off in time to hear the Heron curse us out in that old grouchy voice they all have.

"Man. This place looks like paradise." Matt said with awe.

I was still skeptical. I kept turning around and checking over my shoulders to be sure nothing was creeping up behind us.

We grabbed our gear and headed down to the water's edge. There were a handful of dead trees standing around us. Matt made the comment that if the fish didn't bite at least we had plenty of trees to push over. That was something we enjoyed doing behind his house and we sometimes did it at Mr. Gann's pond if we got bored enough. We munched on granola bars and sipped on Capri Sun's that Matt had snuck along. He couldn't have more than one or they'd jack his sugar up. I was careful to keep a watch on what he ate and drank because the last thing I wanted was to have to carry his butt back to the house after he'd entered a diabetic coma.

We finished off our snacks and placed our trash in a pile near a stump. We'd clean up when were done. That's one thing I can say about us is we always left where we fished the same way we found it. Of course, that probably had much to do with that time our dad's got ticketed by the Game Wardens in Chimney Rock. We got caught tossing an empty corn can and Vienna sausage can into the creek. That's a tale for another day though. The moral of the story is I guess we learned our lesson.

We spent a good hour walking the banks, fishing for bass. Other than a few good bites and something big that Matt missed, we didn't catch a darn thing. While I made my way to the corner of the pond where a small stream filtered in, I noticed something in the mud along the bank. As I came closer, I could tell it was footprints. At first, I thought maybe Matt had wandered over here when I wasn't looking and had made the tracks, but when I looked closely, I noticed I didn't see any shoe tread. That's when I saw the toes. All four of them. The footprints meandered along before trudging out into the water and disappearing. Now mind you this is early fall, so the first thought that entered my mind was *Why in the world would someone be wandering around barefoot out here?* The second thought was, *Who the heck goes swimming in a pond when it's barely sixty degrees outside?*

I hollered at Matt and had him come take a look. He made another joke about the old man living in the abandoned house.

"I don't think no one lives up there. Did you not see how run down that place is?"

"No, not really. I was too busy driving I guess."

"These tracks are weird." I said as I retrieved my phone and snapped some pictures.

We had no luck in bass fishing, so as usual, we resorted to catfishing. I caught a bream, and we shared it for cut bait.

After clipping some bobbers between the eyes of our rods like the old carp fishermen do to know when they get a bite, and situating our rods in the crevice of Y branches, Matt said, "You want to push down some trees while we wait?"

I smiled and said, "Does a bear crap in the woods?"

We walked back up the bank towards the patch of dead pin oaks. I went one way and Matt went another. I found one I thought I could handle and gave it a good shake, keeping a check on the top of course. After a few good shoves it gave way, and I yelled out, "Timber!"

Matt cheered me on as he worked one of his own. I turned my back and went searching for another. I heard the tree crack and then heard Matt screaming for his life. When I turned around, I saw him high stepping through the woods as the big tree fell after him. It bit at his heels before slamming into the ground and breaking into pieces. How he managed to have that thing chase after him that way sure beats the hell out of me. How he outran it is even crazier. He was laughing and screaming like a caveman after having downed a buffalo.

I shook my head and couldn't help but laugh with him.

My laughing stopped at the sound of something grunting from the gulley next to me. I froze in place except for turning my head to look down at where the sound came from. Thick kudzu was spread out everywhere and it must've been a good twenty foot drop off the embankment. I heard movement below me. My pulse quickened and my mouth went dry. A horrible stench wafted into the air. It reminded me of a wet dog after it had just finished rolling in a cow patty. I began to gag.

Whatever was moving around in the kudzu let out a deep and guttural growl. The sound echoed among the pines. Matt stopped laughing. I turned and looked at him. He was like a statue and only stared at me with wide eyes. I motioned with my hand for him to crank the four-wheeler. I watched as he began taking calculated steps towards the ATV.

There was more movement down the hill. Whatever it was, was heavy. I could distinguish the sound of two big feet thumping onto the forest floor. My mind shot back to the tracks in the pond. I could visualize something big and hairy walking out into the pond for an evening swim.

That's probably why it stunk so bad. All that algae and crap had dried onto its fur.

It growled again and every hair on my body stood straight. That's when it bolted up the hill after me. It thrashed through the thicket and was racing towards me faster than I could blink. I made a break for the four-wheeler and heard Matt trying to crank it. The stupid thing sputtered and acted like it wanted to leave us for dead, but as I pounded closer it came to life. I could hear the monster grunting and tearing through the woods after me.

"C'mon! Hurry!" Matt screamed.

He stretched out his hand. I grabbed it and he helped sling me onto the seat behind him. He was already giving the wheeler gas before I was completely on board. I didn't dare look back because all I could imagine seeing was a huge, clawed hand reaching for my jugular. I wrapped my arms around Matt's waist and held on for dear life as he high tailed it out of there. One of my extra rods I'd brought along got its lure snagged in a tree limb. It peeled drag for a good twenty yards before snapping off. I didn't care. A lost fishing lure was the least of my worries at that point. A long trail of line flapped in the wind behind us as Matt aimed for the field. As creepy as that field always was, I'd never longed so much to be back. Anywhere but here in the thick pines with some angry beast thrashing after us.

We finally entered the clearing and Matt shifted into high gear as we bolted towards the hill where the house was instead of traveling along the trail near the wood line. It wasn't until we reached the top of the hill that I finally looked behind us. I patted Matt's gut and yelled for him to stop.

"What? Are you crazy?"

"No, it's alright. Stop for a second."

He did.

Down the hill from where we had just come, a large pine tree swayed side to side as if being shaken by a giant. Was it imitating what we were doing earlier?

"What in the world?" Matt said.

"Alright, that's enough. Let's get home."

He turned around and pushed us onward.

Uncle Trace was about to light a brush pile on fire when we came racing out of the woods to the backyard. Uncle Trace rose from flicking a lighter and looked at us with a hand shielding the sun.

He chuckled when he saw the fishing line trailing behind us. "Yeah, y'all got spooked didn't ya?"

We were both gasping for breath by that point and had trouble describing what had just happened.

"Slow down now. Are you hurt anywhere? Are you both alright?"

We nodded.

"Something...chase...chased us." Matt managed.

The smile disappeared from Uncle Trace's face.

"Matthew. Did you go to the other pond?"

Neither of us said anything.

Uncle Trace clenched his teeth and shook his head, "Boy, I told you not to go down there. Didn't I?"

"Yes sir."

"What happened?"

We did our best to recount the events, but of course it didn't sound as good out loud. You just had to be there to understand it all.

Uncle Trace listened carefully and studied us both with prying eyes. He scratched the back of his neck and said, "I don't want you going in the woods anymore without me." He looked up at us and added, "Is that understood?"

"Yes sir." We said together.

It got quiet among us as Uncle Trace seemed to consider whether he should tell us something or not.

"What is it, Uncle Trace?" I asked.

He swallowed and bit the inside of his jaw. He glanced around to be sure Aunt Amy wasn't listening.

He bent over and placed his hands to his knees. He motioned for us to come closer.

"Come here. This stays between us, okay?"

We both nodded.

"Mr. Gann told me something the other night. I haven't told anyone because I thought he was just pulling my leg like he likes to do. Plus, I think he may have had a little too much to drink. Anyway. Mr. Gann said he saw something the other day when he was cleaning up around the old house."

"You mean the abandoned house that belonged to his parents?" I asked.

Uncle Trace bobbed his head and said, "Yeah. He said he heard something scream down by that pond. When he looked up, he saw a pine tree swaying the way y'all did. Then he said he got to looking and could see something squatted near the wood line watching him. Said he thought it was a bear at first because of how big and dark it was. But he said he knew it wasn't a bear because it stood up and walked on two legs for a good thirty yards before disappearing into the woods. Now he said the whole time he was watching this thing, that pine tree kept swaying."

"There's more than one." Matt said with wonder.

"Exactly."

Uncle Trace's words hung in the air for a moment before he added, "So. That said. I don't want you in the woods anymore without me, okay?"

He didn't have to say it twice. The message was delivered and received.

"And let's keep this between us like I said, alright?"

That was some twenty years ago, and until now, I've kept that promise. The only reason I decided to write this story was because I wanted my kids and grandkids to be able to read it one day. Ever since that day by the pond I've been hesitant about venturing too far into the woods. Nowadays, I never go past the wood line without a gun. If you'd encountered what me and my cousin did that day, I think you'd probably be the same way. You just never know what's lurking in the woods with you.

I know some people who think the woods are like a Disney cartoon, full of Bambi's and Thumpers. I'm not that naïve because I know without a shadow of a doubt . . . somethings out there.

Lie Bumps

Georgetown, SC

1965

Doug Clemmons drove his red Chevy Impala along the dirt road. He grimaced at the sound of rocks pinging off the under carriage. He glanced in the rearview mirror and saw a thick dust trail as he angled his way towards the prospect's home. If he'd known they lived on such a long dirt road, he'd have waited about shining the tires. All that work he'd put into cleaning the car over the weekend would be for nothing after he left this place. Doug shifted his eyes to himself and extended his tongue. The bump was still there. He rolled his tongue over his bottom right canine. A flash of hot pain flared, and he winced. His mind travelled back to the last time he'd seen the dentist. It must've been some twenty years ago when he had his wisdom teeth removed. That was an experience he'd prefer to forget. He'd promised himself he'd never visit a dentist again. But does a dentist deal with tongue bumps? He thought about it for a minute before shrugging and picking his nose.

The road began to snake to the right as an immense cornfield came into view. A scarecrow hung like Christ in the center. Only it wore a potato sack on its head rather than a crown of thorns. Beyond the field, Doug took in the farmer's home. It was a large white, plantation style home with a weathered wrap around porch. The white paint had flaked in multiple spots along the shake siding. A big red barn was to the left with a green tractor parked inside. An old man and woman sat in rocking chairs on the front porch. The scene reminded him of something Norman Rockwell would enjoy looking at.

He eased his Impala into the driveway and passed their leaning mailbox as he did so. The farmer sipped on a glass of tea and offered a nod and wave. Doug returned the gesture and turned down the Elvis tune playing over his radio. He shifted into park and killed the engine. His bulky briefcase full of cookware was stationed in the back seat along with all the sales pamphlets and order forms. Doug stepped out of his vehicle and retrieved what he needed before crossing to the steps of the porch.

"How you do Mr. and Mrs. Wilson?"

Mr. Wilson narrowed his eyes and drew a breath as he sized Doug up from top to bottom. He cleared his throat and sat his glass of tea down on the table next to him.

"Wasn't sure you'd come out here after our last discussion."

"Well, Mr. Wilson, I'm a man of my word. Here I am." Doug said with a smile and ta da motion of his arms.

He looked to Mrs. Wilson whose eyes were glued to the briefcase like a kid staring at a lollipop. Doug grinned and said, "It's a beautiful day out, isn't it?" He didn't wait for an answer but gave his attention to the tractor out in the barn. "That John Deere you have out there, is that a Waterloo Boy?"

"It sure is. I see you know your tractors."

Doug smiled and grunted, "My grandfather had one just like it. His was a 1923 model I believe. I had a toy of it when I was a kid. It's in my office now as we speak."

The effort to build rapport seemed to work as he could see Mr. Wilsons eyes soften just a bit.

"Well, I don't want to hold you any longer than needed. How today is going to go is I'm going to ask a few more questions to get to know more about your situation. After that, I'll explain the different products we offer and how we do business here at Arthur's Cookware and what makes us different. At the end of all that, if I feel we are a good fit for one another and that our products can be beneficial to you, I'll extend an offer for us to do business together. All I need from you at that point is a simple yes or no. Sound fair enough?"

He received blank glares from the old man and woman.

Doug held the silence and forced the old man to finally answer.

"You said something like that last time."

"Yes sir, but you didn't let me finish. If you recall, you stopped me short when you said you were going to your truck to get your scatter gun."

Mrs. Wilson grinned and said, "He didn't mean nothing by it. It's just we've dealt with so many travelling salesmen who just try to take our money. We've seen everything from vacuums, Bibles, television sets, life insurance, you name it. We figured you were just another slimy salesman looking to take advantage of the elderly."

"Well, I can certainly understand why you would feel that way. You are not the only folks I've come across who have felt the same way. But what I have found is that most of them have never encountered a professional salesman who was not trying to sell them anything, but simply offering a solution to the problem they face. My obligation and duty isn't to get you to buy but to help you solve the problem of over spending on less than par cookware. If I could show you a way to save time, energy, and money by getting a great deal on a set of cookware that will be guaranteed to last five times longer than what you currently own, is that something you would be interested in?"

Mrs. Wilson looks at her husband, and they hold eyes for a moment. The two look back at him and the old man says, "If I find out you're just yanking our chains, I'll have my scatter gun pointed at your chest faster than you Yankee boy can say you all. That understood?"

Doug says with a smile, "I'm actually born and raised here in good ole South Carolina, sir. I don't say you all, I say y'all. But yes, that is understood."

"Well, you sure don't seem like it to me."

"Do you mind if we talk in the kitchen for a few minutes?"

The old man dug at some wax in his ear and studied the specimen on his fingertips for a second before answering.

"Bertha, you may want to put some coffee on. I have a sneaking suspicion this'll take more than a few minutes."

"I assure you both it won't take anymore time than necessary."

With that, the Wilsons rose from their rockers and headed for the front door. The old man opened and held the door for his wife. He motioned for Doug to follow.

"Name's Frank by the way. Wife's is Bertha May, but everyone calls her Bertha. You don't have to call us Mr. and Mrs. and all that fancy bullshit." Frank said while holding the screen door open.

Doug nodded and stepped inside with his briefcase.

A victrola played a Buck Owens record somewhere in the shadows. The faint aroma of sweet bread wafted through the air. A curved staircase spiraled to the left. An office door was off the bottom of the stairs. Straight ahead was the kitchen. To the right was the dining room. Buck Owens grew louder as they entered the kitchen. Off from the kitchen was the living area with a sofa, recliner, Magnavox Console TV with wood trim, and the source of the music. A hip height Victrola with horn and crank sat against the wall next to the television. Doug smiled as it reminded him of the one his mother owned. She loved to play Elvis and Chuck Berry on it. Their house was always rocking.

Doug pulled himself from the memory and fixed his eyes on the bar in the kitchen. He raised his briefcase and angled his chin, "May I?"

"Oh yes. Go ahead. Here let me move this pan out of your way." Bertha said as she cleaned off the area.

Doug placed his briefcase atop the bar and popped the locks. He opened it carefully as if it contained a million dollars. Bertha looked on with eager anticipation. He laid the lid back and let the sparkling pots and pans and silverware do their talking. He withdrew the flyers and pamphlets and began his sales presentation.

A half hour later, they'd retreated to the living area for coffee. An hour afterwards and four cups of coffee deep, Doug had convinced Bertha her need for his pots and pans. Frank on the other hand needed a little more selling to. Bertha tugged on his arm and pointed out all the features and qualities that Doug had presented. Frank only sat there chewing on a toothpick, not saying a word. He drilled his steely blue eyes into Doug's soul and prodded.

"We can't afford it. Your prices are too high. Simple as that."

Bertha groaned. "Oh Frank. Don't be like that."

Yeah. Don't be like that Frank. Doug thought.

"Okay. I hear what you're saying but let me ask you this, Frank. Is it price or cost that you're concerned about?"

Frank arched his brows.

Doug looked at Bertha and asked, "Miss Bertha, how many sets of cookware would you say you have purchased in the last five years?"

She chuckled and looked at the floor, "Oh goodness. I'd say half a dozen maybe. I pretty much buy a new set each year because that's about all the life I get out of 'em. I use 'em every day, so they wear out pretty quick."

"Uh huh. And how much would you say you paid for each set?"

"I don't know. Maybe twenty or thirty? Something like that."

"So would you agree then that over the course of the last five years, you've likely already spent a hundred to a hundred and fifty dollars on cookware?"

Bertha looked at Frank then at Doug. She nodded and said, "Yeah, that sounds about right."

"Okay, so based on what you're telling me, I'd say you're focusing on the price of my product when you should be focusing on the cost of my product."

"What's that supposed to mean?" Frank asked with an edge in his voice.

"The price of my product is thirty-nine ninety-nine. Which is higher than what you usually pay for your cookware, would you agree?"

They both nodded.

"However, the cost of my product is much less than what you have already spent in the last five years on your cookware."

"How is that?" Frank asked.

"Because our cookware comes with a five-year guarantee or your money back. So basically, by purchasing my cookware, yes, you may pay a little extra on the price today, but the long-term costs of my cookware are far less expensive than what you are currently spending. Does that idea make sense to you?"

They only stared at him.

"The way I see it. You have two choices. You can continue buying a new set of cookware each year or you can pay an extra ten to twenty dollars now but save yourselves roughly a hundred dollars over the next five years. You catch my drift?"

"Hmph. But how do I know you're not lying about how long those pots and pans last?"

"Well...let me show something Frank." Doug said as he opened up his blazer and dug into his inner pocket. He pulled out a folded stack of paper. On the eight by eleven sheets were the handwritten testimonials of past clients. He opened the papers and sat them down on the coffee table before smoothing out the center crease.

"Take a minute to read over these reviews. I'm going to excuse myself to the restroom if you don't mind."

"Go right ahead honey. It's down the hall. First door on your right."

"Thank you. I won't be just a moment."

Frank held the papers in front of him and looked down his nose through his coke bottle glasses.

"Now hold up a second partner. How do I know you didn't just write all this shit up this morning? How do I know these are real people?"

"Well Frank, I have their telephone numbers right there. You are more than welcome to give them a call. I'm sure they'll be happy to speak with you."

Frank tightened his lips and fixed his eyes on Doug.

"There's a few farmers on that list too. I'm sure you'll have lots to talk about. Please excuse me for a moment."

Doug left the room and wiped his brow. The bump on his tongue pounded like a thumb struck by a hammer. He reached the bathroom and locked the door. He looked in the mirror and stretched out his tongue. The bump had grown to the size of a steel bb. It was red with a white center and hot with fever. He gently touched it with his finger and sucked in air through his teeth as a flash of pain spread across his tongue.

Damn it.

A tear welled in the corner of his eye, and he drew a deep breath.

He pulled away from the mirror and undid his fly. His bladder thanked him for the kind gesture, and he flushed and lowered the seat when he was finished.

As he made his way back down the hall, he heard Frank speaking to someone on the phone. He'd entered the kitchen and stood by the landline attached to the wall.

The old doubtful rascal.

Doug smiled as he passed him.

Frank only glared as he questioned the person on the other line about the legitimacy of Doug's cookware.

Doug sat across from Bertha who was busy looking over the pots and pans.

"Do you have any questions for me at this point, Miss Bertha?"

He watched her give his question some thought before looking up at him and saying, "You know, come to think of it, I do."

"Hit me."

"I see here it says thirty-nine ninety-nine including shipping and handling."

"Uh huh."

"What if I buy this exact set from you? Wouldn't that save the shipping and handling cost?"

He heard Frank hang up the telephone before making his way back from the kitchen.

Doug cleared his throat and adjusted in his seat. He wiped his leg as if swiping off a crumb.

"Well now, that is certainly a possibility Bertha. However, you had told me earlier you wanted this cookware set in pearl white. Are you sure you would prefer the sterling silver over the pearl?"

She looked at Frank then at the cookware.

"What y'all talking about?" Frank asked.

"Bertha here was trying to shave off the shipping and handling charge by settling for my model here rather than the pearl white as she originally wanted."

Frank grunted, "Makes no difference to me as long as the food tastes the same. Would be nice to save a few bucks though if it's possible, I reckon."

The shipping and handling charge Bertha was trying to save was actually where a large portion of Doug's commission stemmed from. It would be a cold day in hell before he reduced his commission like that. If she wanted his display model, then by golly she can have it. The extra chunk of his commission would be a different story. If this was the route she wanted to go, he'd offer to let her have it for half down and the other half due next month. Of course, she would still be charged the shipping and handling fee. Only it would be labeled as a sneaky little interest charge. Bertha gets her cookware. Doug gets his full commission. Tada and abracadabra.

"I tell you folks what...I'll let you have the cookware today for half down. You try it out for thirty days and if you're not completely satisfied, you get your money back. But since I know that won't be the case, we can go ahead and set you up on a payment plan for the other payment which will be due exactly thirty days from now. If you want to cancel, give me a call, I rip up the agreement and will pick up the cookware the same day. Sound fair enough?"

The two looked at each other for a long moment.

Realizing defeat, Frank turned away and huffed.

Bertha looked at Doug and said with a wide grin, "Deal."

They forgot to ask how much the second payment would be.

Doug was out the door and on his way to Charleston before it ever crossed their minds. He crunk up a Muddy Waters song and cruised the interstate for his next appointment. All the while his tongue throbbed like the devil. He was beginning to wonder if a spider had snuck into his mouth last night and stole a bite or something. When he exited the interstate and came to a stop sign, he glanced at himself in the mirror. His heart knocked when he noticed another red bump festering beside the first one.

He cursed and growled.

He had gotten the pestering rascals before but never this bad. This time around was like a hornet had been given free range to roam about his tongue, poking here and there whenever he pleased.

He went through the four way stop and continued towards Main St. His stomach begged for feeding, so when he caught sight of the drive-in diner with a big rotating burger above it, he couldn't resist.

He gave his order to the cute blonde and returned to checking his tongue in the mirror. He had the sudden feeling of being watched. He turned to find an old man and woman staring from the car next to him.

He smiled and shrugged his shoulder, "Doc said it may be rabies."

The man scowled and looked away.

Doug chuckled and went back to examining the bumps. They seemed bigger now than when he was at the stop sign only half hour ago.

What in the hell is happening?

He tried mashing the bumps between his fingers like he was popping a pimple, but the pain was extraordinary. He wiped a tear leaking from the corner of his eye and growled as he pulled away from the mirror.

He rested his arm on the window seal and waited for his burger. The Beach Boys sang *Help me, Rhonda* over the outdoor speakers. The girl comes back with his food. He has to eat on one side of his mouth to avoid the bumps on his tongue. He finishes up and throws his trash away. He sits back into his seat and heads for the interstate. An hour later he'd reached a small, country town by the name of Huger. His prospect, Eileen Fuller, was a seventy-year-old lady who had called the cookware ad in the paper two days prior. After taking a few side roads from town, Doug found himself travelling down a long, narrow road with live oaks on either side. The Spanish Moss hanging over the road looked like melted skin dripping from the tree branches. Doug counted two houses in the last ten minutes along the road. One looked abandoned, the other looked like it was well on its way.

He approached a sharp left curve. Straightening out of it, a white mobile home came into view. It sat on the right-hand side near the road. There was no underpinning so the concrete blocks it sat on were visible. It had red shutters and a red porch. An old 40's model Ford was tucked away to the side within a tall patch of grass and weeds. Free ranging chickens roamed about, pecking at the ground. Three young children with dirt-stained clothes ran with a stick and wheel from around the corner of the home. The youngest of them stopped when she noticed Doug's car. The little girl stared at him as he passed. Her blonde hair was matted with more tangles than a bird nest and Doug even saw leaves and sticks intertwined in it. The two boys, who must've been her older brothers, stopped and looked at Doug. Their faces were caked with dirt and their heads were shaved down to the scalp to likely protect against lice. Doug smiled and offered a wave. The kids didn't return the gesture but only glared at him as he passed.

Doug craned his head and chuckled.

He drove for another few minutes without seeing anyone else. In the distance he noticed a mailbox with the numbers 1313 on it. It leaned too far to one side and all it would take was a stiff breeze to blow it over. A gravel road rested next to it. Doug checked his paperwork to verify the address.

"1313 Maw Die Road. That's the one." He said as he turned down the radio. The road transitioned from dirt to gravel as his tires crunched over the rock. The road descended a little ways before a blue, single story home came into view. A large pond with a dock and gazebo sat to the right of the house. Glass bottles were fixed on the branches of small trees in the front yard. Doug pulled in behind a yellow Volkswagen Beetle. Windchimes and dreamcatchers were scattered about the porch. Various sorts of flowers and rose bushes lined the perimeter of the home. Multicolored stones were placed here and there. Two cats scurried off the porch when he shifted to park.

Doug grabbed his briefcase and exited the Impala. The abundance of windchimes was unsettling for a moment. Something about this place was giving him the willies. It was like the air was heavier here or something. He could feel it pressing down upon his shoulders. He also had the feeling of being watched. He stood next to his car and took in his surroundings. Satisfied there were no prying eyes, he made his way to the front door.

Doug adjusted his tie and cleared his throat. As he was inches from knocking on the door, it opened. The suddenness of it gave him a start. He stepped back and watched as Eileen Fuller came into view. An aroma of burning herbs filled his senses. Eileen was a petite lady, and the hump on her back made her appear even smaller. She smiled to reveal a plethora of missing teeth. The teeth she did manage to have looked rotten. The wart on the tip of her nose had a hair in it and the sight almost made Doug gag.

As if her appearance wasn't bad enough, her raspy, cadaver-like voice sent chills down Doug's spine. He gulped and eyed her carefully as she said, "Why hello there. You must be the cookware salesman. Mr. Clemmons is it? Or should I just call you Doug?"

"Doug is fine." He said though he couldn't recall telling her his last name.

"Well step inside and have a seat. Would you care for a cup of coffee, dear? It's fresh. I ground the beans this morning."

"If it's not too much trouble. That would be great. Thank you."

"No problem at all. You have a seat there, and I'll fetch the coffee."

He watched her waddle towards the kitchen. Her colorful dress almost dragged the ground behind her. He stood there with his briefcase and studied the home for a moment. He found the source of the strong aroma. A bundle of what must've been sage rested on an end table with the end smoldering over a glass bowl. Rocks and crystals were scattered everywhere he looked. He crossed to the couch with its floral pattern and sat down. He moved some crystals and figurines to make room for his briefcase. As he prepared his presentation, he heard Eileen coming back from the kitchen. She was carrying a metal tray and the saucers and mugs rattled loudly.

"Here. Let me help you with that."

Doug stood to assist, but she swatted him away.

"I may look old and feeble, but I can get around better than you think." She said as she sat the tray down next to his briefcase. "There's cream and sugar there if you like."

"Thank you, ma'am."

Doug took a cup and added some cream.

He had second thoughts of drinking the coffee as something about all of this reminded him of Hansel and Gretel. He fought to hold back the grin trying to spread across his face. He sipped the coffee, and a searing pain caused him to grimace when the hot liquid touched his tongue. It was like sticking his tongue into a flame.

"What's the matter my dear?" Eileen asked as she held her mug up about to take a drink herself.

Doug shook his head and grit his teeth.

"You have a bad tooth or something?"

"No. It's these damn bumps on my tongue. Pardon my language ma'am."

"No need for apology. I've heard worse. May I see?"

"Oh, it's nothing."

"You sure didn't act like it was nothing. Come here and let me look."

Feeling like a kid showing his grandma his new boo boo, Doug rose from the couch and bent at the waste in front of Eileen. He stuck out his tongue and let her look.

He watched a crooked grin slowly appear. She began to chuckle.

"Yup. You're a liar alright. That there's proof enough."

He repulsed from her as if slapped across the face. "Do what?"

She looked away and took up her coffee again. "I said you're a liar. Those are lie bumps. Shouldn't be all that surprising considering your profession and all."

Doug stood there with his hands to his hips, searching for a comeback.

"Oh, sit down. Don't get your panties all bunched up."

"Lady, I'm not going to stand here and take these insults. Now, if you'll excuse me, I'm going to gather my things and be on my way."

"Suit yourself. Those bumps won't get any better though. Not without the property remedy. You've done said one too many lies for them just to disappear on their own."

"You're crazy. You know that?" Doug said as he shut his briefcase and clamped the latches. He angled for the door and said, "Thank you for the coffee."

"I can make those bumps go away." The old lady said as he was stepping through the door frame.

Doug paused and stood there with his back to her.

"It'll be like they were never there in the first place."

He turned around to face her.

"Yeah? How's that?"

"Come here and I'll show you."

He breathed deep and studied her for a moment. Giving in, he sat his briefcase down and shut the door.

"That's the spirit. Now, if it's to work, you have to do exactly as I say? Understood?"

"What are you some kind of witch?"

"Not exactly. Now sit down and listen closely."

"If you start communicating with the dead or talking about sacrifices, I'm outta here."

"Oh shut up. I've done told you I'm not a damn witch, okay?"

"Then what are you?"

"Don't worry about it. Do you want to get rid of the bumps or not?"

He narrowed his gaze and sighed.

"Very well. Do you carry a pocketknife?"

"Yeah, why?"

"We'll need it."

"For what?"

She held out her hand and tightened her lips.

He dug in his pocket and placed the knife in her hand.

"Are you left-handed or right-handed?"

"I'm a lefty why?"

"Then you'll need to take this knife and cut a line across your right palm. You'll need to follow the line that runs from the base of your pointer finger all the way down to your wrist below the meaty part of your thumb." She held up her own palm and ran a finger across the line to demonstrate.

"Are you crazy? I'm not cutting myself."

"Well, that's certainly your prerogative, but the bumps will stay until you do as I tell you. It's your choice."

He thought it over for a minute.

"What's after that?"

"I'll tell you once you complete the first step."

They held each other's gaze.

Doug scooted to the edge of his seat and unfolded the blade. He held out his right palm and sank the tip of the knife at the beginning of the line below his pointer as she had said. He squinted and scrunched his nose as he drug the blade across his palm. Blood began to ooze. He reached the bottom of his palm and let out a quick breath. "Now what?"

"Sit the knife down. Take your left hand and rub it in the blood. Then cross your left index and middle fingers thirty times. Each time you do so, say *truth for lies. Truth for lies.* Do it now."

He followed her orders.

After the thirtieth time, he looked up at her and asked, "Now what?"

"Now, you don't lie for thirty days. You should notice the bumps going away by tonight. But remember, you cannot lie for thirty days. It's an oath."

"What happens if I do?"

"You don't want to know."

A FEW WEEKS had passed and true to her word, the bumps on Doug's tongue had disappeared by the time he was ready for bed that night. He has been careful ever since not to fib. However, he may have backslidden this morning. He was meeting with an older couple who reminded him a lot of Frank and Bertha. The wife decided she liked the display cookware and like Bertha, the lady asked if she could save a few bucks on shipping by taking the display. Doug chose his words carefully and it wasn't until he was almost out the door that the old lady began her bombardment of questions. He eventually caved into his carnal ways and told a little white lie. It wasn't a big lie, but it was a lie none the less. Sweat beads broke out on his forehead and he felt a lump form in his throat. The lady had the answers she wanted, and Doug was out the door. He checked his tongue in the mirror as soon as he shut the car door. Nothing had happened.

Yet.

By the time the sun had set, he had that familiar pain flash across his tongue when he took his first bite of supper at the diner. The meatloaf looked so savory and had his mouth watering the second he spotted it on the menu. He'd ordered a side of green beans and mashed potatoes to go with it. Except for a lonely looking old man in overalls and a young courting couple, Doug was the only customer. He cursed when the meatloaf hit his tastebuds. He shut his eyes and wiggled his tongue behind his teeth. A moment later the waitress came over and asked if everything was alright. He told her it was and almost lied to say it was a toothache but caught himself and said he would be okay.

The waitress went into a long story about getting her wisdom teeth removed once and how the dentist had messed her jaw up in the process. Said her jaw clicked for three years after the surgery and it felt like an evil fairy was chiseling on bone every time she chewed or talked.

Doug glared up at her.

"Can I get you anything?"

"I'm good, thanks."

She left and vanished into the kitchen.

Doug looked around the diner at the other customers. They dropped their heads and went back to what they were doing.

Doug stuck his tongue out and felt it with his finger and thumb.

"Dear God." He mumbled.

How had he not felt the huge knot on his tongue? It was five times larger than before. Now that it had been brought to his attention, he could feel it throbbing up against his bottom row of teeth. It had a pulse and with each pump it sent a shockwave of pain. Doug breathed deep and steadied himself. He went back to his meal and was sure to chew on the opposite side. It still hurt like the devil, but his empty stomach pushed him onward.

He finished his supper and left three dollars on the table which would be enough for a about a dollar tip he supposed. He made it back to his car and drove to the motel in Georgetown.

Once there, he tossed his briefcase on the bed and locked the door. He then marched to the bathroom, flicked on the light, and shoved his face in the mirror. He stretched out his tongue and looked in horror as the pulsing bump had grown even larger just since he left the diner. It had spread to cover the entire right front corner of his tongue. It was a feverish red again with a white center to it. He grinded his molars and growled before searching for something to pop it with. He combed through all the drawers, checked the cabinet behind the mirror, but all he could find was a pair of scissors. His heart skipped a beat at the thought of using them.

He cursed aloud. His words were garbled. He cursed again, "I can't eve tock right."

He went back to the bed where his suitcase rested. He dug through it for several minutes before finally coming up with a safety pin tucked away in a side pocket. He went back to the mirror and retrieved his lighter. He held the needle over the flame until it was red. Doug swallowed hard as he took turns looking at the needle and his growing tongue. He smacked his cheek and beat his chest in an effort to gain the courage. He leaned into the mirror and sank the needle into the bulging bump, half expecting it to explode on impact. It didn't. He screamed in agony and forced himself to dig into it, hoping he could dig out the worm like you would a white head. It wasn't working. Blood trickled out and he spit into the sink. The throbbing pain was excruciating. He sat the needle down and placed both hands on the counter. He scratched his cheek and looked down at the pair of scissors on the sink.

"No. Top it Doog."

The scissors were pulling his hand like a magnet. Before he had time to think it over, he had gripped the scissors with his left hand and was pulling out his tongue with his right. It reminded him of a man about to chop the head off a snapping turtle for stew. He'd watched his grandpa and uncles do it before. They'd take hold of the head, stretch it on a log, and whack it right off. His tongue began to writhe as he felt the muscle squirm with anticipation of what was coming. He brought the scissors up to his mouth. He began to moan as he squinted his eyes. Just as he was guiding the tip of his tongue in between the blades, a sharp hiss filled the room. In his horror, he saw something in the mirror that sent a shock jolting through his body. His tongue had split into two and slithered out to touch the mirror. A dark shadow passed behind his shoulder. Doug slammed his eyes shut, ceased up, and squeezed the scissors.

He heard something plop into the sink. He felt warm liquid flood his mouth. He couldn't taste anything, but he could sure feel everything. He screamed again and flashed open his eyes. He looked down to find a squirming piece of bloody tongue wriggling in the sink. It reminded him of a snake with its head chopped off.

"Oh, me Gawd." He somehow managed.

He looked in the mirror. He was a mess. Blood was gushing down his neck and soaking his shirt and blazer. He cursed and grabbed a towel.

His mind flashed to the first aid kit he kept in his car. With the whole corner of a towel stuffed in his mouth, he raced outside and grabbed the first aid kit beneath the passenger seat.

An older fellow with a bear gut and long beard stopped from climbing into his truck to see what all the fuss was about.

"You okay mister?"

Doug looked up with the towel still stuffed in his mouth and waved the man off.

"Suit yourself, you crazy bastard." The old man said before getting into his truck.

Doug rushed back inside with the kit and flung it open. Tape and band aids went flying across the bed. Doug found the gauze and began unrolling it. He took it back to the bathroom and proceeded to wrap his tongue with it until it looked like a nub from a bombing victim. It was so big he couldn't close his mouth all the way.

Gasping for breath, he stepped out of the bathroom and fell on the corner of the bed. He ran a hand through his hair and scratched his head. One thought shouted in the forefront of his mind. He had to go see Eileen. She would know what to do.

A little over an hour later, Doug found himself turning down her gravel road. It was just after nine o'clock when he knocked on her door. The property was dark, and he feared she had already turned in for the night. He had a sudden vision of her stepping out and clutching a double barrel shotgun.

"Ilean. It's me, Doog. I ned you helt." He added as he continued to knock.

"I'm coming."

He heard her patter across the hardwood floor. He stepped back from the door and watched it open.

A crooked grin stretched her wrinkled face.

He furrowed his brows at her and said with a mumble, "What so funny?"

"I knew you would be back."

She waved him inside and motioned towards the couch, "Sit right there, I'll be back."

He did as he was told and waited for her. He could feel a pulse in his tongue as it throbbed with each beat. Nausea began to form as he fought back the pain.

He heard Eileen coming down the hall.

She carried a granite bowl and pestle in one hand and a bunch of herbs and flowers in the other. She had a roll of gauze tape tucked under her arm.

"What's zat?"

"Don't worry about it. How much did you cut off?"

Doug held out his thumb and forefinger, keeping them about three inches apart.

"That much, huh?"

He nodded.

"Did you see the serpents tongue?"

He got quiet and only looked at her. He felt his heart knock hard at the thought of what happened at the motel. He swallowed hard.

"I take that as a yes. What about a shadow? Did you see any shadows?"

He nodded slowly.

Eileen sighed and shook her head.

"I told you not to lie for thirty days. You asked what would happen if you did...well now you know."

Eileen placed some herbs and flower petals into the bowl and began to grind them into a paste with the pestle. She spent a good ten minutes or so mashing everything together.

When she was finished, she sat the bowl aside and looked up at Doug.

"You can take the bandage off now."

He blinked.

"Go on. I'll give you a new one."

He huffed out a breath and began to unravel it. He grimaced as it got closer to the end.

Eileen whistled and said, "My word, you really did a number on that thing didn't you? What did you use, a pair of shears? Goodness gracious."

"Just git on wit it."

"Well alright then. It might hurt a little at first, but you'll heal pretty quick. That is, as long as you don't tell anymore lies." She lowered her chin at him and raised her brows.

He shook his head and said, "No mo."

She chuckled.

She balled up the herb paste and told him to stick his tongue out. He did and she plopped the paste where the missing meat was. He jerked back and yelped.

"Easy now. Keep your tongue out so I can wrap it."

Tears were running down his cheeks.

She finished with the gauze and sat back in her recliner.

"There. All finished. See I told you it wouldn't hurt for long. My guess is you'll be all healed up in a few days. But remember what I said, no lying. Right?"

He nodded.

"What are you looking at me like that for?" She asked him.

He held out his hands, palms up as if asking for an explanation.

"Look. I don't understand it all myself, but I know it's real, okay? You ever read the Bible, Doug?"

He shrugged his shoulders, "A little."

"Well, it talks about the devil being the father of lies. Hell, it was his lie to Eve that led to the original sin. All throughout the scripture you'll find places where it associates the devil with lying. My guess is he must be attracted to those who lie. I mean we all do it, but I think some more than others. I think those bumps are a warning of sorts. It's like they're saying 'hey, you better watch yourself. You've been doing an awful lot of lying lately, may want to tone it down.' You see what happens when you ignore the warning?"

He nodded with wide eyes.

"That's all I'll say about that. You go and get back to wherever it is you came from. I don't want to see you anymore unless you have a free set of cookware, you hear?"

They shared a small laugh.

Doug stood and crossed for the door.

He turned and looked at Eileen as she stood behind him.

"Tank you." He said and hugged her.

Doug got into his car and aimed for Georgetown. He promised aloud that he'd never lie again. Something deep within wondered if that was a lie in and of itself. He gulped at the thought of anything worse than what he'd just experienced.

He wondered if part of his tongue was still wiggling in the sink back at the motel. The thought sent a chill down the back of his neck. *Truth over lies. Truth over lies. Truth over lies.* He repeated the words as he traveled along the lonely interstate.

It Came at Midnight

1932

8 miles south of Texarkana, Texas near the Sulphur River

"Judas Priest, Betsy. Look at what he done did to ya," the weathered old farmer said through a tight jaw as he squatted down by his dying milk cow. He stroked her head and did his best to offer comfort. Her breath was labored as she mooed and squirmed. Deep lashes from claw marks twice the size of his own hands, stretched from her neck to her hind quarters. Blood pooled onto the dirt, turning it to a thick red mush.

Alfred Hickins sighed and rose to his feet. With a thirty ought six rifle propped on the hip of his overalls, barrel pointing to the amber hue of a Texas sunrise, Alfred retrieved his handkerchief and wiped his brow.

"I tell ya right now, I'm going to find this sorry rascal and I'ma put em in tha grave when I do. I promise ya that Betsy. He gonna pay for what he done to ya."

Alfred drew a deep breath and levered a round into the chamber, then lowered his rifle's aim. The metallic metal of the trigger kissed his finger. He pulled and sent the shot crackling through the air.

Alfred cursed the vile creature who'd done such a thing, then strode to his horse, climbed into the saddle, and headed back to the house to get his boys. He'd need help taking care of Betsy. At least her death wouldn't be in vain. Adding to the others, there should be enough meat to get them through the winter.

It'd been the third time in the last month he'd been forced to put one of his animals out of its misery. The other two were shredded just like Betsy. Though he'd never seen the culprit, he'd often heard its god-awful cries late into the night. Deep and grotesque, it sent a chill down his back every time. He shuddered to think of such a thing that could make that sort of sound.

Alfred and his boys had set more bear traps than he could count and had yet to have any luck. But Alfred had another idea, and he vowed that tonight would be the night he put an end to it all.

One way or another, he was going to kill the darned thing and send it back to the pits of hell where it belongs.

ALFRED AND HIS sons, Ralph and Clyde, spent most of the day setting traps and lining the barn with wire and bells to create a self-made alarm system. The day was ebbing away as the sun began to tuck its face below the horizon, painting the sky with splashes of orange, purple, and blue. A swift breeze wafted by, caressing the men's faces as they stood in the pasture looking back to the old weather-beaten barn. Their paint chipping farmhouse with large porches and windows sat to the right of the barn.

Alfred removed his hat and pulled out a handkerchief to wipe his brow once more.

"Whadaya think this thing is Pa?" asked Ralph as he spat away a gush of peach tobacco juice.

Alfred sighed and wagged his head while fanning himself with his hat, "I don't know son. But I know before yens mama died . . . she'd talk a lot about feeling somfen evil lurking in these here pastures. Said she often felt like she's being watched or what not. Now I can't say for certain, but I think I know what she was talken bout. Yes sur, I've felt somfen myself a time or two. What it is, I caint say, but it's more than just flesh and bones, that I know."

"Pa, c'mon now, don't go a talking like that—" Clyde said, but Alfred cut him short.

"Like what, Son? You got any better ideas?" he said with a quick snap of his head, drilling his beady brown eyes into his soul, "Don't go a telling me what to believe or think. If you'd heard what I heard out there those nights, and heard what ya mama was saying, instead of being—"

"Daddy don't go there. Please. We done told ya we's sorry for not being around then, but we here now and that's all that matters. Right?" said Ralph.

Alfred drew a deep breath, not looking at either of them standing to his right and left.

A moment passed.

"You're right. That's all that matters. Whatever this thing is . . . we gonna git it tonight. Which means we a sleeping on tha porch with rifles within arm's reach."

Ralph and Clyde nodded.

"Alright den . . . let's herd em into the barn and get ready for what's coming."

Alfred marched onward toward the cattle and horses, his sons following behind.

AFTER GETTING the herd into the barn and locking them in the stalls, Alfred and his boys enjoyed a quick supper of left-over cornbread, red beans, fried taters, cabbage, and milk, then moved to the porch and waited.

The strike of a match caught Alfred's attention. He turned in his rocking chair and looked to Clyde who sat a few feet to the left of him with his hands cupped near his mouth in an effort to light his wooden pipe.

"Boy, put that out. That thing'll smell ya and turn back round."

"Pa, it's just peach tobacco, I'll make it quick."

"No, you want either, put that thing out. I ain't taking no chances of spooking it off."

Clyde sighed and wagged his head, then shook out the flame.

"Well can I at least chew it?" Clyde asked with a tightness in his voice.

Alfred tossed his hand in a half wave to his son and toyed with a toothpick extending from his lips.

A sweet aroma of peach lifted in the air as Clyde retrieved a pack of tobacco from the pocket in his denim overalls and dug his fingers in, pulling out leafy strings and packing it away in his jaw.

With the sun now resting till morning, the night bugs sang to their hearts desire. Cicadas, crickets, and whatever else lurked in the trees and bushes. An owl hooted in the distance, competing with a pack of coyotes howling at the full moon.

"That there is what's killing ya cows," Ralph said leaning forward in his chair and pointing a finger to the wood line.

"Last I checked, coyotes don't have claws the size of lunch boxes," Alfred said with a scoff.

Ralph tightened his lips and leaned back in his chair, sending it gently rocking and barking out a soft squeak with each shift of his weight.

"Ssshh! Dadburn it boys, ain't I taught yens any sense? Goodness gracious, ya bunch of thick headed goons."

Ralph stopped and gave a side glare to his Pa. Clyde chuckled quietly to himself as his shoulders jarred up and down.

"Whatchu laughing bout? You tha one gonna smoke a pipe while we out here trying to listen for a darn creek devil. You ain't the brightest light in tha bunch either ya know," Ralph said shaking a finger at his brother.

Clyde fattened his lips and waved away his brother's words.

As the night went on, the three found themselves speaking in hush tones as if the creature was listening.

"I think we a wasting our time out here, Pa. We got the barn rigged with the bells, that thing tries and get in, we gonna hear it. Why don't we call it a night and get some rest," said Ralph in a whisper.

"Ssshhh . . . it's gonna come tonight. We gotta be ready for him. We can get our sleep in tha morning. I'm staying up," Alfred said with his rifle lying across his lap as he slapped at a mosquito trying to steal blood from his neck.

Ralph yawned and nodded his head.

Taking by the contagion, Alfred found himself yawning as well. His eyes suddenly took on that familiar heaviness. He had to stay awake, by devil's hell, he couldn't let the night slip away. He had to be ready when the creature came.

He pulled out his pocket watch, chain dangling from his hand, *12:43.*

He looked to the other side of the locket and stared at a picture of his wife until his eyes became moist. Alfred sniffled and closed the watch, quick to tuck it away.

He gave his long gray beard a good rubbing, marinating his wife's words. He knew the feeling she was talking about. He felt it every time he fed the cattle or lingered on in the pasture after sundown. Something was always watching. Tucked away in the thick wood line as it relished its ability to camouflage itself and watch with curious eyes. His wife was right, there truly was a presence lurking within the shadows. What it was, he couldn't say, but make no mistake it was there.

THE JINGLE of the bells and rough jostling on his shoulder, gave Alfred's heart a start.

Alfred flashed his eyes open and straightened in his chair. He swallowed hard and blinked away the sleep that'd overtaken him. He craned his head upward to see Ralph hunched at the back, eyes bouncing between him and the barn.

"Something's out there," he said in a horsed whisper.

Clyde plunged two shells of buck shot into his double barrel shotgun and snapped it back into place.

The horses stirred and hollered as the cows mooed and kicked at the wooden planks forming their square stalls.

The bells attached to the wire surrounding the barn rattled and jingled like a windchime during a Kansas tornado.

"What in the devil's hell?" Alfred said as he forced himself to his feet. Ralph helped him up by cupping a hand in his armpit.

Just as Alfred was straightening his spine and levering a round into the chamber of his rifle, a piercing wail emitted from the barn. It sent a chill trailing down his spine that caused every hair on his body to stand erect.

His feet were frozen to the porch.

Clyde cursed as his eyes grew wide.

Ralph looked to Alfred, "Daddy . . . what in God's name was that?"

"It's that darned thing your mother talked about."

The piercing shriek lingered on into the dark night as if its creator had an endless supply of air.

Alfred disappeared inside the home in frantic search for a light.

"C'mon! Hurry! Let's get to tha barn!" Alfred said clinching a lantern and hobbling off the porch. His leg was still asleep, so he had to drag it with him.

Ralph and Clyde looked to one another with wide eyes as each gulped then proceeded to join their Pa on the trek to the ruckus taking place in the barn.

Alfred was cussing up a storm through a tight jaw as his boot scraped across the sunbaked ground.

His boys were just behind him with their guns.

The cows screamed with deep, guttural howls, pleading for salvation from the rabid beast. The horses sounded as if they'd broken free from the stall and begun to trample around in the tight confines of the barn.

They reached the edge of the big sliding barn door and rolled it open about half a foot to get a glimpse inside.

Alfred peeked in through the crack.

All he saw was silhouettes of the horses jutting in circles in efforts to allude the beast. Until a patch of light caught his attention. On the opposite end of the barn was a large, jagged hole which allowed the moonlight to pour inside.

The thing had torn a hole straight through the wood, ripping it away, splinter by splinter.

"Whadaya see? Whadaya see?" Clyde asked.

Alfred pulled back, "Get ready. I think he's still in there."

Alfred wrapped a hand around the barn door, "C'mon, don't just stand there, help me get it open!"

His boys broke from their stiffness and pushed the door open, sending it gliding along its squeaky track. It rolled open about the length of a T-model Ford. Alfred stretched the lantern out past him, just above his head. Light swam into the darkness, licking away the shadows. The horses still stirred in the center as they kicked and screamed with panting breaths.

It was the loud smacking and eating sound of lips and teeth that tore through the air, louder than all the chaos.

Alfred's hair stood straight along his neck as a thousand cold bumps festered down his arms.

His eyes fell to the ground, trying to peer past the stomping feet of the horses as they trampled by them. He squinted his eyes and inched closer, shoving the lantern further along. The light reached where the sounds emitted, and the legs of a horse filled his vision. The horse lay on its side with its back facing the men. The smacking, slurping sounds grew louder. Alfred took another step forward with the lantern held high in his left hand and the rifle clinched in his right.

The amber light of the lantern reached the full body of the horse . . . and in that instant, everything went still. An eerie silence filled the barn. The rummaging horses stalled and stood with drooping heads, catching their breaths. But the smacking continued.

"What is i—" Ralph tried to ask, but his words were cut short at the sight of an ashy, inky black, hairless body jutting its head over the horse. It was crouched on its calves and its bloody hands with sharp talons were resting on its knees.

Alfred had finally seen it. It wasn't no bear or mountain lion, or coyote as many had claimed. No . . . it was something evil, just as his wife had said.

The thing glared at them with snarled lips. The men were frozen as neither could say a word.

The thing sat there, blood smeared around its face, with big black eyes staring into their souls.

Alfred cursed then said, "For heaven's sake . . . it's the devil!"

The instant he aimed his weapon and put pressure on the trigger, the thing pounced, bolting from the horse, straight for the men. Alfred fired, lost the grip on the lantern, sending it crashing to the earth, exploding into a small puddle of flame before burning out, leaving the men in the dark.

A booming blast from Clyde's double barrel ripped through the air, banging against Alfred's ear drums. The loud crack of a rifle rang out from Ralph's bolt action. Alfred managed to get two shots off, before being pinned to the ground.

The creature landed on his chest, snarled its lips to reveal teeth dripping with saliva over his face. He felt his chest pop under the weight of the beast. It felt like a horse had fallen on him. His breath was snuffed away as his lungs begged for mercy.

Another booming blast from Clyde's scatter gun sounded off followed by the clicking and clanking of Ralph chambering another round.

It was too late.

Alfred's world had begun to falter, turning black as sound began to ebb away, decibel by decibel.

Distant memories of childhood and life flashed before his eyes. This is it . . . he'd succumbed to the beast. The thing of mystery had stolen his last breath. His body went numb and weightless as he drifted away into a sea of memories.

He left this world for the next.

52 years later

1984

THE NATIVE AMERICAN shaman gasped as he stumbled backwards, crashing for the ground, having to be caught by his grandson.

His body went limp as the grandson eased him to his haunches.

"Is he okay? What happened?" asked the husband, dressed in jeans and a button-down shirt with a cowboy hat. His blonde-haired wife clinched to his arm, long yellow dress fluttering with the Texas breeze.

The chiseled faced grandson crouched next to his grandfather and looked up at the man, "I think he saw what's been giving you trouble, Mr. Hensley."

Rod Hensley rubbed the back of his neck and looked to his wife, then placed an armed around her shoulders and kissed the top of her head.

"It's gonna be all right honey."

His eyes went to their ranch style house sitting behind them with its big porch and windows.

"Are you okay, Grandpa?"

The old man swallowed hard and tried to catch his breath. His eyes were still clinched tight. He slowly began to nod his head. Without opening his eyes, he said, "Help me to my feet, Ben."

Ben reached an arm around him and attempted to lift him. Rod Hensley left his wife's side and offered a hand to the men.

Grunting and sucking in air with labored breaths as the feather tied in his long black hair danced with the wind, the old man opened his eyes.

"I know the reason for your troubles," he waited a beat as all of their eyes were glued to his, "This ground is cursed by a Skinwalker."

Ben's eyes flashed wide as his mouth dangled open at his grandpa's words.

The old man nodded and drew a long breath, "He's haunting this land, seeking to avenge his death and the blood that was once shed here. He will continue to stalk and torment anyone who lives here until a peace offering is made. This we must do if you want to save your lives and any of those who come here after us. The Skinwalker is an evil creature from the unseen realm. This is nothing to play around with. We must act fast."

Rod and his wife were silent for a moment as they processed the old Native's words.

"Mr. Wolfe, what are you going to do?" Rod finally asked.

The old man's eyes shifted to the barn, "Follow me."

The four of them marched away as Mr. Wolfe instructed Ben to gather wood for a small fire. As Ben wandered off in search of kindling, Mr. Wolfe spoke over his shoulder to Rod and his wife Evelynn, "I'll need a few strands of each of your hair, and a few drops of blood too."

"Blood?"

Mr. Wolfe nodded and continued for the barn.

Evelynn pulled her hand to her mouth, eyes wide.

Rod placed his arm around her and gave a good squeeze as they followed the old man.

"Can we go in?" Mr. Wolfe asked as he reached the rolling barn door.

Rod bobbed his head and proceeded to push the door open, rolling it along its track.

Mr. Wolfe straightened as the door opened, shutting his eyes, he flinched as his face twisted and tightened.

Ben came striding back with an armful of sticks.

"Grandpa, is everything okay?"

No answer.

The muscles and veins along Mr. Wolfe's neck were taut as the flesh blushed with rising blood pressure. He jerked and grunted, stumbling backwards.

Ben steadied him.

Mr. Wolfe relaxed and lowered his head.

"We will need to do it in the center of the barn," he pulled his head up and looked to Rod, "Got any matches?"

He nodded and retrieved a pack from his jean pocket.

"Make it quick, so we don't choke out the horses," Rod said as he passed the matches to Ben.

"It'll be quick. Please, sit down," said Mr. Wolfe as he lowered himself down with a grunt.

Within minutes, they had a small fire going.

Mr. Wolfe pulled out a pocketknife and looked at Rod and Evelynn, "Hair first. We'll do the blood last."

Rod gulped and looked at Evelynn.

She closed her eyes, took a long breath, then nodded.

Rod pulled a few strands from the side of his head and cut them away, then passed the hair to the old man and gave Evelynn the knife to do the same.

Now holding both the strands of hair in hand, Mr. Wolfe said, "Okay, let's begin."

He shut his eyes and looked heavenward as the flame crackled and hissed at their feet.

Rod glanced at the three of them and was the last to shut his eyes.

"We think you Great Creator for giving us life and all the good things in it. We are eternally grateful for your power and goodness. For you are the Light in whom there is no darkness. And where you are the darkness cannot be. You vanquish the darkness as a light licks up the shadows of a room. We ask you Father, that you'd fill this place with that very light and rid the evil that abides here. We ask that you come and take away this present darkness. Light of the World, come."

With that, he entered a chant in his Native tongue.

Humda um, da yeh, oh wa.

Then he opened his eyes and sprinkled the hair over the dancing flame.

The grandson leaned near to Rod and whispered, "Look."

Rod opened his eyes, then nudged Evelynn.

They watched as the old man rubbed his fingers free of the hair. It took to flame and rose in small embers to the rafters of the barn, burning out before they reached the ceiling. The odor of burnt hair filled the air.

Humda um, da yeh, oh wa.

The old man nodded and the grandson whispered again to Rod's ear, "He need's the blood now."

Rod gave him a long look, then rubbed his brow and reached for the knife lying on the ground next to his wife.

As the Indian sang his chant, a quick breeze gusted through the open door, sending the flame swaying side to side in quick motions.

Mr. Wolfe quickened his chant.

"What's happening?" Rod asked.

"You must hurry!" the grandson pleaded.

Humda um, da yeh, oh wa.

Faster the old man chanted.

The wind picked up speed, rushing and whooshing about the room.

The flame leaned to one side, almost being extinguished. The grandson rushed to shield it the best he could.

"Hurry!" His voice strained as he yelled over his grandfather's chant and the howling wind.

Rod took a deep breath and made a small cut along the meaty part of his elbow, just above the muscle. He winced and watched as blood began to trickle out, oozing down his arm.

"Good. Now give the knife to her and come here. Quick!"

Rod passed the knife to Evelynn. He watched as she made a similar cut near her own elbow. Rod then rushed to the grandson's side. Evelynn wasn't far behind.

"Now say the chant with us and drip the blood onto the fire," the grandson said with his face twisted and tilted from the heat of the flame.

Humda um, da yeh, oh wa.

They all began to say in unison as Rod and Evelynn leaned near the flame and squeezed and shook their arms, sending droplets of blood falling into the fire.

The instant the blood landed the wind began to rip around the room even faster as the sound of its howl quickly faded into a piercing shriek like that of a banshee.

"Shut your eyes! Don't look! Whatever you do, don't look!" Ben yelled.

Rod slammed his eyes.

The sounds in the barn could send ice water throughout anyone's veins. The horses stirred and screamed, huffing out blasts of air.

The sound of teeth clicking in a loud clack like fingernails tapping on glass, entered the room.

Humda um, da yeh, oh wa.

Louder and faster the Indian's chanted. Rod and Evelynn doing their best to keep pace.

Heavy foot falls thudded in the dirt next to them, accompanied with deep, raspy breaths coming from mucus filled lungs.

Rod's entire body began to tremble, and he could feel Evelynn shaking beside him. Her voice came in thin whimpers as she sniffled through the chant.

A deep, gut wrenching, demonic roar emitted only feet from them, rattling their chests and innards.

"Don't look!" Ben pleaded once more.

Humda um, da yeh, oh wa!

The devilish shriek continued.

Rod could feel something leaning close, staring into his soul. Hot, sulfurous breath rushed against his face, turning his stomach from the acrid odor. Rod coughed into the crevice of an elbow. Loud clicking teeth were only inches away.

Mr. Wolfe stopped the chant and returned to English, "In the name of the Great Creator, Jesus Christ, Light of the World who resides within me, I command you to leave this land and go back to hell from which you came!" The man's voice was strong and boomed with authority.

"Nooooo!" the beast shrieked.

"In the name of the Creator, Jesus Christ . . . I command you to leave! Now!"

The creature let out a thick, gravel filled roar. The air grew thin as the wind whooshed around and did its best to snuff out the flame.

A bright flash blasted into the room, sending rays of pure white light slamming against their closed eyelids. The room fell silent.

The wind dropped.

The horses settled.

The flame recovered.

Oxygen returned to its true form.

A moment passed, before the old man said in a low, soft voice, "It's okay. You can open your eyes now. It's finished."

Dead Awake

Savannah Bird was a jovial twenty-year-old who was a psychology major in her third year of study at LSU. For spring break, she, her boyfriend Jake, and a handful of their closest friends went to New Orleans for the week. On the third night around two in the morning the crew had just left a bar and was heading back to the hotel when Savannah stumbled into a vagabond begging for change on the corner of Bourbon and French Street. The old lady wore tattered clothes and cheap jewelry. Her skin was sagging, and she stunk to high heavens. Savannah apologized for the occurrence, but the old lady only glared at her with searing eyes. Savannah felt a chill run down her spine as she found herself locked in the woman's gaze.

The gypsy looking woman held out a cup of loose change and rattled it at Savannah. The old lady scowled at her again when Savannah shook her head.

Jake took Savannah's hand and turned to usher her away, but the old lady seized Savannah's arm and yanked her from Jake's grip. With the suddenness of a viper's strike, the old lady plucked a grouping of hair from Savannah's scalp. She yelped and watched in shock as the old lady rubbed the hair and began to chant.

"What the hell, old lady? What's your problem?"

The lady smiled to show rotting teeth and spoke in what could have been Latin.

Jake and the others wrinkled their brows.

Savannah couldn't move. Her flesh tingled as a sizzling flash of heat flooded over her. Her cheeks flushed and she felt her pulse thump strong in her neck. Her vision blurred for a moment before she felt Jake whisk her away. She felt herself go limp as Jake and her friend, Courtney, dragged her around the block.

The old lady cackled while rubbing the hair between her fingers. Savannah watched her until she faded to black as her eyelids closed without her command.

By the time they had reached the hotel, her body was ravaged with fever. Her eyes had rolled to the back of her head, and tremors had overtaken her. A half hour later, Jake and their friends rushed her to the ER.

Savannah was declared dead within two hours.

THE FUNERAL WAS held three days later. Jake sat in the front row of the church along with Savannah's parents and younger sister. The songs had been sung, a brief word spoken from a close friend, and now the Rabbi had just taken the stage to begin his message.

Within five minutes of the eulogy, everyone began to hear noises coming from the casket.

SHE COULD HEAR a man talking. His voice seemed to echo in the far reaches of her mind. Her vision was as black as night. The air was acrid and humid. It reminded her of the inside of a locked car during a summer day. Her body felt weak, drained, and lifeless. It took all she had to open her eyes. Her spatial awareness came into focus. Her elbows were tucked tight to her ribs and her hands were folded above her naval. She swallowed and a thick, slimy glob slithered down the back of her throat. She felt it land in the pit of her empty gut. A bout of nausea rushed her, and she jerked a hand to her mouth to ward it off. Her elbow popped when she did so. She felt the silk cloth caress her flesh. Her mind was groggy, but she was slowly beginning to awaken.

Where am I? Am I at the hospital? Why is the power out?

When she went to get up, she banged her head against the wood. Her eyes flashed wide.

Why am I in a box?

The man's voice went silent followed by a crowd of gasps and murmurs.

What kind of sick joke is this?

She pressed outward with all her might. She felt the box begin to rock.

There's more gasping and wailing.

Oh my God! It's a casket! Is this my funeral?

She began to scream as she beat against her coffin.

INSIDE THE SANCTUARY people made a wild break for the exit. The lamenters screamed and cried as they tripped over one another.

Jake jolted to his feet and backpedaled down the aisle. His eyes were locked onto the casket as it had begun to shake. The cloth skirt around the bottom of the table swayed with the rocking. The pastor had stepped from the stage and uttered prayers as he looked on in horror at what was unfolding before them.

The casket popped and creaked loudly when the door started to lift. It was soon flung open before Savannah Bird began crawling out of it. She stood in front of her casket with her hands to her sides. The pastor had fled, leaving only her boyfriend, parents, and sister in the sanctuary.

SAVANNAH BIRD'S story had made international news as soon as that night. Her parents were hounded by reporters and journalists seeking answers. They had rushed her to the hospital shortly after the initial shock had worn from seeing her crawl out of her own casket. The doctors were as baffled as the rest of them. Growing up, Savannah was raised in a strict and devout Jewish home. She strayed from her parents teaching in high school and moved out the day she turned eighteen. Due to their religion, her parents refused an autopsy or the embalming of their daughter so as not to desecrate her body. Doctors explained to her that that simple decision may have been what ultimately saved her life. The only explanation doctors were able to give her was a condition known as the Lazarus Syndrome. Named after the same Lazarus in the Bible whom Jesus had raised from the dead. Doctors described it as the spontaneous return of a normal cardiac rhythm after failed attempts at resuscitation.

Doctors monitored her at the hospital for three more days but were unable to find any sign of distress or illness in her body. She was as healthy as any twenty-year-old should be. During her hospital stay she had begged for a nice juicy, rare steak. She had never been much of a meat eater before, so her cry for a rare steak had caught the family off guard. Nevertheless, on the day she made it home from the hospital, her family planned a steak dinner. Jake and her parents ensured it was served rare just as she had requested. After saying grace, they watched as she began devouring the steak like a cavewoman. Her mother had told her to mind her manners. She grinned and apologized. She dabbed her chin with a napkin and went back to eating. This time only at a slightly slower pace.

Jake sat next to her at an angle and studied her the entire time. He sipped his glass of water as she stabbed another piece of meat. He swallowed an ice cube, and it slid awkwardly down his throat as it jabbed his esophagus.

"So, what was it like being dead?" Her younger sister, Aubrey, asked her.

Their mother scolded her for asking such a thing at the table.

"I'm sorry. I mean I'm only asking what we all want to know."

Savannah swallowed a piece of steak and said with a full cheek, "It's alright mom. She's right. I'm sure you're all wondering the same thing. Well. To tell you the truth. I don't remember. It was kind of like sleeping, I guess. I mean the last thing I remember is falling asleep on the street of New Orleans before waking up in my coffin."

Their mother covered her lips with the pads of her four fingers. She shook her head as tears slipped down her face.

Their dad cleared his throat and asked, "You don't remember dreaming or anything?"

Savannah thought for a moment then wagged her head, "No. No, I never dreamed. It was just...black."

Jake sat with his arms crossed and his chin cradled in a hand. He studied her, listening to every word she spoke, watching her every mannerism. Something about this whole thing felt off to him. He struggled to place a finger on what it was, but for the life of him he couldn't get rid of the nagging feeling that something just wasn't right. His mind kept returning to the night of her death when she had bumped into that old lady on the street. Had the lady done something to her? Put a curse on her or something? It's nuts to think that way, but it's also nuts to believe his girlfriend climbed out of the coffin by herself.

"I don't know how to explain it, but I feel so much more alive now. It's like my soul is lighter, more awake I guess for lack of a better term. It's weird. I just feel so different. But in a good way if that makes sense."

Her father reached across the table and squeezed her hand, "It makes total sense honey. Praise God you're alive."

Jake forced a fake smile and continued to observe her.

Even her eyes seemed off. Their contrast was darker. Her brown eyes were almost black it seemed. Her voice had a sandpaper-like rasp to it. He studied his thoughts as he watched her consume the raw meat. She smacked her lips and smiled at him.

He smiled back.

God, something just isn't right.

He left about an hour later to allow her time with the family. The rest of the night he couldn't get her off his mind. He replayed everything in his head until he finally fell asleep on the couch. He dreamed about her every time he drifted away. He kept rewatching from the center of the church aisle as she climbed out of the casket. He jolted awake twice through the night when he saw her gray, decomposed corpse push open the lid and walk down the aisle towards him with an outstretched hand. Her flesh hung like ribbons as dirt and sticks were matted in her hair. Dark, thick veins ran across her skin like lightning strikes. She called for him with a deep, gravelly voice that wasn't her own. Her eyes were blacker than the night sky. Her pupils shined like stars as they beamed into his soul. In his dreams, he was frozen to the floor and could only stand there as she drew near him. She began to whisper the closer she got. She seized his arm and leaned in close to his face. He awoke when she started whispering in his ear. He felt her warm breath and smelt the rancidness of her. The putrid odor turned his gut. He woke up screaming until it felt like his throat was bleeding.

The last time he woke, he checked his phone to see if she ever texted him back from when he'd said goodnight. She did. Her text read: *Love you too honey bear. Can't wait to see you tomorrow. XOXO.*

The text made his brow wrinkle. She had never called him that before. He stared at the screen for a few moments before placing his phone on the coffee table and fighting to go back to sleep. He tossed and turned most of the night but managed to avoid seeing her in his dreams.

He called her the next morning around ten but couldn't reach her. He texted her but never heard back. He thought it was odd, but figured she must be busy with family, so he didn't try her again until later in the day. Worry began to seep in the longer the day went. When night came and she still hadn't responded, he made plans to visit the next day.

That night around three in the morning he was woken to the same dream he'd had the previous night. Only this time it wasn't Savannah he saw crawl out of the coffin, but the old woman from New Orleans. Her long, gray hair stretched to her knees, and she reached for him with long, crusty fingernails that looked like claws. She whispered something in his ear, but it was in another language. She cackled when he began to scream.

That morning at nine he tried calling and texting but got no answer. It was a little after nine thirty when he pulled into the Bird family's driveway. This was Friday so he thought it was odd to find both her parents' cars at home. He figured they would be at work. Especially her dad. He owned his own real estate brokerage and hardly ever missed days at work. He rationalized that maybe they had both taken the week off to be with Savannah. That made enough sense to him. He pushed the questions to the back of his mind and made his way to the front door. He pressed the doorbell and waited.

A moment passed and no one answered. He tried the bell again.

Nothing.

He leaned into the side windowpane of the door and cupped his hands around the glass. He couldn't hear any footsteps and didn't see any movement.

What the hell?

He knocked on the glass and pressed the bell twice more.

Panic began setting in as his pulse quickened.

He pulled out his phone and dialed her number. It went straight to voicemail this time. He tried her again. Same thing.

As he was about to call 911, he heard the door click. He stepped back and watched as it swung open with a gentle beckoning. No one was there. The faint sound of old music lingered in the air. Sounded like it travelled from a vinyl record. It had that static tone to it. He swallowed and peered into the home.

"Hello?" he called.

Only the 40's music answered.

He stepped inside and scanned the home.

"Hello? It's me. Jake."

He shut the door and locked it behind himself.

The music seemed to come from somewhere upstairs.

He eased his way through the home, stealing glances this way and that as he went. As he passed the kitchen, he noticed the table was set in the dining room. Dirty plates and empty wine glasses adorned the tablecloth. He took note and continued through the house.

He reached the bottom of the spiral staircase and stared towards the loft where Savannah's bedroom was located. The music continued.

The stairs creaked with every step.

His heart thumped hard. His mouth went dry. His palms were slick with sweat. He could smell candles burning.

Jake reached the top and began creeping his way down the hall towards the music. Savannah's bedroom door was cracked open.

He slid along the wall to her room. Once there, he extended a hand and gave the door a gentle nudge.

His heart was smashed with a sledgehammer at the sight before him. Savannah stood in the middle of her room with her parents and sister lying on the floor below her within a blood drawn circle. Candles filled the room. On the nightstand. On the dresser. In the floor. Everywhere he looked there were candles.

He trained his eyes to her parents and sister. They laid with their arms crossed and hands over top one another. Their eyes were closed. Savannah stood in the center with her back to him. She had let her hair down and it drooped in unkempt waves.

"Dear God, what have you done?"

She didn't answer. She just stood there with her shoulders slumped and staring at the floor.

He stepped closer and knelt to check the pulse of Mr. Bird. He's alive. It's like he's asleep. Jake patted his cheek but got no response. He lifted his eye lids and watched the pupils dilate. The man was comatose. Jake glanced at Mrs. Bird and Aubrey. He could see they were breathing, but it was super shallow.

He stood to his feet and studied Savannah. He side stepped to stand in front of her. Her eyes were closed but a wry grin stretched her face. It sent a shiver down his back as it was caressed with a ghostly finger. Goose flesh spread over his arms and legs. The hairs on his neck straightened.

He reached out a trembling hand toward her cheek. Her eyes flashed opened and she snapped her head towards him. She seized his hand and sank her teeth deep into his flesh. Jake screamed and yanked away from her. He felt her teeth tear through tendon and heard the bone crunch. She'd bit off his pointer finger. Taken with shock, he clutched his hand and stared at it while screaming with agony. He watched her chew on his finger as if it were a thick piece of beef jerky.

Jake held his hand close to his gut and wrapped it into his shirt to stop the spurting blood. He cursed and yelled at her, "What is the matter with you? What did she do to you?"

Savannah swallowed the finger and said with a grin, "What do you mean honey bear? It was just a love bite."

"The hell it was."

"Oh, don't be so grumpy. You should be grateful it was just one."

He stared at her and marveled at what she had become. Her eyes were black. Her voice was raspy and harsh. Her skin was pale with a purple tint. His blood oozed down her chin. He watched her lick it away as her tongue protruded out, slithering like a serpent as it had an unnatural length to it.

He crossed over to the nightstand where the victrola turntable played the record. He gave it a good kick and the music screeched to a halt.

He pulled out his necklace from beneath his shirt and clutched the cross pendant as he approached her. He watched her eyes twitch as she stared at his hand.

He crossed himself with it and uttered a quick prayer of strength. One his grandma had taught him when he was just a kid.

He looked deep into her eyes and said with conviction, "I want Savannah back. You give her back right now!"

His voice roared through the home.

She smiled at him and began to laugh. Her voice turned high as it blended into the old lady's voice. Her laughter quickly turned to that of a cackle.

A chill washed over him as he recalled the lady's laughter that night in New Orleans. He watched as her face shifted into the old lady's for a brief second like a passing shadow.

"You can't have her. She's dead. Remember?"

"No, she's not. I know she's in there. You get out of there, right now! You hear me? RIGHT NOW."

He flashed his cross at her and she hissed. Her lips peeled back to show rows and rows of teeth.

"Get out of her! Now!" He stepped closer and pressed his cross to her chest. It sizzled there as smoke rose into the air. He commanded her to leave again and pressed the cross harder to her chest. She began to shake violently. Her head snapped back, and the old woman let out a piercing shriek. A rush of air filled the room to lift the curtains and extinguish the candles. The wind whispered in the room before exiting the door it came through.

Her voice fell silent, and her body went limp.

He caught her in his arms.

His injured hand throbbed as he held her.

She rested there as if asleep.

He lowered the two of them to the floor. He brushed her hair with his good hand and spoke soothing words to her. He watched as she slowly opened her eyes. Savannah stared up at him. Her voice stuck to her throat as she asked, "What happened?"

Savannah was back.

Jake smiled and said, "It's a long story," then dialed 911.

As the already bizarre, headline gripping story was making waves across the world, the turn of recent events only added to the buzz. Upon investigation, detectives discovered that Mr. and Mrs. Bird along with Savannah's younger sister, Aubrey, were given high doses of the sleeping aid, Ambien. The ER doctors had to pump their stomachs to prevent any long turn effects. After evaluating the case and Savannah's behavior, the lead investigator suggested Savannah be placed in a mental health behavioral clinic where she could receive the proper treatment. The DA agreed. Three days later Savannah was driven up to Baton Rouge Behavioral Hospital. She was placed under a ninety-day watch and treatment plan to insure her recovery. During this time Savannah would undergo numerous evaluations to track her progress. Jake and her family were allowed to visit twice a month.

After witnessing what he had, Jake took a deep dive into various subjects surrounding Savannah's story. He researched everything from Near Death Experiences, The Lazarus Syndrome and the story in the Bible, ghosts, witches, curses, and everything in between. Late one night after having spent the evening researching and reading story after story, he stumbled upon a webpage dedicated to ghost stories of New Orleans. He found the page intriguing and spent the next half hour or more scanning its contents. He found himself nodding away in the chair. He was ready to click off his desk lamp and crawl into bed, but he made a quick swipe down the page and felt his heart skip a beat. Staring back at him from a black and white, crinkled photograph was the old lady they encountered on the street.

Her dark eyes hooked his soul, and he felt his body turn ridged. The air in the room dropped twenty degrees. His breath became labored. Sweat beaded on his forehead. He swallowed and began reading.

Her name was Deborah Fontane. She was executed in 1947 after being tried and convicted of murder and cannibalism. She was a known gypsy and psychic who made her living reading palms and foretelling futures on the streets of New Orleans up until her arrest in 47'. Many people claimed she became entangled with witchcraft or voodoo during her later years. She went from being a kind, harmless old lady to a cold, ruthless witch. Her business quickly dwindled due to lack of clientele. From 44' to 46', countless women had disappeared only to be discovered days later partially eaten. Many claimed there must be a wild animal roaming the streets at night. Others said the devil himself was to blame. It wasn't until Deborah was caught in the act of feasting on a victim that she was arrested. She was executed less than five months after her arrest. In total, she was accused and convicted of over a dozen murders. Her death didn't stop her from roaming the streets late into the night. Countless stories had been told through the years of people spotting her wandering the sidewalks where she once conducted business.

During the spring of 54' when a serial killer had taken to the streets, many blamed the deaths on the ghost of Deborah Fontane. For years, business on that side of town suffered as her story spread. The great flooding of 62' only added to the folklore. Many were led to believe Deborah had cursed the city and all who occupied it. Rumors of her wickedness were spread again after the devastation of Hurricane Katrina as many claimed to have seen her walking up and down the streets only days prior.

Jake finished reading the page and leaned back in his chair. He glanced over his shoulder as the room seemed to hold someone other than himself. He could feel a million invisible eyes piercing the back of his head. He could almost feel a warm breath upon his neck. He shivered and gripped himself in a hug, rubbing his elbows. He saved the page to his favorites and turned his computer down for the night.

He crawled into bed and started to turn off the lamp but thought better of it.

The next day he drove over to the behavioral clinic to visit Savannah. This was only his second visit as she was still in her first month of treatment. A nurse escorted him to her room. They had to pass through a long hallway with rooms on each side. Savannah's room was at the furthest end. Screams filled the air. Some people beat upon their door and glared into the lookout glass like raged zombies. During his last visit a man had to be sedated by a husky nurse to keep him from scratching his wrists. The nurse and two others had rushed past Jake and his escort to bolt inside a room where Jake caught glimpse of blood spatter and heard the man wailing.

"You have thirty minutes. Your time begins now. Press the button next to the door when you hear the beeping."

The lady's words tug at his drifting mind. He clears his throat and nods his thanks.

The door opens with a hiss.

Savannah stands in the center of the room with her arms crossed. She smiles wide and rushes to meet him. She wraps her arms around him and squeezes his neck. Jake hugs her back.

"I'm so glad to see you. Thank you for coming."

"It's good to see you too. How are you feeling?" He asks her after giving her a kiss.

"I'm feeling better. My head is clearing from the fog. I'm able to think straight now."

"That's good."

Savannah moves a folded blanket from her bed and makes room for them to sit.

She scootches next to him and leans into his side. He places his arm around her. They talk that way for the next half hour. He debated rather he should tell her of his findings on Deborah Fontane, but ultimately decided against it. At least for now.

The beeping began. Savannah squeezed him tight and buried her head into his ribs.

They told of their love for one another and made plans for things to do once she was released.

"You know you can always take a few summer classes to make up for the lost t—"

Jake's words were cut short by sharp pain in his arm. He yelped and jumped away from her. She'd bitten his arm. His mind was instantly flooded with a flashback to when she'd taken his finger. His missing digit would forever be a reminder of that night. He pulled away and glared at her. Panting for breath and lost for words.

Savannah smiled and said with pure innocence, "What? It was just a love bite?"

Creature in the Shadows

Summer of 1985
In the boondocks of South Carolina

The sounds of night were in abundance. Tree frogs screaming from scratchy throats, cicadas singing into the dark sky, and a lonely hoot owl calling out to a lost friend. I remember how muggy the air was. It was so hot I could feel the sweat trickle down my back like rain descending a glass window. I was only nine at the time, but I will never forget the night I first heard the scream and what happened in the following weeks during the summer of '85. That's when I knew we weren't the only ones who liked to play in the woods. If only we'd have known what truly lurked beyond the shadows.

We'd hear screams late in the night once the coyotes settled among the leaves. My brother, sister and I would run to Mom and Dad's room, yelling about how the wailing woman was wandering about the night again. Dad always said it was just a bobcat and that we had nothing to worry about, so we'd reluctantly crawl back to our room to avoid having to pass by the kitchen window. It was at that window where my sister Claire said she saw the big hairy man peeping in while hiding in the shadows. She was only five at the time, so we really didn't think too much of it until we started hearing the wailing woman. It wasn't long afterwards that we finally saw her.

My brother Hunter was twelve, and Claire was six. It was a sweltering summer night and it'd been a few months since we heard any screams. We were so caught up in our game of hide-n-go-seek that the wailing woman or the man in the shadows never crossed our minds.

We'd wandered a good way from the house and weren't too far from Dark Swamp. We lived about thirty miles to the nearest town of Swamp Booger Hill. Looking back on it, I never realized how far out in the boondock's we lived until now.

Anyhow, after my sister and I were found by our brother, Hunter, we took off tearing through the woods, trying to reach the big Oak which was base. Hunter was right on our tails. I could almost feel his hand grasping my shirt. The forest was alive with all its occupants as the tree frogs and cicadas screeched with urgency. A huge bullfrog croaked somewhere in the swamp. The odor of a wet dog mixed with a soured cow patty began to sting my nose the closer we got to the tall oak. It got so bad I had to hide my face beneath the neck of my shirt, and I can remember Claire coughing and gagging.

I turned one last time to see how close Hunter was, and I'll never forget the look in his eyes. It was as if my brother's soul was crawling from his eyes to fly to that crescent moon high in the darkening sky. He'd stopped dead in his tracks with his jaw stretching lower and lower with each passing second.

Then came the loudest piercing scream I'd ever heard my sister make.

I yanked my head around to see what had them so worked up and in the mere second that I caught a glimpse of this thing, my life slammed to a screeching halt as my heart sank to my bowels.

There it was. The wailing woman. The man in the shadows. Gosh. I'll never be able to rid that sight from my mind. It still gives me chills as I write this all these years later.

Night Terrors

The thing that sticks out to me the most though, is how black its eyes were. There really wasn't any white to them, just solid black. The thing was massive, taller than any man I've ever seen. It stood there for a good ten seconds or more, just staring into our souls. Then without warning, it slung its head to the moon and let out a gut twisting shriek that pierced our hearts and rattled our bones. Whew. Look at me, I've got goosebumps now just telling you about it.

It ended its howl then barged off into the woods, plowing past trees like a tank. I can still hear those heavy feet slapping against the earth.

We took off in the opposite direction, screaming to the tops of our lungs, racing for home, and longing for Mom and Dad's embrace.

Obviously hearing our blood curdling screams, Mom and Dad met us in the yard as we stumbled out of the wood line.

I crashed into Dad's arms with tears soaking my cheeks and shirt as my breath escaped my lungs. My heart was knocking against my ribcage as I gasped for words.

"What is it? What is it? What happened?" Dad kept asking, but all we could do was cry. Even Hunter was crying he was so scared and shook up by this thing.

We tried telling Mom and Dad about what we saw, but neither of them believed us. Mom said it must've been a bear and Dad kept saying it was probably some homeless man or something. But after much convincing, he agreed to search the woods the next morning.

I remember the entire night, me, Hunter and Claire sat in the corner of our room under a bed sheet with a flashlight. We even hung a blanket over our window so the hairy man couldn't peep in.

I don't think any of us slept until the sun came up. We each had big bags under our eyes the next day.

Dad was gone when we awoke. Mom said he left at sunrise to go sit in his tree stand until noon.

The whole time he was gone, I remember we stayed right by Mama's side. It wasn't until a few hours later that we heard the first shot, then came the wailing woman. The creature in the shadows screamed from a deep slimy throat, a sound so disturbing that every hair on your body was forced to stand at attention. Tiny bumps spread across my flesh in rapid succession.

Two more shots rang out followed by another. Us kids were cradled tight against Mama as we whimpered at the sounds coming from the woods.

I remember being so afraid for Dad, thinking the thing may have gotten a hold of him or something. We were all crying in fear of what may have happened. It was about thirty minutes before he came barging through the front door, nearly giving us all a heart attack. We each jolted and gasped. He could barely breathe as his heart must've been flying a hundred miles an hour. His eyes were wide and bulged. After catching his breath, he was finally able to tell us what happened.

He said he kept hearing something rustle in the brush but thought it must've been a squirrel, so he didn't pay it much attention. That is until he heard the thing grunt. He said he knew then that whatever it was, was something he'd never seen or heard before. A loud thrashing in the bush tugged his attention to his two o'clock. He had to squint his eyes to be sure he was seeing right. The creature was on all fours laying low to the ground with its big hairy legs spread across the earth like a spider and its massive cone head tilted to my dad at an awkward angle.

As he fumbled to raise his rifle, it leaped to its feet and took two quick steps in an angry charge before my dad fired off a round followed by the others.

The creature jolted back as it took each one and let out the wail that we'd heard so many times in the past. Dad said it then barged off into the thicket, tearing through limbs and trees as if they were toothpicks. After my dad shot it, the wailing woman ceased at night and the man in the shadows quit peeping in our windows. For about six months we had peace and rest. It didn't last long though.

The wailing woman, the stinky odors, the window peeper, and the feelings of being watched in the yard all started back. All our cats and dogs came up missing, our chicken coop got busted into, and even two of our goats disappeared. We started finding big footprints all around the house and even found a few muddy ones on our porch one time too.

Numerous times we were woken to something smacking against the side of the house, shifting it among its foundation. Mom had to keep the blinds and curtains closed on the windows, especially when she washed dishes. Three separate times she caught the hairy man peeping in on her.

We couldn't step foot out of the house after sundown without having large rocks thrown at us. All through the night you'd hear pebbles and pinecones knock against the tin roof before rolling down to the earth. None of us, including Mom and Dad could get any sleep. We finally had to move.

Couldn't have been a year or so later when we found out that the family that moved into the place after us, went missing and was never seen again.

To this day no one knows what happened.

I think I know.

Randall Lane

Curse of Crow Creek

I was ten years old when my parents finally told me the truth about the GTK. It was during the fall of 2014, just after his arrest. Two years prior to that was when we moved into our house near Crow Creek which was about twenty minutes from Georgetown. From the first night we moved in, weird things began to happen.

Our home was an older three-bedroom, two bath that butted next to a grove of pines. The first night we stayed there, I heard someone scream in the woods. It was a blood-curdling, God awful scream. The kind that gives you goosebumps. I remember I leapt out of bed and rushed down the hall to my parents' room. I banged my pinky toe on the frame of their door on the way in. I told them what happened, but when we stepped outside to listen, all we heard was the neighbor's dog barking and a horde of cicadas buzzing. I knew I really heard that scream. I wasn't crazy and I wasn't dreaming.

As time wore on, I met and began playing with the neighborhood kids. When we weren't busy playing the Xbox, we'd go outside and play football or baseball until we became bored and decided to venture into the woods to play hide-n-go-seek. A fishing pond rested on the other side of the grove of pines and when we tired of hide-n-go-seek, we'd sometimes venture to it.

I remember my dad taking me there a few times to catch bream and catfish. The longer we lived there, the closer I became to the kids in the neighborhood. In 2013, I began tagging along with them to the pond to fish off the dock. We were usually accompanied by at least one of our parents of course, but there were a few times we snuck off without them. It was creepy walking through the woods to get there. I always felt like someone was crouching up behind me and about to snatch me up. Or like someone was hiding and peeping around a pine tree at us. Those woods just seemed to carry an eerie presence with them.

This one time I remember us playing in the woods just a little before sunset. It was me and Rusty's turn to count. We had our faces buried against a pine tree and were rattling off the numbers like you do. I heard something rustle the leaves in front of us. I figured it was Brandon or maybe Julie running by, so I resisted the urge to look. The leaves crunched again, and this time it sounded heavier. I stopped counting and so did Rusty. I looked at him and he looked at me. A question lingered in his eyes. I leaned around the tree and looked for the source of the sound. No one was there. A sparrow hopped from one branch to another and then took to flight. Rusty and I looked at each other, grinned, and shook our heads. We returned to counting but were stopped when we began to hear someone chanting just above a whisper.

All sin begins within and there is no cure without atonement.

I duck out from behind the tree in time to catch glimpse of a man, clothed in a white gown with his back to us, ambling along through the woods. He was bald on top, and his head hung low with despair as he drug his feet over the leaves and twigs. He continued to chant those words, *all sin begins within and there is no cure without atonement.*

Rusty and I made a bolt for it. Dodging branches, leaping over logs, and panting for our next breath as we tore our way toward the clearing. It felt like the trees were leaning toward us, about to reach out and grab us. Briars and thorn bushes stung our legs, but we didn't care. We just had to make it out of there. Anywhere but in those woods felt safe.

We tumbled out from the wood line and into my backyard. We hunched over and rested our palms to our knees, trying to catch our breath. Then it dawned on us. What about the others? We called out to them. One by one, they emerged. We told them about what we saw, but none of them believed us. They thought we were playing a prank. I wish we were.

ABOUT A WEEK after that, I was awoken to the sound of a vicious dog fight just outside my window. I crawled out of bed and groped through my darkened room toward my moon lit window. I reached it and put on my glasses. The dogs are still going at each other's throats, growling with gnawing, and gnashing of teeth. My window was damp with early morning dew, but I could see a blur moving about our back yard. I could make out the two dogs. All I could see was they're big, and that one was white and the other was black.

I break from my window and dash for my parent's room. I jostle them awake and convince them to look outside at the two fighting dogs. I drag them to the dining room which has floor to ceiling windows angled to the backyard. I can still hear the dogs growling like rabid beasts. I see Mom and Dad squint as they look toward the noise. All the neighborhood dogs are going crazy in the distance.

"My goodness. What in the devil?" Dad says as he goes to crack open the back door.

"No. What are you doing?" Mom says and grabs his arm.

"I'm going to try to scare them off before they kill each other."

The growling and gnashing get louder when the door opens. A cold gust sweeps in some dead leaves. One of the dogs whimpers. My dad screams at them, "Hey. Getouttahere!"

As I cling tight to my mom, I manage to peep between my dad to see the two dogs running off into the pines. The black one disappears into the shadows. The white one turns and looks at us before vanishing around the side of the house.

I hear the other dogs howling and barking up the street. A man's voice can be heard shouting at them.

Dad comes back inside and shuts the door. He chuckles and says, "Them stupid dogs have done woken the whole neighborhood. It sounds like a friggin' circus out there."

"Yeah, I heard Mr. Brigley screaming at them." Mom says.

"He'll shoot them. Rusty said he thinks that's what happened to his dog, Dan. He thinks Mr. Brigley got him." I say to them.

"It wouldn't surprise me." Dad says.

"Who do you think they belong to?" Mom asks him.

"Heck if I know. They were some pretty dogs though. Looked like they were mixed with wolf or something. I guess maybe a type of Husky mix."

"Yeah."

"Well, let's get back to bed. You have school in the morning, boy." Dad says as he rubs a hand over my head, disheveling my hair.

The rest of the night I tossed and turned, dreaming of those two dogs. One black. One white. Where did they come from? Where did they go? Later in the night I thought I heard one howling, but I couldn't tell if I was dreaming or not.

A FEW WEEKS after that night, I was catfishing with my friends and our dads at the pond by the pines. It was a Friday night and must've been just a little before midnight. We'd had fun catching little bream and small catfish, but our dads were determined to catch a big one for us.

As the night wore on, us kids became bored, so we decided to fill our socks with rocks and toss them into the night sky in hopes of a bat swooping down and locking claws with the cotton covered stones. It was something my dad told us he did when he was a kid. What we were going to do if we caught one of the suckers, we didn't know. At least it'd be something we'd never forget. I mean how many people ever see a bat up close? Not that many if you ask me.

I remember it was a muggy night in September, and the moon was full as it reflected upon the rippling water. Bull frogs croaked, mosquitos' bit, crickets whirred, and cicadas sung. The wind brought a welcome breeze as it bristled through the trees. The grass was cool beneath our feet as we played along the bank. A pack of coyotes cackled in another land, and I wondered if those two fighting dogs were among them.

While I chewed on a snicker's bar, I watched Rusty and Brandon take turns throwing their heavy socks into the air. As I watched one of the socks fall to the earth, I heard Dad get excited. The kind of excitement he gets when a fish is tempted with his bait. I turn and see him crouching up to his rod which rests in a **Y** shape made from a tree branch.

"Hey. Look. He's getting a bite." I say to Rusty and Brandon.

We walk over and stand around him. The tip of Dad's fishing rod gets yanked hard. Dad flinches and almost goes to snatch it up but stops himself short just as the rod returns to form.

"Dang, that was good bite there." says Rusty's dad.

"Yeah. It sure was. I'm trying to be patient though. I want to be sure he has time to eat the whole bream." Dad says. "He'll let me know when he's ready to brawl."

And he did. Within a dozen seconds of Dad's words, the fish hit again. This time he makes a dash for it and begins peeling off drag hard and fast. Dad yanks the rod up and sets the hook.

"Fish on!" He says with a big grin.

He reels and pulls for a second to be sure the hook was in, then looks to us boys, grins, and says, "C'mon over here. Y'all can take turns getting this one in. It's going to be a nice one."

I smile and reach out for the rod. I take my turn fighting and then pass it off to Rusty. He reels him in a little further and then Dad says, "Alright now, let Brandon have a crack at it."

Brandon takes his turn and by now the fish is almost in. Dad goes closer to the water's edge, having to step down a small embankment to get there. He watches Brandon's line zig zag through the water.

"Alright, keep ya line tight now."

The fish comes to the surface and makes a big splash. We all ooh and ahh as excited laughter pours out from us.

Dad takes hold of the line. "Hey, can someone get a light for me. It's dark down here."

"Yeah, I'm trying. My phone's acting up," says Brandon's dad.

Rusty's dad says, "I left mine at home. I don't have anything."

I hear the fish splash again, but I don't see anything. I hear Dad grunt as if reaching out for it. Then I hear him scream like I've never heard before and have yet to hear since.

"What is it? What happened?" One of the dads asked.

I hear my dad scrambling up the embankment. Brandon's dad gets his phone working, and the flashlight app comes on. Dad gasps for air. I hear the fish splash loud as Brandon tries to keep the line tight. The fish makes a last-ditch effort and breaks for it, snapping the line. We didn't much care at that point. Brandon tossed the rod down and we all ran over to meet Dad. He climbs up the embankment with his fingers covered in mud, and his face washed white in sheer terror. His eyes are huge, and his mouth hangs open as he tries to catch his breath. He collapses onto the grass and rolls onto his back.

We hover over him.

"What is it?" Rusty's dad asks.

In between gasps, Dad manages to say, "There's a . . . dead . . . body down there. I . . . saw him. He floated up . . . to me."

It was like someone had just tossed a bucket of ice water on me. I felt my skin tense and crawl with cold chills. None of us said a word for what seemed like minutes but was likely only a few seconds. Brandon's dad breaks the silence and speaks from a dry throat, "You saw what down there?"

Dad pulls in a long breath, opens his eyes, and says with both palms to his forehead, "I saw a boy. He floated up to me, face first. He's down there. I know he is."

He stands to his feet and together we all walk over to the edge. We look down at the darkened embankment. Brandon's dad shines his phone. The water ripples back our reflection. There were no dead bodies anywhere.

"I saw him, I swear." Dad says as he rubs his face which is slick with sweat.

Our dads spent the next fifteen minutes or more combing through the water and searching along the bank. They never found the floating body, and we never landed a big catfish. Our night of fishing was over.

For the rest of the school year, I was questioned about the ghost of the Crow Creek pond. The rumors of it being haunted had spread through town like a raging fire. Everyone was always asking us what we saw. My dad didn't like talking about it and avoided the questions as best he could. He said the guys at work even teased him about it. Mom's friends were always asking her how he was doing. It was like they were afraid he would end up like that scary movie with Jack Nicholson. The one where he sticks his head through the bathroom door.

Whatever it was my dad saw, it affected him in such a way that made me tremble to think of something so scary that could do that to a grown man. Not just any grown man, but one who I knew to be fearless and manly in all sorts and fashions. What did he really see down there? In a way, I hope I never find out.

SOMETIME DURING the fall of 2014, I remember there was a lot of talk going around about the person they called the GTK. He was like a legend to everyone. Reminded me of the headless horseman with the town of Sleepy Hallow. I'd heard some things from my friends about this guy, but up until that point I never really understood what was so interesting about this GTK fellow.

Then one day as I was riding along with my parents on the way back from the grocery store, I heard someone on the radio talking about the GTK and how they believed he may be back or something. As the Georgetown Paper Mill billowed smoak in the distance, I remember asking Mom who the GTK was. She turned the radio to another station and said he was a very bad man who I didn't need to worry about. After I continued to question her and Dad about him, she finally said, "He killed some people around here a long time ago, but he's gone now. All of this new stuff is just some sick lunatic trying to scare people." She looked over to Dad as he drove us through town. "Right, honey?"

He looked at her out of the corner of his eye, swallowed, and said, "Uh, yeah." Then he looked up into the rearview mirror at me. "Yeah, you don't have to worry about him. He's probably dead by now anyway. The boogeyman may have gotten him. At least I hope so."

"The kids at school are saying people think he's coming back to Georgetown. Do you think he will, Dad?"

Dad adjusted his hands on the wheel and searched for the right words. After a moment of digging, he said, "No."

And that was that.

While I hoped it was true that the boogeyman had gotten him, I knew by the way my parents were acting neither of them believed it. I didn't think the rest of the town did either because for about a month leading up to the GTK's arrest, Georgetown had become like London during the nineteenth century in fear of another attack by Jack the Ripper. My friend's parents quit letting them hang out with me as much. We were all forbidden from playing in the woods or fishing in the pond behind our neighborhood. I remember my mom would often stay up late talking to my friend's mothers. I wasn't allowed to ride the bus anymore. Mom or sometimes Dad began taking me back and forth every day. I noticed a lot of other parents did the same as all the school buses were riding thin.

One night I came downstairs from doing homework to find Dad cleaning his shotgun and rifle in the living room. It was something I'd never seen him do before. I sat in awe as he finished what he was doing. I could tell he was nervous with me and his guns being in the same room together. At that time, I'd been deer and turkey hunting with him for about two or three years, but the guns were still off limits to me. He said when I got my first pimple, he'd show me how to shoot the big guns. Until then, I had to settle for the red rider bb gun.

Though I was only ten years old, I knew something wasn't right. Something had everyone scared. As the days grew shorter and the nights wore longer, I began to wonder if there was coming a day when the darkness would remain. Like the way the streets darken beneath a storm cloud, I could sense something was coming. I just didn't know what.

IT WASN'T UNTIL a few weeks later I learned the truth about the GTK. I remember my mom came and picked me up early from school. I knew from the look on her face that something had happened. I felt my gut tense and my heart constrict as I prepared for bad news. Had something happened to Dad? Did one of my grandparents die? Did our cat get run over? What happened?

I buckle my seat belt and ask her why she's picking me up early.

She dodged the question by asking what I wanted for lunch.

"Uh, I don't know. McDonald's, I guess. Mom, what's going on?"

She swallows and scratches the back of her head. She bites her bottom lip and takes in a breath. Feeling my questioning eyes, she glances over at me as she navigates traffic.

"There's something I need to tell you."

"Okay?" I ask with fear controlling my voice.

"You've been asking us about the GTK, right?"

"Yeah?"

"Well, we found out this morning they caught him."

"They caught him? Like the real guy? *The* GTK?"

She bobs her head.

"Where at?"

"Up in Holden Beach. It's almost two hours from here."

"Really?"

"Yeah. Your Dad and I felt it was important that you hear it from us instead of hearing crazy rumors at school. We can watch the news when we get home."

"Yeah. Well, I'm glad they caught him. What do you think he was doing in Holden Beach?"

"They don't know yet." She looks over at me, "Hunter, this was an evil man. You're going to hear all sorts of things about him. Some of it true, some of it just stupid stuff to scare people. We're going to do our best to tell you the truth. At least the things we think you're old enough to hear."

"Okay."

"Okay. Good." She wipes her face again. "So, McDonald's, huh?"

I nod.

I finished one McDouble on the way home and was halfway through my second when we walked through our front door. Mom sets her keys and pocketbook onto the kitchen counter, then walks into the living room and turns on the tv. I follow her and sit next to her on the ottoman. As I sit chewing my lunch, the news is busy showing a lady reporter near what looks like the beach somewhere. Big, grassy dunes sit off behind her right shoulder. The wind plays with her hair as she keeps having to pull it from her face. Seagulls fly around in the background.

"Just over there in those woods is where the missing Rebecca Randolph was discovered last night shortly after eight o'clock. The man in the sketch, which was aired last week, is suspected of being the one many have called, *The GTK*."

With that, the screen cuts to a picture of the sketch as the reporter begins narrating. At that moment, I understood the kind of fear my dad encountered the night he claimed to have seen the boy in the pond. As the picture of the GTK appeared, I found it hard to breathe.

My heart sank into my stomach, and I felt glued to the ottoman.

My dad had said that day in the car that he hoped the boogeyman had gotten the GTK. Judging by the amount of terror the sketch gave, it was more like he'd gotten the boogeyman and turned into an even scarier version of him. That face and those eyes were the things nightmares are made of. I felt my fingers and knees begin to tremble. It was looking into the eyes of the devil. I'll never forget it for as long as I live.

My mother and I both jolted when her phone began to ring. She got up and walked into the kitchen. I followed and clung tight to her side. I felt if she left me in the room with that man on the tv, he'd somehow climb through the screen and eat me.

Over the following days and weeks, my parents did their best to inform me of the truth about the GTK. But I don't think neither of us were prepared for the things we'd soon learn.

Could this be the real GTK?

Like how the GTK grew up in the neighborhood on the other side of the pines behind my house. It was also where his father's cult was born. The one they say was called, *for the greater good.* The pond we fished in was where the GTK claimed to have once dumped a body. It was the body of a boy his father's cult had murdered. The boy had been reported missing for over twenty-five years until the GTK confessed after his arrest. The boy's name was Will Abercrombie. I believe that is who my dad saw that night.

I also believe it was the GTK's dad or one of the cult member's ghost that me and Rusty saw that day while playing hide-n-go-seek in the woods. I still haven't figured things out about those two dogs that were fighting in our backyard that night, but every once in a while, I'll hear them howl outside my window.

After the GTK's arrest it was like we could all breathe again. You could feel the change in the air. It was like the sun was peeking out from behind a cloud on a cold winter's day to spread a little warmth. The atmosphere had shifted, and fear was vanquished, disappearing like a passing shadow. Darkness no longer crept upon the earth. Light had come and pushed it aside like a candle flame licking away the blackness of a room, and for that I was grateful.

We ended up moving to Myrtle Beach shortly after we learned of our nearness to the GTK's origin. Now every time I hear a dog howl at the moon, my mind goes back to our days in Georgetown as I remember the things that happened during those two short years of my life.

The Man without a Face

Ashley Weber had seen the man without a face for as long as her memory would allow. Her parents and grandparents said she began speaking to him soon after her tongue gained its agility. She'd sit for hours playing with her dolls while laughing and giggling to an unseen presence. When questioned about who she was talking to, she'd say, "The man without a face." The way she said it, in such calm matter of fact expression, would lead you to believe this *man without a face* was as common as anyone else Ashley may encounter throughout the day. When asked where he was, Ashley would often raise a finger and point to the nearest seat, whether it be a couch, a recliner, or bar stool and say, "He's sitting right there, watching." Her words would of course be scrambled and slurred like a toothless drunk, but you'd get the picture. To Ashley Weber's family, the man without a face seemed like an imaginary friend. Something a lot of kids are prone to have. Only Ashley's stayed with her as she aged.

All through grade school he hung around. Often lingering by the playground and standing by the edge of the lot watching her. Then he'd visit her at night. She'd awake to the sound of scratching. Like a pencil scraping across a notepad. She'd find the man without a face standing over her bed, stalking her.

When Ashley turned eight, she began to notice that when the man without a face came around, things tended to happen.

Like the time her grandmother died of a sudden heart attack two weeks after Ashley saw the man in her grandma's kitchen. Or like the time she learned her mother was pregnant with her baby brother exactly one week after seeing the man mingled in with the church choir. She saw the man standing in the canned soup aisle at the supermarket shortly before the family dog was hit by a car. There was another time she watched him cross a pedestrian walkway at the university. That was one week before she met her future husband in her English 305 class.

The last time she remembers seeing the man was two days before her baby brother died in a boating accident on the Waccamaw River. That was three years ago.

She's seen her fair share of psychiatrists and psychologists over the years and though she's managed to avoid becoming a diagnosed schizophrenic, she's been given about every type of medication the doctors can prescribe.

She's even spoke to a few mediums over the years, and all but one seemed to be what they're often portrayed as in the movies, a nut case. But the one that wasn't, told her this man without a face was nothing more than her spirit guide. One sent from above to watch her and guide through this life. Well, at least he was good at half his job. Watching.

Ashley Weber is gathering term papers and lecture notes in her office. She stuffs them away in her shoulder bag as her phone lies on her desk showing a picture of her husband, Ben.

"How was the writing this morning?" She asks.

"It was good. I knocked out fifteen hundred words. I was aiming for two thousand, but once I reached fifteen, it was like banging my head against a cactus."

"Ouch," Ashley says with a chuckle. "Well don't worry it'll come to you. It always does."

"I know. Well how did your kids do on the exam?"

"They did okay. The average was an eighty-two. That was pulled down some though by the four frat boys I was telling you about. The highest between them was a sixty-eight."

"Whew."

"Yeah, that's what I said. What time did you say your agent would call?"

"She said she's speaking with the guys at Penguin at one and would call me some time after three or so."

"Well, I'm sure she'll have some good news. Anyone who reads this series and gets to know Detective Crawford is not going to want to put it down. The characters are well developed, the plot is thick, the tension is there, and we did a good job of editing I think. I really took my time with this one. Which I really didn't catch that much, and neither did Ryan."

"I hope you're right Ashley. It'd sure be nice to get this series published with someone like Penguin. If we get this deal, you could work a part time schedule if you liked. It'd give us more time to focus on building a family."

Ashley takes a moment to answer. "We can cross that bridge when we get there." She looks at her watch. "I need to get going. Class starts in ten."

"Okay, sweetie. I'm going to take a break for a bit, maybe take a walk or something to try to poke my brain. I'll have dinner ready for you when you get home. Have a good lecture. Love you babe."

"Thanks, hon. Love you too. Bye." Ashley zips her bag and ends the call. The picture of her husband fades away. She pockets her phone and exits her office, locking the door behind her.

The three to three fifty English 459 lecture is her last of the day. She walks down the hall of the Edwards College of Humanities and Fine Arts building, passing a sea of students and faculty. All walking with their necks craned at an angle to their phones. Ashley had read an article not too long ago about how more and more young people are developing something called, "Devil's Horn" which is a buildup of calcium at the back part of the skull where the neck muscles and tendons connect. X-rays show a little pointy piece of bone sticking out like a tiny finger. God help us. Ashley pushes away these thoughts as she angles down a flight of stairs for room 107.

She passes students sitting in the window seals with their book bags resting on the cream and pepper colored tile. Their eyes glued to their screens, while unbeknownst to them their bodies work to build the "Devil's Horn."

The windows give view of a beautiful courtyard that is decorated with little Sago palms which are dwarfed by the larger Sabal's. A water fountain sits in the center. The sand colored stone masonry work reminds Ashley of something from the Roman Empire. Students move around it like ants navigating a rock in their path.

Ashley opens the door to room 107. It's built like an auditorium with the seats designing a half circle which angles down toward the podium, computer, white board, and large screen for power points.

Three students from the prior class are busy speaking with Professor Dawkins about their History 265 exam. Professor Dawkins stands by a small table after having taken his thumb drive and packed his bag. As he discusses the exam with the three students, Ashley walks down the steps and sets her bag behind the podium. She inserts her flash drive into the Dell computer tower and as it boots up she reaches for the remote for the projector and powers it on.

Professor Dawkins finishes with the students and turns to Ashley as she's now busy scribbling important due dates on the white board. As Dawkin's History students filter out, Ashley's English students filter in.

"How are we today, Doctor Weber?" Professor Dawkins asks as he secures the shoulder strap to his brown leather bag. His gray hair is pulled tight into a ponytail with his graying beard stretching past his neckline. He's seen his share of rowdy days and has lived to tell about it. He's told of a few of them to Ashley before, but boy does he know his history. He can spout dates and events like his life depended upon it. In a way, it did. His financial life at least.

Ashley caps the blue marker and turns to say, "I'm well and yourself?"

"Like a fat man looking in a skinny mirror. Happy as can be."

Ashley snickers and shakes her head. "I've never heard that one before."

"It's something my grandpa used to say. He was a mess."

"It sounds like it."

"Hey how's Ben's books doing? I'm halfway through the last one he wrote. I'm going to be bored until the next one's ready."

"Oh really?" she says with a grin. She tosses her single braid of hair over her right shoulder then crosses her arms and says, "That's good to hear. Yeah, he's expecting a call from his agent soon. We're hoping for some good news."

"Oh really? Well, that's good. Have you ever thought of writing a book? I read your articles in the Coastal Buzz. You're a mighty fine writer yourself."

"Oh, well thank you. I write short stories from time to time, but I've never tried my hand at a novel. I've seen what my husband goes through, so I've tried to spare myself the pain." The image of Ben banging his head into a cactus plays in her mind's eye.

Dawkins chuckles and says, "Yeah, it's not easy that's for sure. Give it some thought though. You never know, you might like it. Then maybe you and your husband could write mystery books together. Wouldn't that be something?"

"Huh, yeah it would, wouldn't it?"

"Never know." Dawkins adjusts his shoulder bag and glances about the room. "Well, must be getting close to three, looks like they're packing in. I'll see you Wednesday if I don't see you before then. And tell Ben I said to hurry up and get Detective Crawford on another case."

She smiles, "I sure will. Have a good day."

He gives her a three-finger salute and makes his way up the stairs for the door.

Ashley sighs and rubs her face. Her husband's potential deal with Penguin taking up most of the space in her head. His agent had said she'd negotiate a three-book deal, which would be enough to get the Crawford series up and running. This could be the big break they've been hoping for.

The idea which Professor Dawkins had tossed up played in her mind too. Could she write a novel? No. She doesn't have the patience for one. That was one characteristic of her husband that'd really drawn her to him. Unlike her, he seemed to be born with an uncanny sense of patience. Whether it was turning up the radio when stuck in traffic or examining how the wind plays with the leaves during a rainstorm, Ben was different.

It'd probably be best if she remained on the editing side of things for a while. Afterall, it was a pretty cool job because she got to see what no one else ever saw, Ben's rough drafts. And by sorting through the slush of words, she felt a deeper connection to him. As he shared his soul on the page, she soaked it all into her own. The two made a great team together and it'd be nice to be the editor wife of a famous author one day. Like Stephen King's wife. If it wasn't for her, King may have never been published. It was his wife who found a crumpled ball of paper in his trash bin with the word Carrie written at the top. After reading it and convincing her husband to not give it up, it went on to fetch them both almost a quarter of a million dollars. And that was in the seventies.

So, yeah she'd be okay with a job like that. Just as long as neither of them took to drugs or liquor the way a lot of writers do. If they could manage to avoid those sort of pitfalls and vices . . . yeah, maybe they could do alright for themselves. She could get her parent's the big house they'd always wanted. She could help send her nieces and nephews to college. Give some money to charity . . .

Professor Weber?

They could invest in some real estate and stock to protect themselves from inflation . . .

"Professor Weber?"

"Huh?" she shakes her head, pinches her tear ducts, and looks up to her class of students.

"I was just wondering if we were getting our tests back today?" asks Courtney from the second row.

"I'm sorry. Yes, I have them with me right here." Ashley walks over to the podium where she had the papers stacked beside the monitor. She picks up the stack and angles back to the table where she begins sorting the tests.

"You can come get them as I call your name."

Starting with the last names that began with A and working her way down, one by one the students came for their tests.

Ashley looked up when she made it to the letter L. She barely noticed it at first, but it was just enough to catch her attention. As a line of three or four students made their way up and down the center aisle, a big black shadow appeared in the seats halfway up the rows. Like a black speck on a pair of glasses, the shadow was a blur at first, but as Ashley blinked and looked past the students, it came into focus. There he was. Sitting in the third row, two seats from the center aisle. The man without a face. His long, slender frame sits with a straight spine, his hands folded in his lap. His face is blank and stained a mix shade of gray and purple. The eyes and nose are mostly gone. All that remains are two small holes for nostrils and a badly disfigured mouth which hangs crooked with thin lips.

Ashley gasps and covers her mouth. She squeezes her eyes and bites down hard on her molars.

"Are you alright?" Courtney asks as she stands waiting for her graded test. "Professor, you don't look so good."

Nausea sweeps over her, and her gut churns up past meals. Ashley feels sweat beads mount upon her forehead. Her cheeks flush and her head spins like an off-balance turntable playing a scratched record.

"Excuse me." Ashley manages to say as she gets to her feet and staggards out the emergency door to her left. The door shuts loudly behind her as she stumbles outside. She steps off the small path of sidewalk and pukes into the grass. She can hear students walking and talking around the other side of the building. Water fountains sound in the distance. Birds sing and light in the trees around her.

A yellow jetliner, with the name *Spirit* written in blue on it, flies over head among the clouds. The engine roars and resonates within her chest.

With her hands to her knees, she catches her breath and wipes her mouth with the heel of her hand. Oh, dear God. Not him again. Please, not again. Though she knows he's come to bring good tidings in the past, there' been plenty other times he's appeared to give news of impending death or doom. It was those times that played in the forefront of her mind.

Ben! Oh Jesus, no.

She wipes her mouth again and retrieves her phone. It rings and rings then goes to voicemail.

He said he was going for a walk when they hung up. What if he gets hit by a car, or gets kidnapped? Well that's not really a thing is it? What do they call it when it's an adult they take? Or what if he has a sudden heart attack like her grandmother did?

She dials him again as all these thoughts rage in her brain.

Oh, please pick up. Please.

On the third ring he answers. "Hey hon. Is everything—"

"Ben, where are you?"

"What's the matter? I thought you had your lec—"

"Where are you?"

"I'm at home. I just used the bathroom and was about to take a walk. Honey, what's the matter? You're scaring me."

"Don't go anywhere. Stay home. Do you feel okay? Sit down and check your pulse, will you?"

"Ashley, what is this? What's going on?"

"I saw him."

Ben goes quiet for a moment on the other end.

"Who?" Judging by the tone in his voice, she knew he knew.

"The man without a face."

THAT WAS TWO years ago. That same night was when Ben's agent called to tell them Penguin purchased the paperback rights to the Crawford series. It was the three-book deal that his agent had said she was working for. Ben and Ashley are currently editing the second of the three.

Two months after her sighting of the man in her classroom, the couple learned they were expecting. Ainsley is now fifteen months and in that funny stage of speaking gibberish and stumbling around with chubby, wrinkled legs. She has her daddy's nose with her mama's eyes and lips, coupled with a head full of blonde fuzz.

Even with the generous advances, Ashley and Ben still choose to live a modest life. They live in a home that meets their needs and offers the things they've always wanted. Like the in-ground swimming pool and the luscious back yard with the pergola and stone fire pit for the family get to togethers.

The Weber's are nothing fancy. They give and invest more than they spend. They never waste their money on things that doesn't bring value to themselves or others. And with their wise investments, Ainsley and her children will never have money problems unless they choose to. Though, Ashley and Ben won't just hand them everything on a golden platter, they're going to teach them how to be wise with their money and how to do things the right way.

When she's not editing the next installment of the Detective Crawford mystery series, Ashley finds herself still teaching English at Coastal Carolina. Though now she's only part time. Seeing Ben go from struggling to put together a paragraph to crafting full length best-selling novels, Ashley believes whole heartedly that the craft of writing is something that can be learned and shouldn't be something that's viewed as either you have or you don't. She loves what she does, and she feels a calling to help teach a new generation of writers. But boy does she look forward to going home to see Ben and Ainsley each day when class is over.

Something that scares her more than anything though, especially now that Ainsley is learning words, is she'll come home one day to find her seated in the living room, playing with dolls and talking to an invisible stranger. Will Ainsley see him too when she gets older? The question turns her stomach.

Ashley hasn't seen the man since that day in her classroom. Ashley hopes and prays that will be the last of him. She has most of the big things in life checked off the list, so what worries her most is that the next time he appears it'll be to warn of coming doom.

It's currently her last day of classes before fall break and Ashley is trudging along through her second to last lecture of the day. As she works her way through chapter thirteen of the textbook, highlighting the bullet points on the power point with a laser, something evil brews in the parking lot.

DRESSED IN A long black trench coat, which conceals a pump action shotgun and a *.9mm* pistol, is Kane Cheraw.

He's a sophomore computer science major who also happens to play on the club lacrosse team. He has no criminal record, is not attune to loud parties, and has never started a fight. He guesses he's left that up for others to do all these years. Like his dad or the bullies who tortured him all through junior high and high school.

Today is when things change. No more will Kane Cheraw stay quiet, laying low to be other's door mat. No. Today is the day things begin to change. People are oblivious to what's coming. Like residents of a coastal town in the eighteenth century before a category five hurricane. Kane Cheraw feels a rush of adrenaline and power sweep over him. He draws a deep breath, steadies his nerves which are strung tight like guitar strings, exhales, and begins the trek for the Edwards building.

TWENTY TILL FOUR and Ashley is still going strong. When she's not going over the power point, she's busy scribbling notes upon the whiteboard. She caps the blue marker and turns to her class. "Readers read fiction for two reasons: 1) They're interested in the characters, and 2) They're interested in the story. Now any book which has either of these two elements will be readable, but a book which has both dynamic and relatable characters, coupled with an intriguing story and plot, will be—"

She stops at the sound of a loud pop coming from somewhere within the building. Just as she begins looking around the classroom to ask if the others heard it too, her heart gets a jolt at who's standing in the center aisle. His long, lanky frame is motionless like a statue. Ashley feels herself freeze into place. The hair on her neck and arms straighten. Here he is again, the man without a face.

There's another pop, but this time it's followed by screaming. At this moment, things enter into a crawl. Time slows, sound ebbs, but the man still stands before her. She sees her students tense with shock in her peripheral. Ashley's eyes are glued to the man without a face as thoughts of her family flash before her mind. The names of her students begin popping up in her head.

Boom!

More screams. Things become chaotic.

She watches as the man without a face, slowly lifts his hand to the exit door. Ashley blinks hard and feels herself flinch. Time returns to reality and sound is now crisp. She hears some of her student's crying and murmuring. Most of them are now standing to their feet with their eyes glued to the door at the top of the stairs behind them.

Ashley breathes in rhythm with her pounding heart. Her breath comes in quick puffs through her mouth. The man without a face has vanished.

Boom!

Ashley looks to her students and bites out a loud whisper through clinched teeth while shoving her pointer finger to the exit door, "Run!"

Boom!

It's getting closer and it no longer sounds like a handgun. The blast is too dense.

Ashley rushes to the exit door and swings it open. She waves her students out as they begin to flood down from their seats, bee lining for the door.

Tears. Screaming. Gun fire. Chaos.

With more than half of her students now outside the classroom, she holds the door for the others. Six more pass through.

It's become eerily quiet. There's no more gun shots and it doesn't sound like anymore screaming beyond the door entering the room.

Five students remain. They each come rushing for the exit. Sun light filters in and spreads across Ashley's sandals, warming her feet. As she waves the last of her students out, the door at the top of the stairs burst open.

A young man with dark glasses and a black trench coat steps in clutching a shotgun. She watches as he raises the gun and aims it to her gut. It all happens so fast. She sees an orange burst of light fill the shadow he stands in, followed by a resounding boom which rattles her chest. Fire spreads across her body.

Two months later

THE DEVASTING AND senseless shooting that occurred that otherwise calm, quiet afternoon in October, ended up claiming the lives of six students and two professors, while injuring over a dozen more. Kane Cheraw's rampage was finally put to an end by a courageous campus police officer who stormed into the Edwards building to confront Cheraw. The two exchanged gunfire briefly before the officer managed to deliver a lethal shot.

Since that day, Professor Ashley Weber has been bound to three days a week of physical therapy. The wounds she suffered that day severely damaged most of her kneecap, splintering a large portion of it into tiny bone fragments. The doctors said if Cheraw had shot her in the gut she wouldn't have survived. If it weren't for the fast-acting aid which she received from one of her students who happened to be a combat veteran from the war in Iraq, the doctors said she'd lost her leg completely.

The tourniquet saved her leg and also saved her life from bleeding out.

The investigators say after having watched the footage and interviewed witnesses and survivors, Kane Cheraw began in his own classroom where he had a world religion elective course. He walked in with no sign of emotion, his eyes black and dilated. He emptied his weapons (a pump action shotgun and a *.9mm* pistol) and proceeded to the next room.

Ashley's was the fourth and last that he entered before being taken out by the campus police officer.

Once Ashley had recovered enough to carry on conversation, she told Ben about seeing the man without a face just before Cheraw burst into her classroom. She also asked around her relatives if they knew anything about this man. It was her aunt Grace that told her of Grandpa John.

Aunt Grace revealed to her that Grandpa John, as many of the relatives called him, was a descendant on her Father's side who fell victim to a nasty bombing during his service in World War One. He and his platoon were killed by a series of mortars while battling in the trenches of Germany. Though no one in the family has ever seen the man which Ashley describes, Aunt Grace was able to show Ashley photos of Grandpa John before he left for war. His stature and lanky frame were identical to the man Ashley has seen since her childhood, only this man had his face.

Ashley went on to order an Ancestry kit to document the details for herself. After some thorough digging, she was able to confirm everything Aunt Grace had told her. She has the diagram of the family tree along with photos of Grandpa John all stuffed together in a large binder. The new revelation was comforting to Ashley. She now feels a sense of relief, like as if after all these years, she'd finally been introduced to the man who for so long had came and went like the seasons. With each of his appearances, she knew to either expect the sun light of spring, or the gloom of winter.

Now on a paid sabbatical and accompanied by crutches, Ashley spends most of her days when not in therapy either with Ainsley or with Ben's latest manuscript.

It's now one in the afternoon and as the birds gather forage to last them through the coming winter, Ashley hobbles her way into the living room with a copy of chapter twenty-seven from the second book in the Detective Crawford series. Ben sits in the floor with Ainsley as she tinkers with her doll house. A kiddie show plays over the television. The one with all the ponies and animals that Ainsley likes.

Ben sees Ashley making her way in and rises to help her.

"Honey. I've told you you don't have to do this. The editors can handle it. You really need to be getting your rest."

"I know. I enjoy doing it though. I want to be a part of this. I need something to keep my mind occupied anyway. It helps me cope."

Ben smiles with his mouth closed and lets out a breath. He kisses her and says, "You're an angel, you know that?"

She smiles back and passes him the manuscript. "You may reconsider after reading my edits."

"That bad?" Ben asks with concern.

She smacks him on the chest with the back of her hand, "Relax. I'm kidding."

"Don't do that. You scared me."

They chuckle as he helps her to the couch. They sit down next to each other and Ben begins skimming over Ashley's red markings.

Ainsley staggers around the doll house. The new length to her hair is bound neatly in a cute red bow. She speaks in gibberish in between smiling with her baby teeth.

Ashley leans back into the couch and rests her forearm across her face. Ben reads quietly to himself, miming Ashley's corrections.

"Oh goodness, how did I not see that?" he says before thumbing to another page.

Feeling a headache coming on as the meds begin to ebb and allow the pain in her knee to return, Ashley says beneath her forearm, "Honey, can you turn that down a notch?"

"Yeah, sure. You okay?"

Ainsley chuckles at something.

"Yeah, I'm fine. I think the meds are wearing off. What time is it?"

Ben turns the volume down and glances at his watch, "Going on one thirty."

"Yeah, it's time to take another pain killer."

"No. No. Dawn do dat. No. No." At first Ashley thought her baby girl was telling her daddy not to turn the tv down, but when she didn't hear Ben say anything back, she decided to remove her arm and see what the fuss was about.

She looks to Ben to find him looking quietly at his daughter. Ashley looks to Ainsley and sees her looking to the recliner in the corner of the room. Ainsley smiles and tilts her head in that direction. She sits down with a thump and begins kicking her feet about the hardwood floor. Her little pink pajamas scrubbing back and forth.

She smiles big and begins to laugh as her little fingers tug at her toes. Then she says with delightful bobs of her head, "Ah-huh. Ah-huh."

Ashley feels her pulse quicken. All her memories of the man without a face (or Grandpa John as he's now known) flood her mind. Will her daughter carry on this tradition? If so, which season of life has Grandpa John come to bare witness of? Will it be a fortune of gloom or one of light? Within enough days, they'll all know.

Ashley looks to the empty recliner where she can half imagine Grandpa John sitting this very moment. She smiles gently, closes her eyes, and looks to heaven. She nods her head and says a prayer for good things to come. Ashley swallows the lump in her throat and wipes a tear from her cheek.

She and Ben have much to teach her. At least she'll always have someone who'll give her a heads up in life when something big is coming. Though Ashley had originally felt it was a curse to be visited by this man, she now feels a sense of comfort in knowing someone is always watching out for them. The man without a face who she finally has a name for, Grandpa John.

Randall Lane

The Coven of
Bloody Pond Road

Having had the chance to speak with my family and a few of the neighbors over the years, I must say, I'm surprised my parents bought the place having known about its history. Granted they didn't know everything, but they certainly knew enough. Like the neighbors hearing beating drums in the wee hours of the night, sightings of long-haired women cloaked in white night gowns dancing in the fields amongst totem poles with colored ribbons floating in the breeze.

Then of course the tale about those two teen lovers who'd cruised up the long windy hill in search of a secluded spot, wandering off in the field behind the house, only to find a chair placed in the center of the path with a baby doll wrapped in a plastic trash bag up to its neck so it could peep at those that passed. The boy and girl fled down the hill and found some friends to go back with. What they found is still talk among the locals to this day. The doll and chair were shredded in a million pieces as if some wild woman or raged animal had taken to it, tossing pieces here and there as white cotton and plastic sprinkled the old, dead field.

I didn't hear that story or the others until years after our time at the Big Red House. That's what we call it. What everyone calls it because it looks like it's been splashed with a pale of blood that'd tilted from the sky.

Anyhow, that's just a few of the things I didn't know about the place when we moved in. But it didn't take long to figure out things were different at the Big Red House. If only I knew then what I know now.

44 years ago

2 miles south of Bishopville, SC

November 8, 1975

10:43 a.m.

WE MOVED IN ON A SATURDAY. I'd just turned fourteen. The sun was tucked away behind a thick overcast and I remember it was cold enough to see my breath. My younger sister, Debra, and I had yet to see the place as Mom and Dad wanted it to be a surprise. Dad had finally gotten the promotion he'd sought after and with Mom settling into a nice job at the bank downtown, it allowed them the freedom to take a chance on the Big Red House.

Cruising along in Dad's 1970 Ford Station Wagon, baby blue with the wooden panel down the side, we jammed to CCR's *Tombstone Shadow.* He and Mom described the property again as we traveled. Lady, our full-blooded white and brown Border Collie, rode between me and Debra in the back. A small carry crate loaded with our three meowing cats, Jules, Tiger, and Cougar, sat in the far back next to our luggage.

Mom spotted the mailbox and said as she pointed, "Welp . . . here we are. Get ready to see your new home." Excitement poured out of her as she was all giddy with that big jubilant smile of hers. Gosh, I miss seeing that.

Dad knocked down his turn signal and applied the brakes. We passed a grove of trees, and a decent sized fishing pond came into view. It rested at the bottom of the hill, just off the road. An elderly black man and woman with cane poles were standing on the bank a good ways down from us. They waved as we turned off Bloody Pond Road and began the windy accent to the two-car garage waiting at the top. Cedar trees lined the pavement on both sides. Woods to the left, water to the right.

"That there is Mr. and Mrs. Rice. They've been fishing in this pond since they were kids. I told the realtor I saw no reason for that to stop. Your mother and I met them the other day. They're really sweet people. You'll both like them," Dad said as we putted along the hill. CCR was still going as Fogerty sung to the rhythm of the beat.

A flock of grouchy crows stirred from a tree and streaked in front of us, cawing as they flapped, catching the breeze, and taking flight.

Cresting the hill, the two-car garage sat to the left with the Big Red House sitting across from it on the right. Dad backed in near the sidewalk leading to the front porch.

The lot was surrounded by a grove of pines which outlined it like a fence. Far in the back was a large field. Pasture like, really. Grassy and flat. Tall weedy grass on the outside with a path of flattened tire marked grass in the center.

Two Ravens sat along the ridge of the house, watching us as we climbed out of the Station Wagon.

The roar of tires against the asphalt emitted below us as I watched a green pick-up truck with wooden rails on the back pass by the pond.

A dog barked in the distance and the smell of burning trash stung my nose. Must be the neighbors.

I followed Dad to the back of the car and watched as he opened the hatch. He tossed me a suitcase. He was grinning from ear to ear. His blond hair and beard made him look like one of the Allman Brothers. I remember he was dressed in brown corduroy pants with a burgundy turtleneck sweater and a beige sports coat. He smiled and said, "You're gonna love it here."

I caught the suitcase with a grunt and asked, "How much of the land do we own?"

He smiled even bigger, "All of it."

Mom and Debra were walking along the brick path leading to the porch, their shoes clacking as they went. Lady bounded happily behind them, brushing against their legs.

Dad sat the crate with the cats on the ground and held a suitcase in one hand then shut the hatch with the other. He picked up the crate as Jules and the other two cried for freedom. He nudged his chin to the house and prodded me onward.

The porch was wide and spacious with plenty of seating and rocking chairs. White wooden bannisters and railing accentuated the red paint covering the exterior. The view from up here was wonderful. The long, grassy knoll leading to the pond would be perfect for some summer fun. I could just picture myself riding my bike down the hill, hitting a ramp and skyrocketing over the glistening water, splashing in the deep.

"I see they remembered my chairs," Mom said, "Oh and my wreath too."

"Yeah, the movers done pretty good. Better than the last boneheads we had," said Dad as he sat the suitcase down and fumbled in his tight pocket.

He retrieved a small set of keys and crossed for the door.

"Well, you two ready to see the new homestead?" he said looking over his shoulder at me and Debra with the key slotted in the hole.

We bobbed and grinned.

He turned the key and slid the deadbolt away. He gave the door a little push to get it going. We rushed inside. A frigid gust of air banged against my face, chilling my cheeks.

"Whew!" I remember saying as I gripped my shoulders and shimmied in place.

Dad chuckled and said, "Yeah, I got to crank up some heat."

The home was dark with brown walls, salt and peppered tile floors, and a loft overhead with wooden railing. The stairs sat to the right covered in beige carpet with a wooden handrail and swirly black iron spindles running skyward. The movers had all of Mom's pictures and decorative trees where she wanted them. A big golden chandelier over the foyer lit up as I heard Mom flick the switch behind me.

The living room was straight ahead.

Our burnt orange sofa sat between a black leather recliner and Mom's peach colored reading chair under the tall lamp. A wooden coffee table sat in front of the sofa atop a furry looking rug.

The kitchen was adjacent to the living area, off to the right.

"Well, what do you think?" Mom asked.

"It's nice," said Debra.

"Where are our rooms?" I asked.

Mom tossed her chin upward and smiled, "The loft."

Me and Debra bolted for the stairs, fussing over who'd get the biggest room. I boasted it should be since I was the oldest, but she got me back by saying since she was a lady, she should get the better of the two. I lost my argument there, so that's how I ended up with the green room. Yeah, the ugly . . . green . . . room.

The walls were a sickly looking and after a few days, I convinced Mom that it needed another color. I think I went with an off white or something. Anything was better than that ugly green. My window overlooked the backyard and from the high vantage point, offered a nice view of the field as well. I saw a lot of deer from there.

Mom and Dad showed us around the rest of the house, but I stopped them when we passed through the kitchen. I pointed to a door and asked, "Where's that go?"

"Oh, that's the basement. I haven't got the key for it yet. Best not mess with it until I get the key and have a chance to see what's down there," Dad said before patting my shoulder and adding, "C'mon, check out how big the bathrooms are."

I nodded but kept my eye on the door as we left the kitchen.

After Mom and Dad were finished showing us the place, Deb and I went outside to explore the lay of the land. Lady sat at the door waiting for us.

Off the back porch was a large concrete slab with an in-ground swimming pool. It was empty now, except for the leaves and green stagnant water puddled at one end.

"C'mon, let's see what's out here," my sister said as she nudged my arm and tilted her head to the path leading out to the field.

I have no problem admitting that back then, despite her being a few years younger, she was always the bravest of the two. Not that I was a scaredy cat or anything, but

Deb never seemed to spook much. That of course all changed after having moved into the Big Red House.

And it got its start that first day when we found those graves out in the field.

As she ran along singing to one of the Bee Gees songs, without a care in the world, I tagged behind with my hands tucked away in my pockets, I watched as my breath steamed thicker and thicker into the air. Lady strode next to me.

I turned back to see how far we'd gone. The Big Red House looked like a toy from the monopoly game by this point. As I was turning back around to say something to Deb, I heard her stop and gasp.

She stood frozen, not saying a word.

To the left of us was a spot about the size of our living room where the grass was cut short and lined with numerous piles of rocks, each with upside down wooden crosses staked at one end. The graves weren't very big, maybe the size of a guitar or something. Definitely not big enough to house a human. At least not an adult that is. But there must've been about dozen or more lined side by side across this patch of ground, forming a circle. In the center was a large rock fire pit with three big circular holes dug in the ground around it. It was big enough for a telephone pole to rest.

Lady took on a defensive stance and began to bark and growl.

"Donnie . . . tell me what the heck this is."

I couldn't speak. I stood frozen next to Deb.

After a moment had passed of us just staring at the site of what felt like sacred ground, Deb finally muttered out, "Let's head back."

I nodded and placed my arm around her shoulders, pulling her to the house as I glanced about the field and woods to be sure we weren't being watched. Because it sure felt like we were.

We reached the house and found Mom and Dad kissing in the kitchen. They looked like two teens caught in a school closet. They jumped from each other's embrace, giggling.

"What is it? What's got you all shook up?" Dad asked.

I swallowed hard and said with a pointed thumb, "We found something in the field."

Mom craned her head, "What did you find?"

"Looks like graves. It's creepy. You need to go see it," said Deb.

Dad sighed and placed his hands to his hips, "I told John to take care of all that. He was supposed to clean it up last week," he cursed and rubbed the back of his neck.

"It's just a bunch of teenagers messing around, that's all. There's nothing to worry about," Mom said.

But somehow, I wasn't sure I believed her.

TWO WEEKS HAD PASSED since we moved in and other than the weird stuff we found in the field, nothing weird had happened. Until the day Dad finally got the key for the basement.

Must've been on the weekend, because I remember it was just me and Dad there at the house. I think Mom and Deb were out shopping or something.

"Well . . . let's see what's down here shall we?" Dad said with a grin as he held and twirled the key in front of his sparkling brown eyes.

He popped the key in and gave the knob a twist. The door creaked open and swung over a set of dusty stairs. An overhead drawstring light dangled about eye level.

Dad pulled it and after a moment of thinking the bulb was bad, it stuttered and winked on to light the stairway.

"C'mon," Dad said as he flicked my chest with the back of his hand.

I gulped and followed tightly behind him.

The steps were wooden and worn as they creaked under our weight. I half expected us to crash to the ground at any moment.

We reached the bottom and stepped off the last board, planting our feet to the concrete floor. The light from the dangling bulb at the top stopped just inches in front of us, leaving the imagination to gander at what lurked in the shadows.

A stale, earthy odor filled the air. You could tell it'd been a while since this place had seen the light. A rat squeaked and scurried away, giving our hearts a start at the sound of those little feet clambering to gain traction before bumping into what sounded like a paint can.

"Ah hah," Dad said as I heard him pull on another stringed bulb. But neither he nor I were prepared for what our eyes were about to show us.

Dad gasped and cursed. Ashamedly, I think I probably yelped like a little girl. But hey, don't get all macho on me now, you would've too if you'd been there.

Pinned to the wall were numerous goat and deer skins sprawled out with the hooves and heads still attached, some with horns, some without. A long table was pressed tight against the same wall, covered in unlit candles and small animal skulls. Snake skins were tossed here and there, dangling off each end of the table. But in the center of this table was a large wooden statue of a burly man wearing a ram's head. The horns spiraled and snaked their way heavenward as it stood with a finger pointing north. An array of herbs, bundled grasses, and other organic looking plants dangled from the floor joist.

My heart pounded like a drum. My skin crawled as if a thousand maggots were living beneath it. My spine shivered, causing my hands and feet to tremble.

On the floor in front of this table was about a half dozen poles decorated in colorful ribbons. I'd later learn they were totem poles.

Dad cursed and said, "Get out of here. Go on git!"

He didn't have to tell me twice.

I bolted up the steps.

I stood at the top in between the door frame catching my breath. Dad came thudding up the stairs not far behind me, cursing and wagging his head.

He reached the top, sighed and slammed the door shut behind him.

"Donnie . . . listen to me," he bent at the knee a bit and placed his hands on my shoulders, "You can't tell your mother or sister about this, okay? They'll be scared out of their wits. Right?"

I nodded with my eyes trained to the door.

"Hey. Hey. Listen to me. Not a word. Okay?"

I dipped my chin.

"We'll need to get that stuff out of there before they get back."

"What? What are we going to do with it?"

"Burn it. Alls I know to do unless you got a better idea."

"What is all that anyway?"

He sighed, "Listen . . . we were going to tell you both, we just didn't want to have to tell you this soon. There's a rumor that a clan of witches used to live here—"

"What!"

"Hang on, let me finish."

"Dad—"

"There's no use in getting all worked up about, it's just a load of crap anyway. Can't bother ya if you don't believe in it, right?"

I scoffed and dropped my head.

"Hey. Hey. It's just stupid stuff, ya know. None of it's real. Just . . . mumbo jumbo, right?"

"Does this have something to do with those graves out there?"

He didn't answer. I watched as he searched for words.

"Does it?"

"Maybe. I don't know. Look, we need to get down there and get this stuff out back so we can burn it."

"You sure that's a good idea? I mean what if we make someone mad," by someone of course I really meant *something*.

"They'll never know. They can't care too much about it anyways or else they wouldn't have left it. Right?"

I nodded.

"C'mon. Give me a hand."

And so, for the next few hours, Dad and I toted that crap from the basement and plopped it out back near a wood pile that needed burning.

We were able to get it lit about half an hour before Mom and Deb pulled in. Though they didn't know that day what we did, it wouldn't be long before they'd find out.

<hr>

SOON AFTER MINE AND DAD'S discovery, two of our cats went missing. Figured it must've been coyotes or something. Then I came down with a stomach bug and that's when the nightmares began.

They'd vary, but mostly consisted of me, Deb, and Lady out in the field at night. The moon would be full and glowing, dogs would be barking in the distance, crows cawing from above, and a hot fire crackling behind us. I'd turn around to see hundreds of men and women dressed in long white gowns with ram heads, dancing around the flame, singing in an unknown language. One of the women would be holding Jules and Cougar high in the air, staring to the stars. My feet would move without my consent like they do sometimes in a dream, but I'd stop when the long-haired lady would realize I was there. She'd snap her to me and that's when we'd bolt back for the house. The people wearing the ram heads would be right behind us growling and hissing, reaching out with bony fingers as they tried to snatch us up. I'd wake in a panic, gasping for breath, drenched in sweat, and doing my best to peer through the darkness to be sure no one was in the room with me.

One night I had that dream, but it wasn't the being chased that woke me, it was someone whispering my name. I swear it sounded like someone was standing right in front of my face, whispering, "Donnn-iiiieeeeeee."

I was overtaken by a wave of nausea and had to rush to the toilet to release it.

That wasn't the only time it happened either. I'd often wake between the hours of two and four in the morning to the sound of that same voice calling my name, followed by the sudden onset of nausea.

I asked Debra about it once, but she said she never experienced anything like that. I guess I was the only one.

I REMEMBER ONE EVENING we were piling into the Station Wagon about to head to town when a special delivery mail truck trudged up the driveway. Dad climbed out of the driver's seat and met the man between the two vehicles. After a few words, he passed Dad a bulky manila envelope. I watched out the back window as Dad stared at the package, exchanging glances towards us and the thing he held in his hands. After a moment he came back to the car, sat down, and held the envelope between he and Mom.

"What is it?" Mom asked.

Dad tapped it, pointing to the top left corner.

"The Coven," Mom read slow and timid like.

She felt the bulk of it.

Dad opened it.

He peered in, then stuck in a hand.

He retrieved a wooden human figurine with dried grass for hair.

A white rolled note was attached with a string to its little hand.

Dad took a breath and unrolled the note. Reading it to himself at first.

"What's it say?" Mom asked.

Dad twitched his brows and craned his head, then passed her the note.

"'You shouldn't have done that.' Done what? What are they talking about? Harold?"

And so, that's when he confessed to Mom and Debra about what we found in the basement.

Mom came down with a migraine that lasted for days, and Dad had to miss work to tend to her. Then he got a weird bug too. Ran a high fever and couldn't keep his food down. Deb stepped on a nail out back and I had the same nightmare every time I shut my eyes. It was a rough week to say the least.

AFTER THAT WEEK HAD PASSED, I found myself tossed in the middle of another nightmare. This one was like the others I'd had where me, Deb, and Lady were out in the field with the goat head monsters. Only this time they never knew we were there.

I remember watching as they performed some type of ceremony. A ritual or what have you. They were gathered around the fire all dressed in white with the ram heads sitting atop their shoulders, totem poles standing tall among them with fluttering ribbons, as one of the witches clutched a small lamb.

The lamb bleated and begged for mercy, but the cruel bystanders paid no mind as they looked on in their dazed rhythmic chant while swaying side to side.

I remember how white and spotless this lamb was. White as snow. Pure.

I turned my head as the person holding it retrieved a knife. The lamb was still bleating, it let out a loud screech then went silent. I couldn't look.

A gust of wind rushed among us, causing the grass and flame to bow in reverence. The onlookers chanted even louder and swayed faster and faster.

I peeked through my fingers. The once spotless lamb was now covered in red, and I watched as a streak of blood trickled from its neck. I was surrounded by a chaotic darkness, so thick I could feel it choking my breath. But the instant that drop of blood splashed to the ground, a bolt of white lightning crackled, striking the dancing flame, sending out spidery webs of energy streaking across the ground. I watched as it reached my feet, giving me a jolt as it climbed my body. I went numb, my sight filled with light and that's when I heard the voice, *Fear not, the blood of the lamb has overcome.*

Those words were overshadowed by the sound of beating drums. I was confused because I couldn't remember seeing any drums among us in my dream. But the drums grew louder. Then as if gripped by a fist that was pulling me from my slumber, I was awoken.

The drums continued to beat.

I sat in my bed, drenched in sweat, lungs begging for breath. But the drums beat on.

My eyes grew wide.

They were really out there, weren't they?

I twisted to the edge of my bed, feet scraping the floor. I rubbed my eyes and listened.

The drumbeats continued.

I stood and crossed to my window in slow, gliding strides. An orange glowing light grew the closer I got. My hands rested on the window seal as I pressed my cheek against the glass, peering out into the field.

My heart knocked at the sight.

My entire body was drenched in a splash of ice water.

A large flame licked the heavens as three silhouettes danced about the field.

I stumbled backwards, crashed to the floor, and scrambled for the door. My heart began to beat to the rhythm of the drums as my lungs labored for breath.

Foot thuds pounded up the steps and down the hall. My door swung open, crashing into my back.

"What is it?"

I heard Dad's voice ask.

I couldn't speak. I only pointed.

He crossed to the window.

Mom entered and knelt beside me, offering soothing words.

Deb came in and limped to Dad at the window.

Their voices were mute. All I could hear at that moment was the drums, my pounding heart, and that voice, *Fear not, the blood of the lamb has overcome.*

Mom snapped her fingers in my face, bringing me back.

"Hey, what happened?"

I tried to answer, but my words were jumbled and cut off by Dad bolting out the door saying, "Everyone get dressed. We got visitors."

"What?" Mom called.

I heard Dad fumbling through drawers in their bedroom.

"What is it sweetie?" Mom asked Deb who still stood by the window, gazing into the field. When she wouldn't answer, Mom rose to see for herself. I heard Dad coming back up the stairs. He entered the room the same time Mom saw the fire and dancers in the field.

"Who is that? Do you think it's them?"

Dad craned his head, "I don't know, but I need to go find out. Here, take this and stay here with the kids," he said passing her a double barrel shotgun and box of shells. He shoved a large revolver down the back of his pants.

Mom said with a strained voice, "Honey, please. Just call the police."

"Barb, I'll call before I go, but it'll take half an hour for them to get all the way out here."

"Dad let me come with you," I blurted.

He looked at me as he held Mom by the shoulders. He squinted his eyes, giving it some thought.

"You need to stay here with your mama and sister. They need you more than I do. I'll be fine."

"Dad, please. I have to go with you," I said standing.

Seeing my resolve and bravery I think he caught glimpse of his little boy becoming a man.

He tightened his lips and nodded, "Get you a coat and shoes, it's pretty chilly out there."

I rummaged through my closet and found what I could.

Dad called the police department in Hartsville which was fifteen miles away as the crow flew and about a thirty-minute drive taking the back roads. We hugged Mom and Deb, then headed for the Station Wagon.

Dad turned over the ignition and shifted into gear. We putted along, easing around the side of the house, heading for the path leading to the field. He kept his headlamps off and followed the moonlight. The flame licked higher in the distance as it danced over the tall grass.

We took our time, riding over small bumps and dodging mud holes. After a few minutes, we'd came within walking distance and could see the flame and totem poles sticking out of the darkness. Dad rolled his window down and hung his head out, listening. Quiet. Just the crackling flame, crickets, wind, the purring engine, and our tires rolling over the grass.

Dad eased on the brake and shifted to park, then popped open the door and stepped out. I did the same, keeping my right hand on the door frame as I stood in the gap.

The dancers were nowhere to be found.

"C'mon," Dad said in a whisper as he tilted his head.

I eased around the front of the car and strode alongside him to the crackling fire. We followed the high grass, taking cover against it as we sneaked along in a half crouch. We came to the end and peered around.

The air was knocked from my lungs. My heart skipped a beat. Dad was quiet too.

Three long haired women dressed in white flowing night gowns were knelt on their hands and knees, palms stretched forth on the ground in front of them, heads tucked to their guts in a form of worship. Silent and still. Small, bongo type drums were within arm's reach of them.

I could see something hairy lying in front of them, but I couldn't make it out. That is until I straightened my legs next to Dad.

My heart felt like it'd taken a round from the shotgun he'd given Mom. My soul filled with grief at the sight of Lady lying sprawled out next to the flame. As good as dead.

Tears sprang to my eyes, my jaw clinched tight.

"You sorry pieces of crap!" I belted through a cracked voice, taking strides towards the three of them. Dad swung his arm in front of me, barring me from going any further.

The women didn't budge.

"Who are you? What do you want?" Dad called out.

The woman in the center stirred, rising to her feet. Her dark hair dangled to the back of her knees. She spun on her heels, slow and steady, craning towards us like an owl. Her head was lowered so that we couldn't see her face at first.

Her two friends were still motionless on the ground.

Dad and I stared at her, not flinching a muscle.

She began to raise her head in a slow sweep, hair dangling in her face. She brought her hand to her eyes and raked back strands of hair, revealing her face. Her sharp features were old and ravaged with deep wrinkles snaking this way and that. Her face was blank and void of a soul. Then I watched as her lips quivered, stretching into a wide grin, glaring at us with icy eyes.

"Who are you? What do you want?"

"We want our land and home back. You never should have taken it from us."

"What? We didn't take anything from you. We bought his place with our own money."

"At half price after the foreclosure," her words sharp and piercing, "Give us back what's ours or else we take what's yours," her eyes shifted to me.

"No, you hold it right there lady, don't you dare threaten me or my fam—"

Before Dad could finish, she jerked her head and belted out an ear-piercing wail, long and screechy like. She took three quick strides straight for me.

I heard Dad reach in the back of his pants.

"The blood of the lamb has overcome!" I yelled.

She stopped and said through gritted teeth, "What did you just say?"

"The blood of the lamb has overcome!"

The wind gusted, lapping against the flame, sending an array of orange embers scattering to the sky.

Her face twisted in utter terror, "Don't you ever say that! You hear me? Ever!"

But I said it again and again. Each time the words came out of my mouth, she acted as if I were dousing acid on her. She stumbled backwards on wobbly legs.

I belted it again.

Her two friends on the ground let out loud screeches.

"Go on, git! Get outta here, you hear!" Dad screamed.

"Give us back our home and land and you'll never hear from us again."

A moment passed.

"If I do, I better not ever have any problems like this again. Understood?"

She pulled her two friends up by the arms. They staggered to their feet, standing next to her.

"You won't. Not with your boy talking like that," she said glancing at me.

"Give us time to find another place. You can have your home and land back. I better not ever see or hear from you again. Now, get out of here," Dad said with a thrust of his chin and wave of his hand.

After a prolonged stare down, they disappeared into the woods. White gowns and long hair fluttering in the wind.

The fire crackling as the breeze tickled the ribbons hanging from the totem poles.

I raced over to Lady and knelt beside her.

She was still breathing but seemed to be asleep.

I stroked her head and searched for a wound but couldn't find one.

"C'mon, let's get her back to the house. Maybe they just drugged her," said Dad as he lifted her in his arms.

I followed behind him, glancing over my shoulders towards the wood line, wondering if the women were watching us.

We reached the car, Dad sat Lady in the back seat, then sat behind the wheel and shifted to gear.

On the way back to the house, Dad asked, "Where did you hear that from?"

"What?"

"The blood of the lamb has overcome."

"The voice said it in my dream."

Then I told him about the Lamb and lightning.

WITHIN A FEW WEEKS we found another place, packed our bags and bolted out of Dodge, leaving behind the Big Red House for the Coven of Bloody Pond Road.

The witches bought the place back shortly after it went up for sale. And soon after they were back, the neighbors said the late-night drumming began.

My nightmares ceased after that night and I've yet to have one since. Knock on wood.

Everyone once and awhile, I'll take a cruise down Bloody Pond Road with CCR jamming over the speakers. I particularly like listening to *Long as I can see the light* as I pass by and gander. Of course, it's so grown up now, you can hardly recognize the place. The windows are boarded with graffiti-stricken plywood and the grass on the long knoll is almost as tall as the house. It's a real eye sore.

I'll never forget our short stay at that place. I learned a lot during those days. For the first time, I witnessed true evil and good. Darkness and Light. I knew from that day forward that there is more to life than just the tangible. Something unseen to the natural eye. Behind the veil if you will.

My time at the Big Red House changed my life. I graduated high school and went to Bible college in the Midwest, evangelized for a few years, and came back home to pastor Abundant Life Church here in Hartsville. Mom and Dad were faithful members up till their passing. Debra and her family are now members and help to keep me on track. I've got a wonderful wife and two kids along with a full bloodied Border Collie named Lady. I'm living my best life and I spend my days talking about the power of the blood from that Lamb in my dream.

So, is darkness real? You betcha. Do I fear it? Nope. Because when you know the Light, there's no need to fear the dark.

The Watcher in

the Woods

"The hairy men among the Giant Cedars of old are to be honored and feared. For they are not only charged with guarding us in our walk among the earth, but they take no issue in spreading the prideful among us as dried weed in a passing breeze. Stay humble and never challenge such authority."
- **Kosumi Windburn**
Elder of the Yurok Tribe

The cry of a raven gave my heart a start as it pulled my attention away from the mysterious odor that had me baffled. I looked skyward to see him latched to a branch while he watched with a twitchy move of his head. The crow's breath steamed into the air with each caw. It felt more like a warning than anything. He stirred and took flight, disappearing deeper into the woods.

A snowflake landed on my cheek, reminding me of my hood with the Velcro strap that would cover my chin. I wasted no time putting it to use. The snow continued to flutter to the earth, giving it a good dusting. The crunching of my boots became louder by the hour as the snow grew deeper along my journey to Cashman's Creek. It was fed by the Kootenai River.

The Salmon had yet to make their annual spawning run into the tributary streams, and with the calendar approaching November, the DNR made it my job to figure out why. I have my speculations that it's due to the lack of plankton and crawfish in the river, which took a hit when those jerks over at Helton Printers dumped all that excess ink and dye in the water. Lucky enough, some good Samaritans came forth and brought it to our attention. With the number of fines slapped on them, maybe old man Helton will think twice about such a careless act.

Anyhow, with all the equipment I'm tagging along, I'm sure I should be able to get to the bottom of the mystery.

I paused my trek to catch my breath. I unbuttoned the front pocket of my feather stuffed vest and unwrinkled the map. I gave a quick glance over the map and coordinates.

A flock of Canadian Geese flew overhead. Their wings cut through the air with a whop and swoosh. A few mocked me with their horsed laughter.

Man, the scenery up here in these parts of the woods is just . . . indescribable. It's hard to put it into words.

Beautiful snow-capped mountains, the vast valley peeking out from the snow-covered trees, frosted rocks by the creeks and rivers, the gentle ripple from the flowing stream, the squirrels barking their displeasure of my presence . . . ahh . . . nature at its finest.

I returned to the map and pulled out my compass. That sickening odor returned. I've smelled it once before in Idaho. It's such a strange smell. Hard to describe. Almost like a wet dog rolled up in a soured rug with a cow patty. It wasn't just the odor this time that had me stumped. It was the eerie feeling of being watched that accompanied it. Like someone was standing over my shoulder, looming over me, and glaring into my soul. An eerie chill washed over me.

The sound of an engine roared in the distance. At first, I thought it may just be my imagination. I was on private game land and as far as I knew, no one should've been out there. Must be a warden making his rounds or something. Or so I thought.

The roaring grew louder from the valley and scratched at my curiosity. A hill about twenty yards to my right looked like a good vantage point. I refolded my map and pocketed it along with the compass, before heading for the small ridge.

The engine stopped and the sound of three doors shutting along with two distinct voices, told me it wasn't DNR. They were close whoever it was. I made it to the ridge, squatted on my calves, and peaked over to view the valley. A black pick-up truck along with three men filled my vision.

My heart sank at the sight of two of the men walking behind another, one of them aiming a sawed-offed shotgun to the back of the third. The man stumbled through the snow as they shoved him onward.

I swallowed the lump in my throat and ducked behind the ridge. I pressed my back to the snow-covered leaves and pine needles. My pulse soared as my heart began to knock hard against my chest. Icy adrenaline trailed down my spine. Each breath became a gasp as it steamed into the air.

My mind went back to the Raven. He'd tried to warn me.

"Shut up!!! You knew you owed us. You've been dodging me ever since. I don't want to hear it! This'll be a warning to the others," one of the men said.

The captive man grunted as if he'd taken a blow to the back from the butt of the gun. I heard him crash to the ground and begin to plead for his life. His voice twisted in fear and choked with emotion.

I fumbled for my phone and texted Jerry back at the lab. I raised my head to give another peak.

Ca-chink!

The shucking of the shotgun sent a shudder throughout my entire body.

Dear God, I'm about to witness a murder!

The moment my eyes rose past the ridgeline, the man took a booming blast, shoving him to the snow. The echo of the blast scattered through the trees, ringing my ears.

The men chuckled at the bloodied mess of a man lying before them. The tone in their voices was demonic. How could someone commit cold-blooded murder and then laugh it off like a joke? What kind of sick people are they?

I took cover once again and looked at my phone. As I busied myself with attempting to place it on silent . . . it rang. My heart stopped as I sat frozen in the snow. It rang out again before I managed to silence it.

"Hey!!!"

I sat motionless and unable to move in fear of being heard or seen. Their footsteps thudding up the hill through the snow gave me no choice. I rose to my feet and with my head tucked beneath my shoulders, I made a break for it. One quick glance over my right shoulder and my eyes met the man with shotgun staggering his way up the hill aiming the barrel of that 12-gauge from about 30 yards away right at my face.

He fired. I ducked.

Bark from a tall pine just to my right splintered against my cheek.

"Oh, we got you now boy!"

The man with the gun screamed in excitement as the other laughed out loud in mid-chase.

My heart pounded against my chest, my vision blurred from all the jarring up and down, a drop of blood trickled to the snow beneath me.

Did I get shot?

Now panicked, I began checking myself for any leaking wound. It wasn't until I checked my face in mid-sprint, that I noticed the painful oozing lump on my cheek. I must've taken a pellet back there and I guess my adrenaline alleviated me of the pain.

My eyes darted to and fro through the forest, searching for a place to hide. My mind swam with a million thoughts.

I can't stop. I have to keep running and create distance. He has a shotgun, not a rifle. I had somewhat of an advantage.

My lungs were burning and screaming in protest at the sudden influx of cold mountain air.

Boom!

Another blast. This one scattered snow about three yards to my left. He shucked another round and fired again.

Boom!

This one landed just behind me and peppered my ankles. I flinched and yelped then managed to hobble to a rocky edge with a sloping descent. It was my only hope for creating distance between myself and the reaper toting a scatter gun instead of a scythe. I'd rather take my chances of tumbling down the cliff than to leave my life in the hands of these deranged hillbillies.

Boom!

This blast knocked me to my knees as it tore through my right shoulder.

"Yeah! You got em! Haha! You got em!"

On my hands and knees, I forced myself to crawl to the edge. The angled descent was steeper than I'd imagined, but I didn't have much choice. I had to reach the ledge. It was my only hope. My only chance for salvation.

I dug my fingers into the cold soil and pulled closer. My blood stained the pure snow.

The shucking of the shotgun couldn't have been 5 yards behind me.

He spoke through an cold, emotionless voice, "Stand to your feet and face me or I'll blow your head off right here and now."

Trembling with labored breath and painful oozing wounds, I forced myself to my feet and turned slow enough for my life to flash before my eyes.

This is it.

Murdered in the wooded hills of Montana by a duo of crazed inbreds. Not the way I envisioned my departure. Are we ever right about our death, though? Who is?

I thought about my wife, my kids, my brother, my parents. Tears flooded my eyes as my whole body filled with dread. My heart was being pulled to the earth as if a cinder block was tied to it. Already I was being pulled to the grave. Just get it over with, put me out of my misery.

Two men dressed in heavy Carhart jackets and overalls stood before me, each wearing crooked grins with wild, hazy looking eyes. Their pupils were blacker than the night sky.

"Looks like you were at the wrong place at the wrong time," he mocked as he trained the gun at my abdomen.

I shut my eyes and braced myself to meet my maker.

The scraping of bark filled the air as a rustle above me sent splintered bark covering my head. A loud grunt and demonic roar sent a chill down my spine.

The look on the men's faces said it all. I jerked my head heavenward. The sight took my balance, sending me tumbling backwards over the ledge.

The last thing I saw was a ginormous, hair covered man come thudding to the earth in mid-swipe at the two men.

Then my world turned upside down and blackness filled my sight.

JERRY SAYS it took the search crew 18 hours to find me as my phone and GPS were smashed during the fall. Said it was sixty-two foot down the side of Avery's Peak to the bottom of that ravine.

As luck would have it, most of my tumble was cushioned by the thick canopy of trees. But even with that, I still managed to break my collarbone, wrist, knee and two ribs. Not to mention the wounds from the shot gun. The last one in which collapsed my right lung. I also suffered a concussion.

Which is a big reason why no one seems to believe me about what I saw. They all claim it was a Grizzly that shredded the men.

Said one guy was picked apart limb by limb, as it took them three days to piece him back together.

The other, they found twenty feet in a pine, missing his head. Doesn't sound like a Grizzly to me.

Which is what I keep trying to tell them, but they won't have it. Despite me having a Ph.D. in Wildlife Biology, the Police and Wardens are taking the title of expert in this case.

All I know is I got to get back out there and figure out what the heck this thing is. I've never seen anything like it, and I sure is heck never learned about it in the textbooks.

The size of this creature was enormous. I mean it was a living, breathing giant. And that roar . . . whew . . . it'll stick with me the rest of my life. I don't know what it was, but one thing's for certain, now I know what's been watching me all these years. Turns out I wasn't the only one in the woods.

Lucinda

The acrid odor of being kept in the dark and unused for a decade, lingered still. Spiders, bugs, and dust had been the home's only occupants since 2008. At least that was what the realtor had said. Their closing was on a Friday, and they were settled in by the following Thursday. The place needed some work, but with Jack's new job and salary it wasn't anything the two couldn't handle. Carrie was hesitant at first on the move to San Francisco. But Jack's promotion was just too good to pass up. Within five years, if they did their money right, they'd have enough to semi retire if they wanted to. San Francisco certainly wouldn't be their forever home, but if they stuck to their plan, it could lead them to it when the time is right. San Fransisco was also far enough away from North Carolina that Carrie hoped the nightmare that had accompanied them there wouldn't follow.

She had wished with all the busyness and chaos, their daughter's little friend would get lost with a box of needless Tupperware. Carrie and Jack knew it'd all be in Mandy's best interest. Ever since her brother passed in the accident, she'd taken up with a stuffed teddy bear which she'd named Lucy.

It didn't end with the teddy bear though. Often times, little six-year-old Mandy would force Jack and Carrie to leave a spot at the dinner table for her imaginary friend.

At first it was cute and almost heart wrenching. Figuring it was just the child's way of not feeling alone since the loss of her twin brother, Carrie allowed it.

Mandy was sure to grow out of it eventually. All kids go through a spell, even Carrie herself could remember having such a friend as a child. Her name was Lucinda. She was a close confidant and even all these years later, she still finds herself . . .

"Hey Carrie, you mind giving me a hand?"

Jack's voice grunted as he peeked around the heavy box gripped in the basket of his arms. He'd tried angling for the steps but couldn't quite kick the front door shut with his heel.

Carrie blinked away the daze that'd settled over her. That's when she felt the hot sear of raw flesh. She removed the washcloth and stared at the palm left hand. It was red and blistered. Lost in her thoughts, she'd rubbed away the first layer of skin upon washing and drying from her labor with the flower garden.

Her light denim overhaul shorts were stained with soil near the midsection, the arm of her white tee wore a small tare it'd received while she ducked under a strand of barbed wire. She'd had the handy man place it there to keep the deer and varmints out. The handy man had also planted a few tomato plants and some other vegetables a month before they moved in so things would be ripe when they got there.

"Ooh," Carrie winced as she removed her red and white bandana that controlled her rippled brown hair. After sucking the heat from the wound, she wrapped it tight and crossed to shut the door behind her husband.

"What'd you do this time?" asked Jack.

"Oh nothing. Just nicked myself on the wire in the flower garden."

"Babe, I told you we don't need that. We're not in the Country anymore, remember? This is San Francisco, not Raleigh. These folks probably couldn't tell a deer from a racoon anyhow."

Carrie smirked and batted her eyes. Still keeping pressure on her hand.

"Well, it eases my mind to know I'm keeping the creatures out. At least I don't have to worry."

Jack tightened his lips, tilted his head, and thudded up the steps. Carrie was just behind his heels.

Mandy's voice tapered from the hall. She giggled and mumbled. Jack and Carrie stopped in the middle of the stairs and peered through the railing at their daughter.

She sat Indian style in the hallway of the loft wearing a pink dress covered in lilies. She lifted what mimicked an 18th century porcelain tea pitcher that Queen Elizabeth would have been proud of. Only if it wasn't plastic. Carrie watched as Mandy finished pouring an invisible liquid into her cup, then stretched and filled the cup across from her. She lifted the cup of tea, pinky extended like proper folk, smiled, and took a few fake sips while snickering at her invisible friend. She sat the cup down next to her knee and smiled at the unseen presence.

Carrie heard Jack mumbling under his breath and could feel the tension building within him. She tried to reach and squeeze his arm, but he was already in motion. He cleared his throat and took the last step.

"Having a tea party?"

Mandy flinched. She was quick to shift her gaze from the empty place across from her. Mandy and Jack locked eyes for a moment.

She stuttered and mumbled, searching for words. In a panic she rushed to clean up. Gathering the empty cups and pitchers in her arms as if they were alive and attempting to flee. She knocked a few over as they clanked their plastic against the hardwood floor.

"No-no, I was counting them. I thought I lost some,"

she said with gleaming eyes and a bright smile that could melt the hardest of hearts. It sure had a way of melting her daddy's. Jack sat the box down, gripped his back and angled to Mandy. Carrie watched as her daughter sat the teacups down before Jack lifted her in his arms and began to tell of all the fun things to do in San Francisco. From trolley rides to seal watching, the Golden Gate Bridge, you name it. Once finished, Mandy squeezed his neck, resting her head on his shoulder, eyes fixed to Carrie's. A thin grin stretched across Mandy's lips, her eyes were less than gleaming and more like . . . plotting.

A chill slithered down Carrie's spine.

She shook it away, denying what her gut was screaming. Mandy would never . . . no! Mandy would never do such a thing! Not *her* daughter!

Carrie cleared her throat and clasped her hands.

"Hey. I could use some help in the garden, who's ready to plant some tulips?"

"Yeah-yeah. Me-me. Ooh can we plant the rose bushes too?" Mandy asked with glee as Jack lowered her to the floor.

"Yeah, we'll see. How about you go ahead and get changed into some play clothes and we'll head out there?"

Mandy fired off down the hall, feet pitter pattering along the wood. It creaked and popped as she did so and popped again when Jack angled for Carrie.

"This'll be great honey. We're going to love it here. We'll be wishing we'd moved out here sooner," Jack said as he took Carrie in his arms. She watched as his dark blue eyes took on that sparkle that'd first drew her. Like a moth to a flame. He grinned and gave her a passionate kiss.

She kissed him back, then pulled away.

"We just have to be careful," she said as a feeling of

dread had filled her soul, weighing down her heart.

Jack sighed and placed his hands to his hips, eyes going to the floor. He rubbed the nape of his neck.

"Carrie. Please tell me it's over. Please. I can't go through this again."

"You saw her, just like I did. Lucy didn't stay in Raleigh. She followed us here."

"Oh, for heaven's sake, you can't be serious."

"Jack, we've been here for two days and she's already taken the tomatoes," she said with her eyes falling to the floor, her voice just above a whisper, "That's why I put up the barbed wire."

"What?"

Carrie raised her vision and sighed. She wiped away a tear. She hated herself for saying that last line. She didn't really mean to say it, but her soul was screaming so loud, it just came out.

"Let's go to the kitchen. I don't want Mandy hearing this."

"Hearing what?" Jack asked.

Carrie tightened her lips and crossed for the stairs, she raised a finger and motioned for her husband to follow.

Thudding down the stairs behind her, he asked, "What is it? What have you been hiding?"

Carrie remained silent. Jack sighed out a huff of hot air.

They reached the kitchen and Carrie took a seat at the wooden table. Jack sat next to her.

Carrie took a deep breath and looked Jack in the eye.

"What? Tell me." Jack said with raised brows.

"Honey, do you know how my parents owned the plantation home near the water in Charleston?"

"Yeah? What about it?"

"I grew up there."

"What? You told me you grew up in Florida with your aunt and uncle."

"That's only half the truth. I never told you about what really happened to my parents and why I had to live with Aunt Frances and Uncle James."

"Babe, what have you been hiding?"

Taken with emotion, it took all she had to gather herself and tell the rest.

Jack took her in his arms and squeezed her.

"No matter what this isn't going to change anything. You're still my girl and I still love you. Okay? Now tell me, what is it?"

Carrie pulled away and sniffled, then pushed out a long breath.

"My parents didn't die in a car wreck."

Jack scrunched his brows and craned his neck.

"I . . . ki . . . ki . . ." the words just wouldn't form.

The blood from Jack's face began to drain.

She gathered enough courage and strength and blurted out through a strained, raspy whisper, "I killed them!"

Jack gasped and jolted from the chair, sending it screeching across the floor before toppling over and smacking the hardwood.

"Lucy didn't start with Mandy. She started with me."

Jack was covering his mouth, eyes wide in horror as he pressed his back tight against the wall, staring at his wife.

"When I was six, my parents and I moved into the plantation home which was given to my dad after Grandma died. We moved in to keep it from getting run down. None of my dad's siblings would do it, so we did. It wasn't long after we'd moved in, I started seeing this little girl. I'd be out in the yard playing by the swing set or playing with my dolls and I'd get the feeling I was being watched. I would look up and see her standing by the wood line, just watching me. It went on like this for the first few days, and then she finally walked over and joined me. From that day until the night it happened, we were best friends."

"Who is she?"

"Her name is Lucinda. She is the youngest daughter of a slave family owned by my ancestors during the early 1800's. Her mother was the housekeeper and her father worked in the fields."

"What happened?"

"Well, Lucinda loved tomatoes and was terrible about stealing them from the garden. She was warned more than once by my distant grandmother not to take anymore, or she'd be taken to the whipping post. It kept her at bay for a while, but she eventually went back to taking tomatoes. My grandmother's son caught her red handed one day in the garden but made her a deal. He wouldn't tell on her as long as she did him some favors. The pour girl was only twelve."

"Dear God," Jack said with misty eyes.

"It went on for some time, until she finally got the nerve to tell her parents. Her father was enraged and immediately went to confront the man. His wife followed him and begged him not to get involved. She knew what would happen. They beat her father to death, killed the mother and her siblings, and then wrapped Lucinda to a tree with barbed wire, leaving her for the buzzards to feast on while she was still alive."

A moment passed.

"She made you kill your parents out of revenge."

"Authorities sent me to live with my aunt and uncle in Florida since I was so young when it happened. I had to go twice a week to visit different therapists until I became a teenager. Two weeks after my thirteenth birthday, my aunt and uncle said I started creeping into their bedroom at night and would stand by their bedside not saying a word."

"Just like Mandy has been doing. Why are you just now telling me this?"

"They said they couldn't handle my strange behavior, so they gave me up to a foster family."

"So, your parents didn't die in the car wreck . . . you really killed them."

Carrie nodded, wiping her eyes. She unwrapped her hand.

"I didn't cut myself on the barbed wire out there. I rubbed the scar raw with a rag in the kitchen," she held her hand up to show Jack the scar stretching from the web of her pointer and thumb to her palm.

"You said you got that scar from a piece of glass when you were young."

Carrie shook her head and said, "That's where the knife cut me as I stabbed my parents in their sleep." Emotion choked her voice.

She looked up to see Jack standing with his arms crossed, pale faced, and swallowing hard while looking like he can't decide whether to offer comfort or flee for his life.

"Lucy is Lucinda and now she's after our daughter. She won't stop until every member of the bloodline is dead. I'm from a cursed breed Jack. I'm cursed and because of my family's sin so is Mandy."

"Oh my God!" Jack said with a face twisted in panic and terror.

"What?"

"Did she kill Jackson? She did, didn't she? Didn't she?"

Carrie dropped her head and began to sob. Her shoulders jolted up and down.

"He didn't die in his sleep. Mandy smothered him!"

"Honey, please. We don't know that."

"And now she's going to try and kill us!" Jack paced the floor next to the windows looking out to the small back yard where Carrie's garden was.

He stopped and glared out the window then angled closer, leaning down for better viewing.

Carrie rose from her seat and crossed next to her husband to see what held his attention.

It was Mandy.

She was standing at the edge of the garden, staring at the barbed wire fence.

"She won't cross it," Carrie mumbled.

They watched as Mandy stood there like a statue, hands dangling by her sides, hair fluttering in the wind along her back.

"What do we do?" Jack asked.

Carrie was silent.

Mandy was moving, turning her head slowly like an owl. Her head twisted as she looked over her shoulder at Carrie and Jack. A long, tight grin stretched her face, she lifted her hand and waved.

"She knows. What do we do?' Jack asked again but this time turning to his wife.

Carrie heard him grunt as she sank the blade deep into his gut. Warm blood oozed around her hand. Jack muttered out a string of unintelligible words as his face was twisted in shock and pain.

Carrie plunged the knife deeper, rotating it, tearing away at his internal organs, piece by piece.

Something had come over her, she was torn. Half of her was screaming in horror at what was taking place by the work of her hands. Why would she kill Jack? She loved him. He's her soulmate. Why! But an internal rage was burning hotter than the flames of hell. Her blood was boiling. She'd never felt such anger and hate. It overtook her. She'd lost all control. Jack swayed to the right, then collapsed to the floor. Dead.

Carrie pulled her eyes to the window.

Mandy smiled with a toothy grin. Satisfied.

Carrie felt her hand being pulled to the veins along her left wrist. She didn't look. Her eyes were fixed on her smiling daughter. She felt her entire body begin to quiver, her teeth chattered, her heart pounded, and she couldn't stop the blade from pressing into her flesh. Her soul screamed from a place deep within. Begging her not to do it. Begging her to put the knife down and render aid to her dying husband.

She felt the pressure of the blade sink deeper. Her eyes still tight on her daughter through the window. Carrie struggled but managed to pull her eyes shut.

A door slammed upstairs. It sounded like Mandy's room.

At first the voice was just a whisper, a distant memory. But then it came charging back with force.

The Light shined in the darkness, and the darkness did not understand it. Jesus is that light folks. Just say His name and the darkness flees.

She heard the preacher's voice in the far corners of her mind. Pastor Welkie was his name. An old preacher at the church her aunt and uncle took her to as a child.

She felt her mouth clinch and seal tight.

With her muscles taut and ligaments stretched thin, she forced with all her might . . . her mouth popped open, and she blurted the name . . . Jesus!

A gut-wrenching screech pierced the air as every door in the home slammed shut. The cabinets knocked as they banged against the wood in quick succession.

"Jesus! Fill this place with your light! Show me your light!"

A loud roar of rushing air entered the room. Carrie's flesh took on a hot, tingling sensation, as her heart filled with a warmth that not even a mother's embrace could rival.

A bright flash of white light blasted into the room, forcing her to cover her eyes to keep from going blind. A loud hum followed.

Every ounce of evil disintegrated in that instant. The entire atmosphere had shifted. Light had entered, and the darkness was forced to flee.

The home took on an eerie hush.

Her heart was pounding as her blood pulsed through her veins.

She caught her breath and peaked through an eye lid. The cabinet doors in the kitchen were left open. She looked outside the window. Mandy was gone.

She looked at her wrist, the blade was still there, but it hadn't moved. There was just a small droplet of blood snaking down her skin, nothing worth worrying about. Her eyes then dropped to Jack who lay on the floor at her feet. She dropped to a crouch next to him and checked his pulse. It was there, but weak. Blood trickled out of him and pooled onto the hardwood floor.

Carrie stood to her feet and rushed to grab a kitchen towel from one of the cabinets. She crashed back beside Jack and shoved the wad of towels to his gut. He jerked and began to groan.

Tears blurred her vision and soaked the floor. She retrieved the cell phone from her pocket and pounded out 911.

The operator had to tell her more than once to calm down and catch her breath because she couldn't understand what she was trying to say. Carrie managed to gather herself enough to blurt out the address and plead for help. That's when she heard her daughter's voice call from the loft.

Carrie jerked her head. The operator was still speaking, but Carrie dropped the phone by Jack's side. She stood to her feet, swallowed a long gulp, and slowly made her way to the stairs leading to the loft.

"Mama . . . mama," Mandy's voice was strained with emotion, choked with tears.

Carrie reached the start of the stairs and had to steady her gasping breath and knocking heart. She drew a long breath, then lifted a foot onto the wood of the first step. It creaked under her weight as she took slow, steady strides to the top.

Creeeeeeaaaakkkkk.

"Mommy . . . Mommy," the voice cried.

Carrie strode to the door and placed her hand around the knob. She shut her eyes and said a silent prayer. She twisted the knob and pushed it open. The door creaked and swung on old hinges. Carrie's heart dropped to the floor at the sight before her. The sound of a distant siren grew in the distance.

Her daughter Mandy lay sound asleep in bed, tucked beneath the covers with little hands folded under her head. But it was what was placed at the foot of Mandy's bed that caused Carrie to be taken with enough fear to drop her dead.

A basket full of tomatoes. Filled to the brim.

Carrie gasped and stumbled into the door frame. Mandy stirred and rose from the bed, looking into her mama's eyes.

"What's the matter, Mommy?"

Carrie's legs grew like a drunken sailor. Everything

went dim. Her sight turned black.

Silence.

Three Months Later

San Francisco County Behavioral Health Center

CLOTHED IN WHITE from head to toe and in desperate need of a shower, Carrie Myers finds herself seated in the visiting room. A corded phone is next to her ear as a thick glass separates her from Jack and Mandy.

"You look good babe. I mean that. You seem better than last time. The meds still working?" said Jack.

Carrie nodded and wiped her nose as she sniffled.

"Stay strong. We'll get through this."

Carrie swallowed hard and gave him a soft smile.

"Look what I drew for you, Mommy."

Carrie looked with misty eyes at Mandy. She sat in her daddy's lap with a wide smile, holding out a piece of paper containing a crayon drawing of the family out in the yard. The house in San Francisco sat behind them and an out of place patch of woods was beside them.

"There's you, and me, and Daddy," she said slowly, drawing out her words like a typical six-year-old.

"Thank you, sweetie. I needed that. Can I have it?"

Mandy shot her a quick glance and wagged her head, "Not until I'm finished. Then I'll think about it."

"That's fine. When you're ready. I'll keep an empty place on my wall for it."

Jack grinned and took in a long breath, "Well sweetie, I guess we better get going. Don't want your mother to miss her dinner. Tell Mommy bye."

Tears welled in Carrie's eyes as she kissed her hand

and placed it against the glass. Mandy returned the gesture. Jack did the same.

"I love you. I always have and I always will," Carrie said with tears streaking down her face.

Jack wiped his eyes and picked up Mandy. She wrapped her arms around his neck.

"It's going to be okay. Stay strong Carrie. I love you. No matter what. You'll always be my girl," Jack said with a strained voice.

Carrie nodded and covered her mouth.

Jack breathed deep and turned to walk away.

Mandy waved from Jack's back as he strode off. She held the drawing in her hand.

Carrie's heart was being ripped in two.

The change in Mandy's eye put her emotions in check. She had that look again. It was the first time she'd seen it since that day.

Mandy raised the piece of paper containing her drawing.

Carrie stood and pressed against the glass, straining her eyes.

Mandy pointed at the wood line in the drawing. Her face twisted into a tight grin.

That's when she saw her. A dark figure about the size of a child. Lucinda. She was standing at the edge of the woods, watching. It wasn't over, she had to warn—

"Jack! Jaaaccckk!" Carrie cried as she beat upon the glass. But it was too late, he'd already rounded the corner. Mandy's big grin was the last thing she saw.

A nurse rushed to Carrie's side to calm her.

She fell into a deep sob at the realization that Lucinda not only wanted to end Carrie's blood line, but she also wanted to end the life of every male she came in contact with. And at the moment, Jack was next in line.

"God please protect them. Please don't let anything happen to them," Carrie pleaded with hot tears streaking down her cheeks.

The nurse brushed away strands of Carrie's blonde hair which dangled in front of her face and said, "It's okay dear. Just breathe for me okay. It's alright now."

Carrie began to pray for the urgent protection of her family. Her voice quivering, her body trembling, she couldn't stop the tears. The nurse prodded her away from the glass and steadied her as they stumbled towards the long hallway leading to the bedrooms.

The whole way to her room, Carrie prayed and pleaded for God to show Jack the paper Mandy had drawn. If he could just see the drawing and see Lucinda standing by the woods . . . then he'd know it wasn't over.

REACHING THE CAR and getting Mandy belted into the backseat, Jack asked, "What'd you draw for mama?"

"Nothing."

"Huh?" Jack wrinkled his brow. "Let me see. I won't show her until you're ready."

Mandy wagged her head and tucked the paper away beside her.

"Mandy. Sweetie, let me see the paper."

Again, she wagged her head.

Jack drew a deep breath and sighed it out. He could feel is blood pressure rising, warming his cheeks.

"Let me see the paper," his voice stern, his eyes meaning business.

Mandy glared back, then slowly began to wag her head.

Jack huffed and stretched across her to reach for the paper, fighting it from her closed fists.

"Ow!" Jack belted and then cursed. He smacked her on the leg before he even realized it.

With the paper in hand, he pulled back into the sunlight outside the car and began to turn his forearm over. A trickle of blood oozed from the bite mark.

"You bit me! Why would you bite me?"

She didn't say anything. Her eyes seared into his, but they went deeper, they pierced his soul.

"That's it! I'm taking you where I should have taken you long ago."

He slammed the door and marched towards the driver's side. While turning over the ignition, Mandy asked in a tight, emotionless voice, "Where are you taking me?"

"To a priest. That's where!"

A moment passed.

He heard her sniffle. He glanced in the rearview mirror. Her head was hanging low, palms to her face.

"I'm sorry, Daddy. Daddy, I'm sorry. Please don't take me."

"Honey, I have to. I should've already taken you. I should've listened to your mother. It'll be okay. You're going to be fine. We just need to get you some help. Okay?"

She didn't answer.

"Mandy, sweetie, I'm going to get you some help. Okay?"

"I don't need no help!" her voice deep and raspy at once.

Jack's flesh leapt from the bone, his heart knocked against his chest, he shot a glance at the mirror, but he didn't see Mandy. He saw something otherworldly.

He slammed his foot on the gas pedal, sending the needle jutting to the right. The engine roared as he sent the tires grabbing at the asphalt.

A deep, eerie laugh emitted from the back seat, penetrating his soul.

"Dear God! Help me. Help my daughter."

He raced to a nearby church. Any church. Anything that contradicted the unholy creature sitting in his back seat.

His eyes found a steeple. Salvation was near.

TUCKED AWAY IN her bedroom, knelt on her knees, hands clasped tight, elbows propped on her bed, Carrie was in earnest prayer for her family. Hot tears soaked the white comforter as her lips sent out petitions. She stayed like this for at least an hour it seemed.

"Please God, shine your light like you did at the house. The darkness can't stand against your light. There is no evil greater than your goodness and there is no darkness stronger than your light. Please, shine your light Lord."

A moment passed. The room was quiet. She felt numb, but she knew something was happening in the unseen world. A peace wafted through her spirit.

She opened her eyes and gasped. Sucking in air as if she'd just surfaced from the depths of the ocean. Her heart was wrapped in the warm embrace. The Light had come. A gentle smile stretched her lips.

The loud jingle of a phone gave her heart a start.

She heard a nurse lift it from its cradle in the doctor's office down the hall.

Heels clicked down the hall. Carrie rose and sat on her bed. The nurse stopped outside her room and gave a quick knuckle wrap on the door, "Ms. Carrie, your husband needs to speak with you."

Carrie nodded and stood to her feet, then followed the nurse back to the office where the phone awaited. She entered the room behind the nurse. The nurse pointed to the phone lying beside its cradle on the desk.

Carrie picked it up.

"Hello?"

"Carrie! You have to sit down. You won't believe this."

"Jack, where are you?"

"I'm at uh . . . Abundant Life Church. The big one off Arrieta Street. You know, with the big white steeple?"

"Yeah. Is Mandy okay?"

"She is now I think."

"Let me talk to her."

"Hang on."

Static wrinkled against the receiver.

"Hello? Mama?"

"Hey baby, how are you feeling?"

"I'm kind of tired. I just woke up. But I guess what I dreamed?"

"You just woke up?"

"Yeah I—"

Jack's voice cut in, "She doesn't remember anything that happened other than the dream. Honey, I took her to a church. The person who I took in there was not our daughter. But she's back now. Listen to the dream she had."

"Yeah, so I had this dream that I was standing in a garden with Lucy. We were picking tomatoes off the vine and eating them, when this big man dressed in white walked up. He was smiling really big and he was even glowing with a bright light. He squatted down and stretched out his hands. We both ran and jumped into his arms. He hugged us tight. And we all laughed. He was so nice. I felt so safe when he hugged me, he was really big and strong. And really nice."

Carrie wiped the tears streaking down her face, and sniffled, "That was the light of the world, honey. He saved you."

Haunted Treasures

Earl and Scarlet Crothers had always been drawn to antiques and things of the past. Upon retiring from their jobs at the hospital, where Scarlet was a nurse and Earl was a business consultant and accountant, they decided to take the plunge and open an antique shop of their own. They found the perfect building in downtown Aynor. It was a quaint brick building with just the right amount of old southern charm. Having paid cash for their plantation style home located less than ten minutes away, the two thousand a month lease for the building fit nicely within their monthly budget. They soon filed for their business license and registered an LLC under the name, *Crothers Antiques*. The two had run the place successfully for three years without any hiccups. That is until that old woman brought in an old picture of a farm and a withered jewelry box from the late nineteenth century. That's when all hell broke loose, and the ghosts were unleashed.

It started innocently enough when Earl began hearing the floorboards creak above. He played it off and assumed it was Scarlet moving around in the office upstairs where she often tinkered with arts and crafts that sold in the store as a bonus. The noises began two weeks after they had bought the picture and jewelry box from the old lady. One day while Earl and Scarlet were speaking with a customer about an old oil lantern, the floors creaked above them. Earl and Scarlet looked at each other and scrunched their brows. They didn't say anything in front of the customer, but as soon as they left, Earl and Scarlet made their way upstairs.

"That was heavy whatever it was." Said Scarlet.

"I've heard it before, but I thought it was you messing in the file cabinets or something," Earl said as he climbed the stairs. His knees popped and ached as he went.

Scarlet was right behind him, "You heard that noise while I was up here?"

"Yeah. I didn't think much of it though at the time."

"You don't think someone could've snuck into the attic or something do you?"

Earl snorted and said, "Woman, you watch too many crime shows."

"I'm serious. What if we have a hooligan living up there or something?"

"We don't have no hooligan in the attic. Lord have mercy, Scarlet. You can think up about anything, can't ya?"

As Earl was finishing his words, they reached the top of the stairs. While Scarlet was in mid reply, her voice was cut off by the loud creaking coming from her office.

They looked at each other with wide eyes.

Earl gulped and trained his vision to Scarlet's office door.

Together they crept down the hall and eased up to the door. They crouched there and listened.

Earl's heart thumped hard as he felt his blood speeding through his veins. He licked his lips and swallowed.

Creeeeaaaakkkkkk!

Scarlet gasped and put a hand to her mouth.

Earl took hold of the door handle.

Creeeeaaaakkkkkk!

"Earl, no. What are you doing?" Scarlet hissed through clenched teeth.

He twisted the knob and shoved the door. It swung freely to reveal the small office. The room was empty except for the file cabinets, totes of beads, desk, and computer.

Earl and Scarlet combed the room for ten minutes but never found anyone or anything out of place. Earl even went on to search the attic at Scarlet's request. They were the building's only occupants.

A few days later, Earl and Scarlet found a piece of China shattered in the floor when they opened the store that morning. Earl ran back the security footage and he and Scarlet stared in disbelief as they watched the glass plate slide off the shelf as if dragged by a phantom's hand.

"There is no way that plate slid off on its own. You know how heavy it was. After all this time, why did it just now fall off?"

Earl tightened his lips and shook his head before saying, "Maybe a customer had looked at it and didn't place it back right?"

Scarlet scoffed, "No. No, it's not possible. You saw it when it fell off of there. It was dragged. Something dragged it."

Earl pinched his tear ducts and sighed.

A moment passes between.

"You know I haven't said anything, but I've felt something here." Scarlet said.

Earl removed his hand and looked at her with questioning eyes.

She bobbed her head and said, "I thought I was just creeping myself out because I've been thinking a lot about ghosts lately." She shook her head, "There's something here. I've felt it."

"What do you mean?"

"I don't know how to describe it, other than I've sensed a presence. It's kind of like the feeling of being watched, you know. It's like when I'm up there working, I'm not the only one in the room. It feels like someone is standing in the corner watching me. I just get an eerie feeling."

Earl scratches his neck and says, "I think we are overthinking things here. We've both had our minds on ghosts here lately and I think our minds are searching anything to label as a haunt."

"I hope you're right, but something in my gut tells me there's more to it than that."

A week passed without incident.

On Tuesday morning of that week, Earl was busy unloading a shipment of goods they had won at an online estate sale. As Earl was dragging a box around the back of the glass showcase, he heard Scarlet call his name from the other side of the store.

"Hold on, I'm coming."

"Earl. Come here."

"I'm coming, just give me a second."

Earl straightened his spine and winced before angling towards the pictures and book section of the store where it sounded like Scarlet had called from. As he rounded the corner and passed through the open-door frame, he looked up in time to catch glimpse of a silhouette of a woman with long hair disappear behind a bookshelf. He wrinkled his brow and stopped in his tracks. The store wouldn't open for another forty-five minutes and to his knowledge, he and Scarlet were the only two there.

He rubbed his hand over his face and glanced about the store while blinking his eyes. He returned his attention to the place where the lady had stood. He rubbed his eyes before investigating. He crept along and listened. His eyes darted this way and that in search of the woman. Earl came to the end of the bookshelf and peered around it. No one was there.

Something seized his arm. Earl screamed and spun around with a balled fist ready to sink into someone's face.

It was Scarlet.

Earl cursed and gasped for breath.

Scarlet started laughing.

"You scared the shit out of me."

"I noticed. What were you doing peeping around the bookcase like that?"

Earl dropped his eyes and shook his head.

"What were you doing?"

He ignored her question and answered with one of his own, "Did you call my name?"

Scarlet scrunched her face and eyed him carefully.

"No. Why?"

"You did too. Don't lie."

"I'm not lying. I didn't call your name."

Earl gulped and looked back to where the lady had been just moments ago.

"What happened?"

Earl felt her hand on his arm. He turned to her and told her everything. She hugged him when he finished. He kissed her head and said, "Sorry I didn't believe you. You were right. I don't think we're the only ones here anymore."

A week later, Earl was woken late in the night to the sound of something knocking on the walls in their home. He thought it was a dream at first. He laid there on his back for a few minutes and listened.

Knock. Knock. Knock.

Earl angled his brows then looked over at Scarlet who was sound asleep. He rose and twisted to the side of the bed. He looked back at Scarlet. She shifted one of her legs and snored. Earl slid into his slippers and put on his robe.

Knock. Knock. Knock.

It was faint, but it sounded like knuckle wraps behind the wall somewhere. Rain played upon the roof and lightning flashed in the distance. Thunder grumbled and light filtered in through the windows with each strike. Earl felt a cold draft waft through the hallway when he exited their bedroom. The hardwood creaked beneath him as he sought the source of the sound.

Knock. Knock.

The hallway lit from a lightning strike and the window curtain fluttered with the draft. *Where in the world is the draft coming from?* He wondered. It chilled his cheeks and caused him to blink as his eyes began to water.

The knocking continued. His heart thumped hard. The wind howled past the eaves. Rain pelted the window as he passed it. The lingering aroma of the baked salmon they had for dinner hung in the air. Now that it was brought to his attention, he felt a tiny flake of salmon wedged in a bottom molar. He ran his tongue over it and kept moving towards the sound.

He peered through the darkness to the door at the end of the hall. They always kept the room closed but for some reason the door was left open. Must be where the draft is coming from.

Knock...........Knock.

Earl narrowed his brows as he stared at the door ahead. The knocks were louder but growing further apart. He braced a little more at the knees and continued to creep closer to the room. They had used it as a guest bedroom for when the family visited from out of town.

The room was hardly used, and Earl couldn't remember the last time he'd been in there. Scarlet must've changed the sheets or something and left the door open. That didn't explain the knocking sounds that were drawing him closer like a moth to a flame though, did it?

He was now only feet away from the door frame. Earl pressed his back to the wall and slid closer. He peeked into the room and continued to ease his way inside. The bed and nightstand came into view. His heart jumped when his eyes caught movement.

The window was left open, and the curtains waved at him like a cape on a ghost. As his eyes were trained to the window, the bedroom door slammed shut behind him. He yelped and spun around. He crossed to the door and tried the handle. It wouldn't give. He was locked inside. Someone had lured him in and locked him up.

What about Scarlet? Oh God, no!

Earl began pounding on the door and screaming for Scarlet. His head spun as his breath escaped faster than he could take it in. He began to hyperventilate. Earl cursed and beat on the door. Blood pulsed in his ears. His heart drummed deeply to the point where his chest began to ache.

Earrrrllllll!

The voice was raspy and spoke in a whisper. It was muffled as if it were hiding behind something.

His eyes widened. A cold chill washed over him as it felt like a ghost had tickled his spine. Gooseflesh rifled over his arms. His breath caught in his throat.

Earrrrrllllll!

He squeezed his eyes shut and pounded harder on the door.

He could hear movement behind him. It sounded like feet shuffling or dragging over the floor.

He screamed for Scarlet as it felt like his heart would explode any moment. He kept jimmying the door handle, but it just wouldn't give. The movement behind him had stopped. He opened his eyes and listened.

All he could hear was the rain and wind.

A hand seized his shoulder. It pinched him in the collarbone and sent him crumbling to the cold floor. He caught a glimpse of a silhouette with long hair just before Scarlet shoved the door open and sent it crashing into his thigh.

He was still screaming when Scarlet bent to tend to him. His whole body trembled. He couldn't speak or think. Scarlet helped him stand to his feet. He gathered himself enough to talk. The two hardly slept the rest of the night. The woman from the store had followed them home. Or so they thought.

A few days had passed of no activity either at the store or at home. Earl and Scarlet were just beginning to return to their normal sleep pattern when Earl had the first dream.

The dream began with Earl standing at the top of the stairs leading to their basement. He could hear a young female crying out followed by heavy feet thudding from the kitchen. Earl watched as a hulking man dressed in a white shirt and overhauls marched through the kitchen with the woman draped over his shoulder. She screamed and beat upon his back but he paid her no mind. Earl yearned to stop the man but could only spectate as we sometimes do in dreams. He watched as the man swung open the basement door. The woman shrieked and pounded at his back. The man chuckled. Earl watched as the big man took the girl from his shoulder and tossed her down the stairwell, into the darkened basement.

The dream then flashed so Earl was standing in the dismal basement with its earthen floor. Across the room from him was a man and woman lit by a dim lantern. This was a different man than the one who'd tossed the girl. He watched as the two dragged the young woman by her arms toward the back wall of the basement. Earl angled closer. A wheel barrel full of mortar sat to the right next to a pile of bricks. The young female screamed and thrashed as the man and woman sat her down against the wall. They bound her to a pipe running down the wall. Earl could only see the young woman's face through the shadows, but could tell by her voice, she may have been mentally handicapped. The poor woman begged and pleaded with her two captors, but they paid her no mind as they busied themselves with the brick and mortar.

Dear God! They're going to block her in!

Earl rushed forward but was stopped just short of the man and woman as if caught in quicksand. He was stuck like we often are in our dreams. He was forced to watch in in horror as the young woman wailed and fought to break free. All the while, her two conspirators worked to wall her in. One block at a time.

Earl awoke with a gasp as he jolted up from bed. The sheets were drenched with sweat and sticking to him. Earl's heart raced as his breath escaped in gasps and steamed into the air. The room was like an ice box as the air bit his cheeks and lips. He batted his eyes and cold tears leaked down his face. The room was also pitch black. Earl peered through the darkness to see the ceiling fan wasn't turning. He looked at the alarm clock. It was black. He turned to look at Scarlet but froze when he caught the silhouette of the woman standing in the corner of their room. Her back was to them so her long dark hair hung over her white gown. Earl could hear her sniffling. He swallowed hard and felt his lips trembling.

Earl reached out a blind hand and began to joust his wife. He felt her stir. He glanced down to her and saw her blinking and rubbing away the slag from her eyes.

"What's the matter?"

Earl looked back to the corner of their room.

The woman had vanished and so had the chill.

Earl rubbed his face and crashed back to the bed. He draped an arm over his eyes and caught his breath.

"What happened? Is the power out? Are you okay? Are you having chest pains? Is your face going numb?" Scarlet said as she hovered over him.

"No. No. Honey, it's not that."

"Then what is it?"

"I saw the woman."

Scarlet went quiet.

Earl rose from bed and twisted to the side to let his feet dangle. He wiped his face with both hands before standing.

He turned to find Scarlet glancing about the room as if searching for their ghost. The two locked eyes.

"What do you mean you saw her?"

"It started with a dream. Someone was blocking her inside a wall while . . ." his voice trailed off as he took a gulp at the knot that was forming. "Jesus. While she was still alive."

Scarlet gasped and placed a hand to her heart.

Earl nodded.

"You've always said you felt something in the basement wasn't right. I think that's maybe where she is."

"Oh my God, Earl. Should we call the police?"

He waved her off and said, "No. They're not going to waste their time with a nightmare. We'll need to give em more than that."

"What do you mean?" Scarlet asked as Earl was pushing an arm through his robe.

"I mean I'm going to go down there and have a look. Besides, I need to check the breaker box anyhow."

Scarlet scrambled from bed, "You're not leaving me here in the dark."

Earl took up his phone from the nightstand and thumbed to the flashlight app. He shined it at Scarlet, "Alright then, let's go."

Together the two crept through the darkened home. Scarlet clung to Earl's arm as he led them downstairs. They reached the kitchen and angled for the basement door. Earl shined his light on it and drew a deep breath. He felt Scarlet squeeze his arm.

Earl took hold of the doorknob and pushed it open. The door swung over the stairwell with a creak. He shined his light down the stairs half expecting the woman to streak past the bottom risers.

The two began the descent.

Dust particles floated in front of the phone's light. The stairs moaned with each step. The temperature began to drop the further they descended. The air was musty and stale. A cobweb draped from the ceiling. They reached the bottom of the stairwell and observed their surroundings as Earl shone the light about the room. Storage boxes and tubs lined the far wall on the left. He also had shelves full of tools here and there. He stopped when he reached the back corner.

He lifted a finger and said, "Over there. I think that's where they were at."

"Are you sure?"

"I'm pretty sure. Let's check the breaker box first though before I start looking around over there."

With Scarlet clinging tight to his side, they crossed to the breaker box. Earl scanned his light over it but found no tripped breakers.

He turned to Scarlet and said, "Maybe a car crashed into a pole or something."

"Or a limb fell on a line."

"Could have."

They turned around and angled for the back corner.

Once there, Earl took his time combing over the wall, checking the bricks for any unusual patterns. Unable to find anything, he turned to Scarlet and said, "I know she's back there. This is where I saw them block her in."

"Why is she just now letting us know? After all this time, why now?"

Earl shrugged his shoulders and said, "I don't know, but I'll go crazy if I don't tear into that to see what's back there."

Scarlet sighed and tightened her lips. "Alright, but just a small enough hole so we can peek in, right?"

Earl bobbed his head and crossed for where his shovels, rakes, and sledgehammer were.

He passed Scarlet his phone and reared back the sledgehammer. His first swing glanced off the brick.

"You'll have to do better than that, podna."

Earl rolled his eyes and took another swing. This one connected and bit a chunk out of the wall. Pieces flew and scattered across the floor. Earl reared back again and struck the brick. Another chunk exploded. Again, he swung the hammer. Again. Again. Again.

Ten minutes or so had passed and Earl was gasping for air. His arms felt like anchor chains. Nothing but dead weight. He had done just enough damage to pierce a hole in the wall about the size of a basketball. Just big enough for you to poke your head through and squeeze a hand in to shine a light.

Earl sat the hammer down and bent at the waist with his hands to his knees. After gathering himself, he straightened his spine and reached for his phone.

Scarlet passed it to him and said, "What if she grabs your head while you're peeking back there."

Earl wrinkled his brows and said, "Geez, that's encouraging."

"I'm just saying."

Earl pushed the thought to the far reaches of his mind and inched up to the opening. He swallowed. He shined the light at the hole and saw about a two-foot gap between the walls. Just enough space for a body, he thought.

He cursed and stuck his head through the entrance. He wiggled and had his hand right next to his chin. He looked to the right and saw nothing but dust, spiders, and cobwebs. He coughed. He grimaced as he turned to look to his left. As he angled the light down the small tunnel between the walls, his heart leaped within him when about ten feet down his eyes found the skeleton. She sat on her haunches and had her knees drawn close to her. Her bottom jaw was drooped open like in mid scream. She still had strands of hair.

Earl cursed and scrambled out of the hole.

"What? What is it?"

His breath escaped him. His heart pounded. He coughed again as he held his hands to his knees.

Scarlet tended to him as she continued to ask what had him so worked up.

Wheezing, he rose up and pointed a finger to the hole, "She's back there. They really did that to that poor girl. Christ Almighty, they did it just like I saw in my dream."

Earl began to cry as Scarlet hugged and soothed him.

An hour later, a Sheriff's Deputy arrived followed shortly by a plethora of others. The fire department came and finished tearing down the fake wall. All the while being careful not to crush the skeleton. Earl and Scarlet watched as they removed her body with respect and reverence. They placed the woman in a body bag and wheeled her to the coroner's van.

After a week of investigating, the coroner and police were able to place a name to the skeleton.

Clara Elizabeth Jordan

She was between nineteen- and twenty-five-years old judging by her bone structure. Courthouse records show she was mentally challenged and often had prolonged stays at the mental asylum in Florence. Health records show no diagnosis other than her being partially deaf and prone to psychotic breakdowns. In today's world, she would have likely been considered autistic or a victim of Asperger's syndrome. Of course, back then no one knew what those things were, so most doctors believed they could electrify the mind back into order and ram a needle through the patient's eye to clear their head. Unfortunately, according to health records, it seems Clara suffered that exact treatment. Electrocutions, lobotomy's, you name it. After unsuccessful treatments, doctors at the mental asylum in Florence lost patience with Clara and sent back to live with her parents and older brother.

Judging by the circumstances, it appears her family lost patience with her as well before blocking her in between the walls.

Courthouse records show her family were tobacco farmers and quite known in the community. They had run the family business for decades and had expanded through the years. Her father was chairman of the board in Aynor and had even run for mayor one year. Afflicted with their daughter's undiagnosed behavior, they likely couldn't bare for her to ruin their reputation of being upstanding members of the small town. In 1892, Clara Jordan disappeared. Police records show the family claimed she ran off into the woods late one night and was never found again. A small search party was organized and lasted for a week before the Jordan's called off the efforts.

Clara Jordan was no longer their problem.

Found next to her skeleton that night was a small jewelry box. It caught Earl and Scarlet's attention when the detectives retrieved it. It looked almost identical to the one they currently had in their store. The one the old woman had brought in a few weeks ago before all this happened.

Earl looked at his wife and saw she was thinking the same thing. That jewelry box they had at the store must've roused the girl from the grave. Which means she must've been hanging around to have taken notice of it. That jewelry box had woken her from her rest.

Earl and Scarlet kept both jewelry boxes as a remembrance to Clara. They have them both high on a shelf at their store.

A few days after Clara's discovery, she visited Earl in another dream. In the dream, Earl was sitting in a rocker on a big front porch overlooking fields of tobacco. The wind brushed his cheeks with graceful strokes. The air was cool and void of humidity. It reminded Earl of Earl y fall. He watched as the breeze played upon the dead leaf pile in the yard, picking and sending a few skittering across the gravel driveway. The sun began its ascension, and all the little birds took notice as they sang to their heart's content. As the sun was beginning to peek out over the fields, he heard another rocking chair squeaking next to him. He turned his head and found Clara gently rocking back and forth. She wore a pure white dress and had her long dark hair draped over her shoulder. She sat with her legs crossed and had her hands folded in her lap. She looked over at Earl, grinned to reveal cute dimples, and dipped her head.

Earl awoke to the sound of three knocks coming from the basement. He listened for a little while longer but never heard them again.

He smiled and whispered, "Rest well, Clara."

Earl closed his eyes and went back to sleep.

The knockings never returned and neither did Clara to Earl's dreams.

The Tony Hole

I heard the thumb latch click on the front door. The door jimmied a bit before someone started knocking. Our three yorkies, Peanut, Britney, and Kayley yapped and jolted from my parents' room. I could hear their toenails clicking on the hardwood before they stopped at the top of the staircase. The knocking came again. I rose from bed and rubbed my eyes. I could hear my mom and dad talking as my dad marched down the steps to the door. By now, I was coming down the hall. I found my mom standing at the top of the stairs tying a knot in her robe. She glared down at the door. I went and stood next to her and followed her gaze. I saw the hulking back of my father as he unlocked the door. My brother was on the other side and gasped for breath. His girlfriend, Danielle, cried into her hands. Her brother, Chad, who was a good friend of my brother, walked in circles with his hands to his head.

"What's wrong? What happened?" My dad asked. As he stepped outside.

My mom called out as she made her way down the steps, "What's going on, Will?"

She cracked the door and listened. I stood tight against her and eaves dropped.

I'd never heard my brother that frightened before. I knew something bad must've happened, but I had no idea what.

"We. We were waiting for the the dogs down near the Tony Hole. It sounded like they were right next to it. So, we drove over there and . . ." He trailed off and swallowed hard to find the words.

"And? Is everyone alright?" My dad asked.

My brother nodded and continued.

"We pulled up and cut the truck off to listen. We sat there for a while and didn't hear the dogs no more, so I crunk the truck back up and started to back out of there when Daniele and Chad started screaming. I turned around and that's when I saw him."

"Saw who?"

"Tony."

I remember a chill running over my spine when he said his name. My whole life I had heard stories of why everyone on our road calls that one spot at the creek, The Tony Hole. You had to go down a long side trail that followed the perimeter of Old Man Dixon's cornfield before reaching the back where Crowder's Creek ran. You would then have to follow a narrow path through the woods that came out at a set of three dilapidated, log cabins. The cabins supposedly belonged to Old Man Dixon's great grandfather and was used to house his slaves. He had given them each a share of the profits from the harvest along with an acre of land, shelter, and a decent wage. The slaves respected and loved Harvey Dixon as he treated them all as family and all he asked in return was for them to help him and his sons with preparing the harvest with which he ran the family business. One slave in particular, Harvey Dixon regarded as his own son. The man's name was Tony Dye. When Harvey Dixon fell ill and his two sons decided to start their own ventures outside of the family business, it was Tony Dye who Harvey left in charge of the farm. Harvey Dixon granted another ten acres along with forty percent of the business to Tony as long as he promised to take care of things when Harvey passed. Tony agreed.

A few months later, as Harvey Dixon lay dying in bed, Tony and his sons were catfishing late one night at the creek next to the cabins where they lived. With Harvey's son's becoming envious of Tony upon learning of their father's wishes, the two men decided to teach Tony a lesson. The two Dixon brothers sneaked up on Tony and his sons and overtook the man. As one brother held Tony's arms, the other pummeled his face and gut. Tony broke away at one point and got in two good licks on one of the brothers before the other kicked him from behind and sent him sprawling into the creek. Having just taken a beating and never learning to swim, Tony quickly succumbed to the current. His body was discovered the next day, floating face down along the creek bank.

My brother's story pulled me back to the present.

"I saw him standing in the headlights, dressed in a white baggy shirt and fishing jeans rolled at the cuff with holes in them. He stared at us. Then the lights went out on my truck. The battery was dead. I tried cranking it, but it wouldn't even try. I got out with my light and gun and stepped in front of the truck. Danielle and Chad were screaming for me to get back inside, but something in me just had to see if it was really him. It was like I was being drawn by something. I couldn't help it. I just had to see."

I gripped tighter to my mama and listened.

"As I walked through the field toward the creek bank, a gust of wind picked up and all the reeds bent over like they were bowing to something."

My brother shut his eyes and scratched the back of his neck before continuing, "I had an eerie feeling turn in my gut. I felt like I was being watched or something. I don't know how else to explain it. I kept walking closer to the water's edge. I reached the top of the bank and shined my light down at the water . . ."

He trailed off again and drew a deep breath.

"What did you see?" My dad asked.

"It was a body."

My mom gasped.

"What?" My dad said.

My brother nodded, "They were wearing a baggy white shirt like the slaves wore. It looked like a black man. He was floating face down with his arms spread out. I only got to see it for a few seconds because my light went dead like my truck. I turned and bolted out of there. Danielle and Chad had the truck locked when I got back. I hopped in and tried the ignition again. It crunk right up like nothing had ever happened. We peeled out and headed this way. I even left my coon dogs down there."

Things got quiet for a moment as everyone was deep in thought. I could hear cicadas singing from the trees and tree frogs screeching from the woods.

My dad cleared his throat and said, "And you're sure that's what you saw?"

My brother stared at the ground with wide eyes as he nodded and said, "I know for a fact I saw a body down there." He looked up at Danielle and Chad and said, "We all saw him standing there in the head lights."

"Do you think we should go back to check on things? Make sure they ain't no one down there in need of help. You probably need to get your dogs anyway."

"Are you sure that's a good idea, Will? Shouldn't you just call the sheriff instead?" My mom asked.

Chad spoke for the first time and said, "I'm not going back there. Huh uh. No way man. You can forget it."

"Me either. I'll never go back there." Danielle added.

"We'll be fine honey. I don't want to involve the sheriff unless we have to," Dad turned back around and said to Danielle and Chad, "Alright, well we can take you two home before we go." He looked to my brother and added, "Johnathan, you want to drop them off and meet me at Old Man Dixon's?"

"Yeah. Bring some extra lights with you and be sure to bring your gun too."

"Alright, well give me time to get dressed, and I'll meet you over there in about half an hour."

As my dad stepped back inside, I began to plead with him. "Can I go with you? Please? Please? I want to go."

He looked at mom.

"Not without me you're not." She said.

It was just after midnight when my parents and I backed up our driveway in Dad's old dodge pickup to head for the Tony Hole. I rode in between them on the bench seat. We bypassed Old Man Dixon's driveway and angled for the long dirt road about fifty yards past his house. We found my brother waiting there in his truck. We followed him as the road led to Old Man Dixon's hundred-acre cornfield. If you continued following it, it would lead you to the back of the field where the crop turned to woods next to the creek bank. We eased our way along the narrow road by the cornfield. The cab of the truck bounced as we ran over roots and potholes. A light mist began to descend. Dad's wiper blades screeched as they swiped the droplets aside. Dad had the windows cracked slightly, and I could hear the cicadas screeching. A hoot owl called out nearby. I watched my brother apply his brakes as we reached the place where he said he saw Tony. Dad put the truck in park and killed the engine. He stepped out and shut the door. He spoke through the cracked window, "Stay here with your mama, Son."

"You're not leaving us here." My mama said as she opened the truck door. I slid over and hopped out with her.

Dad sighed and clicked on his flashlight. I saw he had his pistol holstered on his hip.

"So, this is where you first saw him?" My dad asked my brother.

I watched Johnathan shut his door and click on a light of his own, "Yeah. Right over there." He pointed the light over a patch of old reeds near the wood line. A narrow deer trail cut through the middle of them.

I clung tight to my mama as we followed my dad and brother along the path. A briar struck me on the arm. Another poked my cheek. Something rustled in the woods. I yelped and squeezed my mama's arm so hard she cried out, "Ow! Cameron, let go. You're hurting me."

We regrouped and continued onward. I kept looking behind us as the feeling of an approaching monster loomed in my mind. If I stared into the darkened wood line long enough, I could almost make out a big hairy beast with dripping wet fangs and glowing red eyes. I jerk my eyes away and refocused on the trail ahead.

A pack of coyotes bellowed in the distance. I heard something move in the brush next to us. My dad and brother jerked their light to the sound. I heard dad unholster his pistol. We stood still for a moment and listened. A soft breeze whispered among the reeds and sent them bowing like my brother had described. I gulped and wiped at the sweat forming on my brow. I licked my lips and tasted something salty and copper. The wind ceased and all went still.

We moved again and continued towards the creek. I began to hear water rippling over the rocks as we neared the edge of the bank. We stood along the edge and watched as my dad and brother shined their lights down at the creek.

"I know I saw him floating right there. It was plain as day. He was right there. I promise you."

My dad walked further up the creek and swiped his light this way and that. My brother went the other way. My mama and me stood in the middle and took turns glancing at the end of their lights beam. Satisfied there weren't any bodies floating along the creek bank, they came back towards us. As they were nearing, a branch snapped across the creek. Both of their lights jerked in that direction. In what couldn't have been more than two seconds before the light went out, a family of five dressed in white gowns stood there staring at us. My mama let out a sound I had never heard her make before. The instant the lights went out, we all bolted back for the trucks.

I remember the truck fishtailing as the tires finally grabbed asphalt. My brother was right behind us.

We didn't talk about what we saw until the next day. Which happened to fall on a Saturday, so my brother and my parents were all home from school and work. My brother had set his mind on going back there with a snorkel and goggles to see for himself if anything was in the creek. My parents protested his idea of course, but eventually, curiosity got the best of my dad, and he was able to convince my mom to agree to it. So, that morning around ten or so we all headed back to the Tony Hole. I rode with my brother this time as Mom and Dad followed.

My brother had his radio tuned to a classic country station and Merle Haggard sang *Mama Tried.* We had the windows rolled down in his Ford Ranger and the cab bounced as we jostled our way along the trail next to Old Man Dixon's field.

I caught a glimpse of my brother's hand as he reached to turn down the volume.

"What's got you so quiet over there, huh? Still thinking about last night?"

The truth was, I had never stopped thinking about it. I couldn't have slept for maybe an hour or two at the most. Even when I did drift off, I only dreamed of the people we saw across the creek. They were the same people I had been secretly drawing pictures of for the past six months after they started visiting my window at night.

I turned and looked at my brother, debating whether I should tell him or not.

"What's the matter?"

I swallowed hard before reaching into my back pocket. I took out a folded piece of paper and held it on each end to stretch it tight.

"What is this?"

"Just look at it."

"I am. It looks like the people from last night. You done good."

"I drew that last week."

I felt him apply the brakes.

"You did what now?"

"I said I drew this last week. I have a stack tucked away in my closet. I started last fall."

My brother started laughing and shook his head, "Oh, you had me going for a minute there, Cam. You really did."

I folded the paper and tucked it back in my pocket.

"It started with a tap on my window."

My brother stopped laughing. He cleared his throat and listened.

"I would hear it almost every night. Sometimes it'd wake me up at like two or three in the morning. Other times I was too sleepy to look. After a few weeks went by of it tapping on the glass, I started hearing whispers. I could never see where they came from, but I could hear them plain as day."

With his voice sticking to his throat he asked, "What did they say?"

"My name. They would say my name and then ask me to open the window."

"Alright, now you're starting to creep me out a little bit."

I kept going, "A few weeks after the whispers, I woke up late one night to find two of them standing outside the window. They were smiling at me."

"Shit, are you serious? Sorry, I didn't mean to cuss."

"It's alright. Yeah, I don't think this just started though."

"What do you mean?"

"I've always had a weird feeling in our house. I mean, you remember I didn't start sleeping in my own bed until I was like what seven or eight?"

"Yeah, I thought you were going to sleep on that cot next to Mom and Dad until your legs were hanging over the end of it."

"Oh, shut up." I said as I punched his arm.

"Ow, you frogged me."

"I'm being serious though. I've always felt something in our house. And do you remember my imaginary friend I used to have?"

I watched my brother give it some thought.

"Yeah. What did you call him? Tommy wasn't?"

I nodded, "I've been thinking though."

"Yeah, what's that?"

"That's awfully close to Tony, isn't it?"

Johnathan snapped his head at me, "No. You don't really think so, do you?"

"I always said he was a grown up."

"So, you're saying this whole time your imaginary friend was really Tony Dye?"

I shrug my shoulders, "I'm just saying."

My brother cursed again and apologized.

We reached the back of the field, and he eased the truck to a halt. My parents parked next to us.

I looked at my brother and said, "Do me a favor will ya?"

"What's that?"

"Don't tell them what I just told you, okay?"

"As long as you don't tell them I cussed around you."

"Deal."

We shook on it and climbed out of the truck. My brother grabbed a black duffle bag from the bed and walked towards the embankment.

"Did you make sure to get the rope from the building like I said?" My dad asked him.

"Yeah, it's in here." My brother said while shouldering the bag.

"Here take this." I watched as my dad passed him a flashlight.

My mom spoke up, "I don't know about this, y'all. What if you get caught in the current? Then what?"

"Well, that's what the rope's for. We'll tie it into a harness around him like they use in the army when they repel down a building. I'll wrap it around this tree and hold on to it down by the bank."

"I'll be fine, Mom. I'll be careful. I just want to look around and see what's down there."

Moments later my dad was fitting the rope around him, and he was wading into the current. I sat next to my dad and watched as he intertwined his wrist in the rope. My brother descended to about waist deep and turned to look at us through his goggles and snorkel. He gave the okay sign and sunk beneath the surface.

I heard my mom mumble from the top of the bank as we watched bubbles spread across the water's surface. He was down there for about thirty seconds before resurfacing.

"Anything?" I asked.

He shook his head and smacked the flashlight.

"It's darker than I thought down there. Even the light doesn't help much."

He took a deep breath and tried again.

He stayed down longer this time. A second set of bubbles surfaced.

"Will, is he alright?"

No sooner than my mom's words filled the air, the rope jerked. It caught Dad by surprise and tugged him forward.

"What the hell?" I heard him mutter under his breath as he regripped the rope.

My mama began screaming, "Pull him up, Will. Oh my God! PULL HIM UP!"

More bubbles popped at the surface. The rope yanked again. My dad started pulling. I joined in behind him and did the same.

A big patch of bubbles came up and the water began to swirl.

"Here he is." My dad said with a smile in his tone.

I watched as Johnathan broke the surface and gasped for air.

Mama raced down the embankment and nearly tripped trying to get to him. He peeled the goggles off and tossed the snorkel.

"What happened down there?" My dad asked as he stood and wandered to the water's edge to be next to my mama.

My brother coughed and hacked as he waded closer. I noticed something in his right hand but couldn't yet make out what it was.

"I swear I saw a hand down there."

"A hand?" My dad questioned.

"Yeah. I saw it out of the corner of my eye. It was gone when I turned to look, but I found these on the bottom next to a stump."

They jingled when he held them up. It was a ring of keys. They looked old.

"What in the world?" Dad questioned as he reached out to study them.

I nudged closer for a better look. As I strained and watched Dad wipe muddy silt off them, it hit me. I looked at Johnathan and said, "The box."

"Huh?"

I felt everyone's eyes on me at once.

"The box. You know. The one me and Josh found last summer buried behind the cabin."

I saw my brother's eyes light up at my words. "The one we could never open because there was no key."

I nodded and bounded on my feet, "Yeah, the one we kept saying looked like it could belong to the civil war days."

"Do you think these would work it?" Johnathan asked.

"Only one way to find out." Said my dad.

WE GOT BACK to the house, and I rushed to rummage my closet for the box. I knelt on my knees and snatched at anything and everything that wasn't the box, tossing it out onto the floor behind me.

"Boy, you keep going like that and you'll have a mess to clean up when you're done." Said Dad.

"Yeah, and you better not hide it all under the bed like you did last time." Mama added.

I heard the keys jangle behind me as my brother spun them around on his finger.

"Ah ha. Got it." I said as I swiped away the winter coat it was buried under.

It was a rusted and earth warn piece of steal that must've weighed twenty pounds or more. I rolled it onto my lap and turned to my brother, stretching forth my hand. He passed me the keys.

"Here, let's bring it into the kitchen for a minute. Probably could use some WD-40 anyhow." Dad said as he relieved me of the box.

We followed him into the kitchen where Mom laid down a wash towel for the box to rest on. Dad searched beneath the sink and rose with a can of oil. I watched as he extended the red straw and doused the keyhole.

"Alright. That ought to do the trick. Give it a go."

I slipped the first of about a dozen keys into the slot and wiggled. I tightened my lips and shook my head. I tried the next one. Nothing. It wasn't until about the eighth or ninth key that I felt some traction. A grin stretched my face, and I turned to look at everyone.

"Well don't just stand there. Crack that baby open." My brother said as he nudged me on the arm.

I gave the key another turn and could hear the gears click within. The door popped forward to reveal a slight crack. A musty, earthen odor flooded forth. I squinted and pulled on the door.

A small wicker basket sat in the center and a cloth bag rested in it with the top tied closed with a piece of twine. I wrinkled my brow and looked at my brother. He nodded at me. I returned my eyes to the bag and pulled it out to sit it on the towel next to the box. I slowly undid the twine. I could feel my heart palpitate with heightened anticipation. Sweat beaded on my forehead. I swallowed a gulp and dumped the contents of the bag onto the towel. A stack of black and white photos, which were clumped together, tumbled to the right and a wedding band with a string and note attached went to the left.

Dad leaned close and mumbled, "What in the world?"

Mom picked up the wedding band and said, "It's definitely a lady's ring. Too small for a man."

"What does the note say?" My brother asked.

We watched as she uncreased it and began to read, "To whomever fins this here ring, know that it once fitted the love of my life. She has since passed on to the great unknown, yet her spirit lives. My wish would be that should this ring ever be taken from this here box that whoever find the ring bury it beneath the shade of the large oak down by the creek's edge. My love's wish was for the ring to remain with me until my passing. My wish was to bury it with her, but that was not as she had wanted. Upon my death, I ask that this ring be buried where she lies beneath the oak. Her marker is there and there she is also. As we were joined on this earth so shall we be joined in heaven. Our spirits will not find rest until the deed is done."

Mom finished and folded the note back the way it was. Dad picked up the photos and began peeling them apart. I saw his eyes widen as he looked through them.

"What is it?" I asked.

I saw his Adam's Apple bob as he lowered the pictures for us all to see. It was family photos of the five we saw last night. The same five I've seen standing outside my window. It was Tony Dye and his family.

My brother cursed and we all jerked our heads to him.

"Sorry." He said as he shrugged.

A half hour later we were back at the Tony Hole searching for the tall oak by the creek bank. We counted four in total, picked the biggest of the bunch and began sifting the ground for a burial marker.

Mom called out to us, "Hey, I think I have something."

We crowded around her and watched as she swiped away leaves and loose dirt. A small rectangle piece of metal was planted at the base of the tree. I squatted down and wiped the dirt away with my thumb. I grabbed the bottom of my shirt, spit, and scrubbed at the placard.

"What does it say?" Mom asked.

"I can't really make it out much, but it looks like the last name is Dixon."

"Really? Dixon . . . why would she have the Dixon name?" My brother questioned.

"It wasn't uncommon for slaves to take the last name of their owner back then." Dad said.

Mom added, "Yeah, he's right. If Tony was as close to the man as they say, he probably eventually took on the last name. They say he was like a son to the old man."

I continued shining the marker until I could read the rest of it.

"Abigail Dixon Birth 1837 Death 1863."

"That's her. That's Tony's wife. Has to be." My brother said.

I looked up at Mom and said, "Do you have the ring?" She nodded.

Later that night as I lay on my back with my hands behind my head, I thought about the past two days and the months leading up to them. I thought of all the dreams I'd had and the pictures I'd drawn. I remembered all the nightly visits. None of it started until me and my friend, Josh, found that box last fall. After it was taken was when things started. I'd always thought the story behind the Tony Hole was just an old tale all the parents liked to spook the kids and teenagers with. I figured it was just another piece of folklore like kids in England had of the Headless Horseman, or how my parents and their parents before them grew up with the ghost story of Crybaby bridge. I think every small town across America has a place called Crybaby bridge. I know we sure do.

After dazing at the ceiling and watching my ceiling fan make its revolutions, I eventually drifted to sleep sometime after midnight. I was awoken a short while later to the sound of tapping. I woke facing my window. Something I never do. I always turn my back to it, but I guess I must've rolled over in my sleep. I lifted my heavy lids and took a sledgehammer to my heart at the sight before me. I bolted upright and pulled the covers close to my face.

Standing at the other side of the window was Tony and his family. The initial fright slowly dissipated as a soothing calmness filled my heart. I watched as Tony stood with one arm around his wife, Abigail, and his other dangled around his three small children. They smiled at me, and for the first time since this all started, I truly knew they meant me no harm. I could just feel it in my gut. Fear washed from my heart. The youngest of the children raised a hand and waved. I waved back. I locked eyes with Tony for a moment. He smiled and nodded. I returned the gesture and watched as they turned and headed for the wood line before disappearing beneath the light of the moon.

Thank you for reading *Night Terrors!* I hope you enjoyed it as much as I did writing it! If so, I would be grateful if you'd be kind enough to leave a review on Amazon as reviews truly are the life blood of any Author's career.

About the Author

I am a former college baseball player turned writer who thoroughly enjoys the outdoors, whether it be fishing, kayaking, hiking, and exploring new places, or watching a game of America's greatest pastime. I'm an old soul at heart, so I love old music (especially classic rock from CCR, Bob Seger, Bruce Springsteen, or vintage rock and roll from Chuck Berry, Muddy Water's, Elvis, etc) old movies and antique items. I own a Victrola Turntable in case you're not getting the picture yet.

I'm an avid reader and writer of Mystery, Horror, and Suspense. I enjoy reading Stephen King, Ted Dekker, Frank Peretti, Thomas Harris, Steven James, C.J. Box, and James Lee Burke to name a few. I also enjoy a fun/inspiring Southern Story as well such as Where the Crawdads Sing.

I was a top ten finalist in Inkshares 2018 Mystery/Thriller contest. I am a member of the Horror Writers Association. I hold an MBA from Coastal Carolina University and am currently practicing real estate in Myrtle Beach. You can find me on Instagram, Facebook, and YouTube to stay up to date with my latest work.

Instagram: randall_lane31
Facebook: Randall Lane Fiction
YouTube: Randall Lane Fiction
Amazon: Randall Lane Fiction

Other Books Available

If you enjoyed *Night Terrors* then you'll likely enjoy my latest novel *The Reaping* as well. Available on Amazon! The book trailer is posted to my YouTube channel.

Synopsis. Something strange is happening in New England. Over the past 17 years, numerous children have disappeared after each of their parents were discovered brutally murdered and left with taunting notes. With rumors of the man in a black hood who roams the woods at night, to an escaped mental patient from Cushing Island, and a snake handling church with a dark past, veteran Homicide Detective, Laurie Daniels must work through this high stakes enigma to learn who the ghost-like killer really is. The deeper she goes the more she begins to believe the killer may be connected to her past. And a new, horrifying clue emerges . . . Daniels isn't closing in on the killer, but he's closing in on her. Can she catch him before he catches her?

Devil's Den is also available on Amazon. You can check out the book trailer for all my stories on the YouTube Channel.

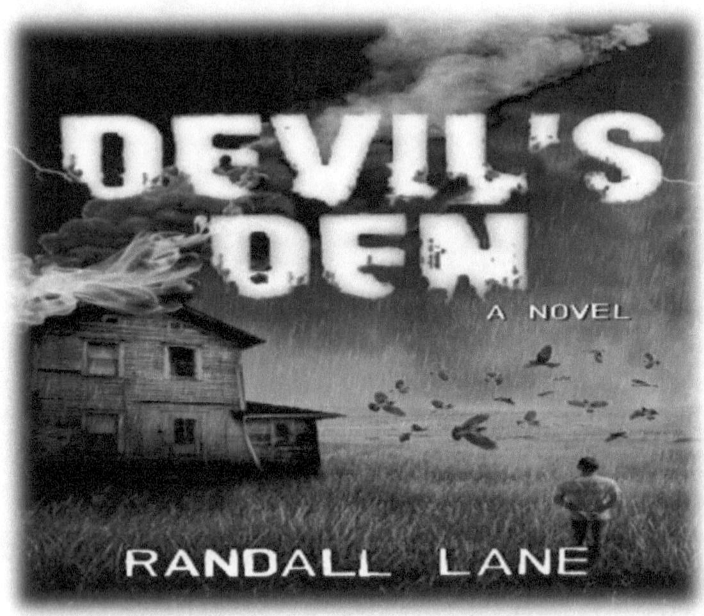

Synopsis. The year is 1989 and as Detectives search for a local serial killer, James and Rebecca Randolph can't help but wonder if it may be Ethan, the new co-worker of James. After causing a horrendous accident at the Georgetown International Paper Mill, Ethan vanishes before further questioning. Locals are quick to term him the GTK or Georgetown Killer. 25 years later, after relocating to Holden Beach, James and Rebecca find themselves once again in the cross hairs of the GTK. As they consult the spiritual guidance of Native American

Friends, they soon learn there is a lot more going on than meets the eye. Embarking on a Journey from Darkness to Light, passing through the Devil's Den along the way, they gain a whole new perspective of the saying, "Good vs Evil."

I also have my novel *Omah*, available on Amazon too! To watch the book trailer, head over to my YouTube channel. (Randall Lane Fiction.)

Synopsis: After a string of mysterious disappearances and encounters in Northern California, Game Wardens are less than surprised when six-year-old Tyler Jacob's vanishes by the South Fork Eel River while fishing with his family. As the family is riddled with guilt and on the verge of losing hope, Native Americans from the local

Yurok Tribe step in to help spread light on the recent events. While pushing through the vast wilderness and majestic Redwood Forest in search of his son, Randy Jacob's soon learns that what he once thought was just a Legend may actually be a living and breathing creature after all. As hours stretch into days and the clock rushes forward, can Tyler be found before it's too late?

Inside Look at Chapter 1

of Randall's next Novel

OLD
GHOSTS
OF THE
VALLEY

A NOVEL

RANDALL LANE

1

Chapel Valley, NC

October 2023

3:33 p.m.

Carol Gore is a fifty-nine-year-old divorced mother of two, who lives alone up in the backcountry of the Blue Ridge Mountains. She has lived in the same house since the early nineties. She and her husband, Steve, moved to the area after he'd picked up a mining job in the town of Chapel Valley. It was also around this time that Carol learned of the Abbott cult. A co-worker from Piggly Wiggly wouldn't shut up about the sweet little Abbott family and its parishioners, so Carol finally relented and accompanied her to an event at the compound. That was all it took for Carol to become hooked.

As Carol thinks back to the moment she first stepped foot on the Abbott compound, she subconsciously rinses off a few glass plates from previous days meals. Skylar, her white Himalayan cat, is busy weaving in and out between her feet. The tickle brings her back just in time to hear the strange noise. Carol thought she'd heard something earlier but only brushed it off as a play upon her ears. Must be the house settling or something, she'd said to herself. Isn't that what we always say? Or at least what we always hope for, right? What if we're wrong though? What if we're not alone during all the times we think we are? What if someone or something . . . lurks within the shadows and watches without our knowing?

As Carol asks herself these questions, she hears it again. The sound is unmistakable this time. The creaking of a floorboard beneath a sturdy, unwelcomed foot. All day she had fought the eerie feeling of being watched. It seems a presence had been hovering just over her shoulder. She's being too paranoid, she'd thought. Things are different now. To think she's still being watched . . . well it'll just end up driving her crazy. She can't allow herself to go on thinking this way. They would end up throwing her away to the place where people drift along in white gowns, while being force fed medicine and whipped into submission. She'll never go back there. She'd made a promise to herself, and she's determined within her heart to keep it.

No amount of self-encouragement can eat away the growing feeling she has of being watched. It is stronger now than ever before. The home is quiet other than the running of the faucet, and the black and white film playing in the living room. Carol stands frozen with her back to the rest of the kitchen. She looks down to find Skylar staring behind her. Together they listen.

Creeeaaak!

Skylar hisses and enters in a low crouch, his ears flare backward, his hair stands straight. Carol feels someone in the room. She turns just enough, so she can scan the room with her peripheral. She goes over the China cabinet full of Grandma's dishes and scans over the kitchen table. Her heart leaps at the big shadow of a man standing in the kitchen's door frame. She gasps and drops a dish. The crash of the shattering glass fills the room. She fights the urge to look directly at the man, knowing that the chance of her survival will quickly diminish should she see his face.

Skylar emits a low growl and backs up to be between Carol and the sink cabinet.

"What do you want?" Carol asks with her words sticking to her throat.

A moment passes.

"You."

Creeeeaaaaak!

The dark man takes a step.

"Stop. Don't come any closer."

He stops.

She grips the sinks hard enough to hurt her fingers.

"Look at me."

She shakes her head.

"Carol."

Her heart sinks at the knowledge of this mystery man knowing her name.

"Carol. You have to look at me. It's very important."

She clamps her eyes shut and shakes her head again.

She hears him breathe deep. He holds it, then sighs.

"I don't want to do this Carol, but I'm afraid I have to. You're leaving me no—"

Carol snatches Skylar up and bolts through the side door of the kitchen for her bedroom. Heavy thuds pound towards her. She slams the door shut and engages the lock. She rushes to move a chest of drawers against the door.

The dark man slams against the door as soon as Carol slides the furniture into place. The door rattles hard on its hinges. She stumbles backwards with one hand to her mouth, and the other reaching blindly for the bed.

Her heart will surely explode any moment as adrenaline courses through her veins in an icy rush. Her legs meet the edge of the bed, and she bruises a heel against the metal railing below. She winces and bends to tend to the pain.

The door rattles hard once more. Skylar growls again before going into a frantic search for cover. Another hard thud pounds against the door.

As Carol rubs her heel, she begins to hear a faint but hoarse whisper coming from under the bed. The scratchy voice stalls her racing heart and sends her body freezing in place. Movement comes from beneath the bed. It sounds like something crawling across the hardwood floor. Carol jerks herself up and looks toward the window. A sudden thought hits her. What an idiot. Last week she'd nailed the windows shut after fearing someone was secretly entering in the night. In her efforts to keep someone out, she ends up trapping herself in. She must break it. She races over to a nightstand and begins to search for something to break the glass.

The whisper under the bed becomes more audible now. Between the thuds against the door, she can make out the words. It's saying, "Come near my dear."

Carol yanks open a drawer to her nightstand and pulls out a hammer she's used for hanging pictures. She tucks her face into the crevice of her elbow and takes a swing. The window shatters. She rakes away the shards along the seal and rushes over to the nightstand. As she begins to swipe away the clutter, lamp and all, the thing beneath the bed growls loudly. Carol catches a glimpse in her peripheral of a long, bony hand reaching out from beneath the bed, aiming for Carol's ankle. She screams and jumps backwards. The thing continues to growl. Its pale fingers fall limp to the hardwood. Its nails make a loud tapping sound.

Carol hurries and places the nightstand beneath the broken window. The door thuds again as she climbs upon the nightstand.

She wiggles through the window and falls to the ground. Her hip barks in protest. She grunts and manages to get to her feet. She hears her bedroom door burst open. She doesn't turn back to look but makes a break for the grove of pines.

Running and stumbling her way into the tree line, she pushes away the swipes of bony branches. Her tender feet scream with every poke and jab from the sticks and pine needles. Her lungs burn like they've been doused with gasoline and lit to a flame. Her breath steams into the frigid air. Running between the pines, she retrieves her cell. Moments later she finds the contact she's looking for and places the call.

Panting and glancing over her shoulder, she waits for her son to answer.

Tales from Uncle Joe

TALES FROM UNCLE JOE
MUTILATIONS
RANDALL LANE
TALES FROM UNCLE JOE
IT ROAMS AT NIGHT
RANDALL LANE

TALES FROM UNCLE JOE
AN INSIDE JOB
RANDALL LANE